No Noble Escape

A Novel

Anton Van Iersel

Démasqué Publications
Munich

ISBN 978-3-9825153-0-4

Book cover design by Christiane Duppé

For my sister Marion,
for the comfort of patience, belonging and trust
that leaves no one a stranger.

And so, to sum it all up, I perceive everything I say as absolutely true, and deficient in nothing whatever, and paint it all in my mind exactly as I want it to be.

Miguel de Cervantes Saavedra, *Don Quixote, Volume 1*

The invitation

The house lights go down and the murmurs and whispering fade out. He can feel his heartbeat quicken, the tension rising up through his body, along his arms, through to the nerves at the tips of his fingers. Jeremy is acutely aware of this incongruous physical response to once familiar pre-performance cues as he moves forward to take his place tonight. But that place is no longer behind a door that will be opened for him when he makes his way to the stage, smiling confidently at welcoming applause for the soloist. Tonight he moves along the isle to his front row dress circle seat, his face behind a mask, hiding what might be an apologetic grin at being late.

Before he settles in, Jeremy's eyes catch the sparkle of lights illuminating note stands in the orchestra pit below him. He sits, closes his eyes, and lets his mind drift back to the night he took his place in the pit under Riccardo's baton two and a half years ago. He had not yet fully recovered from his motorcycle accident. His questionable performance as a substitute first oboist prompted Riccardo backstage to offer him a work retreat. He was invited to work without distractions in the family's vacated ancestral villa in Italy until he recovered his form as an oboe soloist—a politely firm reminder from the conductor that he had to practice a lot harder if he wanted to keep his place in the limelight.

'Old, very old, in the tenth generation of my family. The villa is spacious, and the acoustics are great. You'll find it has a kind of decadent, venerable charm. It would suit you.'

'Because I only appear respectable, but I'm not?'

The conductor knows why he doesn't have Jeremy's full attention. 'Because you may want to avoid over-indulging your charm for a while, until you're back in form?'

Since this was the last performance of La Traviata for the season, a good number from the orchestra and cast were mingling

1

in the backstage lounge, rather than dashing out as they normally would to the nearest pub or bistro.

The creases on Riccardo's round forehead tell Jeremy that this idea of a work retreat is more than just a friendly suggestion; it's a warning that he's being too lax about where his playing is now. 'Look, Riccardo, I'm sorry . . .'

'It happens. I know how unforgiving the oboe can be. I appreciate your stepping in as a substitute at the last minute.'

'I should have known it was much too early,' Jeremy says, massaging his neck with his free hand. He looks around the lounge, sees she is still looking at him while surrounded by other men from the orchestra. He holds her gaze. 'She's quite the flighty courtesan, isn't she Riccardo? Even off stage.'

'I will not introduce you to more indulgence.'

'No need, I think.'

'What about this tour you were talking about? Is it still on?'

'Well, yes, I still have a few months . . . OK, I take your point. It might be a good idea to disappear for a while and push myself harder to get back in form. I struggled in places tonight and I'm very far from where I need to be by November.'

'Then the villa is ideal, and it's yours for as long as you'd like. It's a bit run-down, but perfectly remote. You'll find the villagers keep to themselves; they're somehow removed from people outside, so they'll leave you alone. Ah, Vicky, meet Jeremy Sinclair. He kindly stepped in for tonight's performance.'

'And tripped up in a few places,' Jeremy adds with a demure smile.

'We all make mistakes, Jeremy, and trip up every now and then,' she says, offering him her hand with an unmistakeable invitation in her eyes to stumble into the night with her.

His weak self-discipline at first got the better of him when his affair with her got going. He only took Riccardo up on his offer when it became obvious that Vicky's demands on him were as insatiable as his injuries from the accident were stubborn, both threatening his tour as a soloist; he had to get away and get over his handicaps.

But seclusion changed him, bringing up a sinister seam buried deep below the surface of who he wanted to be, the compulsions compressed and hidden even from himself under his talent, calculated charm, and easy conquest of women. The face he sees in the mirror each morning belongs to a stranger he wants to confront tonight, to demand respite from what that face reflects, what it tells and retells him cannot ever be atoned.

Why is he here? To hear Vicky as Violetta, with Riccardo at the rostrum again tonight. It is as close as Jeremy will ever get to seeing either of them again, as close as he can get to remembering and reconstructing how he changed under circumstances brought about by their presence in his life. La Traviata: this revival of Verdi's most popular opera in Covent Garden is itself a draw. The fact that Vicky has meanwhile been touted as the reborn Maria Callas has filled every seat. He remembers her voice filling every corner of the villa's spacious rooms. 'Fors' è lui. . .' is her signature aria, and she sings it better than anyone, even Callas.

> *Ah, perhaps it is he whom the soul,*
> *lonely in its tumults,*
> *often enjoyed painting*
> *with its hidden colours!*

Since abandoning the villa that night, Jeremy feels as if all colour has faded out of his life. He is trapped inside a sense of pointless loss that obscures everything around him in a permanent greyness. Vicky's voice must break through and take him back deep inside what happened to him then as her hidden colour so he can see and recover that colour as his own.

Applause as Riccardo takes the rostrum. The overture to La Traviata—and the reconstruction of his own brief ill-fated courtship with life in Italy —can begin.

Summer 1995
Italy

Phantom showdown

Could that be the place, up on the hill to his right? He slows down. Riccardo's description of the villa was vague, but there is nothing charming about what he can see from here; it is derelict. Jeremy steps hard on the accelerator, speeding past any thought that after two and a half days on the road he might be in for a grim surprise because the conductor romanticised his family's heritage.

Admittedly, it was a fun trip. He flew to Munich to pick up his new BMW M3 Convertible and spent the day looking around. By late afternoon he found himself in a beer garden on Wiener Platz, sitting next to a lively group. The English he had caught while looking for a seat on the crowded benches belonged to Tammara, a plump but attractive woman who was celebrating a birthday with friends from the university clinic nearby.

She stayed on when the others left, but she was not an easy catch by any means; her fierce temperament pit her against male colleagues—among those who had just gone home—who she claimed undermined her own qualifications as a skin surgeon. Jeremy gave her plenty of time to let off steam—about discrimination, the NHS she fled for more decent conditions, stuffy Krauts—only gradually poking her boiler to find out if there was any heat left for anything else. Gender issues pushed aside, she was pragmatic about what they both did not want to do without; a dinner somewhere was wasting time.

He had too little sleep to cover more than the Brenner Pass the next morning. He spent an afternoon on Lago di Garda and a night in Verona, then made a sprint across the Po Valley for a stop in Florence before the drive here. It was a pleasurable, exhausting journey through a country that has never been on his tour list.

He is now near where the Villa Patricelli must be, and he had better find it soon. It is too bloody hot; his slim-tailored shirt clings to him like cellophane, and his head of thick, wavy hair is a dripping bath mat. He slows almost to a halt to put the roof up and the air conditioner on, just as he arrives at the next track two miles down the road.

'Uphill, on the right, it's barely negotiable, a dirt track with high hedges on both sides,' Riccardo had said.

Jeremy ticks all the boxes, turns in, and moves forward cautiously. There will be no turning back on the narrow, rutted path.

He does not hear the tractor; the chorus of the rousing and romping 'Toasts' chorus from La Traviata is playing full blast on the stereo, and he is too preoccupied handling the jutting rocks and potholes. He misjudges one manoeuvre and jolts from the crunch on the undercarriage of his new BMW. Shit!

As if on cue, the tractor trailer barges through an opening in the hedge on his right, swerving heavily onto the track just a few yards in front of him, carrying workers from the olive groves.

Holy shit! He slams down hard on the brakes and horn. The tractor takes no notice and charges ahead, not bothered by the state of the track, ignoring him.

'A little apology might be in order!' he shouts, thumping the steering wheel. His anger is drowned out by the car stereo and the tractor, and he is rarely this loud. Growing up with a mother who shouted more than she talked, he learnt early how ineffective it is.

He climbs the hill behind the towed trailer and the track improves, but this only counts as half a blessing. Heavy clouds of dust billowing in the wake of the trailer quickly envelop him inside the car. He can hardly see or breathe, coughing uncontrollably as he trails behind.

'You're not getting away with it,' he rasps, this reflex butting in on him with the same compulsion that once pitted him against school bullies he could more wisely have ignored. He will catch up.

When he does, and when his vision eventually penetrates the dust, the workers are not far in front of him, seated higher up on benches mounted in the bed of the trailer. He takes in the shawls and hoods that protect their faces in the fields. What strikes him first is how oddly rigid their heads are, fixed in his direction as if detached from their bodies, which are being jostled about by the bumps. He looks for a reaction to the near collision; none of these hooded phantoms is acknowledging it, no gestures that hint at apology. In fact, there are no gestures between themselves, as if that would be giving something away. And trailing closely behind, he soon becomes acutely aware that every one of the aged faces gradually appearing from under their covers is, without exception, glaring down at him in his car with implacable hostility.

It takes a while for this to infiltrate his consciousness and spike a sense of alarm, like that which fills the momentary suspension of time before an unavoidable collision. And although he has just missed being in one, he still finds himself caught in that same helpless, frightful suspense, unable to steer his mind around a piercing animosity he can neither fathom nor ignore, trapped at the wheel in a mind-numbing spell he cannot shake off, even as the track once again becomes steep and less manageable, calling for his full concentration.

His attention is splintered into too many reflexes triggered at the same time. He cannot break free of their spell as he fights the dust and oppressive heat, dirt-slick sweat dripping down his face as he drives almost blind, ready at any moment to feel another agonising crunch. When he dangerously swerves around a jutting rock, he looks up as he straightens out again as if expecting the near miss to compel a response—any at all—from his stone-faced tormentors. He switches on his wipers to see the trailer more clearly; the splash congeals heavy dust on his windscreen into a muddy smear, forcing him to stop. By the time the window clears, they are farther away, but steadfast in their unrelenting scrutiny.

'Come on, give over,' he silently pleads, making light of his own stupidity with a small shirk of the shoulders and a self-effacing smile. He lifts his hand up from the steering wheel in a cautious wave. Nothing. Still no reaction. Let them go.

He wipes his brow and rubs his eyes as if waking up from a sweaty nightmare. When he looks up, they are out of sight. What a grim bunch. But he could be assuming hostility that was not there. It was not a showdown. It could be the opposite, although that is not too appealing either: he was studiously ignored. It is his first encounter with people Riccardo described as 'removed' from outsiders. The shock of a near collision after long hours of driving and his first taste of the midday heat here distorted the impression they made on him. And these workers have had to endure that same stupefying heat all morning in the groves, so maybe he should give them the benefit of doubt: they are not hostile, just numb, exhausted, senseless, and inhospitable to anything that might delay shade and rest. Perhaps they even deserve some sympathy for their hard life in the fields; that would at least allow him to (make) believe the animosity he saw in their faces was not at all directed at him. He hopes he is on the right track about them, about where this track will lead him, and continues to creep up the hill in his now obscurely black BMW convertible.

Noble facade

Coming out of a slight bend, any doubts are at once dispelled. Ahead, he takes in the sun-bleached facade of a two-storey villa that radiates past wealth and noble pride as much as it reveals, at closer range, that neither exist any longer. As he drives up, he can see the louvred shutters on the tall windows are badly weathered and missing some of their slats, the relief stonework framing the windows is chipped or missing in places, and the sculptured family insignia resting on the pediment of the arched main door is heavily eroded. But ultimately, the precise spatial dimensions and classical sobriety of the whole front defy any impression of spiritless dilapidation. He sees early Renaissance charm, decadently run-down, and lets out a sigh of relief. This must be it. He has arrived.

A quick look around him when he gets out of the car tells him that what had probably once been a charming walled garden in front of the villa was abandoned long ago. A few myrtles, hibiscus, and bougainvillea in blossom cheer up the random remains. Only hardy evergreen shrubs like them have survived amidst the wild grass on the parched soil. Creeper weeds cover the border stones of formally spaced flower beds and obscure the paths between them. But he is not a gardener. It is pretty enough for being wild.

Perched on a slope falling steeply away behind its parapet wall, the garden gives Jeremy full view of the rows of olive trees below that the labourers were working on, and ladders propped against the trees tell him there is still work to be done today.

'Poor peasants.' He spits out the words as he walks along the wall, and at once reminds himself not to be patronising, which he often is when rubbed the wrong way. Even so, the epithet makes his encounter with them feel he need not waste his time thinking about them.

How the people here tick is not his concern. He has come to escape distractions he will likely soon miss while here on his own, never having spent much time away from the hustle and flair of city life, and looking around him now, he can see he could not have put himself farther away from its temptations. His cell phone might nevertheless weaken self-discipline: Vicky has tried four times already. He takes it out, removes the battery, and throws it as far as his damaged elbow can manage. If no one thought he was serious when he said '*incommunicato*!', they will now. He has come here for a purpose, and only one.

However long it takes, he will only be returning home when he has regained command of the instrument that now threatens to defeat him. Almost all the concertos he had mastered since becoming a soloist years ago once again present a challenge. He must ignore doubts that he can again become the sought-after oboist he was before the accident.

His last questionable performance as a substitute first oboist under Riccardo's baton still squeaks at him, like the reed that also turned bad on him that night. He will need many more of them, too, by rehearsals in November. It would be nothing short of a godsend to go back with a few more reliably good ones to get him through the tour than the meagre collection he has. He is booked for better venues than he has ever had.

When he drove through the entrance, the hedge to his right blocked his view of the rubbish tip he now discovers as he peers over that end of the parapet wall. The mound of cascading empty plastic containers, crates, tyres, and split bags of household garbage is shocking. And the nasty truth is his own garbage out here in this remote place will be adding to the heap. He takes in a deep breath, relieved there is no stench to give its hiding place away. He did not expect roses in the garden, either. Nevertheless, his impression of the place so far makes him wary about the state of things inside when he turns away from the groves below to face the villa. It is time to find out.

He strains to hear any sign of life. Where there is waste, there are people, and Riccardo did say the villa's land is leased. The last three generations of Riccardo's family found life in Rome more agreeable, so visits by him and his brothers over the years have been limited to surveying the eighty or so hectares that once earned the villa's fortunes and many village people a meagre

10

livelihood harvesting olive and fruit trees and breeding sheep.

It is their midday break. Lunch, *il pranzo*, followed by a siesta; no one is likely to be around until at least four or five in the afternoon. The tractor driver has deposited his heat-stricken admirers somewhere else, and Jeremy is not in a hurry to meet any of them. He can let himself in and fetches the key from his car.

The front-door terrace above him, supported on columns connected by semicircular arches, forms a portico to the entrance to storerooms below the residence, dug out of the incline on which the villa stands. It makes him feel unbearably hot just to think how cool it would be in there as he climbs the stairs to the left of the portico. A few of the marble steps are cracked from obvious attempts made to remove them for another life, and two of them have been 'successfully replaced' by poorer stone slabs. The mosaic floor of the terrace in front of the door is faded but intact and should be attractive once he has given it a scrub. There is room for a table, and he can already see himself sitting here when it is cooler with a morning coffee. Or a glass of wine in the evening? On either side of the massive front door are tall arched niches, now empty of whatever statues were once there but with two empty wine bottles standing in for the one on the left.

Parched and sweating out his mounting frustration with the door minutes later, he discovers that no matter how far he inserts the long, heavy neck of the key, it wobbles inside the lock and nothing turns. 'Jesus fucking Christ, let me in!' he screams, banging on the door with his left hand, pointlessly turning the key with his right.

'Chi è?'

Jeremy is startled by how threateningly close the man is when he spins his head round to face him. Shorter, but heavily built, with darkly inset eyes and a conspicuously thick nose. A scruffy broad-rimmed cloth cap is pulled over a squarish head held up by a squat neck and broad shoulders with gladiator biceps. A brute to match the gruff voice, and the cap tells him who this is: the tractor driver, the confrontation he told himself he wanted. Jeremy turns hesitantly to face him. His rudimentary Italian will not help. He understands Italian better than the operas and school Latin have

11

taught him to speak it.

He speaks slowly, evenly, trusting his boldness will hold out, pointing to the track and miming a crash with his fists. 'Down there, you crash nearly my car.'

'Ti ho sentito,' the driver says, he had heard Jeremy's car. 'No point in stopping, was there? We missed each other. Now, who are you?'

'Mi chiamo Jeremy . . . amico di Riccardo?'

The brute's blank look makes Jeremy suddenly aware of the useless key in his hand. Wrong place after all? Oh hell . . .

'Riccardo Patricelli? He not informed you?' Jeremy waits.

The driver takes off his cap to scratch his head and wipe his brow. 'We hardly ever see any of them here. Which one is he?'

What a relief. This is the right place. 'Riccardo, il direttore?' This appears to draw another blank. Jeremy briefly mimes a conductor at the podium. 'Sinfonia?'

'Ah, sì, il direttore d'orchestra. I don't ever meet him here. And you? Why are you here?'

'I play the oboe.' Jeremy can only hope he is understood as he gesticulates and stumbles through uncertain vocabulary. 'Sono un solista. I come here to prepare for concerts. Me in bad accident, ugly, very ugly. Motorbike, broke my chest, crushed my arm. I must practice, lots of practice, here, alone.'

'Come mai qui?'

'Perché qui? Idea Riccardo. Sono venuto qui solo per lavoro. Senza . . . distrazione. Senza . . . tentazione. Dolce vita in città molto lontana. Quarantena. Dolce vita arrivederci . . .'

'Vuoi vivere qui?'

'Sì . . . sì . . . solo per un soggiorno breve.'

The driver slaps his cap back on, then adjusts it carefully, looking at him, as if deciding just how short his stay should be. The brute extends a sweaty hand. 'Bene. We forget about before. Unfortunate.'

Jeremy instantly feels the pain shoot up from his right hand as it is gripped brutally hard by one twice the size. Then the crunch. He yells out, yanking his hand away and holding the wrist in his other hand, trying to shake off the cramp in his squashed fingers. 'Bloody hell! That is all I need right now.'

The driver looks away, and when he turns back, Jeremy detects the coda of a smirk on the man's lips. With his arms now folded across his chest, half resting on a sizable belly, the brute's face presents an air of contentment Jeremy would rather ignore.

He closes his eyes for a moment to shut out any suspicion of menace if he intends to stay here. 'Molto molto forza mano,' he says, hoping it means heavy-handed, massaging the hand to that effect.

'Sorry. Out here we forget city people are soft boned,' the driver says, openly smirking this time. 'I won't offer you my hand again. Giorgio. I'm in charge here. Your key is not to this door. Follow me.'

Giorgio leads him down the steps and up the path at the side of the villa, towards the back. As they round the corner, Jeremy takes in the chapel in an overgrown elevated garden beyond a dusty backyard, another small building he later knows to be the baking house, and an open corrugated-roof shed under which the tractor is parked. Next to it, Giorgio's beat-up car.

The rest is chaos. Piles of olive tree offcuts, disused barrels, wooden crates, plastic containers, and broken ladders all randomly scatter the yard's perimeter at the far end. And within clear view, an open compost heap. In front of it, a chained dog. It does not bark but looks at them expectantly, weakly wagging its tail, waiting for an invitation to move towards its master, taking a few cautious steps.

'Torna al tuo posto!' It is Giorgio who barks and points towards the ground. The dog turns back, sits, then lies down, dejected. Jeremy's neighbour points to a door in an annexed building attached to the unornamented back of the villa. 'That is my office. This is your door.'

Jeremy is at last in front of the door that opens with the key in his hand.

Bare comfort

The cliché of a haunted mansion comes to mind when he opens the massive squeaking door, sweeping away the thick spiderweb behind it to enter an empty windowless supply room. The air inside is so cool he almost shivers at the contrast through his soaked shirt. He enters the hall through the next door he opens and continues straight ahead through another heavy oak double door to the reception room—its fireplace, bordered by a decorative stone mantelpiece, the only surviving decorative feature, although it has been sealed off. When are temperatures here cool enough to need it?

He goes straight to the main door entrance, set into the two-feet-thick outer wall, and unbolts it. The heat outside hits him like a blast from an open furnace when he pulls the double door wide open. He at once pushes the doors shut again, resting his back against them and waiting for his eyes to adjust, letting his gaze follow the height of the dimly lit room from floor to ceiling.

As he discovers, all the rooms in the villa have the same terracotta floors and exposed-timber ceilings high above whitewashed walls, which likely cover murals that do not appeal to the present generation of Patricelli. The austere simplicity of this room, now furnished with a sturdy, long, unvarnished table and benches, tells him the villa has been rough-handedly refurbished for short stays by the family after a long period of neglect. But the noble spaciousness of the sparsely furnished room has undeniable appeal compared to the modest dimensions of his apartment in London.

He opens a door to the right of the main entrance. This room is completely dark, and when he finds a light switch, he is stunned. The light is coming from an enormous chandelier suspended directly above a spectacular snooker table. It certainly dwarfs the table he has in his apartment. A complete rack of cues is mounted on one of the wood-panelled walls, and he now sees the louvred

14

windows are additionally curtained floor to ceiling in dark-red velvet. This room has not been touched by time; it is as decadently opulent as when it first came to be. A bronze nameplate from the company that built the table dates it to 1870. The Patricelli certainly had money back then, and Jeremy would have liked to see what Riccardo's ancestors looked like, assuming their portraits once filled the distinct square patches on the walls where pictures have been removed.

His favourite pastime at home in London is right here. While he improves his game on this table, he will get back on top for the tour. It is the perfect balance between something he loves to practice and practice he is inclined to like a lot less, were it not essential for the thrill of performing concerts and the good life he earns from them.

The door to the left of the main entrance leads to what must have been a salon or study; the only furniture in the room is an old roll-top desk against the wall opposite a bank of tall windows. Small drawers, inset behind the desktop, are an ideal place to protect his precious reeds and store tools to make new ones. He claps. The sound is good. This is where he will work: the now music room.

The kitchen, off the hallway next to the stairs, is dominated by a huge, solid, square table—that must be as old as the villa—sitting in the middle of the room. An open fireplace, where cooking probably took place when the villa was built, was later joined by an immovably large wood-burning stove, its front and sides finished in ceramic. A flat, slightly inclined granite wash table with buckets below it sits in the farthest corner of the room. The windows are both high up in the wall facing the courtyard; the servants who once worked here were not to be observed while they suffered the heat when cooking in here. The large, old fridge is unplugged. He prays it still works. The wooden cupboards have everything needed in plain cutlery, pots, and pans to cook and scive a large family—cook! How am I going to cook? Hang on here! Riccardo cannot possibly expect me to cook on a wood stove. There is no charm in that idea at all!

On the wall closest to the kitchen door, he spots telltale signs of cooking above a marble-topped table pushed against it. He eventually finds a two-ring, bottle-gas cooker in a large storeroom off the kitchen. Cooking is going to be a very simple affair, necessarily so. Pasta diet, salads, steak. It will do.

He brings his car round to the back of the villa, unloads it, and is relieved to discover the fridge is cool when he stores away a bag of car-warm assorted snacks, wine, and a bottle of water he half empties with greedy gulps. He is tired, almost dizzy with fatigue when he closes the fridge door.

Two flights of stairs, interrupted by a landing with a window looking out onto the courtyard, take him up to the bedrooms and a white-tiled shower room with a sink. There is no curtain around the shower, no toiletry cabinet; it is primitive, but it is clean. Nothing noble about it, nor all the other rooms he goes through, each sparsely furnished with just beds and a closet for clothes and bed linen. He chooses one of the front corner rooms. It is the only one with a double bed. He strips off his wet shirt and collapses backwards onto the bare mattress with a deep sigh. He closes his eyes and unconsciously strokes his damaged arm, only now digesting his encounter with the tractor, with Giorgio, before dozing off.

The first REM phase, following deep sleep, puts him moments before his crash on the motorbike months ago. He is fast approaching the sign he did not heed then and sees it now, warning him of a side road on his left; it feeds into the one he is on, just after the blind bend he is taking too fast. As he leans into the right-hand curve, he is suddenly confronted with a car turning right into the side road. His bike is going to hit the car side-on.

The impending crash jolts him awake on the bed. He can feel his pulse racing and breathes in short bursts, his eyes wide open. The close call with Giorgio probably triggered it this time, but it has happened a few times since the accident; the trauma specialist in hospital warned not to talk about it or risk revisiting his horror.

When his pulse and breathing slow down and he feels calm again, he stretches both his arms out straight in the air, turning his open palms outwards. This is his fingerwork problem: his right elbow only allows him to twist that palm halfway round, and the wrist is too stiff and inflexible to wriggle it, which he needs to do for certain keys played in quick succession with the fourth and fifth

16

finger; E flat and C to D flat are going to take a lot of adaptation of fingerwork.

He lets his arms flop back onto the bed and finds himself, curiously, in a crucifix position. 'Hail Ms Mary full of Grace, remember me? You'd better bloody well put things right again.'

Siesta awakening

It is late afternoon, and while Jeremy sleeps, the tractor gets ready to return to the groves, the workers taking their places on the trailer and talking amongst themselves.

'What's he doing here?'

'The brothers probably sent him.'

'What a show-off. Look at that fancy car, will you?'

'All city people are show-offs.'

'So, has he been sent?'

'Why do any of the brothers ever come back here?'

'To check up on us.'

'To make sure they're still making money—on our backs.'

'Like they have for the last 300 years.'

'Don't remind us.'

Giorgio hears them through the door to his office and comes out to take the driver's seat on the tractor.

'Giorgio, is he here to check up on us?'

The Patricelli brothers visited two years ago, and they were not happy with the family's share of the olive oil revenue they are entitled to as part of the leasehold. Giorgio is fed up with the lot of them, but especially Riccardo. Does that idiot really think more can be had from what he is doing here? The workers he can get out here are meanwhile old and too slow, which forces him to start picking earlier than he wants to these days. If he waits until the olives are at their peak oil yield, the harvest window is too small, especially picking by hand. There are still a couple of months to go, but there's no harm in reminding everyone they are going to be repeating the long days forced on them last year.

'I don't know, maybe. He says he's a musician, but he is a friend of phoney Riccardo, so who knows?' Giorgio starts the engine. 'Now, let's finish our inspection and set the traps down there today. There is rain coming, so we can expect plenty of flies, and we must be ready for them.'

18

The noise of the tractor outside his window ends Jeremy's siesta. He feels groggy and his mouth is dry. On his way down to the kitchen for a drink, almost at the landing window, he catches sight of a scruffy, heavy-set young man admiring his car in the courtyard. Admiration is, in fact, too weak to describe how enthralled the scruff is, caressing the contours of the car body and ignoring the heavy dust as his palms stroke the car slowly along its length. Jeremy is a car enthusiast, but this devotional intimacy is too embarrassing to watch, although he cannot help doing so. He stands back from the window and goes back up a few steps to avoid detection.

Fabio has always wanted his own Alfa Romeo. It has taken him years to save up a deposit from his pay at the canning factory where he works in winter, before shearing time. Since he now works there part-time all year round he can just scrape up the monthly payments for the coupe; living at home to help with the sheep costs him nothing. But his mother will not have it. She just does not understand wanting anything that is not a necessity or that tests God's goodwill, which is why the five of them live in a makeshift two-room stone dwelling just up the hill.

This BMW is real competition to the Alfa, Fabio thinks. He brushes the dust off on his trousers and tries the door handle on the driver's side. It's open! He looks up at the villa to check it is safe. Did he just spot feet on the stairs behind that window? Is he being watched? Car owners can be touchy. The owner of this totally neglected beauty should hide in shame; it is filthy. He would take better care of it, would show more respect for a car like this. With his knee, he clicks the door shut again and leans forward to look through the car window. He burns to drive a car like this, to feel its speed in the wind through his hair with the roof down. He lets his hand trail along the body to the front of the bonnet, and then he wanders off.

Panorama

Jeremy came up to the roof terrace of the villa to catch the last rays of the sunset that now bathe the breathtaking view in an orange gold he cannot compare with any sunset he has seen before. From every corner of the terrace, which tops the entire villa, he can see the barren golden-brown rounded peaks of the Sabina Hills around him, skirted below by rows of silver-green olive trees, clusters of pine, cypress, oak, and ash, flowering shrubs, and grassland. The nearby village straddles a long ridge higher up opposite him across the valley. He can make out a steep dirt track that leads across to it; he has the wrong sort of car for this rural outpost.

By the time it is dusk, he is at the bottom of his first glass of wine. The siesta did him good, the air is pleasantly warm, and the scenery rewards his long journey here. The idea of staying feels more positive and less like a sacrifice of the pleasures Riccardo persuaded him to leave behind to work here alone. An hour of practice he promised himself after his nap still awaits him downstairs.

As he turns to go, his attention is drawn by sheep being led out into the fields from their shaded enclosure next to a stone dwelling farther up the track behind the villa. He is quickly inspired by the fading sound of their bleating departure to add something to this pastoral setting, make it his own, lift it out of reach of the urban noise he has left behind him. Oboe d'amore would be perfect, and he goes to fetch it; Bach's 'Sinfonia in D' is his standard encore piece.

Jeremy does not realise it, but he has an audience. Fabio's mother sits in the kitchen reading aloud with difficulty from a psalm she is trying to memorise when she hears him through the open window and stops absently swatting flies from her face to listen. In the fields Fabio's father stops singing to his sheep in his low nasal voice when the music upstages him and takes over his audience. Even though Jeremy is not aware of it, the sound of his oboe floods the valley from the villa rooftop, just as the barking does that will keep him awake well into the night. Even people in the village might hear him if they listened closely, not counting the loud men in the bar playing out their last decisive round of cards for the day and Isabella, diligently practicing her English on her bed in her tiny bedroom, headphones plugged in, quietly repeating sentences from an old cassette recorder.

However inspired Jeremy's impromptu performance, he found it hard to stabilise the sweeping melody of the sinfonia through a grounded force from his abdomen. His ribs still hurt too much, putting enormous pressure on his thorax to sustain the long low notes. He rubs the pain away from his tendon-squeezed thyroid and briefly inspects the reed he has used. It held out better than he expected, but it was definitely not responsive enough for any kind of subtle modulation.

Reeds are the only reason he had to delay his start as a soloist. His career depends on them, but every time he takes out his tools to work on another segment of cane, failure clings to him like a clumsy glove he cannot shake off. It was made long ago by his clinging mother, and he still struggles to peel it off, still hears her insist in graveyard tones that failure is the price he must pay for his sins. Just what those sins were she never said, nor did she punish him for anything he did—or did not do—to provoke some form of retribution. As a boy, he goaded his teachers incessantly but was not punished for being thrown out of school. His mother ruled over his life through guilt, and in the absence of punishment, it resonated with him like tinnitus.

As far as she was concerned, his insecurity and unworthiness were the direct consequence of his not seeking salvation; only a pure spirit could prevail. He tried to make her—not her bitter threats of failure—part of his life and finally did give in, becoming an altar boy to please her, only to discover that Catholic teaching assumes everyone sins and everyone can be forgiven. But it was already too late to convert him to the idea of forgiveness and he would not let the Church decide what sin is, or punishment. Like

21

the stars out tonight, his link to either was light years away from anything he could feel, and the idea that his behaviour would first have consequences after this life was beyond cynical. He left the Church. And although he has often been irresponsible, he does not see anything he has done as sinful, and he probably never will unless he is one day punished in the here and now for something he himself feels is unforgivingly evil.

He later took up music and was naturally gifted, but he denied it vehemently when the music academy selected him, convinced he would fail as his mother predicted before he even started. Jansen somehow saw behind his negativity and took him on, soon irreversibly convinced of his talent. Realising his self-chastisement would not deter his amicable instructor, Jeremy reinvented himself. Fictional past achievements that made him worthy of admiration made him someone he could be proud of, his good looks helping him to notch up conquests over women with careless abandon.

Even so, his student days were anything but carefree. Every less than perfect performance at the academy was a reminder that his insincerity and conceit went hand in hand with having chosen the most unyielding wind instrument there is to pursue his musical career, provoking likely failure in becoming the soloist Jansen was sure he would be.

He succeeded and overcame his fear, replacing failure with the magical, electrifying symbiosis he feels in front of an audience urging him on to move and inspire them. Even if the piece tonight demanded 150 per cent from him, to deliver just 85 per cent of his best, he will not be thwarted by his injuries, and tonight, at least, the reed's stubbornness yielded to his will. He must not allow the penance he must pay for each mediocre reed to become severe. If the guilt of failure is inbred and unavoidable, the oboe must give a voice to forgiveness. That is, after all, the only faith he needs.

In one last look at the clear night sky, unable to remember any of his classroom astronomy warriors, he can see he may face mental battles here with his mother once more, confrontations she devised to keep him small and doubting his worth, and he has kept at a safe distance by losing himself in the distractions of the city, where the stars are not even visible.

First encounters

He feels slightly guilty about not coming outside yesterday to meet the young man admiring his car. This spotless car can only be his doing, inside too; Jeremy forgot to lock it. Why did the car freak bother? The effort is pointless on the roads around here. What is the scruffy car worshipper after?

He sees the door to the office is open, the tractor parked outside it. He looks in through the door on Giorgio's broad back. He is sticking Post-it notes on a large-scale map of the property, swapping their positions around and mumbling under his breath. The man's irritability is palpable even before Jeremy offers a cautious 'buongiorno'.

Giorgio does not turn around. He speaks as if he couldn't care less how well he is understood: fast, angrily, staccato.

'Tell Riccardo he can forget about higher production. The people I can find here are too old for the job. Two with bad backs, two with bad knees, and two that simply called off work today. I might be facing an invasion of fruit flies. There's no one to help me. How can I protect 3,000 trees if I have no people?'

Getting the gist of this tirade, it is obvious to Jeremy that Giorgio wants to let off steam from whatever pressure he is under from Riccardo, who is obviously more involved with what goes on here than Jeremy thought. What can he do to calm the man down? Repetition helps; you take a deep breath, go through the notes slowly, and then repeat again in the right tempi.

'What you want me tell Riccardo. Lentamente. So I understand.'

'Tell him what you want,' Giorgio says belligerently. 'Whatever you came to find out.'

'I only come now to ask about the boy who cleaned my car.'

'Fabio. Slow, lazy boy, crazy about fast cars.'

'I noticed.'

'Don't let him drive it, whatever you do. That's what he wants.'

'Should I pay him, then?'

23

'Only people who do an honest day's work should get paid.' Giorgio turns his attention back to the map on the wall, ending the conversation.

Jeremy leaves the doorway with a meek 'buona fortuna', aware that what he does is probably not considered work by Giorgio and his overworked labourers. Amen. He promised he would keep to himself anyway. Only, he and Giorgio are sharing the same property, and this unfriendliness makes him feel out of place, uncomfortable, as if it is something he should find a way to correct. Maybe it would help make some sort of connection if he read up on olives, showed an interest in what is going on here. He approaches the dog to give it a comforting pat, but it at once cowers away from him.

Just outside the gate to the villa, he faces the choice of going back down to the main trunk road to find a paved one leading to the village or up the track he saw from the terrace last night, which would be the more direct option. He is now on another deeply rutted test of his patience, but the dust is behind him this time and he makes fast progress, soon enjoying the driving challenge, taking the few short smooth stretches at speed before braking hard to inch forward where necessary. Presto, andante—and when he hits the first tarmac—allegro, passing a bar and entering the village square almost before he realises it.

He parks next to an old immaculately kept yellow Fiat 500, the Cinquecento, an iconic car he sees complements the austere simplicity of the parochial church in front of it; its sober front pediment and arched doorway and window are outlined in the same yellow against a coral-pink facade. The houses around the square, with their weathered louvered windows and unpainted plaster, are drab by comparison; the assorted bare bricks of the two-storey building housing the bar reveal an original structure that has been successively built on over the years with purely practical intentions. Not an attractive village, he concludes, disappointed in his anticipation of a more rustic atmosphere to match the villa he assumes first brought the village into being.

He briefly admires the Cinquecento. When he looks around the square, he cannot help but notice that all the other cars he sees around him are older models, much older models, some better cared for than others. More vintage poverty than vintage pride, he thinks, and he goes for a coffee in the hope of finding out what this sort of village could possibly have to offer him before venturing any farther into it.

It is mid-morning. The bar is empty of men doing an honest day's work, he reminds himself, and he interrupts the owner reading his newspaper on a stool behind the counter. His cheery 'buongiorno' is met with the nod of a head briefly appearing over the top of the page and going back down again. He would walk out on such a rude response in London, but he decides in the barman's favour that he is being treated as a local whose presence and patience at this time of day are casually taken for granted. When the paper reluctantly closes and the barman gets up, Jeremy puts on a modest smile and asks for an espresso.

While the black brew trickles down into the cup, he asks the barman's back where he can buy groceries. 'Alimentari qui?'

Without turning to face him the barman says, 'Down the main street, butcher on your right, farther on, the rest.' And presenting the cup, he adds, 'Cinque-cento.' Courtesy is as plentiful here as what one lira could buy.

The coffee that he drinks under the still-mild sun on the steps of the small bar terrace is as he likes it: bitter. Getting to know the locals will hopefully not leave the same taste. He has been made to feel unwelcome by everyone since he arrived.

The square is eerily quiet. The benches in the shade of olive trees next to the church are empty. He has seen no one, although the parked cars suggest there are people around. A half-open pair of shutters on the first floor of the building opposite are drawn closed, and he suspects he is under observation. It rekindles a smouldering antagonism, taking him back to when he was the target of teachers who wanted him out, wanted to catch him out doing something in class he should not be doing.

He takes a last sip of coffee, puts down the cup, clasps his hands behind his head, and arches his back, his chest out, smiling. Catch me.

What a beautiful smile, she thinks, what a handsome man. Not too much macho muscle but nimbly lean, dressed in casually elegant clothes. Isabella knows a lot about clothes she cannot afford from the countless pictures pasted on her walls, pictures that would make her part of the cosmopolitan world beyond her reach. Now this world has come to her. The English prince has come to take her away.

The momentary fantasy is so childish she giggles. There is no way she could even meet him to find out what he is like. He is staying at the villa, which puts him out of bounds, and in the village all eyes are on her, anxious if she shows the slightest interest in anyone other than Marco. To be seen alone with this nice-looking stranger would not just raise eyebrows.

Just about everyone, including her parents, insist Marco is her ideal match and they will make a perfect couple one day. It has become a promise she is expected to keep, and she cannot find a way out of it, since it is her own fault everybody thinks that way. She made the mistake of pretending to be in love with him at the age of thirteen when TV soaps she closely followed at the time made her want to find out what it would feel like to be in a relationship. In real life, she soon lost interest and dropped the slippery addiction; love dramas were not for her. Although she feels she is forcing herself to hang out with Marco sometimes, it avoids another drama at home with her mother, who still worships the idea that she and Marco will 'grow together'. But she has either grown up faster than he has, or he has stayed behind, completely unaware of the gap. She has not given in to him, and he has respected that, sure enough in his boyish pride not to chase her and more than confident she will give in eventually. She is not at all sure she will ever want to.

Her indecision about him is not just from the gap between them but from the bigger gaping question of what alternatives she has now that she is nineteen. She does not want to land up simply being the mother of babies created by 'the village's best-looking couple', according to her mother. That is not enough. Her mother meets any of her cautiously voiced doubts with: 'Give it time, Bella, you will see.' Her father's approach is painfully blunt, maybe only because Marco's father is a friend and partner at the card table: 'What are you waiting for?'

Imagining what it would be like to meet a real man of the world who is much older than she is makes her feel a bit childish, even.

She pulls the shutters in and practices anyway. 'I am *so* pleased to meet you. I am so *pleased* to meet you. I am so pleased to meet *you*. Where are you from?' The stylishly sleek chariot he drives reminds her she does not have a clue about people in his world: living in style, with plenty of money.

Jeremy stands, stretching his body before he nimbly scoops up the empty cup and strides purposefully into the bar, coming back out moments later to return to his car. As if out of nowhere, there are now three older boys on scooters clustered around it. The trio's obvious leader is slightly taller than the others, self-assured, sporting a half-open shirt. He is very aware his looks outshine his companions, who by comparison appear slouched and sloppily dressed.

Marco is always carefully groomed, and his doting mother has always made sure he is never short of clean, washed, and pressed clothes. Demonstrating his superior status to the *Inglese* when he approaches, Marco moves closer to the car, leaving his companions just behind him.

'A che velocità va?' he asks quickly, his chin pointing dismissively at the car.

Jeremy stops in his tracks before reaching his car. He refuses to accept not being acknowledged by anyone with a civil greeting, and this cocky sod's jutting-jaw arrogance is just not on. 'Buongiorno,' he says, holding a false smile and the awkward pause it causes even if that marks him as a condescending senior insisting on a respectful reply.

The gang leader locks into his forced smile—not to do so would be giving in—then briefly exchanges looks with his mates and turns back to face him. 'Hello,' he offers, hanging on the word, drawing it out.

'You speak English?' Jeremy asks.

'Preferisco l'italiano,' Marco says, sharing a smirk with his friends.

Are these young studs wanting to take the piss?

You like the car?' Jeremy asks. 'Ti piace la macchina?'

The boyish macho combs his fingers through thick, slick black hair and takes his time to let his eyes follow the length of the car. 'E' davvero . . . "flash",' he says, just short of a sneer on his invented English word.

'È un complimento?'

'Forse sì, forse no.'

'I see. Maybe yes—if you can drive it? Maybe no—if you can't drive, only look at it?'

'I know how to drive,' the head stud says, 'but who wants to drive on the wrong side? E' stupido.'

Jeremy shrugs. 'I'm used to it.'

'I could never get used to doing something stupid.'

Even his poor grasp of Italian tells Jeremy he has just been called stupid. 'Capisco. Is English stupid, too?'

'Non abbiamo bisogno dell'inglese. Ci capiamo l'un l'altro.'

They do not need English. They understand each other and have no desire to understand him. Fine. Jeremy raises his hands, gesturing he cannot help them in that case, punctuating what is the end of the exchange for him with a bleep from his car as he unlocks it with his remote key. 'Preferisco l'inglese,' he says, reaching for the door.

'How fast?' the big shot asks in English.

'Why do you want to know?'

'I was thinking of buying one.' The mock-serious reply—in Italian again—sparks laughter from Marco's mates which he glances back to acknowledge. 'But with the driver on the correct side,' he adds, prompting another outburst.

Jeremy pretends to join in the laughter. Time for him to take the piss. He makes a sweeping gesture at the car, taps it with his hand like a practiced salesman. 'OK, signore, permetta introduzione.'

'Per favore!' Marco says.

'Sí! Sí!' the others join in.

Jeremy rattles off a few of the BMW's specs in English he knows will stump them. 'This convertible has a naturally aspirated three-litre inline-six engine featuring double VANOS, Motronic engine management, and a six-speed sequential gearbox—'

'Stop! Cosa succede?' Marco cuts in.

'Oh, so sorry. How utterly silly of me. English is obviously beyond your capacity,' Jeremy continues in English, pretending to reproach himself.

'Non capisco niente!'

'Scusate. Non capisci l'inglese? *Solo* l'italiano? Che stupido . . . da parte mia. Velocità maxima?'

'Sì.'

'Il tuo scooterino moltiplicato per . . . dieci? 240.'

Marco takes in this put-down with a swipe over his face, nods back at his mates, and they all restart their scooters. 'Really? That's definitely not my speed. No, really, it's too . . . slow!' And with that the gang ride off, hooting and howling their delight at getting the better of him.

He watches them go. How on earth did he end up bragging about his car? What a stupid, childish thing to do. He gets in and collects his thoughts for a moment without starting the engine. He let himself be provoked. The boy's cockiness takes him back to his own at that age, when he took the piss out of anyone who came off as too superior for his liking. But was his insistence on civility just now what the boy objected to? It is much more likely that he is simply too 'flash' for this cheerless place. While lost in thought, he starts the engine and begins to reverse.

'Hey! Attento! Guarda dove vai!'

Jeremy's brakes squeak to a stop. The old, stooped man behind him is shocked but unharmed. Window shutters open.

He jumps out of the car and goes to him, apologising profusely 'Sorry! Scusate! Non ho visto. Tutto bene?' He lightly touches the old man's shoulder, and his hand is brusquely brushed away followed by unpleasant mumbles he cannot catch as the man wanders off. Window shutters close, but he can sense all eyes through them are still on him.

The day is off to a bad start. Maybe he should avoid the village, take a long drive instead to a supermarket in a bigger town somewhere else. But wait, he thinks, what's up with me? I'm a guest of the family that gave the square I'm on its name, aren't I? I have been invited to appear on their stage. I will not bow out now like a lame actor afraid of his audience. If I'm an unwanted outsider, I'll play my role up front, make *them* squirm before I do, and stay blind to what goes on behind me. But maybe not when I'm driving, he reminds himself.

Dom Pietro has been expecting the visitor, a friend of Riccardo's. Alessia already put him in the picture of the stranger's arrival yesterday, says the *estraneo* is a show-off. Let them all make up their own minds—for the time being. What he sees out of the window of the rectory directly beside the church confirms his assumptions about the company the once-devout Patricelli keep these days. The expensive fancy car was sure to be a magnet for the younger ones in the village, like Marco, Ramiro, and Francesco.

How he hates extravagance! How hard he has worked to drill out any temptation for it in the village. It is rare his followers, set back here from pleasure-hunting iniquities they cannot afford, are confronted with big-city bait on their own doorstep. But the boys outside are not all over the car, and that is a good sign. The man's showy appearance tells him how well parents under his guidance have guarded younger ones against infectious, frivolous, material wants, the gadgets and brand fashion no one needs.

His credo is restraint against all unnecessary possessions. Only restraint avoids envy, levels the playing field, prevents poor people from borrowing beyond their means, and makes sure no one feels left out; only restraint leaves something—from the near hand-to-mouth income of his followers—to donate to the Church so he can keep his parish going and stall the bishop's threat to close this loyal outpost of believers he has so carefully nurtured.

He sees the English visitor admiring his dependable Cinquecento; it sets an example, copied by almost everyone in the village, of his own frugality. He wants how he lives to edify God's will, to preserve what has been given to him and not covet more. That is what he preaches, what he learnt from his devout father, who showed him how strict discipline in the ways of God allowed him to stand above the extraneous worries, wants, and accompanying crime of the poor Naples community he grew up in. The Church has always been his home, his sanctuary, his life. He was teased about his piety, and his faith grew stronger. He was already convinced of his calling by the time he reached puberty.

Outside of his seminary in America, which put his faith in the institution of the Church to the test, he has never doubted his decision. He has learnt to ignore the Church's preoccupation with itself and its wealth. Following in the footsteps of his father, he has always had the mission to establish genuine faith and correct the weaknesses, temptations, and envy that harm the community, by dedicating himself to the spiritual guidance and morality that protects everyone in it.

The truth is, keeping the right balance in any community is everything but easy. God's standards are strict, and he represents them, fervently, but he cannot control who does or does not heed them in the spirit intended. He was determined to achieve more than the perfunctory worship he witnessed in America—here in the village, too, when he first arrived. He may have encouraged women like Alessia too strongly, and the older women in his congregation who have nothing much to live on other than their faith, but the small devout following he started with have given his congregation conviction and cohesion. Although moral discipline, which comes naturally with people's understanding of God's will, should not lead villagers to judge each other's morality, turning their backs on each other, or on people of lesser faith who might consider a return to the rural life their grandparents or parents once fled for the city. The village is shrinking.

And intolerance is growing. He was shocked when rumours circulated that Signor Accardi took home more than only his salary each month from his new government job. They were good Catholics—Mass every Sunday without fail. Whether or not their piety was real, many deprived villagers saw the family's less modest lifestyle after Signor Accardi landed the job as profane self-indulgence. The back-stabbing response the family faced should have warned him of an overzealous strain in his congregation he must contain, while at the same time it told him why *everyone* in this poor community would do best to show absolute moderation. He should have intervened but told himself the rumours would die eventually. They did not. It was an ugly mess and a big loss when the large family, silently ostracised, decided to pack up and leave, bleeding the village of three generations, and donations he badly needed for the upkeep of the church, school, and nursery. He had not taken confessions from anyone that would get him to the bottom of where some corrective guidance was needed.

The phone rings while he is observing Riccardo's friend in his car. The announced call is punctual.

'Salve, Signor Accardi.'

'Salve, Padre. You received my letter?'

'I did, yes. I deeply regret the rumours.'

'Rumours? Someone has since called my office. I have been accused of taking bribes in my job!'

'Stop!' Divine intervention. He crosses himself. Riccardo's friend is off to a bad start in the village. The near accident is sure to make the rounds. 'Sorry,' the priest continues. 'I was distracted . . . something outside. I'm not sure I understood what you just said.'

The rumours were just the beginning. Signor Accardi has been under investigation for corruption after an anonymous caller to his government ministry voiced suspicions that he was taking bribes from growers subsidised by the government. Someone has gone too far.

'But that is ridiculous!' the priest confirms.

'Jealous libel, Padre, not just rumour! And there is, obviously, no evidence!' Signor Accardi shouts down the phone at him. 'But do you know *why* it sticks, how I landed this job? My predecessor did take bribes! The crackdown on corruption you read about in the papers has everyone hysterical here. My work has been investigated. They went through my accounts, even my private ones.'

'So, you're cleared, of course.'

'Of course! But that doesn't erase suspicion, does it? This libel must be uncovered, removed. I'm filing a case against an unknown in your congregation.'

'I'm sure that won't be necessary. Give me some time.'

'I finally landed a job, Padre, which allowed my family more than a hand-to-mouth existence, allowed me to visit a bank. I know you don't approve of people borrowing money, but allow me to remind you of what I contributed to our—to your church. I also spent money on things I always wanted to give to my family. That is not a sin. Look at what all that preaching about the virtues of self-denial and frugality in the eyes of God has done to how people think in the village. Now you must fix it. Get me a confession, signed by whoever it is, or I will be taking all your slandering vigilantes to court.' Signor Accardi hangs up.

Dom Pietro knows his next sermon must address the issue of envy and slander before they divide and weaken his congregation. The ugly mess he chose to ignore is far from over.

Speedy promise

Jeremy is not even remotely a competent cook and most often eats out in London. Not surprisingly, the village offers nothing so conveniently pleasurable. Having only two gas burners to cook on does not make things easier. His veal chop from the *Macelleria* is frying on one burner, some zucchini on the other, while his waiting potato mash gets cold. The zucchini joins the chop so he can reheat the mash, and he raises his glass to toast his first cooked meal in his new home. The wine, from the village winery(!), is cheaper per litre than petrol. Served very cold, it is palatable, in the medieval sense of being better than polluted water, so he will drink it, pesticides and all, and adapt to local tastes. Or as a nod to the woman who told him where the local stuff comes from when he by accident discovered her selling fresh fruit and vegetables out of a makeshift lean-to beside her small house. Locals knew why the village *Allementari* had little to sell but the basics and where to find what they needed. He had to find out for himself.

He did not get more than a barely civil reception anywhere. Removed would be a polite way of describing how he was acknowledged at all. His status as a stranger here already carries a stigma not even his most charming smile can change. But the old veggie lady was friendly and helpful. She already knew who he is, so everyone else must somehow be in the know.

'Ah yes,' the signora enthused, she had heard him playing the night before while relaxing in her back garden, which looks out onto the valley. 'So beautiful!' she said, granny eyes sparkling. 'What more could I want from life?' While he pondered what else he might buy that he would know how to cook, she asked him if there is something more he might want. He was not sure, he said. 'But you must be rich,' she said, puzzled, pointing at his car. He had to laugh and assured her there was nothing more he needed in life, except maybe some more tomatoes.

She was talkative while she packaged and weighed them. 'My son, God bless him, takes care of me now I am alone. He brings me what I sell here every day before he goes to work. God gave me everything I need. I do not envy other people who have more.' He found this assertion naively touching; it also told him that being rich, by their definition, made him stick out like a sore thumb everyone wanted to squeeze. The poor woman did not know how to add up his bill and asked him to do so. 'Don't worry,' she said, 'my son always checks them in the evening.'

The parsley root with a bit of fried garlic in the mash—delicious he now confirms—was her suggestion when he admitted being a poor cook, recommending also that he take the basil she gave him out of its pot, separate the roots, and plant them in manure. The small plant would grow into a bush! He would have to think about that one.

In a back room of the annex behind Giorgio's office, he discovered all sorts of useful old furniture from generations of Patricelli, including the weathered table and chairs he hauled out, assuming the now-scrubbed terrace is where they belong when the family visits. He has just about finished enjoying his first meal while going over the piece by Crusell he intends to tackle that evening when his car washer appears on the steps to the terrace.

'Buonasera. Lei disturbo?'

He cannot completely hide his irritation at the timing of this visit but returns the greeting, reminding himself to be personable; the scruffy car maniac, Fabio, he remembers, has manners at least. He decides to get straight to the issue he would rather put off. 'Buonasera. And thank you to clean my car.'

Without invitation, fearing he will not get one, Fabio introduces himself as the shepherd neighbour and quickly takes a chair at the table. 'Such a fantastic car. It was very dirty. It should be looked after properly.'

'I'm sorry, these roads, it's not clean, again.'

'No problem! Tomorrow. I love your car.'

'No, please, don't bother yourself again. It was very kind of you, but the roads—'

'I know some good roads! You like to drive fast, no?'

'No. Not here.'

'Not fast? In this car? Let me show you!'

The open question is whether Fabio means to show him the

roads or how to drive fast. 'I'll take you for a drive sometime.'

'I can drive.'

'On the wrong side? No, sorry. It's stupid, I know, but I am used to it.'

Fabio takes in a deep breath, his puffy face full of real disappointment. His head sags, resting on a propped-up elbow, and then swings up again. 'It doesn't matter. It's an automatic! You can show me. You like Alfa?'

Jeremy is very surprised to learn that the son of the bitterly poor family up the track somehow sees himself buying an upmarket Alfa Romeo, a consuming interest the car fanatic appears prepared to spend his last penny on. While he pretends to listen to endless details with an occasional nod, his thoughts drift back to his embarrassment by the village boys. Would they see a local 'flash' car the same way? Let Fabio find out if and when the time comes. Too late to correct himself, he realises a careless nod at some point tacitly indicated he would let Fabio take the wheel of the BMW to compare its handling with the Alfa model the fat boy claims to have test-driven.

'Tomorrow?' Fabio asks.

He will find excuses. 'No, not tomorrow. Sorry. I must practice.' And to underscore his point, he lifts the notes he was studying. 'I am musician. I have concerts. I must practice.'

'Of course. I see. No problem.'

Rebel altar boy

The next day while Jeremy is having breakfast on the terrace in the early morning sun, Fabio passes by on the path to the villa entrance, beeping and waving to him on his moped. He returns the gesture half-heartedly before he returns to examining the reeds that he takes out one by one from their felt-lined case. Despite changing them three times last night, he was unable to fully control the staccato runs in Crusell's allegro vivace. The practice frustrated him, pissed him off, even if he knows the composer wrote for the oboe as if it were a clarinet, presenting him with a tough-lipped challenge. He broke the session off early. Using his few remaining concert reeds for practice is not an option, even if attempting new ones threatens to throw him into despondency about playing at all. The sense of defeat he knows so well was echoed by the dogs howling across the valley last night, fighting for supremacy over their own darkness and uncertainty as he lay awake, unable to silence their shared distress.

Woken by noise in the courtyard this morning, Jeremy felt that fitful mood stir to life once more at the sight of the family-built chapel through his window, reminding him of the beliefs that had robbed him of his mother and turned her against him, feeding the latent fear of failure she prophesied and he has never been able to appease.

The truth is, the altar boy is not dead, despite everything he has done to ignore the stranglehold of his mother's Catholic lynching. 'Whatever you do as a human being,' Father Robinson warned when he finally left the Church, 'you have already pledged your soul to God through us, and it will never find salvation without our proper guidance.' That put an end to his association with the Church. His sincere attempt to belong to it for his mother's sake was met with coercion, and he would have nothing to do with it, just as he has learnt to steer clear of any attempts by women to coerce him into a relationship, intending to 'improve' him.

He is surprised by an inclination to look inside the chapel. What bothered him almost as much as its ridiculous doctrines were the hypocrisy and pretence he saw in the Church's wealth and ostentatious rituals. Were its monumental churches really there in praise of the Almighty or to impose a dictatorial view of people's smallness? Perhaps the intimacy of a small chapel, built by a family for the practice of its faith, would help him clear away some of his hatred for the genuflective obedience demanded of him by his mother and Father Robinson. Maybe there is something like genuine belief, and if he can find some way to at least find sympathy for its existence in other people's salvation fantasy, he might clear away some of the emotional debris that has accumulated in his life around his cynical stand-off with the Church. He clears the table.

Once out the back entrance, he is immediately intercepted by Fabio's mother in the courtyard.

'Please, Signore, do not encourage my Fabio. It is wrong!' she implores, pointing at his car.

The BMW is spotlessly clean, again. He shakes his head in disbelief. 'But no, signora. It is not right. I told him I do not want this.'

'No? It's true? God bless you. God protect him. He only thinks of cars.'

'Alfa.'

'He told you? He is possessed. You must stop him!'

Assuming she is a strong believer, not wanting any part in this, he raises his hand up to the sky. 'Only He can do that.'

'It is true. I pray every day for it. We are poor. He already had an accident. We do not need a car anymore. It is too dangerous.'

Fabio's mother goes off with her basket to the baking house, a slim plume of smoke rising from its short chimney. It is an appealing artifact of how earlier generations of Patricelli must have lived here, in rural self-sufficient isolation, although maybe they did not enjoy it that much if his own sentiments are anything to go by.

He approaches the epicentre of their advertised beliefs and

circles the chapel, negotiating the bush and weeds around it. It is certainly bigger than one family would need to practice their religion, in the middle of nowhere at that. He stands back to examine the facade of the chapel. The depictions of salvation and adulation that adorn any Catholic church are replaced here by the family coat of arms, upstaging the cross for space in the triangular pediment above the doorway. Half-eroded statues of the chapel's founding couple occupy alcoves on either side of the entrance. Maybe this was not built to show how devout they were? From the outside at least, the family predominates, makes a show of piety. The place was more likely a disclaimer against rural anonymity, put here to connect to the power of the Church that in those days ruled over everything, to proclaim the family's allegiance and elevate its importance more than its faith.

He watches his step when he opens the door and glances down on the threshold: marble with gold inlays, again depicting the Patricelli couple in portrait profile. What perverse ostentation. On Jeremy's cynical threshold to faith, it is a fitting statement of Catholicism he knows: marbled in profane conceit, seamed by false gratitude. After creating the wealth to build this place, the nobles' indentured workers were probably obliged to worship here so that in every moment of their lives, they should feel that the power of their masters was second to none, and then came God. Father Robinson, wanting to indenture him to the Church, could be seen as noble, too.

What remains of the chapel he enters has something he nevertheless finds authentic in spirit. Its decay dissolves the fake piety that built it. It has denied that piety the right to endure, and what is left is cleansed of its origins; there is nothing left to celebrate its noble pretentions, nothing the eye is now grateful for. Rain from the leaking roof and broken dome above the small altar has smeared the family's whitewash faith on cracked plaster walls; a broken display case houses what remains of an ornate nativity scene; enormous cobwebs glisten in the sunlight coming through a broken stained-glass window depicting the Virgin Mary, or what is left of her; bird droppings cake the pews the family once sat on. And prominently placed in the middle of the chapel before the altar is a slightly elevated structure topped by a hinged marble slab;

the dedication inscribed in cast metal characters, half of which are now missing, is indecipherable. The entrance to the family crypt, the legacy, is anonymous. That fits, he thinks.

The beautifully intact hand-printed bible he finds lying open on the pulpit has somehow survived the state of absolute decay he sees around him. He looks at it closely. The craftsmanship is fascinating, he must admit, slowly turning the elaborately illustrated pages of script. What is this doing here? It must be worth a fortune.

'It's comforting that God's words defy decay.' A deep voice in English speaks to Jeremy's back with insistent authority from the entrance. It has a familiar ring to it.

'It's a shame Latin has hardly ever been any use in comforting people,' Jeremy says and turns to face a priest. He guessed right. 'At least not the less learned, like myself.'

'I admit, insistence on Latin has been seen by some as too high-minded.'

'Authoritarian at any rate, keeping the devout guessing with repeat-after-me rituals.'

'The word of God is the authority,' the priest says.

Jeremy makes a broad sweep with his arms. 'Then maybe this place shows how Church authority crumbled by keeping His holy followers in the dark for centuries. I don't think the Almighty can be happy if His words only bend the ear of a Latin-blessed minority.'

'Or to see anything built in His name in this state. Do I guess correctly that you're a disgruntled Catholic?'

'Not practicing your beliefs, obviously.'

'I'm Dom Pietro, the priest of this parish.'

'Jeremy. My apologies. I cannot keep my mouth shut sometimes.'

'Let's call it a strong outside opinion. Depending on how many more you have, it's forgiven.'

'My mother was a viciously devout Catholic and left me scarred, I'm afraid. No insult to yourself intended.'

'None taken, Jeremiah.'

'Not me. I neither weep nor prophesize about anything. The prophet was a favourite of my mother's. She was probably more preoccupied than he was with the punishment of sins.'

'Was—meaning she's no longer with us?'

'She died five years ago of overzealous tumours, cancer.'

'My sympathies. Is your father devout?'

'Ran away when he lost his job. His excuse for staying away from the private purgatory my mother called home.'

'Is that what persuaded you to stay away from us as well?'

'Let's just say I don't regret it and leave it there.'

'I'm sorry to hear that, Jeremy. I know how hard it is for each of us to find the right balance in obeying God's will. What is meant to hold people together can sometimes pull them apart from each other. I've seen that happen to families, and in communities. It's really sad to see, but nobody ever said keeping their faith was easy.'

Jeremy needs to change the subject, aware that this very corpulent round-collared reminder of his Catholic past is begging him to baulk. 'Your English is excellent.'

'I did my seminary training in the States. I thought it would be useful to my mission to have a command of the world's lingua franca. Unfortunately, my bronchial condition left me only the choice of a dry parish, also linguistically.'

'I was in the village yesterday. And my Italian is primitive, unfortunately.'

'I tried to introduce English in the school when I came here. But parents were not happy about their children speaking to each other without them understanding anything.'

'And now? English is everywhere.'

'And still not here. The present generation doesn't seem to have any motivation either to make their own children learn it.'

'Two generations? You've been here a while.'

'Yes. And any opportunity to keep up my English is rare.'

'Isn't false modesty half the sin of pride?'

'I'm certainly not guilty of overconfidence, the other half. Riccardo tells me you are a colleague, a musician.'

'An oboist, yes. You spoke to him?'

'Oh, yes. I guess this visit to announce your arrival here is a bit late. I can assume now, though, that didn't matter.'

'It took a while to clear the dust, I would say. Giorgio at first claimed not to know who Riccardo is.'

'That's because the two of them, how should I put it . . .?'

'Avoid each other?'

'Do not share good company. They prefer to communicate through me.'

Jeremy looks for a clean spot to sit on one of the front pews, and the priest replaces him at the pulpit to examine the bible himself.

'This is exquisite, isn't it? Quite beautiful,' the priest says.

Having heard nothing from Riccardo about Giorgio or the conductor's dealings with this priest, Jeremy wants to find out more if he can, and is soon irritated by audible mumbling in Latin. 'Giorgio is worried about the harvest. I think he's under pressure from Riccardo.'

Still turning the pages slowly, the priest answers without looking up. 'Giorgio is always worried about the harvest, always complaining about his lease arrangement now that Riccardo is holding him to it. As you probably know, Riccardo is the only Patricelli to take an interest in this place in three generations. He only wants to earn enough from the land to restore what can be preserved before it is lost for good.'

'Well, this place is certainly not worth saving anymore.'

Dom Pietro's full attention bears down on him from the pulpit. 'I don't agree. It is essential to preserve what praises God. This dishonours us all in His eyes. Restoring what the Patricelli lying underneath here built to practice their faith will show that it can always be brought back to life, even if it's neglected for decades.'

Maybe that argument goes down well with people he already preaches to, but he is way off target if he aims to stem the flow of people happy to leave the Church to its own self-preservation. 'Aren't there enough churches standing already? Congregations are shrinking everywhere.'

'Not in my parish.'

'Well, allow me another outside opinion. I doubt restoring another church is the inspiration people need nowadays to keep their faith.' Jeremy gets up. 'Can I invite you for a coffee, an opportunity to practice your English?'

'Sure, thanks. I could really use some practice dealing with disgruntled Catholics.'

As they move together to the door, Jeremy steps aside to usher the priest out before him. 'Don't even try to restore me. My foundations are meanwhile too weak.'

Dom Pietro excuses himself as they enter the villa and heads straight through the kitchen to the maids' toilet behind it, letting him know, indirectly, that his status as a newcomer is preceded by the priest's longer acquaintance with the family. He is preparing the coffee when the priest returns.

'The oboe. What a fascinating instrument. Doesn't the whole orchestra tune to you? I was just thinking how great it would be if my words to my congregation inspired them the same way.'

'Striking the right note is not what counts. I have no control over whether the musicians play in harmony afterwards.'

'I guess that's what it's all about, you're right. It's a shame that some people who come in on Sunday only come to rehearse the Communion of their faith in God. They're not spiritually involved. They're out of tune, and that does kind of disturb the harmony.'

'In my experience, everything depends on whether the conductor has the energy and foresight to bring musicians together to follow his interpretation of the music. Maybe we don't know each other well enough for me to be this candid, but all the priests I've met were the opposite of inspiring.'

'So, you broke away and became a soloist.'

'I found out only after I became one that being a soloist was in fact less gruelling than serving in an orchestra, where you repeat passages over and over again like endless rosaries, following a rehearsal plan that ignores the strain of playing the oboe for hours in one stretch.'

'I wasn't talking about your life as a musician, Jeremy, more about your perception of faith. God's prophecy—even for soloists in this liberal, materialistic society—can be an inspiration if we see it for what it really is: a way to fulfil our need for inner harmony when we can follow a common score—without too many different interpretations.'

'I will not be persuaded back into the pit, by any conductor. Let's go out to the front terrace.'

Jeremy is surprised by the priest's resilience. Maybe this priest is not faking faith, even if he also belongs to a Church that is more devoted to obedience to its own canon than anything else. He has no haughtiness to rebel against if the priest's belief is genuine.

Sitting on the terrace, they both watch the trailer as it leaves, heading down the path beside the villa. They were discussing the region's history.

'So, when the Apostolic Church had the say around here, the leaseholds of the peasant farmers were taken away? And the land sold to aristocrats like the Patricelli?'

'I can't deny that what happened around here to the farmers back then is a very shameful chapter in local history. But it wasn't all bad, you know. Many nobles like the Patricelli were devout and helped to develop the region. They didn't just rake it in, they gave something back.'

'After turning small leaseholders into labourers, they built churches and kept the people on their knees. They didn't look so happy just now about their lot in life.'

'Working the land is an identity, Jeremy, a tradition. Most people around here haven't ever known anything else. As an urban man, you may not understand why some people prefer it, no matter what conditions are imposed on them. It keeps them closer to the soil, the essentials of life, and the humility they want God to see in them.'

'They're too worn out to work anymore, according to Giorgio.'

'Do you not wonder, then, where they find the strength to carry on?'

'Ah, of course, it's their deep-rooted faith. I'm sure they are delighted to work at minimum wage so there is enough money to restore the chapel built 300 years ago under the same conditions. History repeats itself.'

'Sceptical views are fine, cynical ones are not. I won't allow you to turn my hopes into exploitation.'

'And I won't question your own sincerity, Dom Pietro. I just ask myself why the Church spends its enormous wealth, above all, to preserve itself as an institution for its own sake at the cost of denying benevolence that people like those we just saw could use. It's completely out of touch with the needs of its followers.'

'People in all walks of life have always needed places to worship, places to bring their body and spirit together. If you can't follow that, then all we have built, and perform every day in our churches to create that unity, is meaningless. The church is where belief really begins, Jeremy, where we can share Communion, renew our faith, confess, and cleanse ourselves of our sins.'

'I'm not following you on that path, sorry.'

'Sins can be forgiven, Jeremy.'

'I'm the outsider, remember? If my sins are real, I opt for punishment in the here and now.'

They talk on to lunchtime. It surprises Jeremy how reluctant the priest is to talk to him about the people in the village, a reluctance that hints at resignation, although he is sure that cannot be the case.

'Most in the village are poor day labourers, pickers, you were right about that. And when they grow old without a safety net, they get anxious their children will leave them, and feel pretty dejected when they do. It gets harder and harder to persuade them that what they've got is already enough because strong faith and our common sanctity are all we need to preserve and protect us through this life.'

'I must say, the villagers I have come across so far are extremely unapproachable, whatever they're protecting.'

'That will pass. We rarely get strangers around here. There's nothing here to appeal to people like you—or younger couples. My biggest worry is that the younger generation we still have will leave the village for far-fetched material dreams they'll likely never reach.'

Deflecting the finger pointing at his own lifestyle, Jeremy describes how he landed up in the villa. When this leads to the topic of music itself, he discovers the priest knows a great deal more about it than he would have thought. Dom Pietro's collection includes meditative Gregorian chants he enjoys in a reflective mood, 'Das Lied von der Erde' at the other extreme, and of course Bach, Mozart, and Handel.

'I'm often really moved when I listen to the oboe,' the priest says. 'It's like a voice that sometimes insists you listen, and then turns meek; it can be really uplifting, but also sadly comforting. It has a very *spiritual* quality.'

Jeremy doesn't want any *spiritual* connection attached to what he does and digs out an established myth. 'Producing that voice can be very poisonous, you know. Oboists can play for a long time on one breath, but that means they keep stale air in their lungs far longer than is good for them when they play.'

'I see. Yes. It makes sense. Keeping something in for too long that must come out is never good, by my confessional experience.'

'Let's stick to music, please.'

'Forgive me. The association is—'

'Comes with the job.'

'In a manner of speaking, yes.' Bowing to Jeremy's wishes, the priest stays on topic. He says that his record player is getting old now and there is no replacement for it. 'Not everyone is happy to sacrifice their old records for the sake of today's devotion to new gadgets, like CD players. It's a wasteful sin.'

Jeremy is sympathetic at first about the enormous pile of rubbish new electronics are generating. And since he is still happy with his old stereo set, he cannot resist a poke. 'The prophet speaketh! The legacy of a sinning multitude shall be the salvation of the provident few. A second-hand player will be found.'

'If you make it there at all, Jeremy, you could spend a long time in real purgatory for language like that.'

Lunchtime presents itself early when Fabio's mother climbs the steps to give Jeremy a very warm fresh pizza from the oven that at once spikes his hunger with an aromatic whiff of oregano. What strikes him when he takes it and thanks her with a deep appreciative sniff is how anxious she appears to be. She greets Dom Pietro quietly and hastily, pointlessly brushing down her full-front apron as she does so. The priest takes her nervous behaviour in his stride, obviously accustomed to the venerable divide. The poor woman is quick to shame herself for having missed the previous Sunday's Mass, offering reasons he could not understand in her heavy slang. She is visibly relieved at the understanding nods Dom Pietro gives her and at his absolution when she finishes.

'God is aware of your devotion, do not worry.' Dom Pietro crosses himself and nods her away.

'Do all of the villagers trot to Mass every Sunday?' Jeremy asks when she leaves.

'You had a Catholic upbringing at least, Jeremy. You know the rules.'

Jeremy picks up the pizza. 'I'm hungry, Dom Pietro. Share it with me, even if it is leavened.'

'Don't mock.'

'Sorry, that was a bit yeasty, an unorthodox joke.'

'Also, not funny. Irreverent.'

'OK, I'll now do penance by fixing you something to eat.'

Dom Pietro, sitting alone on the terrace waiting for lunch, realises how starved he has been in the village for the likes of Jeremy's intelligent company, even if what he says is unbearably cynical at times. Should he be concerned that he does not know how to deal with Riccardo's guest? The extreme irreverence towards his Church is getting on his nerves, and it is jarring his conscience that he is inclined to tolerate it, maybe because he has never faced anything like it since he arrived in the village. Is Jeremy's blunt provocation not preferable to Riccardo's fake piousness, pretending he will restore the chapel one day? The two men are strangers to the cloistered faith of the village. Church doctrine is too far removed from their profane everyday realities for either of them to understand the meaning faith puts in people's lives.

He has an intuition that Jeremy's cynical scepticism is more spurious rebellion than irreversible rebuke. His lost soul is in debate with itself, not with him—a contest the soloist compensates for with a life of luxury, chasing the limelight, and most certainly other footloose distractions he will hopefully keep discreetly to himself. If he really has come here to put all of that aside and concentrate on his music, he could become more receptive to convictions he once must have had. It may be wishful thinking, but when a lost soul is up for grabs, it can go either way, and he has not been relegated yet to Jeremy's order of uninspired clergy. If his tolerance is not stretched to the limit, he will do what he can.

A faithful companion

It is Sunday. Breakfasting on the terrace, Jeremy welcomes the peace, even if he is happy to have signs of life around him during the week so he doesn't feel quite so isolated out here on his own. It is not too warm thanks to some clouds. They are the first he has seen since his arrival, but it does not look like rain, so he will take a drive and explore a bit. He can assume that all good Catholics are now at Mass.

Now that he has met the priest a few times in the village, and taken delight in bullying his past into a corner, he has to admit he is curious. The priest had suggested that he is welcome to 'observe a service in the provincial nest', to which he replied that he was not inclined to 'witness the reprimanding authority of the Church' he knew. His curiosity is not strong enough to cope with any ritual reincarnation of his mother's legacy, especially since he is likely to feel even more uncomfortable under the eyes of Dom Pietro's cohort. Leaving in the middle of Mass would only further justify the bigotry that has meanwhile pilloried him in the village.

So, he will substitute those misgivings with the priest's savvier suggestion of a trattoria in the abbey town farther into the hills, where those who can afford it go on Sunday—after Communion of spirit—for a communion with their stomachs. After so many days of steady practice and one promising attempt at a reed, a good *primi-secondi-dolce* lunch under olive trees, followed by a siesta, seems like a great programme for the day.

Washing up a few dishes in the kitchen, he becomes aware of the dog whimpering in the courtyard. The sound is heart-rending, rising in urgency to an outright howl as he listens, but he cannot see anything from the kitchen's windows high up on the outside walls. He hastily rinses the cup in his hands and goes to the back entrance.

The howling is reduced to a whimper again as soon as he opens the door to scan the courtyard, and when he steps out, the whimpering stops too. He sees the dog he had seen on his arrival, and has seen many times since, outside Giorgio's office. It is again chained up near the compost heap, and he feels guilty not to have noticed the dog's cruel plight before.

He moves cautiously towards the black-and-white mongrel, remembering how it once cowered away from him. It sits unevenly more on its right hind leg. It's a male. His head with overlapping flews and slightly floppy ears all sag forward; the eyes fixed on him are accentuated by a broad white streak between them that flows unevenly from chest and neck, around the nose, to the top of his head. A forlorn creature: his short coat is dull and matted now that Jeremy looks at it more closely.

He talks softly, encouragingly, as he moves forward and recalls a friendly Buddhist monk he met during his quest for an alternative 'fix' to his once-deep post-Catholic anxieties. Those gestures were gentle, welcoming, expressing trust, and he copies them now. He alternately closes his hands in prayer near his chest, places his right hand on his heart, and opens out his arms and the palms of his hands. 'It's OK, mate. Stay calm. Everything is going to be fine. Oh, sorry, non capisci Inglese. Bravo cane. Tranquillo. Tranquillo. Tutto va bene.'

When the back door opened, Fabio held back a bit, having hid behind the large oak at his corner of the courtyard all morning, waiting for the Inglese. Now that he is coming out at the other end of the courtyard, he is heading straight for Giorgio's stupid dog, which has been whining off and on all morning. The dog deserves a beating all right . . . but wait, this is crazy, Fabio thinks. What *is* the Inglese doing? Is he praying for help for the useless mutt?

Everyone knows that dogs can only count their blessings as long as they are useful, even if their only duty is to protect their owner's property, and the scared mongrel in front of this softie cannot even do that. Dogs are bred to serve. You pat them and feed them properly when they do a good job, not otherwise. You show them, like he does, who is the master over their lives, and those are short enough not to bother with anything else. It is pathetic to get sentimental about them; it makes no sense. He cannot watch any more of this stupidity or he will scream. Curse the damn dog. He will have to come back later about the test drive. He will show this man a thing or two when he takes over the wheel. The Inglese is a wimp. He should never be the owner of the BMW, that's for sure; it's wasted on him—he would never trust himself to drive it hard, the way it should be driven.

Jeremy is very close now, crouching and ever so slowly moving a hand towards the dog. His head shrinks downwards, but not away, until it is nearly touching the ground, all four feet still ready to leap away. Domino was just as fearful at first. The older dog was a surprise for his twelfth birthday; his father brought him home from a strays kennel he passed by on his weekly sales route. Jeremy loved the dog. He remembers how painful it was to come home one day and find him gone.

Domino avoided his mother, did not understand why she barked at him through her chain-smoking fumes any time he appeared, throwing her arms about wildly in his direction until he was out of sight. She had Domino put down two years later, declaring it would be a sin to return 'the poor creature already gone mad with loneliness' to the kennel cage, leaving her no choice but to arrange for his dog to find its blessing in another life.

She accused Jeremy of neglecting Domino, a situation she insisted he brought about by his disrespect for school and for the goodness of others God sent to guide and help him. In fact, he had only just become a weekly boarder at his new school—his third in as many years, which was why, he was told, it was decided to board him. Only later did his father admit his fear for Jeremy's sanity, as much as his own, from the mania at home. At the time, though, Jeremy could only blame himself for Domino's death, denying his father's own acknowledged share of guilt for not anticipating this consequence of boarding him.

The first feather-light stroke of his hand behind a floppy ear is the beginning, a chance to call Domino back and redress the sadness Jeremy felt deeply at the time, resurfacing now for this dog, the eyes looking up at his. This reincarnated companion is without water or food. Some of the leftovers from the workers' last meal yesterday have been eaten, but the remains, strewn on the ground near the compost, are now inedible. The roughly cut bottom half of a plastic container that serves as the dog's water bowl is empty. It is thankfully not too hot, but the dog is fully exposed to the sun at this end of the courtyard; his chain is not even long enough to reach the tractor shelter nearby. How can Giorgio treat his dog this way?

By the feel of his coat, the dog has stopped cleaning himself, caring for himself, and no one has cared for him ever. He, too, ignored the dog's plight, remembers the dejected look on this dog's face the very first time he saw him, his fear of his master, and probably everyone else, being far too long denied everything but the absolute basics to exist in his chained circumference of life. It is not just touching to see the dog now enjoying the stronger strokes of his hands, it is a miraculous and mutual relief of old pain. Domino is back. And Jeremy is taken back, feels a surge of the boyish delight he took in his chasing, fetching, wrestling companion—the most positive memory of his childhood he has.

The dog's shallow breathing signals more a need for affection than water. Or maybe it is hard for Domino II to lose either one for the sake of the other, straining against the chain when Jeremy goes inside to fetch some water. In the back room off the kitchen, he finds two old aluminium cooking pans, a deeper one for water, a shallow one for food. He has nothing to fill the shallow pan, he realises, when another miracle occurs. At the back of the deep top shelf of the same cupboard, he discovers a cache of tinned foods. Among the fat white beans, tomato concentrate, and tuna, he finds a tin whose shape he would recognise anywhere: corned beef. It is a curiosity here, with a historic sell-by date, and invaluable. 'Do I hear a dogged bid from the courtyard?' Jeremy calls out. 'Its contents go to . . . Domino II!' He tosses the tin in the air.

In the kitchen he mixes the corned beef with some leftover pasta to stretch it. Domino II is not waiting for him when he goes through the open back door into the courtyard carrying both pans; the dog only looks up from busily licking his coat when Jeremy is within a couple yards of delivering the unbidden prize of an edible lunch.

He sits on the ground with Domino II and watches him eat his meal. He will take care of this dog himself if he can, make him the

Domino he lost, bring him back to life. He would love to unleash the dog, of course, quite confident that this Domino, like his old faithful companion, would never run away while he is around. But he is going out. He could retie the rope so the dog at least has shelter from the sun under the tractor shed, but he will not take any liberties in case Giorgio shows up. Domino, until he can adopt him, is safer from his present master's wrath if he stays put for now; Jeremy cannot do anything more at this point. As if reading his mind, Domino takes a stretch after his last morsel of food, comes over for a moment, accepts a few last strokes over the back of his neck, and wanders over to another spot he favours to lie down. From there Domino looks at him calmly as if to say, 'I'm OK now.'

Jeremy goes back into the villa and collects a few things for his outing. A perfect day for a drive, and because it is just so perfect, he is sure to get another visit from Fabio about the promised drive. The tenacity of the lout is getting on his nerves; he has had to turn him away twice already. Fabio's mother would be horrified if he let her son drive his car, and he would not like to do anything that would close his bakery.

He moves quickly to lock the back door and climb into his BMW, and without putting down the roof, reverses out of his parking spot. Domino, at the opposite end of the courtyard, is sitting erect, motionless, looking at him. *Bravo cane.* He has almost reached the entrance gate when he hears frightened high-pitched barking through the open driver's window and punches the play button on his stereo to drown it out. He also drowns out Fabio calling after him, who he sees in his rear-view mirror bolting out of his house and down the path leading to the courtyard, arms waving and then punching the air in frustration as Jeremy drives off.

Dolce vita
Vita dura

There is no printed menu, but he managed to recognise a few ingredients amongst the choices the old lady rattled off. The rest was potluck: fettuccini with fresh sardines, tomatoes, and large fruity capers—picked from a bush bordering the foot of the terrace of the trattoria—followed by tender roast lamb cooked with herbs, and a gooey lukewarm chocolate cake dessert with accompanying espresso. Dom Pietro was right: the food is unbeatable. An unobstructed view of the undulating valley from this round elevated terrace, propped up on a hillside by high stone walls, is the dream of any tourist in Italy, but he is the only foreigner here.

His small table is surrounded by larger families, the adults talking loudly to each other down long tables while they take turns pulling children onto their laps. It is a welcome touch of suburban chaos. The number plates he saw when he parked his car tell him most of the guests are visiting from Rome, which explains why he sees more younger couples. They would be visiting their parents, the oldest patrons at the table, who have most of the children's lap time. The younger inhabitants of Dom Pietro's Catholic fiefdom probably have no desire to return to the drab place they came from. The rustic appeal he hoped for there is probably waiting for him here in the streets of this historic hilltop abbey town; he will explore a bit before he drives back.

The abbey itself was a fair way out of the town, so a tour there is postponed to the next visit. What he saw while walking through the narrow winding streets of the town charmed him so much he lost track of time. It is late afternoon before he makes his way back to his car. The innocent clouds he saw earlier are now a solid mass of dark grey, and the wind is picking up.

His journey home is under a hefty storm, a solid downpour that makes it difficult to negotiate the winding road awash with mud from the sloping terrain above it. It is almost dark by the time he reaches the track leading up to the villa, which now more resembles a murky torrent, forcing him to inch forward, wipers at top speed, lights on full beam.

He is relieved to reach the entrance without any jolts from the undercarriage, entering the courtyard to park in front of the back door. Coming to a stop, his high beam is pointing directly at Domino, his new companion, seen in quick, clear snapshots through the motion of the windshield wipers, lying in a tight curled ball on the ground, motionless, not acknowledging his arrival for what seems like ages, and then only with a slight lift of his head.

Forget the rain. Jeremy gets out of the car and moves quickly towards the dog. Too quickly. Domino springs up, frightened— and limping. Whatever happened in his absence, the dog is injured, and not only physically. The brief bond they shared some hours ago is gone. If he wants to restore it, he must wait, stay put, until it can creep back into the dog's awareness of who he is. The aluminium pan he left filled with water is far from where he left it, and badly dented out of shape. Kicked. Kicked hard. Domino has been kicked. Hard.

He shares Domino's suffering, trying to reach him by repeating his Buddhist entreaties in the hope of recognition. By the time his wounded friend responds and limps to him, he is completely soaked and chilly himself. The dog, much longer exposed, is visibly shivering. Once confident that some semblance of trust has been restored, Jeremy combs the rooms of the villa and finds some blankets. He cannot excuse Giorgio for keeping Domino helplessly chained up outside without any shelter or food, at the mercy of a frustrated sadist, but taking his new companion inside is off limits—neither the dog nor the villa belongs to him.

When he comes out again, he retrieves a treat for Domino from his car: a bag of bones donated by the old lady who ran the restaurant, who herself has a dog she loves. He reties Domino and they sit under the tractor shed while Domino enjoys his bone, both blanket warm, until it is well after dark, the rain has subsided, and the BMW's battery is almost flat.

L'artigiano e il musicista

It was a successful shopping spree in the large supermarket an hour's drive away. There he found everything he missed in the spartan village *allementari*. Top of his list was a good assortment of food for Domino, which local dog owners did not seem to countenance at all, as well as a wide selection of things that would make life easier cooking for himself, also not countenanced by anyone who values *real* cooking: ready-made pasta sauces, loads of different salami, cured ham, cheese, and pickled things for cold snack meals. He splurged a bit on wine, though he was getting used to an occasional ice-cold glass of the local precursor to vinegar.

Vegetables were the domain of Signora Tendri, as the old veggie lady was now known, and the local *macelleria*—big on local gossip judging from the seemingly permanent group of women sitting there 'waiting' to be served—provided him a choice of veal or lamb, which those waiting probably only afforded themselves when they had a fresh piece of gossip to roast for the dinner table.

Olive oil was a whole new chapter in his scant knowledge of cooking, until Giorgio came along. He would never view the oil the same way again. Jeremy had examined the bottles of olive oil on the shelves in the supermarket and confirmed Giorgio's worst fears about oils of questionable origin posing as the real thing. He would never forget that day in the cellar and how grateful he was down there to encounter a more genial side to Giorgio, who had tried to hide it the day after the storm when he took over Domino's care by default.

Giorgio scorned 'pampering the useless mongrel' but had no objection to Jeremy taking over, although he also made clear that when Jeremy's stay was over, Domino would also be back 'where he belonged'. Jeremy can meanwhile assume that Giorgio's bark is bigger than his bite. The stressed olive grower was no doubt relieved that day that his poor custody of Domino's welfare need no longer hang on his conscience. Domino is now free to roam, find shade and shelter, and as Jeremy had guessed, he does not stray far from the villa and keeps him company any time he is on the terrace. That is where the two of them were one lunchtime when Giorgio appeared, placing a wooden tray of peaches and another of tomatoes on the table.

'Here, these are for you.'

'Oh, well, how very kind of you. They're beautiful. Thank you very much.'

Giorgio was about to turn, ready to leave, as if the gift was an embarrassing necessity, when he spotted the bottle on the table. 'What is that?' he asked angrily. 'Where does it come from? A supermarket?'

Jeremy felt like an idiot for not having asked Giorgio about his olive oil earlier, deciding to use up the bottle he bought in the village on his first day. 'It says extra virgine. That means good quality, doesn't it?'

The bottle was snatched from Jeremy's hands and, after close inspection, thrust in front of his face. 'Look. It says Italian on the label, no? But look, here, in fine print: "extracted from olives from the European Union". This cheap Spanish rubbish is ruining my business!' Giorgio hurled the half-empty bottle, smashing it to pieces against the parapet wall of the garden below. 'Come with me,' the oil baron commanded, grabbing the remains of a loaf of bread off the table and ignoring that Jeremy had only half finished his lunch.

Giorgio marched down the stairs, Jeremy and Domino less eagerly trailing behind, and opened the thick wooden double door beneath the portico leading into the cellar. It was as cool inside as Jeremy had imagined the day he arrived; he shivered briefly at the contrast. What surprised him were the dimensions—the back of the cellar extending beyond the back of the villa—and the pungent smell coming from oil spillage on the dirt floor. Giorgio moved towards the back, pointing at the rows of lidded clay vats, naming the different olive varieties from which the stored oil was produced. 'Frantoio, and here Leccino, and here Canino.' Giorgio then turned around, his arms sweeping wide in praise of his treasure, his voice serious and triumphant: 'This is the real world of cold-pressed extra virgin olive oil.'

It was an enlightening experience. Not only the remarkable difference in taste between the different oils but the Giorgio he now saw: a man transformed from brute to suppliant, who ripped bread roughly from the loaf before dunking it in each ladle sample of oil and presenting him with the dripping mass as if to say 'Here, this is my body, eat', anxious each time to see some reverential sign of approval on his face. Jeremy did not have to pretend; each sample was an exquisite and new taste that would make a gourmet meal out of any piece of bread or simple salad.

There could be no mistaking a man passionate about the quality of his olives and the devotion that went into his work as a 'produttore tradizionale'. Giorgio seemed to forget that Jeremy's competence in Italian was limited, and not wanting to dampen enthusiasm, Jeremy was willing to forget, too, as Giorgio sang praises for the methods he used and cursed the 'fabbrica' competition, lamenting his fight against weather, pests, and the price he got for his cherished oil. The love-hate passion in Giorgio's lengthy rant echoed the rough-edged emotional turnarounds he also now experienced as an impaired oboist fighting the odds against upholding his own reputation. He knew Giorgio, like him, could never imagine doing anything else.

It would be going too far to say this shared devotion to what each does made them friends in the hour or so they spent in the cool cellar, but they did warm to each other, so that he felt more respected as a 'musicista', and Giorgio gladly accepted being an 'artigiano' of his trade. Jeremy saw it as a compliment when he was told he was more inquisitive about the background of the oil than the Patricelli brothers. They did not follow Giorgio's conviction that his methods were the secret to quality that would ultimately fetch its price, that it is better to harvest by hand and produce less by traditional press methods than to maximise the yield by sending a machine-picked crop to a *fabbrica* for extraction. This angered Giorgio, but he would stand his ground, and his tone became surprisingly confidential: perhaps one day the trees he harvested would be his own.

Jeremy smiles as he recalls the meeting now on his way home. He is on the secondary road that takes him to his turn-off for the village—driving through it, across the square, he then only has a short, rough run across the valley home—a shortcut compared with the track he first took off the main trunk road the day he arrived, where Giorgio nearly crashed into his mint BMW; that track is now in even worse condition since the rain. This village bypass is also the road that takes him to the historic abbey and delicious food. He feels hunger at the thought and speeds up. A ready-made pasta will never compare with the fettuccini he had there, but it is too hot anyway to venture that far away; the sun is burning a hole in his scalp.

Isabella turns quickly to look at the car she hears approaching behind her and instantly back again, her heartbeat in overdrive.

Rebel beauty

Since her first sighting of the Englishman in the village, nothing has occupied her imagination more than a chance encounter with him, alone of course. Entertaining that impossibility posed questions she has asked herself repeatedly since, like how much of what she does is left for her to decide. Marco bragged to her about putting down the '*estraneo*', which can only mean he is jealous of this real man, who is no doubt smarter—and better looking? Well, older handsome not boyish handsome.

'I told that arrogant nobody what I thought about his flashy car.'

'Oh really, you speak English now?' she asked.

'Didn't need to.'

'He speaks Italian?'

'Like a two-year-old.'

'That would fit your vocabulary.'

'Are you taking his side?' Marco asked angrily.

'You're bragging, again.'

'Ask the others. They know.'

'I want to know for myself.'

'What?'

'Whether he's arrogant or you're bragging.'

'You don't speak English either.'

'I don't need to, either, you just said.'

'Leave it.'

'Leave it to who? You? You decide what I should think?'

'About him? No. Ask anyone around.'

'We agreed no gossip, remember?'

'This is not about us.'

'No, I guess not. It's about me. People can gossip all they want; I want my own opinion about him.

It felt good to speak her mind, although she then felt it necessary to prop up his ego by meeting up with him the next day at the bar, playing her starring role in the village's perfect-match drama. These showy appearances irritate her; Marco loves them. She is tired of not being seen as a person in her own right. No one ever pays her a compliment on how she looks or for what she says or does; it is always 'Oh, Marco is a lucky man!' as if that should be all that mattered to her.

Her role in the 'golden couple' is her only identity, and she is not happy about that at all. It also makes her unhappy that everyone pretends their run-down village has been good to them and will be for her if she would just accept her position in life. Giving in to Marco would convince everyone that the way things are is the way they should be, as if it is a good idea that things never change. Now that she is old enough, everyone seems to be counting the days until she finally agrees to marry Marco. She feels trapped inside an invisible bubble of expectations that locks her up and denies her a choice in what she wants to do with her life.

Marco's braggy boyishness does not bother her, nor do the secret flirts he always denies as jealous gossip. They more likely tell her how weak her own feelings for him are. What she hates is how he claims a right to her, and this assumption is propped up for him by people who do not really know what he is like and who would not have to deal with gold possibly turning into lead. It will take strength to assert herself, to back out of the relationship, and until she has the courage to face whatever happens when she does, she is stuck.

She wants to feel judged on her good qualities and not just the narrow-minded ideas Dom Pietro's vigilantes have about what being good in life means. They are always breathing down everybody's neck, poking their noses into everybody's business. All they ever talk about is duty to God's will, and they assume they are the only judges. Conforming to their standards is not just about attending Mass on Sunday, which hardly anyone misses. It seems to her that everything she does, anything she openly likes, owns, talks about, or even dreams of, is given a real going-over, like she is wearing an old-fashioned corset that must be tightened regularly to make sure it stays in place. She doesn't need one; she wants to breathe, try out new things, but even the fashion she loves and would wear if she could buy it is considered immodest, indecent, a wasteful sin.

When she discovered a way to learn English on her own, she made it her best-kept secret: it would raise suspicions, questions about what use it is to everybody else's plan for her before she had any options of her own. 'English essential' was what the ad for an export clerk at the canning factory said. Angelina, her girlfriend in the town, provided the cover for today as well as a place to change her clothes before and after the interview.

They used to hang out together every day. She misses her girlfriend's company a lot, admires her, the rebel who quickly became an outcast for wanting to live by her own rules. Angelina did not hesitate to say what she thought and spoke out openly against having to stay a virgin until marriage—although she was a virgin at the time. The padre's vigilantes got to work. Her girlfriend was branded off limits, and her presence was shunned in the village until she fled, warning Isabella not to defend her liberal views until she was ready to fight or flee for whatever she chooses to believe in. After she left, Isabella did face off with her parents about keeping the closest friendship she has, and occasional visits to Angelina are tolerated. She pacifies her mother's doubts with made-up stories when she gets home.

On the bus back home she went over the interview she had that morning, and although disappointed that it did not go well at all, she is proud of herself. This was her first step towards something new, something outside the village and away from the church nursery where she works on alternate mornings, away from the vigilantes who run the place and begin the indoctrination of the toddlers on their path to God before they can even walk properly.

Now she is on the road to the village from the turn-off where she got off the bus, dressed in a suitably plain calf-length pleated skirt and white blouse, her interview outfit folded in an equally plain cloth sack strung over her shoulder. She is inventing her conversation with Angelina as she walks, this time deciding they talked about how much her girlfriend regrets having to leave the village (mostly a lie), how hard she is training as a seamstress (half true), how lonely her girlfriend feels sometimes (mostly true, her boyfriend is a truck driver), and how she begs her to come again soon (convenient exaggeration). She is half in these thoughts when she looks back and sees the car.

Oh please, not today, not in her state. What if he wants to offer her a lift? Alone with him in his car? She picks up her walking pace, hoping not to draw any attention to herself, and dares not look again, but he must have slowed down if he has not passed her yet. She is not ready for this, not in her head, not in this non-outfit, not while a bit sweaty from the heat with unbrushed hair—and he is stopping!

No one in their right mind would willingly be on this road at this time of day, Jeremy thinks when he sees a woman in a loosely flowing skirt far ahead of him, an apparition shimmering in the heat coming off the road. She turns her head very briefly in his direction as he approaches. He slows down. She is very young, very attractive, very modestly dressed, a beautiful figure with a flowing gait, the prize village damsel by the book, and most definitely out of bounds for his early-forties eros. But a close-up is too tempting, and he cannot just pass her by. He will give her a lift to the village if that is where she is heading. There is no harm in showing his snoopers through latticed shutters that their stranger in town is a considerate man to whom they could be more friendly. Driving on the right, he could almost reach out and touch her when he pulls alongside, and they both stop.

'Buongiorno!' He smiles up at her from the driver's seat, back straight, both hands on the wheel, anxious to avoid any likeness with tacky machismo. 'Vivi vicino villaggio?'

'Where do you want to go?' the girl asks, tucking her hair back self-consciously, too shy to meet his eyes for more than a moment.

'Oh, English, that's a relief. My Italian is about as good as a four-year-old's.'

Isabella laughs. That makes him twice as smart as Marco thinks he is. 'That is funny.'

'This heat is not,' the Englishman replies, indicating the passenger seat. 'Hop in. I'll give you a lift.'

Isabella knew this was coming, and it is almost unfriendly not to accept, so she answers as brightly as she can. 'It is OK, thank you anyway. I prefer I walk. I walk from the bus stop often.'

Jeremy watches her walk on, but she moves more hesitantly than before, like she wants to give in but cannot, and he catches on right away: even if she is inclined to trust him, nobody else in the village does, so she cannot arrive there alone with him, especially in his flashy car. 'Just up to the village. I'll drop you off wherever you want.'

Isabella's indecision feels ridiculous to her now that he has stopped her in her tracks; this could be her only chance. He does not seem like the dangerous show-off people say he is. And a twenty-minute walk in scorching heat makes a ride in a luxurious fantasy car too tempting.

Do not stare at her, Jeremy says to himself as the girl walks around the front of the car. He reaches over to push open the passenger door before quickly resuming his position, hands at the wheel, reminding himself that he is only doing her a favour—he must not think anything else. He resists any expansive movements that might seem too forward and waits until she is seated before looking at her fully. She is looking straight ahead, clutching her bag in her lap.

He tugs his own seat belt, giving her a questioning half smile to signal she should fasten hers.

'Oh, sì,' she says, only glancing at him as she puts her bag under her skirt on the footwell in front of her, between her legs, and then reaches for the seat belt.

He sees the wet patch under her right arm when she does so and bends slightly towards her to work the air con on the console as she swivels slightly towards him to find the buckle. 'This should cool things down a bit,' he says.

When he presses the button, a powerful stream of air blows up from the footwell that raises and flips her skirt just over her knee before her belt clicks into place and she can lunge forward to clamp it down.

'Che diavolo!'

'Oh my God! Sorry!' He stabs another button on the console, cancelling the preset he forgot about. Out of the corner of his eye he can see her face has turned crimson, even on her lightly tanned skin. Upright at the wheel again, he waits for her alarm to subside.

'I'm very sorry,' he says quietly, then looks at her profile. 'The car's new, you see. I'm not used to all the controls yet.' He has embarrassed the young goddess next to him. He has bungled being her Good Samaritan. He will drop her off, then go home. But there is no hurry.

Was it a trick, or did it take him by surprise too? Is he the dangerous type? Isabella takes in that thought, decides he is not, then braves a glance at him. 'It is OK,' she says to him. And then thinks to herself: But it is not OK to act like a shrieking schoolgirl, is it? She could kick herself. He is embarrassed. She has messed everything up. What can she say now? 'This car is really cool,' she says.

'Oh, sorry. I can fix that.'

He is reaching for the console. Again! She quickly lifts her right hand from her lap and raises it in a stop sign, almost touching his arm. 'The temperature is fine. It is not my meaning.'

'Ah, I get it. Cool. Well, it's a bit flashy, some people say, but it's very comfortable.'

'Yes. It is. Do not care about jealous people.'

'Would you like some music on our short ride?'

'Si! Yes, I would like it. You are playing? In the music?'

'God forbid, no. I hear myself too much, sometimes even in my sleep, I think,' Jeremy says as he begins searching through his CDs. So, she knows he is a musician, but who knows what else they are saying about him in the village. He looks for a sound that will relax her, something easy-going and not too distracting.

She watches him scroll the tracks and waits for the sound after he makes his pick.

'Here's the one we want,' he says confidently and sits back in his seat.

When was the last time 'we want' included her in something she decided to go along with because *she* really wanted to? He is being very considerate to take her to the edge of the village. After meeting Marco and his gang on the square, he must have guessed she might get into trouble sharing a ride with him and found a way she could accept anyway. He is being careful, for her benefit, so she can enjoy this. She never dared dream she would share a ride in his unbelievable car. The positive impression he made that very first time she saw him from her window is right, then? She thinks so, and listening in silence with her eyes closed for as long as she dares, she smiles, and the car starts moving.

'Mi piace. I like it,' she says to him. In fact, she would not mind at all, she thinks, if this chance meeting, these completely new sensations, lasted longer than a two-minute ride.

'Glad to hear it. My name is Jeremy.'

'My name is Isabella. I am *so pleased* to meet *you*, Jeremy.' She gets it all wrong and has really overdone it.

Her oddly intense sincerity catches him completely off guard. 'Oh please, it's *my* pleasure. Just a favour really—well, maybe more like yours to me . . . for keeping me company. You speak English for a start.'

'Comme?' He is nervous too, she thinks while trying to figure out what he said: he favours her company and her beginners English? That cannot be it. 'My English is not good. Sorry.'

'Your English is fine, really, it is, don't worry,' he says, still a little rocked by his own seesawing. 'Where did you learn it?'

Why had she not thought about it? He could give her secret away, just by accident. 'I teached myself. Please don't say anybody. It is my secret.'

'Secret?'

'I speak English. Top secret. It must be no one knows. Only you, now.'

'No one in the village knows you speak English?'

'No. Also at home, no.'

'Dom Pietro said as much.'

'What? What he say?'

'He told me no one in the village speaks English except him. He does not know you do too.'

He talks with the padre. She must tell him why he must keep her secret. But how to explain it, her life in the village? Can she trust him? She doesn't have the courage, and she needs more English words. 'I am different from the others,' she says simply.

They look at each other openly for the first time.

How true, Jeremy realises. She is very different, and he is at once aware of why that is: he can either be enchanted or aroused when he meets an attractive woman for the first time—it is never both so strongly or simultaneously. 'Move along now, Jeremy, that's a good man,' says the admonishing voice in his head. How can this not be forbidden fruit in his older orchard? He must not even think about reaching for it.

He is glad his driving gives him reason to turn away. 'Well, not including you, the people I've met here seem afraid of me because I'm a stranger, different. So maybe we somehow have something in common.'

'Yes, they are worry about you. They do not know you. You are secret to them. My secret, it is saved?'

'It's safe, yes. My lips are sealed.' He swipes a hand across his lips.

She understands, smiles, and laughs. 'Your English is funny sometimes.'

'My Italian is even more funny, always.'

She laughs lightly, excited. 'You teach me, I teach you! Maybe.'

Is this an invitation to link up? Jeremy asks himself. That would be too good to be true and would definitely put her too close within reach. 'Ma prima devo imparare ancora qualche parola in italiano,' he says, claiming he must first improve his vocabulary.

'Bravo. Meglio di un bambino di quattro anni.'

'Did I pass my first test?'

'My lips are sealed,' she says, though she cannot improve his abominable accent.

They share a good laugh together. Any remaining ice has been broken. But they are already approaching the turn-off to the village, a narrow lane—like a gutter between the houses densely packed on the ridge—that spills out onto the bypass road they are on. He has driven no faster than a chariot drawn by an old lame horse, reluctant to let the moment go, and he senses she is too, fidgeting with the long shoulder strap of her canvas bag without pulling the bag up from the footwell and preparing to get out. It is up to him to make small talk.

'Nothing from here to the abbey but olive trees.'

'Yes, they are many.' She slowly pulls her bag onto her lap, getting ready to get out, when it hits her. That's it! She has to stifle the giggle in her throat. Why not have a secret fantasy adventure to the tree with her own Aginulfo, just for the fun of it? He won't know. 'Do you know about olives?' she asks.

'I recently had a crash course on them—sorry, funny English. A few days ago, I spoke to a man who is very passionate about olives. I know a little about them now.'

'You want to see the biggest olive tree in Europa?'

'Andiamo.'

Slipping into Italian here and there, Isabella on the way there tells him the story of how she began learning English. She had volunteered one day to help clear out the school's storeroom of disused books. She came across a box holding an old compact cassette recorder, tapes, and books—a complete self-teaching course in English. It was not taught at the school while she was there because parents decided it wasn't necessary for anyone living in the village to learn it; they were taught Latin instead.

'No English, Latino! Mumbo jumbo!' She laughs at the odd expression like she did when she first heard it on tape.

He would love to record her laugh. 'Catholic mumbo jumbo,' he says carelessly, recalling Dom Pietro's bogus claim he wanted to introduce English to the village.

'You do not like Catholics?' Isabella asks.

'I am one! But I hate dogma, and Latino,' he says, anxious to extract the nail he has trodden on.

She snuck the box home, stole it (bad Catholic girl), which is why she kept it secret at first. But the more she learnt and thought about what she could do with it, the more she wanted to hide it from everyone else until she is ready. 'È la mia strada verso una vita più grande.'

He sees the eagerness in her opal-green eyes before it quickly disappears.

'It is too early,' she adds more quietly, like an apology with a weak smile.

'So, am I your English guinea pig?'

'Pig? No!' Then seeing him smile, she says, 'Ah, another funny meaning.'

'I am your first test?'

'I must learn more funny English!' She laughs.

And she could use a lesson in body language: he can assume she is just naturally vivacious, but her coy gestures are so seductive he could eat her whole.

'Please go right ahead.'

It sounds like an invitation, her English missing a pause of emphasis after 'right'. He turns into the road and weaves his fingers through his hair, imagining hers and appeasing himself with her smile when he thanks her for helping him discover the scenic countryside. She is curious, wants to know why he is visiting. He omits the accident and explains he needs to practice hard for his upcoming concerts. Her interest in where he is to perform hands him an opportunity to impress her with his own *vita più grande*, but he feels awkward, not wanting to overreach and plonk his large world over her small map.

'A few cities in Europe and some smaller towns,' he says.

'What cities?'

'Amsterdam, Stockholm, Frankfurt, Vienna. Those are the biggest ones.'

'Then you are a man of the world.'

'Isabella, I'm only a musician trying to earn a living.'

He is pretending he is not famous; he wants her to feel OK in his company. No bragging from him. That's nice. She points to the stereo. 'Can I hear the musician?'

'Do you know what the oboe sounds like?'

'I am not sure.'

'Well, I won't mind if it's not your cup of tea—sorry—it's OK if you don't like it. Not everybody does. But this is a very gentle piece.' He chooses the adagio movement he has recently been practicing from Tomaso Albinoni's Concerto in D minor.

It does not take long for Isabella to be overwhelmed by the long, mellow note introducing the oboe; this completely new sound takes her by surprise, urging her to give in to it as the air flows freely through her hair, caressing her face, and the music draws her into a deep sense of joy. What other word, she thinks, could describe this feeling of escape, suddenly free of the worries that tie her up every day, unlocking what seems trapped inside her?

She soon finds herself caught in visions of a different life that stream through her in quick succession, opening her mind to everything at once. Her thoughts strip the music of its contemplative pace; the subtle sway of its sweeping notes coax out of her what she at once knows she has been hiding from, creating a magical warp of awareness. She can feel the epiphanic spell of a new self taking over, an ecstatic rush that empowers her to believe in herself, to leave behind the village girl who wrapped herself in fantasies to escape the anger, fear, or sadness that have defeated her anytime she considered the odds of whether and how she could make a different life for herself. Why shouldn't she? Why has she never trusted herself? Her life can change if she wants it, and this new certainty puts a smile on her face as she listens through the music to what she can be; she must protect the fragile joy it gives her.

She is so serene, he thinks as he watches her listening intently from the corner of his eye. A faint smile takes shape and falls into place on her full lips, barely pleating the corners of her mouth. Any trace of shyness or self-consciousness is now behind her; her bearing is easy, mature, womanly. The music has taken hold of her, leaving her only fleetingly attentive of the countryside they move through, travelling ahead of the immediate, familiar scenery she knows. He wants to smile at her—and suppresses it; to distract her by saying or doing anything would destroy the moment, forcing her to put aside the notes she has let embrace whatever she is thinking.

She is different from the people around her because they are stuck, and she does not want to be, Isabella decides. She will not hide from life because they do, because anything or anyone new to them, like the man beside her, could make it obvious how falsely they live in the village—under a bubble of anxious piety, pretending to be content with their lot. She does not want to pretend being part of that any longer; she wants change. What holds her up must be genuine, as natural to her life as the olive trees they have passed that fend for themselves no matter how little they have to grow on where they were planted.

How grateful she is Jeremy inspired this inner voice to speak, how beautiful his music and thoughtful silence while she listened. But this new magical awakening, about going somewhere with her life, does not involve him. She does not need a prince to rescue her after all.

They reach the tree as Jeremy comes to a well-timed stop on the last notes of the movement. The tree's enormously thick trunk and monumental crown dwarf any thought of irreverent proximity. They sit in silence some distance away from it.

'How did we get here?' she asks.

'There are road signs.'

'I was a little . . .'

'Lost in your thoughts?'

'Sì. É vero. Che bello, Jeremy.' She sighs, feeling really content. 'Che gioia! Grazie. Grazie mille!' On an impulse that completely surprises her, she quickly reaches over and gives him a peck on the cheek.

The token of affection is unexpected, even if she is less shy than she was at first. But it would not be the first time his music led to more than admiration. Jeremy ejects the idea along with the CD and puts it back in its sleeve. 'It is yours, Isabella. I'm very happy you liked it.'

'Quanto sei gentile! I love your music. But I cannot . . . I cannot play it.'

'No Discman?'

'Ah, yes! I will lend from Angelina! Thank you, Jeremy.'

She could also buy one from her savings and hide it—no, why hide it? Maybe his CD, though, for now, which she puts in her bag. When she looks at him again, he is sliding his hands down over his face. 'Cosa c'è, Jeremy?'

'Pity about the road signs.'

Jeremy nods in the direction of the tree. The garish shirts, Bermuda shorts, sneakers, and overweight frames give away the couple as Americans, the type he can spot a mile off in London, even if fast food has equalised the heavyweight competition at home. In the picture the man is taking, the woman is pretending to push the tree to topple it—and three of her could probably do the job.

'Look more toward the camera, hon. That's it. Smile. Great! Now look mean, like you really think you can do it. Fantastic!'

His 'hon' lumbers over to him to have a look at the pictures, and they huddle together over them and laugh, delighted. 'Now you, hon,' she says before she spots them still seated in the car. 'Hey, wait! Maybe those folks in the car could take a picture of us both, like, you know, trying to hug the tree?'

Jeremy and Isabella watch the man waddle towards them.

'Here's your second English lesson for the day,' he says to Isabella.

'Hi there!' the Yank says, still a few yards away. 'Hey, what a car you got! Wow! You own it?'

'It's not a rental,' Jeremy says drily.

'Yeah, guess not. Never seen anything like it. She's a real looker!' The man's focus shifts from Isabella to the bonnet before holding up his camera and addressing him. 'We were wonderin', like, would you . . .?'

'Of course,' Jeremy says. He opens his door.

Isabella's mind is elsewhere, her eyes scanning the bough of the tree. 'Aspetterò qui, Aginulfo.' His puzzled look makes her realise the slip. 'I wait here,' she says and watches them go, wondering what story she can come up with to replace the legend of the prince that inspired her secret flight of fancy to come here with Jeremy. When will she learn?

They are a few paces away from the car when the Yank leans in towards Jeremy. 'I guess she comes with the car, eh?'

'She is my niece.'

'I bet you wish she wasn't.' The man nudges him and laughs at his own overweighted joke.

'Hey, great! Thanks, Mister. Like, this is really nice of you. Come on, hon, let's not keep him waiting,' the bulging starlet says from her place near the tree.

'Just the release button. That's all. The focus, light, it's all automatic, don't worry,' her hon says. The Yank takes up his position on the opposite side of the tree trunk from his wife, forming a colossal group of three.

Jeremy hands back the camera after taking several shots. 'There you go.'

'Hey, these look really great. Thanks a whole bunch,' the Yank says. 'We gotta get goin' here. This wasn't a planned stop. Just saw the signs. Awesome. We still got a bunch of Rome to see by this time tomorrow. We'll let you get back to your . . . niece.'

Isabella has paid little attention to the scene. She used the time to come up with another explanation for Aginulfo, the Lombard prince who scandalously disobeyed the rules of nobility by taking the poor village girl Artemia as his wife. They married under this tree. The story is sure to put ideas in Jeremy's head about why she brought him here. Her flights of fancy, like the TV soaps that led to Marco, only get her into trouble. Even if her role somehow fit the legend—a young village girl with nothing to her name—she would never even consider any romance with him. He has been very cautious so far, and she must avoid anything to encourage him the wrong way. She does not want to be the local Artemia, nor Jeremy to start playing the prince who assumes his attraction to her is all that should matter. She does like him too, though; he is so different to anyone she has met before, and famous even, so it would be exciting to be with him some more—as long as she never forgets that he is also worldly in ways that she, unlike Angelina, is not willing to explore with him just for fun.

'I don't suppose you can blame them,' she hears him say when he comes back to the car. 'After all, it is worth seeing, *and* it's real. Shall we walk about a bit?'

They walk separately around the tree, and he is soon not comfortable she is so distant; he is accustomed to taking charge and closing any gaps with women in his company. But this is an age gap, too, a first for him. How to discover how ripe or unripe she is for any advances? He picks up one of the many olives that have fallen prematurely and examines it to distract himself while she wanders over to the trunk of the tree, and he sees her examining the gnarled bark.

This tree has beat any odds against it, taken care of itself for centuries, Isabella thinks. Can I not manage that for a few decades? On that question she turns to Jeremy. 'Do you like it?'

'Awesome.' He tries to imitate the Yank, but she does not get the joke. 'Molto im*press*ionante.'

'Impressio*nan*te,' she corrects.

'Who is this Aginulfo? I obviously reminded you of whoever it is a couple of minutes ago.'

'The prince from Langobardia.'

'A prince. Charming idea. Your Prince Jeremy.' He bows theatrically, making her laugh.

'It is long ago. He liked this favourite place. When the prince came here, he took musicians to play with him. I thought if you do the same, it would be funny.'

'An open-air concert. Why not? It might even make me some friends in the village.'

'They do not know about you in the village. They are afraid only, of strangers. Do not worry.'

'Well, you, at least, are different from the others, like you said.'

'I am not stuck, that is all.'

Jeremy tries to get her to tell him more about life in the village on their way back, but she is reluctant, as the priest was, he remembers. What she does tell him, though, makes it obvious that Dom Pietro and his Church are in complete control of what goes on in the village. He avoids questions that might take a poke at intimacy he does not yet know how to handle across this age gap. She tells him about the nursery, he talks about Domino and snooker. They distract themselves after a while by selecting tracks to listen to.

As understanding as he might be if she told him more about herself, he is still a stranger to her. The village will always be her home. Isabella wants to change her place inside it, not leave it, or her mother. He is a city man. He comes from a world that fascinates her, the possibilities that can only exist in her imagination. In her real life here, she can only take one step at a time to change things. As the village comes into view on the ridge above them and Jeremy asks where he should drop her off, she suddenly finds herself ready to take the first step.

'I live on Piazzale Patricelli.'

'The village square?'

'Yes.'

'I didn't think . . . perfect. That's on my way too.'

It is meanwhile four in the afternoon. He drives slowly onto the square and pulls up opposite the rectory. 'That was a very nice outing, Isabella. Thank you.'

'Grazie, Jeremy. È stato un bel "lift" . . . dall'autobus?'

'Sì, certo, piacere mio.' He swipes his hand across his lips; he is to pretend they only travelled together from the bus stop.

Their secret is safe. Isabella returns his smile and gets out of the car. While they were driving back, he invited her to play snooker and to hear him practice, but in passing, not waiting for an answer, and she was way too unsure to give him one. Going alone to visit him at the villa? That would be a far more daring step than the one she has just taken. No matter how easy-going he pretends to be, she can see he really likes her. Her own attraction is different, but if she is not careful, that may not be enough to protect boundaries she would never casually cross.

When she reaches down into the car to collect her bag from the back seat, she nevertheless finds herself saying 'ci vediamo' with the same spontaneous affection that prompted the peck on his cheek earlier. She really would like to get to know the man better who made the beautiful music he plays a gift that is now so precious to her.

Jeremy hears her say 'see you again' without waiting for a response before she wanders off. He cannot resist spending a few moments to look at her as she saunters over the square, slinging the bag over her shoulder as she walks, and his gaze would willingly follow her until she reaches her door, but that may be conspicuous. He moves off.

'Oddio, no!' Isabella's mother has been looking out for her daughter off and on for the past two hours and cups her mouth to stifle her alarm at the scene.

At the same time, Dom Pietro observes their arrival outside the rectory window. 'This is not the way to make friends in the village, Jeremy.'

Isabella's father stops shuffling the card deck at the table, his face at once rigid. He elbows Marco's father. Through the bar door they both catch Isabella waving back at the Inglese as he passes by and waves at her from his car.

Isabella turns suddenly away from him, and her hand drops to her side. Jeremy's instincts tell him right away she is in trouble, and he, the Good Samaritan, in this village's version of the parable of neighbourly love, was supposed to be the Levite that left Isabella on the road.

Jeremy would learn a lot more about life in this village if he could sit next to the women talking on the benches beneath the olive trees overlooking the square.

'That's Marco's girl.'

'Our golden girl.'

'How dare she, then?'

'This outsider in a fancy car, he's trouble.'

'He nearly ran over poor old Signor Cappelli.'

'He was parked over there. Races out backwards, like everybody else should be careful, not him.'

'What will her mother say?'

'I keep telling her she should keep Isabella away from Angelina.'

'Isabella is different. Modest. Faithful.'

'Good with the children at the nursery, I hear. Don't worry.'

'Marco will not be happy about this.'

'He knows what he's got. He will not let her get away.'

'God will preserve their promise to each other.'

'There's plenty of time. They're young.'

'We're not.'

'They would have such beautiful children.'

Off-road

Driving home on the dirt track through the valley to the villa, Jeremy is fully aware that the afternoon with Isabella has taken him off-road. This, not the track itself, is jolting him: he should steer clear of her in good time. This is not the smooth ride he knows in his conquests along the straight and narrow, and maybe that's the catch.

No woman recently—upwards of ten over the last three years, he does not count—has taken him so suddenly and dangerously skidding through curves of desire that leave him struggling to keep control. Isn't he supposed to know by now how to negotiate and navigate his feelings for women? Isabella could take him back to those messy, amorous obsessions that left him wrecked ages ago, before he learnt how to brake in good time.

'Ci vediamo,' she said. That already feels like an invitation to think about where to go with her, and his mind is already losing its way exploring. She is too young to share a ride with him. And he must accept that, even if he is totally enchanted by her seamless and reversible metamorphoses—a charming girl one moment, a reflective woman the next—unaware of the indiscriminate way this happens with her coy then serene gestures and expressions, and her laugh. Has he ever been so hooked? He'd better buckle up. And stick to easy roads he knows.

This accelerated longing is a bluff anyway, panic at not having any other prospects in the near future. He will not even pretend she is one. He will head back onto the smooth straight and narrow that ends at a familiar salacious juncture; Vicky, the current engineer of his eros, never fails to put him in high gear, even if their arousal on the way there often skips past sharing any tenderness and leaves him less to be enchanted about. Self-imposed seclusion could lead to a breakdown in his restraint, but if Vicky can join him for a week or so, that should stall him in neutral before he sets off in pursuit of Isabella.

In trouble

When she hears her daughter come in, Isabella's mother finds herself still at the window where she has been standing, thinking about her own past, and feeling a lot older than her mid-fifties. It took her too long to choose the man in her life from the few choices she had then (and Isabella has now). And it took many unsuccessful attempts before Isabella was born. Outside of that manifest blessing from God, she soon recognised He also intended to challenge her in the match she accepted.

She knew beforehand she would have to scrimp and scrape, but her husband had kept his scrappier moods mostly hidden until their life together began. Neither could forgive not being what they had hoped to be for one another, until eventually it was too late to grow together, to find harmony as a couple, although they kept their composure in front of Isabella when she was a child. The older her daughter has become, the more open the anger that has invaded the house. It has been a blessing to see Isabella and Marco start life together so early. Of course they quarrel occasionally, when it cannot be avoided, and what she has just seen is sure to hurt Marco's pride very badly. But they are starting early enough to settle their differences and find the harmony they will need when they are married and have children. It would heal her soul, after her own broken marriage, to see her daughter settle down peacefully near her. She must have more faith that she has been a good mother, with a stronger understanding of Isabella's virtue than her daughter realises.

It turned out to be a good thing she let her watch those TV soap dramas in the afternoon after school years ago. Being so careful by nature, her daughter questioned early on what she should expect for herself when she grew up. It was not hard for her to see, when they talked about it, that the only danger would be to stray from the fold of faith and continuity she found around her. If she could find faith in a match she chose in the village, her

76

home, she would build love far stronger and more lasting than that in the confused and saddening relationships troubling the lives of people on TV. It was not long afterwards that her daughter declared Marco her choice, at thirteen, admittedly too young, but nevertheless it was reassuring that the message had found its rightful place in her adolescent mind.

Of course she is more hesitant about things now that she is older. But is this incident a sign that Isabella could make different choices that would damage her life, like Angelina who deserted her own home? Her daughter has become more private about her relationship with Marco, but that would be natural as she considers her future responsibilities; she was no different, finding strength and guidance in her marriage through prayer. But these visits to her girlfriend, a girl gone wrong and too big for her shoes, may be weakening Isabella's ingrained goodness and resolve, making her appearance in the village with a distressing stranger something she somehow found acceptable.

This is only a minor lapse in her daughter's vigilance she should be made aware of. These fears are unnecessary. No dangerous show-off or morally weak girlfriend will lead Isabella astray—or away. Her own loneliness, and Isabella's, is something she must protect both against.

'Ciao, Mama!' Isabella calls out cheerily to her mother as she enters the small hallway to the apartment, and she continues to talk in the same tone while she quickly ducks into her bedroom to throw the contents of her bag into a drawer. 'I missed the one o'clock bus by two minutes. Imagine that, the one day it left on time!' She closes her door and enters the apartment's main room. 'I hope you didn't worry . . .' When she sees her mother half turned to the window, she knows any attempt at light-hearted normality is futile. She expected as much. 'You did.'

'Worry about you being late?' Her mother turns her head briefly into the room and back outside again: the stoic 'look'.

'Well, yes. Or maybe you were worried and are now angry. You just looked at me like Papa does on one of his bad days.'

'I wasn't worried about you being late.'

'Are you angry then?'

'You could have walked from the bus as you normally do.'

'He offered me a lift from the bus stop. What's wrong with that? He's known in the village by now.'

'You're right, of course, he is *known* in the village.'

'Why does everybody mistrust him? He's a nice person, extremely polite, Mama.'

'Aren't they all, at first.'

'I didn't see any danger.'

'Your beauty is also God's challenge—to your virtue. Protect it.'

'It is not at risk. You know that better than anyone, Mama.'

'He's dangerous, Bella. Arrogant and careless. Marco, Signor Cappelli—in fact anybody I've talked to—won't share your opinion of him, I'm afraid.'

'That doesn't change mine now that I've actually met him. I don't have to accept what other people think.'

'Is that no longer important to you?'

'It's all just hearsay about him.'

'All right. I have my view and you keep yours. You're soon a grown woman.' She holds up her hands in defeat. 'But keep it to yourself. And think about what you'll say to Marco when he hears about it,' her mother adds.

So predictable. Even the slightest thing that might upset the 'lucky man' is taboo. Why should she feel responsible for what he thinks?

'I will tell him the truth. The Inglese offered me a ride in his car from the bus stop, and I accepted it. He was extremely polite and charming . . . and his Italian is atrocious!' She laughs at this to lighten the mood, moving towards the kitchen area. But there is a slight cynical edge to that laugh which her mother did not catch; it belongs to yet another attempt to cast her obedience to a worn-out mould, like the compressed coffee grounds she removes from the moka pot to make a fresh cup.

The built-in kitchen along one wall, a Formica-topped table and wooden chairs, and an old sofa and armchairs are all in the one main room. A crucifix hangs above the television, and pictures of saints and biblical scenes and one of Marco and Isabella as young teens decorate the walls. Isabella's back is to her mother as she prepares the coffee.

'Tell me about your visit. How is Angelina? What did you talk about?' her mother asks.

Isabella lets out a plaintive sigh, relieved not to be facing her mother. 'She misses the village, she says.'

'She says. Or you say, maybe, thinking for her? My guess is you know I would be relieved to hear she regrets her behaviour, misses being here.'

Isabella turns to face her mother. 'What are you saying, Mama?'

'You don't have to make up stories, Isabella. Angelina has chosen a different life for herself. She doesn't belong here, but you do. You must be careful what her thoughts do to your own. I know this distressing mistake with the Inglese is only a careless lapse in your vigilance, but you must be careful.'

'I am careful. That is why I decided, for myself, that it was all right to meet him face to face.'

'You should not only be deciding for yourself. You must think these things through.'

'Mama, please. I'm beginning to feel like I'm not allowed to be me anymore. Do I not have the right to even think differently from what people assume is right for me?'

This is Angelina talking. And the Inglese, who shows no respect for her daughter's virtue, is infecting her with his arrogance towards what matters in their village. 'But what about Marco? You've more than embarrassed him for sure, showing up like you just did in the middle of the village.'

'I have nothing to hide. I would do nothing to hurt Marco, you know that. It's his problem, with his own ego. If he goes around bragging about making a fool out of this stranger, it's his fault if my mistake, as you call it, makes him feel like I'm making a fool out of him.'

Isabella is not her real self; she has always been more forgiving than assertive, as she should be. 'I'm sure if you tell him you're sorry, everything will be all right again,' she says.

Isabella pours out two small espressos. How much should she say—can she say now—about her thoughts in the car, about what really matters to her and what is not all right. 'I warned him about his bragging.'

'And you will cure him of it, I'm sure, as you grow together. As we've said before, he has some catching up to do. All men do. Give it time.'

'You always say so, Mama.'

'What did the Inglese talk about?' her mother asks, breaking a tense silence on what Isabella needs to talk about, on her shame of not being truthful, unable to make her mother her confidant for fear of hurting her. That is what she and Angelina talked about.

'Nothing everyone doesn't know already. He's a musician. We just listened to music. He hardly speaks any Italian.'

They hear her father at the front door, and when he barges into the room, one look at him tells Isabella all she needs to know. It does not come as a surprise. She gets up from the table, as her mother does, ready for anything.

'Don't you know your place in the village?' he says angrily.

'She is going to put things right and apologise to Marco,' her mother says quickly.

'Don't let me catch you with the Inglese again. He is not welcome here. Nobody likes him. Arrogant show-off.'

This is slanted, unfair; nobody even knows who Jeremy is. She must take a stand. 'He's not arrogant, Papa. That is all I wanted to find out, for myself.'

'How dare you.'

Her mother steps between them and faces her father. He grunts to a stop, and Isabella exits quickly to her bedroom, leaving her coffee to go cold.

Her mother's worst fears about the encounter are unfounded maybe, and that is a relief. But it would nevertheless make sense to find out more about the *estraneo* from Dom Pietro, who she heard has already paid him a visit at the villa.

Toss and fetch

He is on his walk with Domino. The dog stays close to his side, looking up for reassurance every now and then as they move up the path, passing by the shepherd's house, heading towards the groves uphill and beyond. Domino is now free, but Jeremy finds himself chained up in thoughts he cannot break out of.

Whatever leads up to him wanting to seduce a woman, the challenge and anticipation have often felt more vital to him than the temporary thrill of pinning it down; he loses interest quickly afterwards, and when he is turned down, he is seldom discouraged from chasing up the next opportunity. But what if seduction, for its own sake, were to be replaced by real desire? What if the anticipation of being able to feel something totally new and vital through Isabella does not go away, is not so easily perishable or discarded, before they meet again? She has got him vacuum-packed, sealed up, inside the question of whether he would make a move on her, given half a chance, if the seal was broken, opening the question. If anything happened between them, he would be forced to run before he is fetched to answer for the soiled reputation of the village's prized beauty.

'Fetch, Domino!' The dog can do his running for him. But when he picks up a stick to throw, Domino darts away from him, misreading his intentions, afraid of being struck. How to show Domino he only intends play? He crouches down, looks at Domino, and puts the stick in his own mouth, earning him a very puzzled look from his playmate. He then takes the stick out of his mouth, throws it a short distance away, runs to pick it up, returns to the same spot, and throws it again. Domino does not catch on with the training method he used on his boyhood dog, and Jeremy gives up after three attempts.

They walk on up the incline. He must focus on other things he can positively anticipate. His concerts, getting the better of the music he has been working on, and Vicky. She accepted his invitation, of course, but not before hurling insults at him down the phone line in the bar, calling him negligent and selfish, before declaring she missed him. Her arrival is farther away than he would like, but her magnetic lust puts him on a predictable orbit, not anything like the subtle gravitational force Isabella is exerting on him. Vicky is mercurial; her maniacal passion, her mood swings, exist on that planet—too near the sun. Her moods create havoc on the concert circuit too, but she always delivers. She is transformed as soon as she enters the opera stage, turning supporting roles into vibrant characters that usurp the peck order of applause due at curtain time. He was standing in for the lead oboist in the pit when they met. Neither wasted any time going into orbit.

Fabio is waiting for them outside his house when they return from the walk. Domino lags behind, coming to a stop at a safe distance.

'My friend here doesn't like you. Sorry. I don't know why,' Jeremy says.

Both know the answer. Fabio dismisses it.

'Maybe because I make my dogs work.'

'Are your dogs not your friends?'

'I am their master. I teach them their duties, not silly games.'

'Dogs like to play. They need to.'

'Your dog doesn't even know how to do that.'

Jeremy is now aware he was seen earlier and can imagine how ridiculous a sight it was. 'They learn quick if they trust you. This dog has no reason to trust anyone.' Jeremy bends down, picks up a stick, and throws it, and to his total delight and amazement, which he hides, Domino rises to the occasion and races after it, returning with it to exactly the spot he set out from. He goes to Domino, gives an encouraging pat, and repeats the exercise, registering disdain written all over the lout's face while he watches, slouched against the door frame.

'I think the test is won,' Jeremy says.

'And what about mine? You promised.'

'It's not possible. Sorry. You are not insured.'

'Do not listen to my mother.'

'She has worry about you. You had an accident.'

'It was not my fault. The police said so.'

'But a man died?'

'It was his mistake! I am not to blame! I am tired of being accused!'

Fabio disappears into the house with a slam of the door.

Fabio was overtaking one tractor downhill just as another tractor entered the same road from the fields, turning uphill without seeing him. Having almost completed the overtake manoeuvre, Fabio hit the rear wheels of the oncoming tractor just as it was turning, tipping it and sending the driver flying over the road guard rails down the sheer drop to the valley below. Fabio had in fact seen the tractor approaching the road before overtaking, sure he would be faster. The car was to blame: too old, too slow.

Kiss me

Marco, too, wants to pretend there is no danger he has overseen, anxious to overtake Isabella, take the lead again. He will not let her humiliate him by cosying up to this show-off with his flash car and fancy ways. No way is he going to settle for any second choices; he has only ever half given in to other willing girls out of frustration with her, and he has never gone all the way. She cannot back out now, and he never will. Her respect in the village depends on keeping her promise to him, on them starting a new family here. He can be forced to be patient as long as she keeps her place behind him; he can see no reason to be lenient about that.

Isabella is getting frustrated with appearances like this one; an apology to Marco can only mean she is afraid to show she has her own mind. Will she do so this time or hide from the truth again for her mother's sake until, hopefully, she sees other options? Marco is too stuck in his own thinking to see the bubble they are under here, too immature to want to avoid a mistake, so she cannot come clean with him and find openness she wants to share with people, and acceptance for who she is. She will not reject Jeremy because he is a stranger; she does not want to be his or anyone else's lover or obedient girlfriend.

Looking at Marco waiting for her on the bench when she closes the door to her house across the square, she knows she has an uphill battle. He is pretending not to be watching out for her. And yes, he seems more than ever like a boy now that she has met Jeremy. She does not want to hurt Marco, if only because he is as innocent as she has been until now of being pushed in a direction they should not go. It is rare that he openly expresses his feelings for her, probably because they are not really what matters to him. It is more her looks compared with the other girls, her continuing 'relationship' with him, the 'promise'. It makes him feel important that all eyes are on them. Her absence would be more a demotion, not so much an ache. But can she really be sure she has not got it all wrong? What if Marco really does care for her more deeply than she thinks? What if he is just too insecure about her, unable to admit it to himself and express his real feelings? She will not find any happiness in the make-believe relationship she once invented for them. If something happened between her and Marco to truly make the match real for her, she would keep it.

'Ciao, Marco,' she says brightly and takes a place beside him, props an arm on the backrest, and ever so slightly runs her fingers though his hair. He leans forward, elbows on knees, and looks up sideways at her, trying on an angry expression that only makes her smile. It will taunt him. She is ready to make his anger real. 'I found your note in the post-box yesterday, as you can see. I liked the ones I found under my books at school better. "Carissima Isabella", not just "Isabella".'

'You started this, not me.'

'What have I started?'

'Questions, about us.'

'Who is asking them? You, I hope. I will answer those.'

'What's up with you?'

'That's too general a question.'

'I'm really angry, Isabella. That should concern you.'

'Oh, but it would, Marco. If I knew what your anger is about.'

'Stop pretending! You know!' He jumps up from the bench.

She wants him to name the accusations. That is how the bubble exists, she sees now, because no one ever dares to own them openly. 'I can see you are angry. So am I, in a way.'

'What are you talking about?'

'I'm fed up with us being forced to watch our steps all the time. People tell us what we should think. What is right, or wrong. You know I would never wrong you. Don't believe them, what they think. Your anger will go away.'

'I know what I think.'

'I'm listening.'

'I have waited. I am yours, and yours only. You are mine, mine only. So, I will not take any risks, even if other people see them first and I don't.'

'And what risk do you, or they, see?'

'You want to be different, like Angelina.'

'She's my girlfriend. I feel close to her. She gave up her virtue for a man she's not sure about. Those are not my choices.'

'But you think it's OK to risk a ride with someone nobody knows, who does not know us, and who does not care what we think about him.'

'I took a ride with someone you don't know, who does not know about our relationship, and who probably would not care what you think about him. Isn't that what you should be worried about? Go on, be yourself, be different.'

'Who is putting these crazy ideas into your head?'

'What's so crazy about having your own thoughts, your own questions, finding your own answers?'

'Is it crazy to protect what we have?'

'I'm sorry I upset you by accepting the ride. I really am. Sit down again, please.' She has made the apology her mother insisted on. What is he going to do with it?

He lurches backwards onto the bench, trying to keep up the manly anger that comes off as even more boyish to her. 'So, you do see that it was wrong,' he says.

'Absolutely. He could have made advances, or more. I didn't know if he would ruin my reputation. But he was just very polite. I was lucky. You read all sorts of horror stories.'

'Then why did you do it?'

'Because the poor Inglese cannot even pick his nose without everybody in the village talking about it. He is under constant observation, and he knows it by now. What more protection could I want? So, I thought, "He's just trying to be friendly."'

'He could still be after you. He's a risk, dangerous.'

Marco is right, of course, if the open invitation to visit the villa cannot be trusted to be just an innocent, friendly interest to meet again. But what if she did give in to the boy next to her? 'I see a much bigger risk for myself,' she says.

'And that is?'

'Let me show you. Kiss me.'

'What? Now? Here?'

'Yes. Show me you will stand by yours only, because you love me and will try to understand me. That's the protection I need as we grow older.'

'Isabella, we've already been together for six years.'

She moves her mouth inescapably close to his. 'Show me the next ten, then.'

He obliges. The kiss feels awkward to him because she is asking for it, and she has never done that before. And in front of everybody looking? She wants to assure everyone they are still together. That should feel doubly right, but it does not. Is she stringing him along? Did she ask the Inglese too? He breaks off the kiss abruptly and lowers his head. He cannot look at her right now.

She gently brushes away his hand on her thigh. Maybe he is not to blame for the kiss feeling really put on, but surely if his feelings for her were genuine, she would still feel something that told her so, a hint of warmth and forgiveness to keep them from moving apart. But that is already happening now. She smiles at him, his lowered head in profile.

'You see the risk? To me, any kiss from you should feel like a sacrament, in communion, with you, with love. That felt like the kiss you give to girls behind my back not thinking I would hear about it.' She stands up. 'Carissimo Marco, the risk, as I see it, is all mine. Maybe you won't ever understand me, even in ten years' time. Should I still feel then like I am yours only?'

'Isabella . . .'

But she does not turn back. He watches her walk confidently across the square with litheness unmatched by any of the other girls. He is unhinged by this new Isabella he does not know, who questions his grip as a man. She can forget her fancy romantic ideas and give him her body, take her place next to him, and not just walk away, like now, because she does not agree with what he thinks. Only then will he listen to her. Those girls meant nothing to him. And why does she bring them up now? Because the Inglese is after her, and she is tempted to get even. She has no idea how dangerous that is. He must find a way to get that man to clear off, back to wherever he comes from. His sort is not welcome here. Maybe he should make him see that more clearly.

Isolated challenges

Having now settled into life in the villa, his days follow a pattern; he would not go so far as to call it a disciplined routine. The rise and fall of the day's heat dictates at different times what he is likely to be doing. He manages to get up most mornings early enough for a small breakfast with Domino on the front terrace.

He uses that time to decide what pieces he will tackle next from the repertoire he is set to play on his upcoming tour. He tries to be methodical about pacing himself, switching between compositions to avoid frustration when certain passages or movements sound either stifled or overwrought after several attempts at them. The divertimento by Crusell, the Swede, with its bright semiquaver runs at the extremes of the oboe's range, demands virtuosity from him he seldom feels up to, a taxing piece of showmanship too many concert organisers latched onto when they heard his recording of it.

Whatever his choice, he seldom feels fluid or expressive—or as aware of what the next notes need from him as once came naturally to him. Dom Pietro was right about it being a spiritual experience, at least when he can sense his mind, body, and the spirit of the music flow intuitively in one stream. Instead, it all feels like conscious effort now to reach a remembered familiarity; an easy dialogue with the instrument or the inner satisfaction of hearing that dialogue take shape as he plays is still missing.

The many repeated runs, wobbly legatos, and scratchy key shifts are a source of frustration. It is hard to ignore the pain through his ribcage that can still stab him out of the blue, puncture the breath he is on. The doctors assume that will eventually ease off. But the stiffness leading down from his crushed elbow to his right wrist, the arm he needs to hold the oboe steady, is irreparable, permanent. That injury makes it impossible to twist all fingers of his right hand so that they are parallel to the keys when he plays them. He misses how naturally he controlled his fingerwork and breathing, leaving him free to find his own articulation as a soloist. He just cannot get inspired; inhibited freedom makes his practice a chore. And while diligence might give him back some confidence, it takes more than that to find his voice again on the oboe.

The other half of that voice, the reed, is his real disability; it kills inspiration where his physical impairments spare him. He needs to stop seeing each botched attempt at making them as confirmation that he does not have the intuition it takes to make a good one. He spends most mornings after breakfast trying to fight off that foregone conclusion, trying to scrape and shave away his destructive conviction that the reed he is working on will give him no more than a mediocre chance to play as he wants, to revel in the fatter notes and scamper through the oboe's register with the dynamism and contrasting subtlety of expression that made him a soloist.

Quite apart from the colour and stability of their tone, most of his reeds are too unresponsive. The pressure he is forced to endure on his lips, thyroid, and tendons in his neck is unbearable. But that's the only way to compensate for his lack of skill in shaping the two blades of carefully hollowed-out cane to vibrate together in a way that creates the voice he wants. His best performance will always depend on having made each reed unique to what he wants to do with it, right down to which one feels right for the composition he plays. The reeds either bless or condemn his voice even before the music begins.

Jansen made him so happy about the progress he made, he did not give much thought to them when he started out, because the strides he made in playing for the first time put aside that da capo curse he had grown up with: he would never succeed at anything he did. He was surprised he got into the academy, but he remained convinced he would ultimately fail, vehemently denying he had any real talent and treating it as a given right to think so whenever he got stuck. He rebelled against Jansen's insistence that he had what it took to be an outstanding oboist. His amiable, unperturbed instructor laughed heartily at his tirades until he saw no point in them either and could laugh too, accept that he was talented, and continue making real progress in his playing.

But the curse returned to do battle with him later because Jansen had nothing to say about making reeds. He left him completely in the dark about how to make and then teethe the oboe's vocal cords to produce the exact sound he wants to hear from them. He rarely has the patience to test the reeds thoroughly before wanting to change them if they do not work the first time. But adjusting the scrape once they are basically finished can easily ruin hours of work. It is a debilitating task, it can really depress him, and there is no one to distract him here, no one to blunt the sharp edge of his impatience.

Thank God for snooker. For an hour or so, after attempts at reeds, he throws open the windows, chalks up, and practices. It is a miracle mood shaker; he never tires of playing and can see his game is improving fast. It is a much larger table than he has at home. He has become a lot more accurate since it takes a lot more precision to pot the ball in the narrow-jawed straight-edged pockets, and he is getting better at cushion shots. His intuition of where his shot will lead him does not betray him on the table, which gives him back some calm and patience. Snooker is the perfect antidote to what defeats him when he makes reeds; it is a welcome timeout when practice frustrates him or just wears him out.

He has too much time on his hands out here. He practices as much as he can after lunch and has a short siesta that takes him past the hottest part of the day. But the idea that he could spend all his time on his music and reeds is illusory. If he does not pace himself, he will be revisiting the panic that took hold of him in the first months after the accident because he was trying too hard, and too soon, to recover his form. There is no one to turn to here, no one to give his ego a boost or even keep him company for a while. He has had no visitors.

It was heart-warming to spy Giorgio giving Domino a quick pat the other day, and his exchanges with the artigiano are cordial now, but there is not a lot of common ground. In this isolation, snooker and walking his faithful companion are his only distractions. And on some evenings lately he found himself drinking too much, wanting to drug himself asleep and mute the unloved dogs howling through the Death Valley of his scorched virility while he lies awake fending off thoughts of Isabella, waiting for Vicky.

He told himself this self-imposed quarantine, this undistracted time alone, would quicken his recovery, and while he has made some progress, knowing it will take a lot longer than he thought is at times chastising, in every sense. At home he would be out and about now, trawling for a catch within easy reach. Here the net pulls up 'ci vediamo', and logically at least that catch must be tossed back; it is tagged with insane paradoxes worthy of Heller's novel *Catch-22*.

He has booked a night in Rome to explore a bit. Vicky would expect him to know his way around when she comes, and he needs a break from isolation in rural tranquillity.

Calling up a miracle

Dom Pietro has decided it is time to check up on Jeremy. Even though he has been spotted in the village only a few times, the gossip and rumours surrounding the *estraneo* are still in high circulation. His intentions towards Isabella when he offered her a ride were probably as innocent as she herself certainly is, but she is maybe not as aware as she should be of what her looks can provoke in men like him. There is no skirting around the temptation he presents, her mother said when she visited the rectory wanting to find out more about the Inglese. He told her not to worry, but maybe he should find out if there is any reason to worry and forestall Jeremy from doing anything more, out of ignorance of the status quo, to provoke the villagers. As for himself, he is somehow grateful—ignoring the cynicism—to take a break in the musician's company from his intellectually dry parish following.

He can hear the oboe clearly as he passes through the gates to the villa and drives his car around to the back entrance, and the sound gives him an idea that could improve Jeremy's reputation and lessen objections to his stay here. He parks up alongside Jeremy's BMW. As always, it is a bit of a struggle to get his bulky frame out of the tiny Fiat Cinquecento. The wheeze in his chest is back by the time he is standing erect. He takes the pause as an excuse to examine the sleek contours and opulent leather interior of the convertible, the micrometre perfection of every seam where parts join, the luxury and elegance surpassing any car he has ever sat in. What would it be like to sit back and feel the breeze, travel quietly through a panoramic view of all God made? A heavenly experience, no doubt—and a man-made temptation that weakens true spiritual resolve against worldly desires. But would he refuse a ride in this car?

The oboe is extremely loud when he enters the back door,

echoing through the open rooms and alternating between high-pitched rapid runs and deep solemn notes. It does not sound like a composition, so it must be some sort of practice exercise. He does not want to disturb; he will wait in the main room outside the door until there is an obvious break.

Jeremy has just taken a seat at the desk and is risking a small scrape on the reed he has been testing when a loud 'salve!' outside the door gives him a start. His scraper slips badly, cutting off too much at the tip of the reed. Oh shit! He holds it up against the bright light from the window. It is ruined.

'Oh, bloody fucking hell, holy shit, Jesus Christ almighty—' The tirade is cut short at the sight of Dom Pietro in the doorway, fingers in his ears. Jeremy cups his hand briefly over his mouth to give the all-clear. 'Do you make a habit of sneaking up on people?'

'I didn't want to disturb your practice, or hear the consequences for that matter. I thought you were having a break. I'm sorry. What have I done?'

'Ruined what promised to be one of the best reeds I've tested for a long time. See? I cut too much right off the tip of the blade. I just wanted to make it slightly easier to play. Now it's unplayable.'

'I'm quite happy to replace it.'

'You cannot. No two are alike. You can't buy one of these. I have to make them, for me, how I play, from scratch, from this.' He hands the priest his mouthpiece and a segment of raw cane. 'It's all very complicated, delicate work. And I'm no good at it, that's the problem.'

'I can see it can't be easy. This from this,' the priest says, holding up the reed and then the segment of cane.

'It is *my* cross, Dom Pietro. I drag it with me from one performance to the next, with no promise of salvation if the reed does not hold out and I cannot carry on. My crap skill in making these will nail me to mediocrity. If I don't get at least a few of them right, that's the end of my solo career. No second coming.'

'Please, Jeremy, cut out the irreverence. You're overdramatising this.'

'Believe you me, I wish I was.'

'Well, I don't think the world will be saved by your music, and that's the only fair comparison.'

'I was illustrating, not comparing.'

'You exasperate me, Jeremy. Have some faith. I will go out on a limb for you. I will now ask the true Saviour you just insulted to bless this piece. You will make a perfect reed from it.'

Jeremy watches Dom Pietro hold up the cane and make a cross in front of it, murmuring a few words in Latin. Satisfied, the priest gives the piece of raw cane back to him. 'Witness God's forgiveness and goodwill. Please mark it so you know which piece it is.'

'I can't say that will give me any more faith in it. But maybe yours is all I need.'

'Neither you nor I can assume His grace.' Dom Pietro takes a seat on Jeremy's chair with a heavy sigh of relief, examining the tools and discarded reeds scattered on the desk. 'But if it is a good one,' he says hesitantly, 'maybe you can use it to play a concert in my church?'

'No blessing from the Church without attached motives. I should have guessed.'

'Oh, no, don't feel obligated. It's just an idea I had listening to you on my way in here. I think my villagers would welcome the chance to find out what you're all about. A small concert is sure to strike the right chord, so to speak. They would see it as a very kind gesture of goodwill, I think. I'm really sorry about this reed.'

Jeremy takes it back and puts it into the oboe. He will see later if it is really buggered. 'I think my reputation precedes me as someone they should keep at arm's length. I certainly don't feel very welcome in the village.'

'I'm sorry to hear that. I can't imagine why.'

'Well, if you can't, how should I know why I'm never even greeted properly? Not the first day, not since—oh, not true, there is one exception: my veggie lady, Signora Tendri.'

'I found the crassness you probably mean very strange myself when I came here. So, I'm pretty sure it's not intentional. The signora is a fine woman, yes. She lost her husband too early but found her faith in others through God.'

'I don't share her faith, I'm afraid, in any other villagers I have met so far. And it's probably too late to change anybody's mind about me, unless I ditch my car, change my wardrobe, and stop trying to make people smile back.'

'Jeremy, you're assuming you're not wanted. The villagers are pretty guarded about newcomers, I'll give you that. But I'm confident things would change if you reach out to them. And I speak from experience. I had a hard time too when I first arrived. Only a few villagers followed my first attempts to revitalise the Church here; it took a while before they saw that pulling the bell rope together made sense to build community spirit. Now they're all behind me. I can assure you the church will be packed. You'll be an inspiration.'

'I dare say no one in the village has even heard the oboe, live, as a solo instrument, which they will probably assume is a clarinet that sounds weird the way I play it. I'm already treated like an odd apparition they're not happy to see. And I'm not keen on them either.'

'Give it a chance, Jeremy. I could use some support getting my congregation in a more positive frame of mind about welcoming people to the village.'

'I cannot play on my own. That would be ridiculous.'

'You've not yet been inside my church, obviously. We do have an organ, donated by the Patricelli, of course, a few generations ago. The bishop at the abbey occasionally sends someone to play a service for us. It can be arranged, I'm sure.'

'I still would rather not. It's what I do for a living. People pay to hear me. It would be a bit like showing off, trying to make myself more popular. That's not me.'

'Oh, Jeremy, you disappoint me.' He turns to look out the window.

'We don't have to agree on everything, do we? OK, we'll make a deal. If the reed *is* good, I'll play.'

'You can't bargain for His grace, Jeremy.'

'A devilish idea, I suppose.'

Dom Pietro turns round sharply. 'If you continue to offend my beliefs with your irreverence, I will join my villagers and keep my distance.'

'Sorry! Sorry. My apologies. It just slipped out. I have nothing against your beliefs. They're strong, I can see that.'

'All I'm after is to give my congregation something uplifting, and your music complements their faith. Like I said last time, it has a spiritual quality.'

'Since my irreverence offends, let's please leave out faith's preeminence in everything too.'

'But you agree maybe that music could break down some barriers?'

'I didn't erect any. If they exist, I cannot break them down.'

'Then let me try.'

'I don't want to be in the limelight, thanks.'

'You already are, Jeremy. I just want to give it a more positive focus.'

'Well, OK, if you're determined to experiment, I'm expecting a visit from a soprano friend of mine, a terrific singer, and if I can get her to accompany me, she would certainly lift people out of their seats.'

'Excellent! What a great idea. It will be a major event!'

'She's a busy opera singer, coming here for a break, so please don't count on it. It would be something impromptu, very improvised.'

'Of course, of course. I'll pray hard that she goes along. And you must come and hear the organ.'

'When?'

'Well, ideally, on the Sunday when the organist comes in a few weeks.'

'Are you having me on? I told you. I haven't been to Mass in twenty plus years. I'm not a practicing Catholic, remember?'

'And I'm not a priest who wants to grab your soul and claim your faith for the Church. As much as I hate to say it, you will not be the only one to just go through the motions. You may take Communion if attendance is otherwise awkward.'

'How generous of you. Will there be a sermon?'

'I don't always. But yes, I have one in mind.'

'Not in Latin, I hope.'

'Not funny. Only the liturgy.'

'*Suscipiat Dominus sacrificium de manibus tuis . . . ad laudem et gloriam nominis sui . . . ad utilitatem quoque nostrum . . . totiusque ecclesiæ suae sanctæ.*'

'Jeremy. No Mass in twenty years. I am surprised.'

'My memory is all that qualified me as an altar boy. And the fact that my mother insisted I be taken on. What's your homily about? Not that I will understand much anyway.'

'The Eighth Commandment.'

'Is this a test? Do not bear false witness. You have a scandal in the village?'

'Overzealous observers, maybe.'

'The faithfully intolerant. I know something about that.'

'Rumours in any community of faith are bad for spiritual morale.'

'And you want me to sit in your church? Give a concert? Look, for your benefit, we should just forget the whole thing.'

'Leave it to me. The villagers shouldn't be intolerant of people just because they're strangers to the way we live here. You can help me change that, and it's important to me.'

'So, I'm the token rebel they have to deal with. I feel really comfortable.'

'I don't want the village to shrink because our moral standards are strict; they make sense—in God's community and everywhere. But I won't allow them to be used to exclude others here.'

'You're very sincere about your faith, Dom Pietro, I'll give you that.'

'I'm happy to hear it, coming from you.'

'I'll do what I can, to help you keep your job.'

'You would have to spoil it. Where's your sincerity?'

'It is famished, needs sustenance. I'm hungry. Stay for lunch. I could use some company for a change.'

'At your service. That is my job, most of the time.'

The sun is now over the crest of the trees that protect the front terrace from direct heat before noon, but Jeremy now has put up an umbrella. Dom Pietro is satisfied with how things are going. He has done his best to bring Jeremy into the fold, as he promised himself he would last time he was sitting here waiting for lunch, and he cannot be disappointed, even if he is wary about the risk involved if their association becomes more public. If Jeremy does anything more to antagonise the sensitivities of his most faithful followers, he might be accused of being too lenient towards brash behaviour he himself has scolded them for from the pulpit.

And Jeremy's behaviour already has everyone worried about

his possible influence on Isabella. According to her mother, the girl has appeared to be having a change of heart since she met him. Any unpredictable movement on that pillar would really rock the foundations of the two families and shake the village.

Why did he even think of bringing Vicky into this, Jeremy asks himself as he prepares a quick pasta-and-salad lunch in the kitchen. Maybe it's time to rebel against the impenetrable people here, give them some grief. Vicky thrives on behaviour that would storm the barricade of intolerance erected by Dom Pietro's villagers, and the priest, genuine in his beliefs or not, obviously helped put it there. They could never become friends, no matter how relieved he is to share the priest's company and still find himself able to stare down the gullible altar boy. It might even be amusing to see the priest perform from his pulpit and watch the man he has casually bantered with bear down on slander on the other side of the village's barricade.

Dog-eared compassion

He takes out the pasta and wine. Dom Pietro sniffs the pasta approvingly before Jeremy returns to the kitchen, comes back out with the salad, takes a seat, and gives Domino an affectionate pat as he settles down next to his chair.

'You found a companion, I see.'

'I had a dog as a boy. A stray, like this one. I'm just taking care of an unloved creature.'

'That's very Christian of you.'

Jeremy takes his time pouring the wine, trying to resist the temptation to put down the cult that indoctrinated his mother. 'I don't think the Christians around here are too concerned for their dogs' welfare. My mother had my dog put down. She said I was guilty of negligence, too, a sin that forced her to catapult my dog into a better afterlife.'

Dom Pietro knows the villagers' dogs are treated miserably but decides not to say anything. He is not comfortable answering the misguided fervour of Jeremy's Catholic mother head on. He takes a forkful of pasta in silence. Is he just hungry again or is this good? He raises his glass. 'You're a good cook, Jeremy. I am surprised.'

'Why am I surprised?'

'Because I'm complimenting you?'

'On a sauce that comes ready-made out of a jar.'

'Oh. I wouldn't have guessed.' The priest puts down his glass, and Jeremy watches him shovel a massive swirl of fettuccini into his mouth. He only cursorily chews his food before he swallows almost whole what he has forked in.

'I normally eat out, in London. Who cooks for you?' Jeremy asks.

'A small group of women in the village take turns. The parish can't afford a housekeeper for me.'

'Well, that's one way to keep up with what is going on in the village I suppose.'

'I don't heed gossip, Jeremy. Only confessions.'

'I'm curious to know who the villagers think I am.'

'A bit surprising coming from a man who is used to standing in the limelight. You're a friend of the Patricelli, a musician, and the new guy in town.'

'That does not answer the question.'

'Ah, true. Gossip is built on subjective ideas, isn't it? I can't help you there.'

'You can, with your own. You've known this village over two generations.'

'What more can I tell you than I have already? The people here are mostly poor rural workers. They depend on continuity, the next generation to keep things going. They are protective of their faith, of what they have here. To them, you belong to city life, a bad influence that corrupts the younger villagers and encourages them to leave.'

'It can't be good for you to be seen in my company, then. What would you say?'

'"The Lord is my shepherd; I shall not want." I'm not worried about my reputation.'

'In the presence of mine enemies? Thou anointest my head with oil. No, Domino.' Jeremy responds to the dog's discreet whimper for a bite and turns him towards the stairs, giving his rear end a light pat. 'Go play.' Domino starts to leave, reluctantly, and turns his head back towards Jeremy before ambling down the stairs. 'So, seriously, in your opinion, what can I do to feel welcome here?'

'Avoid mocking their Church.'

'Loose tongue; I'll cut it out. And then?'

'Reach out as best you can.'

'Why does that feel a little bit like Domino whining for approval, like a dog these people want to control on a leash. Some more wine?' He need not wait for the nod.

'You could see it as a leash or as a chance to grasp their values and the pull of faith you've strayed from.'

'My reasons for bolting are as legitimate as theirs for accepting a collar, so to speak.'

'No one is denying your right to decide for yourself, as they have: to stay clear of distractions and temptations and keep their faith robust, share community with those who keep up awareness of it. That deserves respect, even if you personally might not think much of the conformity they're after together in the practice of their beliefs.'

'That puts you in charge, doesn't it?'

'No, God. His Church. Anything else is insurrection. I seek to inspire, not dictate.'

'Well, that's a welcome change from Catholic history.'

'Don't rile me'—he punctuates his warning with his fork—'by taking a poke at what you think the Church stands for. If piety is a personal choice, conformity in belief is the social soul that protects and guides the community.' He takes a healthy slug of wine. 'It is not a leash. All you have to do is respect that community, think about how what you do affects your neighbours, hopefully to inspire them.'

This is a chance to hear how Isabella fared afterwards; there was sure to have been big objections to her taking a lift with him. 'Well, I do my best. In fact, not long ago, this Good Samaritan rescued one of the prettiest girls he has ever seen off the road in the sweltering midday heat.'

'Noon? It was later in the afternoon. I saw you arrive.'

'Could have been later, I suppose. The heat here at any time of day is too intense for me. Anyway, I don't think it has inspired my "neighbours" to be more friendly.'

'Let's hope your intentions are taken the right way, but they might not be. Isabella has been with Marco for years, and they're not just any couple, they're the "coppia dorata" of the village. A lot of hopes are pinned on them. So, careful.'

'Oh, I see. The golden couple. I could secretly be planning an abduction of the bride-to-be to sin city, is that it? I only offered her a lift. If she knows better, she accepted anyway. Whoever Marco is, she will have to sort it out with him.'

'Marco is the older boy you met on your first day in the village, with two of his friends around your car?'

'Oh, him.'

'Marco is pretty geared up, but Isabella is still holding off. So, you know, everybody in the village is waiting.'

'All eyes on them, then. The big day.'

'Exactly, so her sharing a ride alone with you makes people nervous. Didn't you ask her about herself? She'd be closer than I am to any gossip about you as well.'

'I should have, obviously. In my abysmal Italian? On a two-minute drive?'

'Pity no one speaks English here. Looks like you're stuck with me.'

'Poor me. She was charming about my Italian, though. She said English was abandoned in school here. Don't I remember you saying you tried to introduce it?'

'I did, until the parents decided it was more important for their children to learn the lingua franca of their Church instead. I saw no reason to object, obviously.'

'Well, in the secular world English is pretty essential, I think.'

'In my book, protecting our values is more important.'

'Aren't your ideas for the village a bit narrow-minded? Where is the priest who went to America?'

The priest shakes his head, putting down his fork after the last bite. 'I met people every Sunday over there who practice more communion with their cars, their real estate, their careers, and their unsanctionable relationships than they do with God. They're indulgent.' He downs his remaining wine in one gulp, unaware of any contradiction.

'And doomed I suppose, unless the Church puts indulgences up for sale again.'

The sturdy table rattles as Dom Pietro's free hand slams down on it, followed by the other with his glass. 'I don't need a history lesson from someone who only wants to see where the Church once went wrong. It's history.'

'And redeemed? Really, Dom Pietro, you may be different, sincere in your beliefs, but many in your Church are not, and you know it. The Church should clean up its own act before telling everyone else to clean up theirs.'

Dom Pietro puts his hands on the table, preparing to get up from his chair. 'I am not responsible for the Church you left, Jeremy, but for the worshippers of my village who accept that prayer, self-restraint, and sound morality are what it takes to be ready for the Lord. That is what I, personally, believe in, why I chose to come here to preach, where I would be heard.'

'OK, I hear you, all right? But you forgot tolerance. My own personal experience left a bitter aftertaste in my life. It lingers. Especially if being stigmatised by your villagers feels no different than when I was chastised as a good Catholic boy for trying to be heard myself. Have another glass of wine.'

There is a touch of disappointment in his voice as the priest eases himself back down in his chair. 'Don't let it get you down, Jeremy. The door is always open.'

'Amen. For today, please.'

'Let's try and disarm the villagers. Will the soloist put in an appearance at Mass?'

'To hear the organ, and you, maybe. If it is understood as diplomacy, and not bowing to conformity.'

Jeremy stands up to clear the table and has the stacked plates in his hand when the sound of a scooter and a beep turn his attention to the path leading down from the courtyard at the back of the villa. Fabio, hunched over the handlebars, comes to a dust-swirling stop without greeting him, leaving him enough time to register what is happening. At the end of a rope, attached to the scooter, Fabio is trailing a dead black-and-white dog tied by its front legs. Domino? Jeremy slams down the plates on the table and quickly turns to look again. It is a collie, one of the herding dogs. Fabio sits back on the seat and, smiling broadly, gestures with his hands held in mock prayer towards his dead cargo.

He shouts above the scooter engine, laughing. 'Inutile pregare questo, eh?' No use praying to this one, is there?

Fabio relishes his vindictive moment before it is cut short by Dom Pietro, who slowly shifts his weight to his feet and rises from his chair until standing in clear view above the balustrade of the terrace. The priest looks down on his subject, his presence triggering shock and panic on the lout's face.

'Un peccato, non serve più!' Fabio shouts, not showing any

shame at all as he hits full throttle, back wheel spinning against the drag of his heavy tow and throwing up dust as he moves off, desperate to get away, the dog in rigor mortis scraping and bouncing with eyes wide open behind him.

Jeremy sees Dom Pietro fingering his rosary as his eyes follow the scooter down the path and out of sight beyond the villa's entrance gate. The priest does not share his horror at all, simply looks on with rigid impassivity, contemplating God knows what, certainly not the obscenity in front of him. Jeremy can feel his anger grow until he cannot control it.

'Is this cruel dismissal of life natural for people who live closer to the soil than I do?' Jeremy points at the gate. 'Is that despicable lout someone who deserves any respect? Is this respect for the dead? This, in my eyes, is a sin!' He grabs up the stacked plates. He does not need a second look at this priest. 'I will gladly stay an outsider!' he adds from the doorway, and storms inside to the kitchen.

Jeremy enters the kitchen and puts the plates down on the granite wash table, stretches his arms out against the edge, and lets his head sag. Dom Pietro is no different to the priests Jeremy remembers. They are all cold ritualistic pontificators who ignore the need for true empathy, compassion, or emotion. They treat genuine sympathy like bothersome flies with no place to land, like those hovering around the plates before he rinses them under the tap. He hears Dom Pietro coming through to the kitchen. Should he openly attack the priest for being pitiless? He stays put at the sink, tense, the altar boy awaiting rebuke for his outburst.

Dom Pietro knows the anger directed at him is old, dug up and thrown at him with a vengeance against the Church. Jeremy is obviously reliving his misguided Catholic mother's accusations of negligence and his guilt, brought back in force by the creature just dragged away in front of him. What a pitiful sight it was. Jeremy's anger is justified, but it also makes him blind to the consolation believers find in the everlasting spirit, continuity which comforts both the dying and the bereaved. Maybe this is not the time to tackle that truth with someone whose past has weakened the healing power of faith. He must show the compassion Jeremy only looks for in this life.

He picks up the salad bowl and swills down the sip he sees left in Jeremy's glass before taking what he can safely hold in his chubby hands to the kitchen, where he finds Jeremy bent forward against the wash table, his gaze studying the remnants of their meal moving towards the drain. He places the dishes gently on the kitchen table, moves deliberately but unhurried behind Jeremy, and places a hand on his shoulder. 'I am truly sorry, Jeremy, for what you just experienced.'

'It didn't seem to bother you much.'

When Jeremy turns around to face him, Dom Pietro sees his sympathy is both unexpected and convincing when their eyes lock and he gives Jeremy a faint understanding nod. But rebellion still lurks in those eyes.

'Just don't dare tell me to have faith again. I couldn't be farther away from it,' Jeremy says.

Dom Pietro shakes Jeremy's shoulder in response, but lightly enough to turn his annoyance at this stubborn rejection of faith into an innocent admonishing gesture, accompanied by a rueful smile and what he hopes is a comforting squeeze. 'I'm sorry for the pain you felt.'

Neither of them is in the mood to voice their views as they share an espresso on the terrace, in silence that feels uncomfortable to Jeremy, incompatibilities rattling around in his head like the clatter of cups and teaspoons while Dom Pietro fingers the beads of his rosary. Music, a safe topic, would bring up the concert he now feels disinclined to commit to. It would not be what the priest had in mind, either, if it does not conform with the 'restraint and sound morality' of his cross bearers. Vicky is more than likely to take evil delight in piercing their pious armoury with her devilish stage presence and God-sent voice. She thrives on scandal. More's the pity, maybe, if she decides not to sing.

Dom Pietro is relieved their coffee was peaceful, but the exhaustion he feels as he goes to his car drags him down to an unsettling undercurrent he has fought many times over. Should he be in this job, as Jeremy disrespectfully calls it, if he is unable to genuinely reach people who do not share his deep faith and the real comfort it can offer? He trusts God to heal whatever afflicts

His devoted followers. He knows no other path. He has never felt close to people who do not see the inner peace faith could give them.

Jeremy's rhetorical denials will not give him any chance to stand above the suffering that awakens past pain. Fabio is sure to be punished for his sinful disrespect for the dog, and the boy's mother would know that in her pious heart. Jeremy does not. He is too passionate about this life. As he said when they first met, Jeremy wants any sin to be punished in the here and now, as if he can push God to reveal His plan.

He looks towards the ruined chapel and contemplates going inside it to ask for inspiration, for a peek inside Jeremy's soul that would give him a chance to reach it. But prayer takes strength and concentration he does not have. He goes to his car.

He hates the struggle he has getting into and out of the Cinquecento, an unwelcome reminder of how his weakness for food and wine (much poorer vintage than Jeremy's) has grown his bulk since he bought and restored the car ten years or so ago. The shout of 'padre!' reaches him at the most awkward halfway point, but he knows the siesta he longs for is now delayed. He extracts himself out of the car door before his head is inside.

Giorgio approaches him from the direction of his office, and he watches a strong stride in a body he would prefer to inhabit, even if it is a bit squat. There is a faint smile on the olive grower's lips that he has seldom seen.

'The inspectors have been here. We're through DOP certification. We can finally start bottling last year. Very late, but us small producers always get pushed to the back.'

'Salve, Giorgio. I am happy your efforts have been blessed.'

'Double, Padre. Triple!' Giorgio takes off his cap. 'The quality is so good they suggested we enter this year's competition. Drought down south has cut quantities from last year, so prices are up. I can finally charge what our quality up here is worth.'

'Ah, good to hear it, though it's a shame that this is because your fellow growers elsewhere have suffered.'

Giorgio holds his cap out front with both hands. He looks like an admonished schoolboy but replies with barely concealed irritation. 'Ah, forgive me, Padre. Maybe because of them, I should not be so happy.'

'Of course you should be, Giorgio. But know a blessing when you see one.'

'I do, Padre. I do.'

'Good. I will tell Riccardo. He will be happy at your news. And this year so far? What can I tell him?'

'We had a problem with the unseasonal rain before we could set the traps. But we have been spraying.'

'Flies?'

'Yes. Not unusual. We have them under control.'

'So, let us hope you will again see the favour of His grace. It is precious, isn't it?'

'True, yes, Padre,' Giorgio says, replacing the cap on his head.

'We must never take it for granted and pray for those less fortunate than ourselves. Keep a close eye on your crop, and on your faith, Giorgio. Both are essential. Give thanks. God bless you.'

He can feel his back going as he squeezes into his car, but he is spared the worst—forgiven. Had he looked back as he reached the villa's gate, he would have seen Giorgio shaking his head in excusable exasperation. What the hell does he care about the misfortunes of other growers? He has been on the receiving end of disaster often enough.

Jeremy observed the scene below his bedroom window when he went upstairs to rest for a bit after Dom Pietro left. It surprised him how reserved, even reverent, Giorgio appeared to be in front of the priest. If he can humble the single-minded artigiano that convincingly, there is no doubt the preacher's Church-appointed authority has a hard grip on his followers.

The siesta was restless, his practice afterwards a fiasco he cut short, and with no real joy on the snooker table either, he was left too long an evening stretched out before him. Not even Domino showed up when he went out onto the front terrace with a bottle of wine. He took it up to the roof terrace to watch the sunset and only left after dark with half of a second bottle.

Not home

Isabella is totally unsure about this, and that feeling makes her nervous enough. If she is spotted now in the stifling midday heat along the path that takes her across the valley, she will have trouble explaining herself. Especially since her mother thinks she is with a girlfriend from the nursery. From lunch through to the end of siesta, there is no one about, and wanting to keep the visit secret tells her she is doing something wrong.

She is also not sure why she trusts Jeremy enough to visit him, in his own home, alone. His music must play a big part; she has listened to his CD so many times that part of who he is has become somehow close, soothing, and familiar, sometimes taking her right back to the day he gave it to her. The lively stuff, which must be difficult to play, makes her think about how light-hearted a person he is compared with anyone she meets in the village; the slower bits remind her of how considerate he was in the car, the thrill it gave her to feel confident about herself, and that the sense of openness and joy his music made her see so clearly are the things she wants most. It happened because he let it, did not interrupt her or pry into what she was thinking about while she listened but simply left her the space to be herself, let the magic of the moment take hold of her in a super luxurious car gliding silently through the countryside. He welcomed her as the outsider into his world. It was real, not something she had to imagine being part of, like the soaps on TV.

But what could he see in her, what does she have to offer him, now she is halfway there? He took a real interest in who she is, even if it did not feel right to get too personal. He is probably just lonely out here. She certainly does not want to encourage him to try anything, but she is not too sure she knows what counts, how to behave with a man like him. Her Catholic faith protects her from Marco, who has never made any serious attempts, but Jeremy says he lost his faith in the Church, so that will not count. Are her

110

instincts strong enough? She is here to find self-confidence in his company that feels real and validates her faith in herself, not just something that leaves Marco stunned on the bench. She never wants to hear 'Marco is a lucky man' ever again, or allow herself to be treated as any man's trophy.

Armed with the CD she can pretend she wants to return, she approaches the villa cautiously from the entrance gate and can hardly believe she has never been here. She missed a school outing long ago that came to visit the seat of the family whose name is splattered all over the village, including on the nursery she works in.

The oldest villagers have nothing good to say about the family, their rewritten generosity in local history. Gay Riccardo, prancing around the village like he owned the place, puts her off wanting to know anything more about the present generation. But this is where the *directore d'orchestra* invited Jeremy to stay. Jeremy said it was gutted but still charming inside, but she does not know what that means. And she will not find out today. The villa is all locked up and Jeremy's car is nowhere in sight. She was so full of anticipation that she is a bit lost he is not here.

A dog comes up and crouches on its hind legs beside her, waiting for something to happen to the front door they both stare at. Domino, she remembers, Jeremy's best friend. She crouches down too.

'Non è in casa, Domino.'

She gets a very faint whine in reply that echoes her own sense of a lost purpose. All for nothing. She is not sure she would risk it again.

They go down the stairs together and Isabella heads for the gate. She hears Domino behind her bark twice, and she turns and sees the dog move up the side of the villa, turn to her, and bark again. The dog wants her to follow? As she rounds the back corner of the house, she finds Domino sitting in the courtyard in front of the back door. She tries this door too, lightly tapping the winged angel against the metal plate of the door knocker three times. She and the dog wait for a sign of life inside.

'Niente da fare oggi.'

Looking around her while giving Domino a comforting pat,

Italians: loud, no fancy table setting, neon lights, brilliant food, cheaper drinkable house wine.

After the first half-litre, the southern belles decided the place was 'a whole 'nother experience' they liked and he 'might could' join their tour of the sights the next day. This invitation was accompanied by a squeeze underneath the table from Susan—and maybe another squeeze to Dixie, for as soon as dinner was over, she was suddenly very tired and would not be joining them for a nightcap.

The next day was gruelling. They walked their way through a long list of must-sees in the oppressive heat, escaping frequently into the equally oppressive gilded gaudiness of cool churches. From the Colosseum to St Peter's Basilica to the Fontana de Trevi to the Spanish Steps, with a few palazzi along the way, the girls ticked off their marked territory with a light-hearted diligence and naive enthusiasm he found infectious enough to stay the course. He especially liked the Caravaggio they bumped into along the way. There was no pairing up or reference made to the night before—he had put Susan in a taxi at 2 a.m. In fact, Dixie's attention was the more forward of the two.

They all joined hands to pitch a coin into the fountain, promising they would meet up again someday so he could show them his London, and landed up after the Steps in Caffè Greco, where they miraculously found a free table—their last stop before going to their respective hotels to freshen up before dinner. Susan excused herself, and he soon felt a hand squeeze his thigh.

'Well, ahm, me and Susan are, like, totally close. Like, we share everything? Susan says you're in a really nice hotel. I can't wait to see it.'

Dixie was less his type, but there did not appear to be any diplomatic way out of another long night.

Jeremy is exhausted when he fights his way out of Rome the next day and heads back to the villa. One erotic and one wild one-night stand have tamed his overheated libido sufficiently to accept, almost too readily, the delay in Vicky's arrival she announced on the hotel phone that morning.

'The way you say "that's all right", I wonder whether I should come at all. You don't sound quite as desperate to see me as when you asked me to come—after ignoring me in the first place.'

'Vicky, let's not go back into that. I've been looking forward to having you here ever since you said you could come. As I said, I'm in Rome. I've walked the whole place looking for the best spots to take you. In fact, I'm *your* tag-along relationship at the moment; it's not the other way around. I'm just trying to be patient.'

'I'm sorry, of course you are. You're important to me, Jeremy. And please, don't wear yourself out in Rome. I spent a lot of time there with a cousin of mine in my late teens. I'm more interested in other things we can do together.'

'I know someone who would give everything to see us perform together.'

'Ooh, now that's kinky.'

'Me on the oboe, you singing,' he tells her drily.

'I do that whichever instrument you play.'

'Please, Vicky. I'm asking . . . for a priest, the priest of the village.'

She breaks into hysterical laughter. 'You and a priest? I'm lost for words now.'

The opening in the conversation came up much earlier than he expected, and it was typical of her to twist everything into this image of mangled bed sheets. She has often left him feeling like a toy boy hired for her pleasure, though she insists she genuinely loves to be with him.

'But Jeremy, a priest? That you even let him talk you into this idea is . . . scandalous!'

'Precisely.'

'What are you saying?'

'I don't think these dour villagers have ever seen the likes of you on stage.'

'You want a scandal?'

'I am one already. I could use some company.'

'Jeremy, I don't want any publicity about my visit. I'm visiting the Scala, with a few days' holiday.'

'Are you?'

'What?'

'Invited. Scala.'

'Yes. Violetta.'

'Congratulations!'

'It's not fixed yet. And the role is beginning to feel a bit stale. They might all just walk out.'

'I very much doubt that. But here, in the village, they might even stone you for being too passionate.'

This sent Vicky into peals of wicked laughter. Haughtiness still beat naughtiness, however, so she held off for a long time before she tentatively agreed to put in an impromptu appearance if he wanted her to. There could be no way of knowing if she will sing until the day arrives, he realises now, recalling the conversation in trickling traffic on the drab outskirts of the city. Creeping along, he spots a store in which he 'might could' find a gift for Dom Pietro in honour of his miracle reed.

Unwelcome back

He reaches the track leading up to the villa from the main trunk road, and although he is now familiar with its hazards, he remembers the day he first arrived. Not just by coincidence, he is playing the same La Traviata CD, awakening his memory of that experience. The dust that day was full of obscure antipathy towards him that has still not settled. It clings to him in the village, as inexplicable as on that first day, but it has an almost familiar feel to it now.

He went for Susan and Dixie because Isabella is out of bounds even if she does show up sometime, but it bothers him that he lives in a duality that can so easily put aside feelings of genuine desire for non-committal sex. Hearing Vicky now reminds him that his liaisons with women have mostly been on their terms, leaving authentic sentiments on his part so eroded or misplaced that either he or they discard them, leaving only sex to lend a semblance of substance. The monkish seclusion he returns to now is not an alternative. Keeping to himself will not tell him why the things he feels compelled to do are so out of tune with what he would prefer to want. He cannot trace the dissonance to its source. His music is what he has become: an outward display of harmony, ambition that prevails over rejection and dejection, a cadenza of sensitivities within a composition no one can recognise.

The emptiness he feels as he meanders his way up the track, around obstacles he meanwhile automatically avoids, is gone when he reaches the gate of the villa, greeted by Domino's excited yelps and hopping around on his side of the open car. The dog is beside himself with happiness, and it is infectious. He stops the car in the front garden and gets out to play until the dog's excitement and his own subside. Domino is given his first-ever ride in the passenger seat, where the dog sits up, honourably erect, making Jeremy smile as they drive round to the back of the villa.

Fabio cannot shove his way through to the car door until it is too late for any escape.

'Fabio, wait, please!' Dom Pietro shouts. He wobbles and wheezes his body across the square from the rectory. It takes a while. 'Is this your car?' he asks when he finally draws up to them.

'Sí, Padre,' Fabio replies, unable to manage more than a weak smile, betraying the confidence he would like to show.

'È fantastico, eh? A really good-looking car,' the padre says.

Dom Pietro looks around for confirmation from the boys, the bench ladies who followed him across the square, and other villagers who seemed to appear out of nowhere when they saw him approaching the group. Fabio's unease is more the focus of their attention than his car as the priest circles and studies it, tracing his index finger along its profile admiringly.

'What a beautiful design. Is this what is called aerodynamic?'

'Sí, Padre.'

'Can I have a peek inside?'

Fabio moves away from the door and Dom Pietro peers inside. 'Well, this is incredible. The top speed is 240! Does it really go that fast?'

'I don't know, Padre. It has fast acceleration. I like the design,' Fabio says with obviously forced casualness.

'So do I. Beautiful. I envy you this car, but of course I shouldn't think that way. We must share your happiness today, and hope for our own in some *meaningful* way on another day. I'm sure you've given thanks already for the chance to own a car like this?'

'Of course, Padre. And I saved hard for it.' Fabio looks pointedly at the gang. 'I work. I have a job, plus keeping the sheep.'

'So your mother told me. Then it is paid for? I am impressed.'

'The deposit, yes.'

'Oh! So the dealer lets you drive the car before it's fully paid?'

'He wants to sell cars. That's normal. It's insured,' Fabio says defensively.

'Ah, yes, insurance, very important, in case there's an accident. You must be careful with it, Fabio. We trust you will be. We all know Signor Righi is watching,' Dom Pietro says, looking up to the sky for effect, to the solemn murmurs from the onlookers and a secret snigger amongst Marco's gang.

Fabio is barely able to hold his anger at being censured yet again. 'Excuse me, Padre, I will go now.' He gets in the car, starts the engine with a loud rev, crunches into first gear, and shouts out the window above the noise, 'Signor Righi knows it was his fault, his mistake, not mine! I will not take the blame!'

The gathering clears a path for the car reluctantly, unwilling to let the confrontation end. They watch Fabio turn into a narrow lane off the square. He gives the accelerator an angry punch with his foot, picking up speed fast. Signor Cappelli suddenly appears, walking backwards out of his house, his arm stretched forward to pull shut his main door that opens directly onto the narrow lane. There is no room to manoeuvre, and Fabio brakes hard. The old man blinks hard and moves just quickly enough back into the doorway to save himself. Heads pop out of windows at the screech of tyres, and Signor Cappelli comes back out into the lane angry and shouting. Fabio has already moved on.

'What is this? Ban these murderers from the village!'

The city is far away

Jeremy was anxious to see if his new method was indeed one, with reproducible results, so he got to work on two new reeds the day after Rome. In one morning he had another finished, one still to scrape. He is no longer limited to playing competently; the new reeds give him new confidence. He can now concentrate more on improving his altered coordination to reach the keys, on flowing steadily through trills and legato and staccato runs, and on giving the music his own expression again with a lot less effort.

Days later, with awakened enthusiasm, he is practicing well into lunchtime, gliding through the allegro movement of the Mozart concerto in C major. He has his eyes closed, 'hearing' the orchestra behind him and performing the concert on stage. When he opens them again, she is standing in the doorway.

'So, you don't deny you were at the villa? Fabio's not lying?'
'Why should he? Why should I? I have nothing to hide.'
'You don't even have a CD player.'
'Angelina lent me a Discman.'
'You cannot carry on like this, Bella.'
'What do you mean exactly, carry on?'
'Cosy up to this fancy man.'
'He's a musician. A famous one even. His music really makes me feel good. There is nothing wrong in liking his music.'
'Or his car, his money.'
'Don't be stupid. I don't care what anyone drives, and I don't need anyone else's money. I earn my own, and always will.'
'You can't always. You don't want children now?'
'When I think it's time, yes. Not before then.'
'How long are you going to keep me waiting? Where does that leave me? How do I know when then is?'

'Then is when you can show me you have your own mind, a job, and you understand what matters to me. I'm not in any hurry, obviously.'

'You want me to clear off, don't you?'

'No, Marco. I just won't let other people decide what's right or wrong for me anymore.'

'You don't care about what other people think about you? About us?'

'Just because I want to think for myself, doesn't mean I only think about me and nobody else. But I'm not letting you, or my parents, decide for me.'

'Yours and mine are counting on us starting a family. Look, I'll soon be finished with my training. They'll give us all the help we need until I earn as an electrician.'

'We don't want to live off them, do we? We don't want to live only like they expect us to because we're dependent on them. I don't see any joy in that.'

'What do you want then? Where is our joy?'

'I don't know yet. I'm still unsure about a lot of things. I want to be more open to see what's right for me and then see if we can grow together.'

'You're giving me the shove, Bella. You don't fool me, hiding behind these fancy ideas.'

'Yes, I am giving you a push, Marco, out from under where everybody's mind is already made up about everything. Is yours? Are you open to new ideas?'

'You just want to be open to the Inglese, and that's going to cost you if you carry on, like Angelina.'

'I'm asking you to think about things, and you only accuse and threaten me? Forget it. We can't grow together. You don't even try!'

'How can I when you call everything into question?'

'This is going nowhere.'

She was really close to calling it quits on her tag-along identity, but she always gives him another chance to continue it, as if he could be transformed by some miracle into someone she would want to be together with forever. She did not walk off and leave him, on condition that he would try to be more open-minded. He promised he would try, but he would not be OK with this visit, that's for sure, any more than her parents would be.

She is supposed to be visiting Angelina again, which always unsettles her mother. She tries to keep her calm by promising the village is her home for keeps. That is not a lie, it is what she wants, but it is her mother who would suffer most if she dropped Marco, and her father would make living with them impossible. Forget about the villagers; she is not going to pay the price of being and doing what everyone expects should make her happy. Home is the problem, causing pain there and maybe being forced to leave. Why can people not be happy if she stays but decides for herself what she wants?

Her mother is not completely wrong about the village. Angelina is missing that seam in her life, cutting off the place she grew up in, her parents, people she once thought cared for her, unable to undo the sadness it causes her and free herself to get on in a new life. The old cloth, the old patterns she was used to, still cling to her girlfriend's skin; she is a seamstress with no new material or ideas to work with.

What does she want from where she is going now? Some sort of relief, distraction from it all, sharing a little time with someone who is outside everybody's master plan for her. Driving through the countryside that afternoon inspired her to think differently about that plan. Jeremy treated her with respect despite her coming from the village that has shown him none—and neither herself, really, beneath the expectant toe-the-line smiles of the people around her that deny she has the right to a future of her own making. He at once accepted her, respected why she was hesitant to share the ride, making it possible for her to do so, to do something she wanted to do. And when she asked him to take her to the square, he must have guessed the hit he would take on his own reputation in the village. He did not object or back down; if he had, she probably would not be here. Maybe in the bigger world he comes from it is just more natural to accept people for who they are, without any designs on them. Mama, you cannot be right, she thinks. No challenge today, please. That would be disappointing.

She checks the path behind her yet again to see if she is being followed. She is wearing a loose-fitting white dress and half-open sandals. A broad-rimed straw hat protects her from the worst of the sun. Her appearance has always been important to her, and she wants to look at least as nice as he always does when he visits the village. But she has always been careful in her choices, more discreet than fancy, neither chaste nor revealing too much. Today she avoided any attempt to look like the women on her bedroom wall, but she also does not want Jeremy to think she is a silly village girl with no clue about fashion.

The sound of him playing from somewhere in the villa somehow reassures her she is safe. When she listens to his CD, the music sometimes makes her feel like it is meant for people with more sophisticated tastes than her own, but it does not let her feel inferior or small, in the same way as he is a refined man who makes her feel like a grown-up woman. It is exciting to spend time with him because he is so different: his company is fun, his English makes her laugh, he is considerate and not pushy about what he thinks.

But is she as safe as she believes she is, with a real man? She has never been alone with one, faced the advances that real women deal with, and this visit is secret, so she is on her own, whatever happens. If that scares her, should she be here at all? Is deciding for herself who she can trust not what openness is all about? If this is a mistake, it is not going to make her worse off than her parents and Marco acting like they know who she is. They do not. She is different. They are the ones out of tune with her. Jeremy's music takes her up the steps to the open front door.

She stands on the terrace and listens, her eyes scanning the front of the villa for any observers; she would not hear them. On its own, at close range, the sound of the oboe is penetratingly loud, even a bit aggressive in her ears, less playful, even if it is full of light-hearted strings of notes she likes. He is playing something she recognises from the CD. The door to the room he is playing in is just inside the front door. There is a pause in his playing. She steps quietly into the doorway when he continues.

His eyes are closed. His cheeks are the first thing she notices. They are completely distorted, his lips pressed so tightly together they all but disappear. His neck bulges, his body sways, bounces, bends, then stretches through the notes. He is completely absorbed in his music, and the sight of him playing is pure and incredible drama.

Jeremy has reached his cadenza in the movement. The orchestra gives him the stage. He opens his eyes as he begins. And there she is in the doorway.

She will have caught the surprise in his eyes, but he carries on like he would on stage and in response to the delight that shines in her smile, accelerating and giving expression to his own indulgent pleasure in its unguarded radiance. He holds her gaze, locks into it, does not let it go. He can feel playfulness return to his rendition of the piece, a renewed connection to his music. He does not want to stop and finds new variations to extend his cadenza before ending with a flourish. Isabella claps. He bows.

'Bravo, Jeremy!'

'Thank you. It must sound strange to you without the orchestra. Did you recognise it anyway, from the CD?'

'Yes, I think so. Mozart?'

'Bravo, Isabella. Yes, the concerto.'

'C maggiore.'

'Yes, right again.'

'I have listened many times. I like your music very much.'

'It's this key.' He plays it for her. 'Would you like to try?'

'Oh, no. I can see it is too difficult.'

'You don't have to press anything to start with. Just hold it, like this.'

He takes off her hat, and her dark-brown hair falls in its luxurious full length around her shoulders. She sweeps it back behind her neck, sweeps away the familiarity the gesture implies, takes the oboe from him, and lets him take her hands to put her fingers in the proper positions. The intimacy of the moment, close to each other, catches him out like a teenager with a crush on her. He feels foolish. He steps back a bit.

'There, that looks good. Pull the shoulders back a bit, raise the elbows slightly. Perfect.' Her breasts, profiled in her short-sleeved dress, quickly correct the spell of adolescent timidity.

'And now? How do I play?' she asks.

Isabella reflects for a while on where she is. She is standing on the mosaic-tiled roof of history she knows the Church has rewritten to bury the fear-driven times endured by the villagers. The Patricelli were not noble; they were mean, greedy, and powerful. And this is where they once stood, where she is standing now, observing *their* village on the other side of the valley. From here looking over there, she can sense how hard a struggle village life must have been. She can feel it because the gloom has been passed on, down through each new generation since, including her parents'. How afraid everyone is to change things, how helpless they feel in the place they praise as their home, demanding everyone stick together to protect their inherited dejection.

That is not her, not her at all. She must not let that gloom control her own expectations. Up here, now, she can pretend to be on top of the world, a free spirit, full of the joy she can and will build around her own life. It is so liberating to be here. If she could dance to celebrate, she would. She catches herself almost prancing around the perimeter of the terrace like a prisoner just released. She stops. It feels right but it is girlish. She opens her arms wide and laughs.

'Sono sulla cima del mondo!' She turns towards Jeremy at the opposite side of the terrace behind her and sees his head sunken into his chest.

He had followed her though a heavy squint until the inescapable heat, and the enchanting but fading sight of her carefree movements, coaxed him into a chimera of her dancing along the parapet for him. In that nebulous half-conscious space, he thought he could see through her white dress, the outline of her naked body under sheer fabric penetrated by intense light, before his eyelids shut down, locking the alluring, surreal vision in darkness.

Isabella gently shakes his shoulders, lifts his head with one hand under his chin, and pulls lightly on his earlobe with her other. 'Jeremy?'

She is squatting directly in front of him. For the few moments his semi-conscious reverie survives, the impulse to draw her head to him feels completely natural, but she intercepts his limp outstretched arm before his hand can reach her neck. She pats his hand lightly and places it back on his knee.

'Aspetta un momento. Un colpo di calore. You go in tilt.'

'Yes . . . I suppose so, tilted right over into another world. Not bad at all, though.'

He douses his head under the basin tap in the bathroom on the way back down to the kitchen. His temporary dizziness fades, and he is sufficiently alert to object when she says she will leave and let him rest, casually forcing her hand to stay by taking salad things out of the fridge and putting them on the table as soon as they enter the kitchen before taking a very needy drink of water.

'I'm fine now, really, don't worry. I got so hot so quickly my head went spinning.'

'It can be dangerous.'

'True. It is. I temporarily lost control of my senses.' He has emptied the fridge of just about everything in it and collects the knives, cutting boards, and a big salad bowl. 'You can decide what goes in the toss-up today and what does not belong in the mix,' he says, pointing at the bowl.

'I follow my mama at home. Her choice is more safe.'

'Let's experiment, then. Whatever we mix together is sure to be adventurous.'

She has only ever shared time in the kitchen with her mother, and it is unthinkable her father, or Marco, would ever help prepare a meal. Modern men are obviously different, and this situation is perfectly normal to him. Sharing this private household duty with a man she hardly knows feels a bit awkward, but this must be how people connect in his world, doing things like this together. What fun, after all. Salad is easy enough, there is no need to be shy about what she knows. He is giving her time to make a start by busying himself getting things out for the table.

She chooses the vegetables, slicing everything very thinly like her mother taught her so it all mixes well with her lemon-oil-garlic dressing. She can see he is hopeless in the kitchen, clumsily careful of cutting his fingers, following her instructions as best he can, joking about his own attempts to copy her. It feels good, fun; he makes her feel welcome, appreciated, and more mature than she has ever felt around people in the village.

The salad prepared, they move to the main room, sitting opposite each other on the benches at the long table, away from the sun's heat on the terrace, and without saying so, any observers.

'You give new meaning to my salad days, Isabella, put new life into them. It's great.'

'Thanks to my mama.'

'I can't give her the credit, can I? She wouldn't be pleased, I'm sure.'

'It is better . . . for you . . . I was not here today.'

'For me?'

'No untrue stories about you. They do not know how you are. And they do not want to.'

'Rumours. Yes, well, they don't bother me much. I'm not here forever. But you are, maybe. Some wine?'

She places her hand over her wine glass. 'I do not drink alcohol. Once only. It was to try it.'

'An experiment.'

'Yes, but I go in tilt.'

'Ah, well, that would make two of us today!'

They both laugh, already like familiar friends, she thinks, as he pours her some water and himself some wine.

He holds up his glass, contemplating aloud. 'I'm sure I would never drink again if I got drunk on this stuff from the village. It's quite acid, so it must be served very cold.' He takes a big swig. It tastes even more acid than he remembers, and he squints. 'It's a bit like a bad rumour, really: nobody really likes it but everybody swallows it without thinking. I'm safe with you since you don't drink, but I must be giving the village a hangover. Cheers.'

'You have a funny way to say things. It is like a puzzle to me.'

'OK, then how about this: you don't like rumours and you do not swallow them, like this wine, because they taste sour to you and feel cold. Is that better?'

'Yes. Yes, it is like that. No understanding.'

They both eat for a while in silence, her mind elsewhere.

'Are you understood, Isabella, in the village?'

'If I follow *speranze* of other people, it is OK.'

'So, it's not really OK.'

'I want to change myself in the village, but it is difficult. My girlfriend, Angelina, she try to, but the minds are stuck against her, the bad talk about her never stop, she is refused, so she leaved. I want understanding there is different ways for me. Voglio avere tolleranza, non aspettative su tutto nella mia vita.'

'There must be bad talk about you already because of me.'

'About the lift, it is OK, it does not matter. We meet in private, it is hard to find understanding.'

'So, this is a risk to your reputation, the *aspettative*, expectations people have of you.'

'You have a wrong reputation. But only I find out it is wrong. So only I say to me it is all right to visit.'

'What did Angelina do wrong?'

'She say things people did not like about . . . about the Church.'

'Ah, let me guess. She rebelled against the moral code, conformity.'

'Conformità, sì. La bolla.' She outlines an imaginary bubble with her hands. 'You know what I mean?'

'I think so. The village lives under a bubble.'

'Maybe only me. Because I see it.'

Domino appears in the open doorway to the terrace. His tail wags happily. His slightly tilted head questions today's unusual lunch arrangement, putting him out of bounds.

'My best friend wants to meet you, I think.'

'He cannot come inside?'

'Off limits normally. But go ahead, call him to you.'

She straddles the bench on her side of the table and pats her outside leg. 'Vieni qui . . . vieni . . . Domino, vieni qui!'

The dog goes straight to her when he hears his name.

'You remember his name?' Jeremy asks.

'From the last time . . . in the car, yes.'

'Well, he certainly takes a liking to you. Like he knows you.'

'It is a nice surprise to meet and feel lucky.'

'Are we lucky?'

'How we meet, yes. It is good luck for me. You are a nice man.'

'And you are a charming woman.'

She can feel his eyes on her and does not want to meet his. She gives Domino her undivided attention, thinking about what to say. 'You are mistaken maybe, Jeremy, about me? I do not follow women's ways, like in the city.'

'Isabella, it's more charming when you are the way you are, the way you want to be.'

'It is OK, for you?'

'The city is far away.'

Anton Van Iersel

Snookered

'Hold it, Isabella! You must pot a red ball first before you can score with another colour.'

'But there is no red free to hit.'

'Down the other end of the table?'

There is a red near the left top rail pocket, and the eight at the opposite corner.

'It is too far, Jeremy.'

The cue ball is a far reach from the bottom rail. He demonstrates. 'It's a long shot, yes. My favourite challenge. I have to stretch myself a bit to make this one, but I need the right angle. I practice my shot without striking because I don't want to hit too hard. I am then in position to score big.' He points his cue at the eight ball.

'This is not an easy game you play. OK, I try to follow you.'

Concentrating, Isabella is oblivious to the revealing sight of her legs as she stretches forward onto the table. Jeremy stands behind her.

'Take your time. First focus on your cue, Isabella, what is meant to happen on contact, the path, the speed, what you're aiming for.'

'Aspetta. Aspetta.'

'Take it slowly. Feel the motion of the stroke, sliding smooth and gently in and out again. Does it feel good? Are we ready now?'

'Adesso!' She shoots, frozen, still bent over the table, her eyes following the cue ball as it travels slowly on target. 'Sì . . . sì . . . sì!'

The red is hit precisely at just enough speed to sink it. Isabella's upper body collapses briefly on the table in exaggerated wonder at her feat.

'Un miracolo! My first time, I did it!' she says laughing as she stands again.

'Beautiful, Isabella. You're a natural talent. I'll bet on it. A dream shot.'

'And now?'

'Play again? You get another chance to score.' He points to the

135

eight ball.

'It is more easy, I think.'

'That's the beauty of the game, Isabella. If I'm careful, one good chance leads to the next.'

A while later, Jeremy thinks he should stop the game. Isabella's delight at snooker, a mingling of girlish excitement and earnest concentration whenever he shows her what to do, has put him tantalisingly close to her several times. Her playfulness could easily tempt him to make a play for her. She is cuing off a new frame now, so the game goes on.

What he wouldn't do for a cue that tells him she is ready to break the rack holding them in. But she has only dropped her guard because she is young enough to believe he is good on his word. Holding back presents a paradox: she can now be more carefree, adding to her appeal, while he is forced to be more reserved, cautious, the dupe of their age gap. He must content himself with observing her inconspicuously, tempted and trapped by her careless sense of fun, her unintentional, natural sensuality that seduces and frightens him in its innocence. Any cushioned shot at pocketing her would be amateur, a beginner's stroke leaving nothing for him to play if he misses. She is new to this fickle game. She is ignoring the doubts everyone has about him in good faith. He is a visiting stranger. She is a Catholic village girl, feeling the constraints of what is planned for her but not ready to make the break and see what happens. That makes her consent inviolable. This is not a contest he wants to win, feeling like the victor of a show contest, as he so often has; he wants to set her up to win, too, over whatever holds her back.

She undoes him with each unwittingly provocative pose as she takes her turn at the table, lost in concentration. Every preoccupied pout as she considers her next target, every bright laugh when she pots her shot, teases a desire for her he can barely restrain.

Fabio's sheep show no such restraint. Outside, his flock strays from the path leading to the front gate and out onto their grazing pasture. The sheep have invaded the patches of wild grass and blossoming shrubs of the villa's once-proud front garden; their mouths do what Jeremy's would have liked to do on Isabella's naked skin, but theirs are not a pretty sight as they tirelessly roam, snipping, voracious, bleating with impatient, insatiable hunger, nibbling the ground bare.

This uncontrolled stampede is preventable with a few simple commands to his herd dogs; Fabio is in no hurry to do anything about it. From his favourite spot on the terrace, the Inglese will look onto barren ground, and Fabio is happy to let the man know how little he is respected, how unwelcomed his presence is. Jeremy is home and not coming out. Fabio has news for Marco.

Jeremy is used to hearing the sheep bleating. He only registers after a while how loud, how close they are. He opens one of the drawn shutters to see them demolishing his garden. They are everywhere, moving slowly towards the gate, leaving nothing behind them.

'Wait here, Isabella.'

Jeremy rushes out onto the terrace and down the steps. The sheep scatter away from him at once, a noisy chaotic scramble of bobbing heads in all directions. Fabio is nowhere to be seen. What is going on?

As soon as he caught sight of Jeremy, Fabio stepped back, around the corner of the house. He now walks into view and yells out orders to his herd dogs, who race around the perimeter of the flock forcing them in the direction of the gate. The Inglese is angry; he can see that as he approaches.

'How can you this let happen?'

'I let them out and then had to take a piss. Sorry.'

'Like the hell you are.'

'Why blame me? Blame your useless dog. Mine have everything under control now.'

'You think you're a tough little fucker, don't you?' Jeremy says in English.

'Don't be angry, Signor Jeremy. Sei molto richiesto oggi. Guarda, un altro visitatore.'

The loud commotion of the sheep masked the sound of the

137

tiny Fiat with its bulky driver creeping up from the gate through the flock towards them.

'A nice surprise, no?' Fabio says smiling. 'What will you do now?'

'Mind your business.'

Fabio moves off behind the last of his flock. Jeremy is stumped. He cannot ignore the priest's arrival and go back inside to warn Isabella. If he takes him through the main entrance, she can escape through the courtyard door at the back. Dom Pietro needs time to struggle out of his car after he has parked in front of the villa, giving Jeremy time to compose himself. His greeting is purposefully loud.

'Buongiorno, Dom Pietro! What a nice surprise!'

'You didn't look so happy a moment ago. Is something wrong?'

'Look what the sheep have done to the garden.'

The priest surveys the garden more closely, wipes his brow with a handkerchief. 'It's completely bare! Disgraceful. You had words with him.'

'For all they're worth. The smiling creep pretends it was a lapse of vigilance. It's not. He did this on purpose.'

'He's on the wrong path, that boy.'

'Racing down it.'

'And a real danger in that new car of his.'

'I wouldn't have thought he could afford it.'

'He can't. He borrowed. Also from your example with the BMW, I'm afraid.'

'My arrival here, and his timing, are pure coincidence. He's a fanatic. A car freak. Completely possessed, as his mother says. Let's hope he defaults.'

'An exorcism of sorts I suppose we would all welcome.'

'It's broiling today. Come inside.' Jeremy climbs the first few steps fast that lead to the terrace, bringing him closer to the snooker room window as a last precaution. 'I would invite you to lunch, Dom Pietro, but I've already eaten.' He turns back towards the priest, who struggles to climb the steps, at once out of breath and sweating profusely now in his cassock, looking up at him.

'Isa . . . bella . . .' he falters, struggling for breath. 'Oh my, this is hard on me . . . our prize village girl?'

He must have seen her through the open shutter of the window higher up behind him. Jeremy shrugs in abashed apology, not knowing what on earth to say.

'Her mother . . . she cooked for me today. It was excellent . . . unfortunately.'

He has not seen her, thank God. 'An ice-cold glass of wine won't hurt you,' Jeremy says, instantly relieved.

'I shouldn't.'

'We have something to celebrate.'

It was Isabella's break when the game was interrupted. She briefly followed the commotion outside the window through the half-open shutter, then went back to the table to discover that Jeremy's preceding shot had set her up perfectly. She potted it and went on to the next; a scoring run followed that excited and totally absorbed her. She only realised the sheep had gone when she thought she heard Jeremy on the stairs saying something, about Dom Pietro? She listened closely. English. Jeremy was talking to Dom Pietro as they came up the stairs.

Jeremy returns to the main room from the kitchen and hears Dom Pietro through the previously closed door of the snooker room.

'Non mi scappi, diavoletto!'

Has he found her in there? No. The 'little devil' is a billiard ball hit hard: clack! She is out the back door—a close escape. He puts the serving tray down heavily, pours and takes a big swig, squints, swipes his hand across his mouth, then goes to his music room to collect the plainly wrapped box and place it on the long table in the main room.

'I didn't know you play,' Jeremy says in the doorway to the snooker room.

'Pool, in the States, during my seminary.' Dom Pietro shoots and misses. 'These pockets are much tighter,' he adds.

'It's a different layout. And snooker is not so straightforward. A lot of hide and seek with your opponent,' Jeremy says.

'Who do you play hide and seek with out here?'

'I keep my undisciplined self in check with my saintly cautious alter ego.'

'Which of the two cues I found on the table am I playing with, then?'

'That's your guess.'

'Get the point. I just missed an easy shot. Well, give me a chance to redeem myself: the pink in that corner?' He points to it with his cue.

'That's a difficult shot.'

'Redemption is never easy.'

'Got the point.'

Dom Pietro concentrates. He is obviously at home on the table, despite the barriers posed by his cassock, unbendable bulk, and pudgy hands. The cue ball hits the pink with enough speed and sidespin to sink it with a convincing clunk in the pocket.

'Heavenly. Bravo.'

'Simply a question of faith, Jeremy.'

'Well, it so happens I do have a reason to celebrate yours.'

Afraid to go out and be seen by anyone, Isabella ran upstairs. She checked the closet in this room: it is empty, would hold her easily if need be. Sitting on a bed, she smiles briefly; for a few moments sharing this secret with Jeremy is simply mischievous. But she knows being discovered here would be dire, not only for her but also for her mother. The span between her father's bad days is already shorter than it used to be. She does not want to be responsible for another relapse of his brutal anger.

Her mother's anger is quieter. What comes to the surface more often is bitterness, and having realised as she grew up that she, the child her mother desperately wanted, was the reason her mother married in blind faith, Isabella feels responsible, appeases her, lets her mother cling to the idea she has found someone in Marco. Her parents did not grow together as a couple, even after she was born, as her mother has admitted. There is only argument now, nothing keeping her parents together except for their sacrosanct duty to marriage. They are scratching and scraping their way through.

How can her mother not see she would be taking the same risk with Marco? She is not a blind thirteen-year-old anymore, does not want to share her mother's fate. If there ever was once love between her parents, it is gone, spoilt, long forgotten. The thought of a man wanting her does not call up hopes of affection, trust, understanding. She feels fear, of possession and of disablement. Before she can feel the desire Angelina says belongs to her natural instincts, she feels fear, she sees her father, she feels her mother's loneliness as if it were her own. Could she ever find the trust she needs to give in to anyone? Downstairs are a priest who offers her mother God's cold comforts for her mistaken instincts and a man who probably believes it is simply a question of temporarily ignoring what matters to herself.

She lies back on the bed. There is no way to protect her mother and find her own life. She is always hiding from it. In a pause today there was Jeremy's company, making lunch with him, playing snooker—against a man with enough experience to set her up for a shot at the sort of life he leads. It is an obvious choice, but the game would not last; he would just play along until he was ready to leave and quietly slip away.

Isabella hears the laughter below. She cannot remember ever hearing the priest laugh. Jeremy obviously knows how to deal with him better than anyone in the village. And he is not even a real Catholic, he said. What does this say about Dom Pietro that nobody knows? Her mother says the priest does not like Jeremy. Did she make that up?

'I cannot possibly accept this gift, Jeremy.'

'Why not? You earned it.'

'How?'

'Well, think of it as a lottery.'

'What are you talking about?'

'Let's say I really don't deserve any godsend but got one anyway: the blessing is on your ticket.'

'*Your* faith helped you, not mine. That's why you've now made more than one good reed, as you said.'

'Then share my satisfaction. I can now play more easily and like what I hear, and you can hear records you like more enjoyably. My future as an oboist is safe now. I think it's only fair I save yours as a music lover.'

'This is very generous of you. I'm extremely grateful.' Dom Pietro opens the box. 'It is beautiful.'

'As promised, second-hand.'

Dom Pietro takes out the record player and admires it. 'I presume it's also a consolation prize. Your singer friend said no to the concert?'

'No bargaining with Him, you said.'

'True.'

'Vicky said maybe. Her yes did not entirely convince me.'

'The organist will be coming here to play this coming Sunday. I've already told him. He's delighted.'

'You are confident, I must say. Sounds like you're on an inside line,' Jeremy says, pointing upwards.

'That's what prayer is, Jeremy. You should try it. You can dial direct.'

'I think I'll only get a long-distance echo, or static.'

'I would call it sceptical interference.'

'That's a good one!'

They both laugh.

'So, did Rome live up to your expectations?' the priest asks.

'Oh, yes. I got what I wanted from the visit. Plus, a driving lesson, sore feet, bumping into a Caravaggio or two, and on my way out, your record player.'

'The Basilica?'

'A must-see, of course. Awesome. And a nice, cool break indoors at this time of year.'

'I was hoping for something more intelligent, coming from you.'

'A lot of artists and artisans put their hearts and souls into it. I could see that. From that point of view, a magnificent achievement. You feel really small and inconsequential standing in there. I suppose that was the point, too.'

'A bit extravagant, perhaps.'

'I won't tell on you.'

'I prefer simplicity. I think worship and sanctity are beyond anything we can physically honour. If we want to internalise God's intent, Holy Mass is the most important.'

'Ritual not Ritz. Wrong Church for that.'

It took Jeremy another hour to extricate himself from further debate, which carried on through a return to the snooker table and a bottle of more palatable wine. He is completely worn out as he climbs the stairs to his room for a lie down. When he reaches the upstairs landing, he sees a clear stream of light cutting across the room directly ahead, coming from the half-open door of an interconnected room at the back. Isabella? He finds her sleeping on one of the beds when he reaches the door.

It is a fairy-tale moment, complete kitsch, he knows that, but she really does fit the princess role. Her hair fans out from her peaceful face cupped in one hand, as if composed for a B-movie scene: first shot. Next shot: she is lying on her side and the camera moves down to take in the gentle swell of her breasts, her exposed arm resting behind her back, the shot continuing down over the rise of her slender hips to her legs, carelessly parted, one above the other, exposed upwards of her knees where her plain white dress has slipped. His eros tempts him to think of a gentle caress along them, between them. The first sight of her made him catch his breath, and the longer he looks at her the more he longs to test fate, creep over, sit on the bed, stroke her gently awake, and see what happens. Third shot: her eyes open as he steps into the room. Sorry, prince. She shrieks in alarm and scrambles to pull her dress over her bent knees as she sits bolt upright.

'Sorry! Didn't mean to scare you. I would have called out to you. I didn't expect to find you here,' he says.

Isabella slips into her sandals. 'Oh, Dio mio. I fall asleep. The light! It is not so strong now! What is the time?'

'About four o'clock.'

'Aiuto! Help me. I will miss the bus! I must be on the bus!'

'Don't panic. Everything will be OK.'

His car could not be more conspicuous for the clandestine operation of getting her to the bus. He keeps the roof up and she hides underneath her hat. He hurtles down the track to the main trunk road, tossing them around in their seats as he negotiates the obstacles quickly. The bus stop is a few hundred metres away around a slight bend. He spots the head-boy macho and his scooter just in time as they approach it; Marco is waiting for the bus, looking in the opposite direction towards where it will come from.

'Down!' he says, pushing Isabella's head forward and down just as they drive past the stop.

'Who was it?' she asks when he gently pulls her shoulders back upright.

'Marco. How far to the next stop?'

'Not far.' She pauses. 'So, you know about him.'

'And you, la coppia dorata.'

'Jeremy . . . only for today . . . I wanted to forget I am not so lucky in the village. It is hard to explain.'

'You did already, expectations, aspettative.'

'They stop everything for me.'

'Only so long as you let them. Here we are. And look, the bus is coming. Quick!'

Isabella unbuckles, lightly touches Jeremy's arm before she scrambles out of the car and crosses the road, signalling for the bus to stop.

They look at each other across the road. She smiles until the bus blocks her from view. He moves off to visit the town she is supposed to be coming from. Remembering her lying on the bed only minutes ago, imagining her last smile just now as the one 'afterwards', he feels as hopeless as ever, either facing a bar too high to jump over or, by her rules, set too low to creep under. His lust is teasing him to attempt a Fosbury Flop when he should be practicing limbo.

The bus has only two passengers, neither from the village. Isabella sighs with relief as she takes a seat. The danger is over. Just a few minutes to compose herself. She can trust her natural instincts about Jeremy. She was defenceless. She need not fear he would force his natural instincts on her. And his eyes on her in the snooker room, the long wait before he entered the room from the doorway, thinking she was asleep, tell her those instincts are alive.

She is surprised not to find Marco waiting for her when she gets off the bus. Is he across the road? The bus moves off. She looks around, stays put for a moment, puzzled, then shrugs her shoulders and crosses the road to head home. Marco observes her from across the road, hiding behind a hedge, wanting to surprise her. She looks as though she is . . . expecting someone? Maybe in a BMW? As she approaches, he kick-starts his moped and comes out of hiding.

'Ciao, Marco, what a surprise! How did you know?'

'Your mother. She told me. Are you surprised to see *me*?'

'Yes, and no. On the bus I thought my mother might ask you, after the last time. It's very kind of you.'

'Not such a fancy lift as with the Inglese, is it?'

'I'm happy you're here. I'm tired.' She climbs on the back of the seat, unhappy about the lie.

'He passed by a few minutes ago.'

'So, I did see the car from the bus,' she says above the noise of the scooter.

'What a coincidence, eh?' he shouts as they move off. 'But he was going in the wrong direction. You're lucky today.'

He believes protecting her reputation is what should matter most. He has understood nothing. Wrong direction. How unlucky she is.

How lucky she is to have seen Marco on the benches this afternoon, Isabella's mother thinks. She saw him in a pensive mood on his own and went over to him. He lit up at her idea he should go to meet Isabella at the bus stop. And now here they are, smiling at each other. Everything is going to work out again. Everything is going back to where it should be.

Jeremy returns to the happy yelps of Domino's welcome and an angry argument spilling out into the back courtyard from Fabio's house. He hears the word 'machina' several times. They're shouting so loud in a heavy slang he cannot follow. Not that he needs to. Fabio's trophy car gets a dusting every day, a shining example of reckless pride that ignores his mother's fears and his family's poverty. What a selfish, despicable lout. And for very different reasons he thinks of his own mother, shouting him down for being too proud, too arrogant, wasting the family's money on private schools he in no time was thrown out of. Maybe she thought the same of him. Surely not. It was all in the name of God.

Mass rejection

The church is almost empty when Jeremy goes inside; he sees only a few heads in the pews bowed in prayer. With the bells rung and a few minutes to go till Dom Pietro's curtain call, it is not exactly the full house he was made to believe showed up every Sunday.

The decoration is modest, limited to a few pictures of saints, other Catholic so-and-sos, and depictions of biblical scenes. It does give credence to the preacher's preference for simplicity. Even the cross at the alter is mainly polished wood with modest decorative inlays in gold. The organ is to one side of the chancel, close to where they would perform. The organist, a tall, lean, studious-looking fellow in an oversized jacket, has already taken his seat at the console. He is playing a contemplative intro to the service, a Bach sonata by the sound of it—for his benefit?

The owner of one of the heads bowed in prayer, kneeling on the hassock, sits up and looks around, seemingly as bewildered as he is that so few people are in attendance: Signora Tendri. She sees him and he returns her beaming smile. That warm welcome turns out to be the only friendly face he sees when suddenly people enter the church in droves. The pews all around him fill rapidly. It does not feel intentional at first until he catches glances, murmurs, an agitated nervousness from pews farther away, begrudging looks from people with no other choice in the crowded church than a neighbouring pew. He sits exposed, alone, fighting for composure that is neither aloof nor apology. Either staring down at or purposefully ignoring him, they want him to know he is out of place, an unwelcome intrusion.

Dom Pietro does not know his people; any attempt to reach out to them is ridiculous. The priest's strict control of their lives has turned his followers in on themselves, anxious and distrustful of anyone and anything they see as interference in their observance of conformity. This, then, is not hate; their intolerance is not necessarily felt, but forced. Not one of these people would trust themselves to approach him, the decried outsider, without risking being made to feel like one themselves. A concert would change nothing. It is time to leave; this feels ridiculous, pointless. He is being pilloried by these people.

Despite persistent gossip about her flagrant misconduct involving the man concerned, people nod and smile at Isabella with habitual admiration as she follows her mother to their pew. Her mother sits at once, then kneels in prayer. When she raises her head again, her daughter has still not taken her place.

Isabella has spotted him. It can only be Jeremy. He said he stopped going to church long ago. So, what is he doing here? The padre is pretty good at persuading people they must stay connected with the Church if they want to feel connected in the village. Maybe Jeremy is trying to mend the reputation he unfairly has— for her sake too?—trying to fit in somehow, and this response is shameful. He is sitting in the middle of a long, otherwise completely empty pew, and all the others are packed to avoid him; he is being deliberately isolated, purposefully rejected. He is a Catholic; he has a right to be here and ought to be made to feel welcomed, especially the first time. Does no one remember what the padre has said about leaving differences outside, sharing responsibility for communion of spirit in here? The faces greeting her approvingly quickly appear false, even malevolent, in her imagination: 'See, we've taken care of the infidel.'

She does not know what to do. Their mistrust of him is not based on anything real, but if she does nothing, she is guilty of falling in line behind slander that smears him as immoral, full of himself and his money. She has had to silently endure warnings of him stalking her, without openly laughing at his accusers, knowing it is pointless to contest them. If she wants to be true to herself, here and now, true to what she knows and not what slander insists he is, this is the next step: go over to him, sit beside him, and let everyone see she will not abide their falsity, the hearsay that suffocates her.

'Isabella, what is with you? Sit down.'

'Mama, no one will sit next to him. Why?'

'The Inglese? He is false. Sit. Marco will be here any moment. Know your place!' her mother hisses.

'This place is a church! Not a place to be unkind, to anyone.'

'Your father forbids you . . .'

'. . . my other Papa is in charge in here.'

When he enters, Marco sees Isabella walking down the central aisle, heading towards a pew near the centre, not their regular place. It is the Inglese again! This is the second time she is demeaning him, their vows, in front of everyone! Is it not obvious why the show-off is sitting alone? He is false! Marco wants to rush over and grab Isabella before she reaches the pew, pull her to reason, to her place. But what if she resists? It would be even more humiliating if she refuses to obey him. He finds Isabella's mother; anger is written hard on both of their faces before he turns back outside, slamming the heavy entrance door shut in his fury.

Jeremy was aware his presence in the church might not agree with people who assume only angels of their feather have a right to be here. When Isabella takes a place next to him, he knows this defiance of the sanctimonious community she belongs to will sting her. He cannot help but admire her, although taking a role in this aspect of her being different is not something he really wants.

'Hello, Isabella.'

'Buongiorno, Jeremy.'

The current between them as they stand close to each other feels stronger than ever, although it is fused by an equally strong resistance to this unwelcomed publicity. He does not want to cross any new red lines with Isabella, their celebrated appearance together in his car was enough. That, too, was a mistake, breaking not just the villagers' phobic code of conduct but his own rules: although she may not count as one yet, he normally avoids outside interference by keeping his liaisons under cover, and solidarity in his circles means keeping them that way so that any doubts or controversy attached to either starting or ending them can be settled quietly.

Now she has intervened, openly made a show of her solidarity with him, the outcast, just as he was ready to walk out on any further attempts at diplomatic liaison with this alienating cohort of fanatics. He does not need the village she is fighting to be respected in, on her own terms, with this demonstration.

Looking around him, the attempt is futile, and he does not like being used in her stand-off with these people, whether intentional or not. Her move has less to do with defending his maligned character and more with how she wants to be seen here. This is not about him, or them, but her. It is about her frustration with the people around them, and he could not care less about how they see him. All the same, he cannot very well leave her in the lurch, nor can he deny that her strength of character would shame his own if he did so. He thought he might see her here, keeping their secret alive at a distance. It never occurred to him that his presence, on this stage of her naive proof of selfhood, would put him in this predicament. He would have avoided it entirely.

'This will get you into trouble, Isabella.'

'You say no to Church, Jeremy, but you are here. Why?'

'To make friends. Bad idea. Mea culpa.'

The organ pauses, then takes up the Entrance Hymn. Dom Pietro appears. The service begins.

Dom Pietro always makes a mental note of who is there or not there, and he at once spots Jeremy and Isabella together. All the other pews around them are fully occupied. Why are the two of them alone in the centre of the church?

He turns to venerate the cross and wait for the Entrance to finish. He coaxed Jeremy here; now he could regret it. This scene is divisive, and he warned Jeremy against anything like this with Isabella. Although, he suspects this is her doing; Jeremy must have been alone when she came in and decided to join him. The most steadfast amongst the younger ones, she always comes to Mass, and if not truly devout, she has taken to heart her duty to communion of spirit inside the church he has always insisted on. She cannot know she has sided with a steadfast sceptic to show everybody else she has heard what he preaches.

He would never have thought her popularity in the village would lead her to challenge, a second time, the now confirmed arm-length distance to Jeremy held by everyone in the church who avoided him when they came in. Her behaviour is as incautious as his own invitation to Jeremy. How far is he himself willing, as head of the congregation, to stick his own neck out for the man he wants to persuade back into the fold? Can this rejection be turned around?

He turns back around to face the congregation. It would help if Isabella's mother had joined the two of them. There she is, alone, where she normally sits with her daughter and Marco; he is not here today, or this would not have been allowed to happen.

'*Óminus vobíscum,*' he says, arms outstretched.

'*Et cum spíritu tuo,*' the congregation murmurs

The Penitential Act that follows inspires Jeremy to go through his scorecard with Isabella. His concessions her chaste reluctance have misled her. But that reluctance is not dictated by the discreet cross hanging from her slender neck today, he is sure of that. The Church protects her against unwanted advances from him, and that is almost a provocation to test the validity of how unwanted they are. Is he not deceiving her, and himself, that he will not do so? *Mea culpa.* She has pulled him off his playground, from playing tag with women just for the fun of hearing them squeal when he catches them. Is he not likely to call it quits and run once he has satisfied this runaway attraction for her? *Mea culpa, mea culpa.* If her squeal is heard in the village, it would ruin her reputation, making her a tagalong he would have to take care of. She is not a free-floating city girl who understands what consensual really means: no responsibility. Leaving her stranded would be evil. *Mea máxima culpa.*

She is so stunning, though, whether those full, sensuous lips are smiling, playfully pouting, or drawn tight and straight across in tension, as now. She is obviously nervous about taking the stand she has and exposing herself to uncomfortable criticism and rebuke, questioning her readiness for the fight, no experience with infamy. As innocent as this is, still.

'Siamo tutti e due isolati ora,' she whispers.

Dom Pietro's strong voice fills the church. *Kyrie, eleison!*

'You're upset,' Jeremy says.

'I do not belong them.'

Christie, eleison!

'I don't either. But you should have ignored me. You live here.'

'Non mi nasconderò dietro a chi è falso.'

Kyrie, eleison!

The faces that smiled at her when she came in turned stern when Isabella took her place next to Jeremy. She will not hide behind what is false, their false assumptions, their constant and depreciating scrutiny. Jeremy cautiously steals an occasional glance at her, but they avoid looking at each other openly. She desperately wants to show him calm and composure but can now only think of consequences—her father's rage, her mother's despair, Marco's ugly abuse—the insidious disapproval she will confront in the village now, at the kindergarten.

Glória in excélsis Deo, et in terra pax homínibus bonæ voluntátis . . .

Where is the goodwill you see in your congregation? Jeremy silently asks Dom Pietro's booming voice as it chants a hymn following the Kyrie. He could still leave Mass now, make himself the sole target of these sectarians, confirming the profanity of their pet evildoer and adding acid to their rumours. But it would be Isabella's defeat, and as the cause célèbre in her fight against these misguided zealots, it would be his unwilling departure from anything more between them. Some of the women under their headscarves remind him of his mother. He could have told Isabella earlier how hopeless her battle is against Catholic fanaticism. The empathy and understanding she is looking for will never be found here.

Cum Sancto Spíritu, in glória Dei Patris. Amen.
Orémus.

He admires her courage, but her cause is hopeless. He must desert the obvious incentive to stay put for a reward of his sympathy later that is not part of her protest agenda, making his cause hopeless too.

'Isabella, thanks for trying. I'm sorry. I must leave,' he says.

'No. Stay.'

'These people are stuck, like you said. They will turn against you. I do not want that.'

'Stay. Please. Save my trust.'

Any single-minded escape is aborted when the call to prayer ends; Jeremy missed his chance to slip out quietly when all heads were obediently hunched over, everyone on their knees. And perhaps what follows prayers, he cynically allows himself to think, is in his honour. Dom Pietro reads from none other than Jeremiah, chapter 9: pure master weeper. He cannot understand much of the Italian he hears, but he knows what it is all about, was forced to listen to it being read by his mother anytime she decided he was lying or deceiving her. Good ol' Jeremiah really let loose on the people of Jerusalem before it was lost for its sins—at least according to his prophesy and not factual history.

Dom Pietro, in best form as far as Jeremy can tell, is pounding his congregation with the prophet's warning of God's vengeance against slander. The moral overseer had said he would bear down on its culprits in the village from the pulpit today. Any aptness to his own standing as a victim is coincidental. The priest is just doing some housekeeping.

Jeremy follows Isabella's lead as she bows her head into her chin to whisper under cover of Dom Pietro's voice.

'You understand what he says?' Isabella whispers.

'Jeremy, Jeremiah, we're old friends.'

'He is speak against bad talk, about you I think.'

'He's defending you too, then, now that we're both outcasts.' She has not understood. He discreetly points at himself, then at her. 'Siamo due emarginati,' he whispers, smiling.

Her eyes give away an anxiety his flippancy has mocked; this rebellion is a serious matter for her, no matter how misguided it is. He is making fun of her worst fears, of slander she will likely face now. He has no place in her protected life here, what she will have to deal with when this is over.

'Your trust is safe with me,' he says.

She raises her head. He raises his own, bewildered by the promise he just made to her. What is he pretending he can be? Anything, it seems, that will preserve his chances.

He can follow some of the less formal language of the priest's homily, enough to know it comes down hard again on the topic of slander. Dom Pietro is not just cleaning house, he is scrubbing. His delivery is firebrand emotional, real, him, judgement. Jeremy tries to spot a telltale guilty squirm. There is conformity here amongst the priest's followers all right: none of the congregation are giving anything away. Dom Pietro's Universal Prayer after the homily is devoted to 'toleranza', which in principle defends Isabella's behaviour; her face does seem to lose some of its tension.

He must hand it to Dom Pietro: his Latin is effortless—the Creed recited by heart. His chant, backed up by the organ, is confidently strong; his stage presence is magnetic, dignified but benevolent, authoritative but appealing. His low carefully modulated voice in Latin turns the Mass into a captivating mystical ceremony, not the rushed and perfunctory exercise he remembers. It is ritual at its best; the priest knows what he is doing. He celebrates faith in a power he earnestly believes holds together his cohort, and it is done so beautifully everyone can avoid the issue of how they behave in the here and now altogether.

Jeremy catches a few people peeking at him when a response in Latin is called for, and he can sense Isabella's surprise that he still knows his stuff; he is a bit surprised himself. But that presents him with a Catholic dilemma. If he does not go up to receive Communion, everybody here can assume he is conscious of committing grave sin and has not confessed it. That's a bit of a bore now that he has done so well. If he does go up, it would at least formally remove any grounds for further speculation about his moral character. So, no harm in a sacred snack together if it confounds these other pretenders around him.

It feels different to Isabella. She has received Communion with Marco countless times, but it has never been anything they have shared. Marco makes a show of piety, more devout to his appearance than anything, always attentive to who is looking at them. Jeremy's reverence seems natural, in the moment, without pretence. She can feel his presence next to her while they kneel and wait their turn. For a few moments, it feels to her like a sacred bond: her courage will give him acceptance; his acceptance will give her more courage. She receives the host first. There is a perceptible moment of hesitation before Jeremy receives his, a strong undercurrent between him and the padre. Or did she just imagine it? She feels slightly cheated of knowing something she would like to know about the two of them.

On their way back to their pew, all faces are turned towards them. Some are less hardened, less scornful now. Jeremy notices.

'Well, that did it. You're safe,' he says when they sit down again.

Not with my papa, Isabella thinks as her mother makes her way back from her own Communion. And then her mother surprises her, stops at their pew, moves in, and takes a seat beside her. Isabella is deeply moved when they bow forward for closing prayers.

'Grazie, Mamma. Grazie,' she says.

'È per te, non per lui,' her mother replies.

'Grazie per esserti unita a me,' Jeremy says to Isabella and her mother at the end of the service, hoping it means 'thanks for joining me'. Her mother turns into the aisle and stands there rigidly without a word, her eyes directing Isabella to leave with her.

'Sono felice di averti incontrarto qui,' Isabella says. Her smile is nervous, but she gives Jeremy her hand confidently. 'Ci vediamo presto.'

'Vieni adesso,' her mother orders.

Out of tune

The church empties as quickly as it filled, and Jeremy goes to talk to the organist, Angelo, a soft-spoken type with an endearing squint in his eyes and a fair command of English. Jeremy's intentions, if there is a concert at all, are now less conciliatory, more inclined towards a controversy that would shake things up a bit. He and Angelo talk easily about music and what they might play together, and what Victoria Costanza, alias Vicky, could sing.

'Dio mio! I did not know. She will sing here?'

'You know about her? You know her?'

'Not her. One of her sisters, Adalena. She is religious, only sings in church. There are four of them, all singers.'

'Vicky said. Competition began as soon as she was born.'

'But why here? I do not think these villagers even know who she is.'

'Dom Pietro doesn't either, so it might not turn out to be the healing power of music he expects will bring people together. Vicky is an opera singer, no likeness to anything angelic, if that's what Adalena is all about. I wouldn't be surprised if they all walk out.'

'The people here are strange, I know. It's different here to any other villages I visit. Closed off.'

'That's a polite way of putting it.'

They are discussing music choices when Dom Pietro reappears in church, now dressed in a plain cassock, his voice booming and brimming with confidence as he approaches them. The villagers he spoke to after the service were bewildered by his praise of Isabella for welcoming Jeremy, and by insinuation, his admonishment of them for doing the opposite. He let it be known that Jeremy is a Catholic who he is trying to acquaint with their church. No one should begrudge his presence; he is a very talented musician whose modesty and thanks to God for the talent he has will soon give them a concert to remember.

155

So, the word is out. Standing behind Jeremy is a bit of a gamble on his own reputation, but he has to do something to change attitudes in the village, hopefully without damaging allegiance to his church that he has worked so hard to establish.

'So, is our concert now planned?'

'What a concert it would be, Padre. Nothing like I imagined,' Angelo says.

'We have an idea,' Jeremy says. 'I think a dirge would best catch the mood of the congregation today.'

'We must give them something to take delight in, Jeremy. You will win them over. And Riccardo assures me Victoria's voice is captivating.'

'He knows she's coming here?'

'Why, yes. He did not sound surprised. He laughed. "Typical Jeremy," he said.'

'I told you she's here privately, Dom Pietro. She and Riccardo work together a lot. She'll feel obliged if he asks her to sing here. That's not fair on her.'

'Let us pray for goodwill, wherever it comes from—that is what the concert is all about.'

'I'll leave goodwill to your direct connections. You can leave my own to me. I'm not exactly keen after today.'

'Reach out, Jeremy. I have already put out the word to a few of my congregation today. This is your chance.'

'I don't feel like I have or need one with your congregation, Dom Pietro. They did not, to put it mildly, spike any interest in me to connect with them.'

'Then we must turn the tables around.'

'So, are we going ahead?' Angelo asks.

'God willing.'

'Dom Pietro believes in miracles,' Jeremy says.

'I see Rome's drivers left you a souvenir,' Dom Pietro says before he opens the passenger door.

'What are you talking about?' Jeremy asks.

'This scratch on my side?'

Jeremy goes round the front of his car. There is a long gouge in the body paint down to the metal. 'This is not Rome, Dom

Pietro. I would have noticed by now. And the scratch is too sharp, not from another car, not even in a straight line. This is malicious. A local souvenir that says go home and do not come back here.'

'Are you sure?'

'I'm not tolerated around here, that's for sure.'

'This is distressing.'

'Not everyone heard you out today, obviously. Remember our very first conversation? One member of your congregation, the orchestra you lead, Maestro Dom Pietro, is more than just out of tune. Get in. Let's go.'

He is sharing a ride with Jeremy. He stood up for him, defended Isabella's solidarity with him, and now he is sharing luxury he has preached against for years: all in the name of tolerance, but he might be preaching to half-empty pews soon if he is not careful.

The priest's reputation is already scratched if the ladies on the bench are anything to go by.

'I say the Inglese is false.'

'Like in the psalm: a haughty look and proud heart. That's him.'

'But he knows the Mass.'

'Don't we all? He's just trying to trick us.'

'I'm not convinced, anyway.'

'By the look of things, our padre is.'

'Isabella too. Poor Marco.'

'And her mother?'

'What else could she do? She had to take charge in there. She wants to protect her daughter. She is worried sick, for sure.'

'We should all be. Padre has always criticised luxuries as a weakness. Now he's off with that city show-off in his fancy car.'

'Accusing us of slander? Preaching tolerance?'

'I told you the Inglese was dangerous.'

'I trust our padre. He's not fooled.'

'Then what is he up to?'

'I don't know. But how can we not trust him?'

All is not gold

'Just a few days ago, I thought everything was settled. Now this!'

'What was settled, Mama?' Isabella asks.

'Well, you and Marco, back to normal.'

Isabella knew this was coming. When she and her mother got home, she went straight to her room to lie down for a few minutes to take stock of what happened in church. She did the right thing, and she is proud of it. Jeremy understands her better now, promised she could trust him. Marco did not show up for the service, but he wouldn't understand the reasons she did it anyway and would have tried to stop her. He will be furious when he hears about it, which means he probably already is. Does she even want to argue with him about this? Her mother joined her, unwillingly, but it was a start. Maybe it is time, as hard as it will be on her mother, to be open about what is going on in her mind.

'Mama, there was nothing normal about what happened today. How can we pray forgiveness for our mistakes and reject a man for no reason who comes to worship with us? You see that, don't you?'

'I saw Marco storming out! You rejected him.'

'He was there?'

'He saw you with the Inglese. He left. He felt betrayed, Bella.'

'By what? I only wanted the Inglese—Jeremy—to be treated with respect for taking Communion with us. Isn't that why you joined me?'

'You know very well the Inglese is not welcome here. I did it for you. You're right, of course, church is not the place to show we don't like what the man stands for.'

'How do you know what sort of person he is? I wish you knew . . . we all knew.'

'Maybe Marco doesn't understand you . . . yet. I try to.'

'He never will, Mama.'

'What are you saying?'

Isabella gets up from the table they were sitting at and moves to the window, trying to find the right words.

'Don't make a mistake, Bella,' her mother adds, fearing what she will hear.

'Is it a mistake to want the man who shares your life to share an understanding for who you are, what you think?'

'No. But I don't think anyone in church understood you today.'

'Probably not. But if that includes the padre, who you told me does not like Jeremy, why is he now getting in Jeremy's car?'

Out in the open

'Have you been to see Europe's largest olive tree?' Dom Pietro asks as they pass the turn-off that would take them to it.

'Yes. It's "awesome".'

Jeremy's attempt at the accent reminds the priest of why the site is mentioned in so many guidebooks for American tourists. 'You met some Yanks there?'

'A huge surprise, yes.'

'Well, the tree is popular with them. Local legend says it's the site of a scandalous marriage between a banished medieval Lombard prince and a local peasant damsel he fell in love with. The prince pushed back on his family obligations and tied the knot with her under that tree. It's the Disney story in tourist guides that brings Yanks here, not just the tree.'

So, that is the story, Jeremy thinks. 'How romantic though, don't you think? Maybe Isabella . . . just joking.'

'She is spoken for, and you're no prince.'

'Obviously she doesn't think so either, or she would have kept the venerable distance to me everyone else did in church today. Like my chariot?'

'Sinfully comfortable.'

'We should trade cars.'

'That was an excellent pasta, like the last time. Worth the trip here,' Jeremy says, admiring the terrace views and sipping his wine.

'Even so, it's got nothing on your quick-fix lunch.'

'Be kind to be cruel? Dom Pietro, take it back.'

'I meant it in the spirit of thanksgiving, even if my appetite is a curse.'

'It makes for an imposing figure at the altar. You have a good voice, too. All very convincing. I presume Jeremiah was not in my honour.'

'I'm afraid some of the things I've preached over the years to my followers have backfired and need to be corrected.'

'You sound like a politician covering his tracks.'

'Vigilant obedience to God's will should not mean people only see faults in each other. The slander against neighbours Jeremiah laments recently pushed an entire family out of the village.'

'The village does have an odd way of expressing community spirit, I must say. But I'm immune to slander. I see no fault in anything I've done, or in anyone I've met, assuming I've not met the person who scratched my car. That shows a certain lack of restraint.'

'Someone is envious, obviously. Most of my villagers take pride in denying themselves any luxuries.'

'Oh, so this may simply be someone assuming it will deny me pleasure in being able to afford them.'

'I guess I'm partly to blame if that's the case. I grew up in poverty, Jeremy. My father was a priest too, and he taught me to see austerity as something really closely connected to what God admires in the soul. He believed that hankering after possessions only weakens our own connection to spiritual fulfilment. And it definitely makes sense in a poor community. So, that's what I have always preached in the village.'

'From the pulpit of the Catholic Church, the richest of them all.' Jeremy holds up a hand to stall objection to a poke he could not resist. 'Your intentions may have been good, but it looks to me like you now have an enclave of misguided fanatics on your hands. Something has gone wrong, that's obvious.'

'Getting the balance right in community faith is never easy, Jeremy. I want people to be righteous and to take pride in it. I didn't expect things to turn in the direction they seem to be heading right now. I don't want the sanctity, modesty, and vigilance in the ways of the Lord I have preached to become strictures that exclude people or feed slander against anyone who does not appear to comply. It's the opposite of what I intended for my village. *Mea culpa.*'

They fall silent. Jeremy sees why he likes Dom Pietro and dislikes him. His straightforwardness, his honesty, presents a candid side of the priest probably no one else in the village knows;

it must be a privilege. But it is also the priest's fear of losing his influence, his authority, that makes him turn a blind eye to intolerance that cements his congregation in the name of protecting their church.

'Doesn't it look bad, coming out to lunch with me? It couldn't be clearer after today that everyone else thinks it would be better for their souls to keep me out,' Jeremy says.

'Today you became one of my congregants.'

'Not a regular fixture, Dom Pietro, that's for sure.'

'I don't want you treated differently from anyone else. That's my message.'

'It may well backfire. Like voluntary conformity, which you now admit is at least distorted. What's the point in me giving a concert now we know how popular I am?'

'I had no idea you would be given the cold shoulder, Jeremy. I can't harass them to be more tolerant.'

'Your sermon told a different story.'

'It was a homily to a village that is shrinking, into itself, unable to accept others for who they are. I must get the villagers to see that. I must get them back to a more sensible practice of their faith, turn them around. You could help me inspire a different attitude.'

'By turning the other cheek, in a popularity contest?'

'With your music. It's a message through you from God to show goodwill for the talent he gave you.'

'I'm not *that* good.'

'The most popular girl in the village stood up for you today, Jeremy. Make it worthwhile for Isabella that she ignored the whole congregation to welcome you into our church.'

'I suppose that makes her your only ally so far in a return to "sensible faith". She seemed quite nervous next to me; no doubt she's worried about falling out with everybody she knows. She could use your support, I think.'

'I've got her back. It was a reminder to work harder on attitudes. In your case, I have no idea what being back in church means to you, what moral attitudes I'm defending.'

'It was a one-time experiment, so that makes two of us.'

The bill when it came was only for one. The old lady remembered him but would not let him pay for the padre.

'You should have come in civvies,' Jeremy says.

'The dog collar is obligatory, and around here it always obliges people to be generous. Which is why I can't afford to eat out too often.'

As they were leaving, the old lady gave Jeremy a bag of treats for Domino.

'It's nice to feel welcome for a change,' Jeremy says as he places the bag behind his seat in the car while Dom Pietro slowly lowers his weight into his seat, expecting something to give.

'Things will change for the better,' Dom Pietro says, although Jeremy is sure the heavy sigh itself belongs more to the relief of not experiencing an expected spike of pain. 'Maybe you can drive a little slower on our return?'

On the wrong side

It was Alessia. And the padre himself inspired her defamation of Accardi. While she was preparing lunch for him one day, she asked him to read to her from the local paper. Dom Pietro obliged, never knowing what to talk about with her, a simple older widow who spends her worn-out days on the fields and in the church pew—praying, resigned, bitter, like so many in the village who idolise him for giving merit to their poverty and now believe being better off can only be achieved by deceit. The subject of the paper's lead article was yet another disclosure of corruption: it was a bad year for the crops, local government officials took kickbacks on generous subsidies given to complicit growers, and workers like Alessia got nothing except less work and less pay. Accardi was a revolt against privilege that meant only she and others like her suffered. Her ancestors had it better, owned the land they worked on. Dom Pietro was reminded of his debate with Jeremy.

While she prepared his lunch, he drew up a statement for Signor Accardi. He read it to her, she signed, and then she rushed out in tears.

The revelation that she is almost illiterate, barely able to scratch her own signature, is disquieting. He has known her for thirty years or so and never realised. Beyond the mostly petty sins they choose to confess, how much does he know about the people in his village? Where is his human connection to them? What has he missed of what is going on outside the church? The rift Jeremy caused at Mass was an unwelcome surprise, but shouldn't he have seen it coming?

Jeremy is not a presence people can tidy away, ignore in their lives. Jeremy projects wants and personal freedoms his faithful have suppressed or denied themselves. Dom Pietro sees how both Jeremy and Accardi question the faith he wished to instil, devotion that elevates those suffering the same poor circumstances he grew up with. But as much as it offers protection and meaning to his villagers, it can also turn humility into a rule to exclude anyone who does not share the hardship that gave faith its substance, inviting slander and envy. Faith that lacks virtue is meaningless.

Of course there is more to Jeremy's bad reputation than that. Whether or not it is justified to question the sceptic's morality, he must be careful about taking sides with a man he knows too little about. Alessia says Jeremy is prying Isabella away. That must be in village circulation after Mass last Sunday. No doubt Jeremy is attracted to the girl. And there is no telling how steadfast a man of undefined morality would be, given a chance. But Jeremy is far too intelligent to start anything reckless with a girl half his age. That said, the golden couple is losing its shine, and that is more than a scratch on the village's bodywork.

Fixation

Since his lunch with Dom Pietro a week ago, Jeremy has seen no one. No phone calls either. He has avoided the village. It is difficult being on his own all the time, but Dom Pietro's fiefdom, despite his being privily private with the priest, would still pull up the drawbridges when he shows up, and that makes him feel worse. He is becoming cynical about being somewhere he is not liked, about the priest's ridiculous efforts to reclaim him for the Church, to use him on fake friendly terms to mollify the doctrinaire Catholic attitudes that brought his faithful to heel. The priest is deceiving himself if he thinks he can reverse the bigotry drawing down on the bell rope he installed.

Isabella wants the priest to succeed. So far, she is Dom Pietro's only ally, and she has made Jeremy hers. He was not happy being used as her trumpet at Mass to herald the end of the gleeful intolerance around her. She is deceiving herself, too. He has no interest in her cause unless she can find cause with him to ignore what is keeping them apart. He would not like to meet up accidently, and definitely not if Marco is with her, which is really why he has stayed away from the village. She has seduced his mind into making her a lover before she is one. He could not bear the sight of them together. That means waiting, day after day, for her to show up at the villa again. He has put in a lot of practice these past few days. He can really say he is almost back in form—even better, at times, now he has reeds he can trust.

But she is always there. Her presence is so strong he can hardly think of anything else when he is not practicing, and even then he thinks of her: the unguarded radiance of her smile as she listened, her perfect body, full breasts, the magic of freeing her hair from under her hat, the intimacy of that moment, so close to undressing her.

And their game in here. Reimagining her is a constant during this solitary snooker session after his morning music practice each day, and it is always his 'undisciplined self' that reinvents the game, even before he racks up, ready to give in to an often-repeated vision of what he wanted to happen that day.

He takes the break as a smash-and-pray shot, hitting the racked balls with enough power in the stroke to scatter them as widely as possible around the table, giving her, his novice opponent, as many scoring options as possible. There are a few easier ones, but he has Isabella choose a long option that stretches her over the table to reach it. He hears himself coaching her through the shot, remembering the wicked—no, lewd—inuendo he allowed himself to stall making a real move on her, as he does now in his imagination and has done so many times with his eyes shut, frozen in the same position she was in to take the shot.

He approaches her from behind, places a hand on her hip. She lets his hand glide down the smooth skin of her exposed leg, stretched out and up as she leans over the table to take the shot. He hears her giggle softly, nervously admitting her willingness, before she turns to him. He presses her against the table and bends forward to kiss her, his practiced fingers undoing the first button of her blouse as she lies back on the baize. But this time the uncertainty he has often seen on her imagined face at this point in his fantasies reminds him of the last time he failed to see how insecure she truly is.

'Your trust is safe with me.'

His promise to her at Mass yanks him bolt upright. How can he pretend he wants to protect that trust? He must break this fixation on her. Her doubts are driving him mad wanting to clear them off the table. Game over! He throws the cue down hard on the table. It bounces off violently to the floor. The balls scatter. He watches them, spellbound by the chaos, until they come to rest. The eight he was aiming to pot is on the edge of the pocket he was aiming for. Hanging there, waiting for her to pot it. She would. He can hear her delighted laugh.

What created this obsession with her? When has he ever been so seduced by the mere thought of a woman? She is barely a woman! She has him reeling in a dilemma he cannot escape. He cannot stop thinking she would give in to him if he could raise her self-confidence, coax her into pocketing her chaste doubts, but any attempt at spinning that idea—even in his imagination—makes him recoil at how easily he is ready to forget integrity just to have what he wants. He said he could be trusted. Is there any sincerity in what he feels for her? Can he concede the game?

He storms out of the snooker room, angry it is no longer his alone, slamming the door on his fear of losing control. He grabs his keys and wallet off the kitchen table and goes to his car. He needs space, a fast, forgiving stream of air.

Domino does not ask if he wants company, does not wait to be invited, and jumps in the car as soon as he opens the door.

'OK, Domino, but no panicking when we pick up speed. And fasten your seat belt.'

The silly thought, as his roof opens up, puts a smile on Jeremy's face.

The chase

Right time, right place: Fabio laughs triumphantly when he sees the car ahead. The road is perfect, the race is on.

No, wait, hang back. Is this real? His eyes open wide, his mouth creases into a sneer. He sees the dog sitting upright in the passenger seat. He sees the Inglese talking to the dog.

'Well, mate,' Jeremy says, looking over at Domino, 'I'm in a bit of a fix. I'm really stuck on that young lady you really like. But Vicky is coming in a few days and could ruin everything. I have no desire to see her, to put up with her antics, mood swings. Sex is just routine with her now, especially her craving for—'

Jeremy is interrupted abruptly by the blare of a horn behind him; the bright-red car approaches fast until it hangs on his rear bumper. Fabio's repeated revving of the engine makes it clear he wants to race. This road through the valley to the abbey is dangerous, as Jeremy discovered when he misjudged an unmarked tight curve on the way there with Dom Pietro, not even driving fast by his standards. He brakes lightly, just enough to put his braking lights on and not get rammed. No race, you idiot.

The brake lights trick Fabio into braking harder, he falls behind but quickly catches up. The Inglese is angrily waving his arms at him to overtake, leave him alone. Fabio has no intention of doing so; he has waited too long for this chance. He rolls down the passenger window and on a straight stretch drives alongside the BMW.

He shouts out the window, past Domino, at Jeremy, 'Ehi, dov'è Isabella oggi? No time for your secret lover? Only for this stupid dog?'

Domino barks as if he understood. Jeremy gives Fabio the finger and sees an opportunity to shake him up a bit. He keeps

169

their cars abreast for as long as he dares before braking just in time to let Fabio back in the driving lane ahead of him and avoid oncoming cars, their headlights blinking wildly at the lunatic in the Alfa.

The lunatic takes a deep breath. That was a nasty trap. But two can play that game. His time will come.

Jeremy had completely forgotten that Fabio was a witness to Isabella's visit. 'That shithead in front of us has a nasty bit of meat for the village vultures to gnaw on,' Jeremy says to Domino. It could really create a stink in her life in the village, and his stay here. If it is still a secret, the loudmouth is taunting him with it now.

The road is clear again. Fabio cannot be trying the same trick on him? He is signalling Jeremy to come alongside in the overtaking lane, to talk window to window at closer range, right-hand to left-hand drive.

'What do you want? A race? Think of your mother!' Jeremy shouts.

Fabio gives him the finger in reply. 'Scared, are you? Your secret is only safe if I lose. First to the abbey! Let's go!' Fabio revs his engine and his tires screech as he takes off.

The stake is a joke, a childish attempt to coerce him. But he would love to put the fat boy in his place, shame him where it will hurt him most, and Jeremy finds himself accelerating, challenged by the racing thrill. He catches up quickly with the Alfa, but the speed soon gets insane; the idiot does not seem to know the road he is on. Or maybe he does? Maybe this is the speed freak's daily test circuit—when he can afford the petrol.

Let the reckless bastard win, Jeremy decides, lets up on the chase and lags far behind. He will not give chase. Isabella's visit to the villa is her problem; he does not have a reputation in the village to protect if Fabio talks. He would not be on this road if it was not driving him mad he must accept her attraction for him is purely chaste curiosity.

Jeremy's anger at his obsession with her soon presses his foot down on the accelerator again, doing what he came out to do, has always done when anything or anyone holds him back: test the limits of what he dares. Aggressive speed is today's elixir as he sets off. Forgetting he has a passenger with nothing to hold on to, he takes a tight curve at faster than safe speed, throwing Domino hard sideways against the passenger door. Domino yelps, whines, his eyes pinched in fear.

The dog's helpless whining continues into the next straight stretch of road. Jeremy tries to ignore how pitifully it vocalises this futile attempt to distract himself: daredevil speed will not put him ahead of the unstable emotions that are overtaking him. He feels helpless against them. He slows down again.

But speed's cure-all aggression stays in his bloodstream, makes him an angry loser. Left free to choose another outlet, it becomes hostile; his own unintended cruelty to his frightened companion quickly fuels a turbocharged compulsion to avenge Domino's tormentor, Fabio, for his taunting deliberate cruelty and arrogance, and his disrespect for life. Still driving, Jeremy reaches over to Domino.

'OK, mate? No seat belt, eh? Down you go then. That's it. What do you say we go after the bastard that kicked you?'

Domino, settling in unwillingly but obediently, stops whining, looks up at him from the footwell. The dog looks down, then up again, giving him a deep throaty growl. The race is on. Jeremy will leave Fabio trailing behind in an inferior car until the presumptuous racing ace is forced to give up, defeated at the wheel of his precious, shiny new car. Jeremy's pent-up animosity as he again sets off at speed quickly closes the distance between their cars.

Fabio has not seen the BMW in his rear-view mirror for at least two kilometres and is sure the wimp backed down, pampering his stupid mut again. But the next look in the mirror tells him he has got it all wrong. The BMW is approaching very fast around the curve he has just left.

The low, wide wheelbase and wide tyres of the convertible give Jeremy the advantage on curves; he can feel their secure grip on the road as he rounds the one he is on and then spots Fabio accelerating ahead of him. The Alfa will have to go slower through the next curve, so he can easily close the gap between them.

A delivery van on that next bend puts them both in a new starting position. Coming out of the bend, Fabio has the advantage of being able to see around the slow-moving vehicle earlier than

Jeremy, whose seat is on the wrong side. Ready to resume the race, Jeremy pulls out to follow close behind Fabio as soon as he starts to overtake the van. He is almost clear of the van himself when Fabio moves back in but holds a position that gives Jeremy no room to slip back in behind him. Caught by his own trick, Jeremy knows Fabio will not do as he did earlier and allow him to accelerate past the Alfa to avoid head-on collision with a fast-approaching car. He has to brake hard to get in behind the van. Fabio races off.

'You nasty bastard!' Jeremy shouts after him. A string of oncoming cars keeps him stuck behind the van for some time, building his anger and frustration, until it cuts out any sane logic in what he is doing. When he does overtake, Fabio is nowhere to be seen. 'You're not getting away with this.'

A minute or so later he spots Fabio ahead, driving slowly and waiting for him, taking off again as soon as the BMW appears. But Jeremy is soon tagging the rear bumper of the Alfa, goading his rival to drive faster and faster. The wannabe ace driver blocks any attempts to overtake, and if he does not block, Jeremy knows there is something coming. He falls far enough back to sight any oncoming cars, and on a straight, when he can safely pull out and check if it is clear, he floors the accelerator.

Fabio sees the BMW fall behind, but only seconds later, the car is no longer in his rear-view mirror—the Inglese is already in his blind spot; it is too late to move out and block him. The two cars are neck and neck, competing for advantage at dangerous speed on the patchwork road surface. Hitting a serious dip or bump could put either car out of control, sending one or both of them off in a fatal crash.

Jeremy at once recognises the next bend ahead from when it gave him and Dom Pietro a fright on their trip to lunch at the trattoria. Line of sight of the road past the jutting rock formation makes the bend appear harmless, but Jeremy knows the road sharply turns in on itself to round a gorge hidden behind the rock. There is little time left to slow down and safely take the extreme right curve. Jeremy brakes hard and falls far behind. Fabio does not take the cue of danger ahead, his eyes more focused on the road surface.

The Inglese is such a sissy, Fabio thinks, but as he reaches the outcrop, he realises too late that he has mistaken the curve for another one. At his winning speed he loses traction on the road surface and his car skids out of control before it smashes clean through an already-damaged section of guard rail on the far side of the road. He flies head-on into the deep ravine.

Jeremy hears the collision. 'Oh, fuck!'

Moments later, barely in control of his own car, he sees the open gap in the guard rail as he takes the same sharp curve. The massive explosion of an ignited petrol tank at the bottom of the ravine during his slow drive around it numbs Jeremy. He continues driving. What just happened did not happen.

Fabio had a few seconds to think the same thing before the front of the Alfa hit the slope of the gorge. The car somersaulted, the roof crushed on top of him on the second impact, and the fuel tank exploded on a jutting rock while the wreck slid down the slope rear end first.

Out of the ravine on an open road, the reality trickles into Jeremy's conscience. It is not his distress that reaches him first but his complicity. He is at once aware of it, alert. He must get off this road. He takes the first opportunity he comes across, climbing up to the ridge of the valley and then along it on a narrow tarmac road in the opposite direction. Homeward bound.

'We're in deep shit, Domino.'

After several minutes the valley broadens into gentle slopes covered in fruit and olive trees. He comes across the sign and follows it to the olive tree, reminding himself of his cautious behaviour with Isabella there. He is not compulsive. His recklessness was provoked. Fabio took things too far. He must calm down before he returns to the villa. As soon as he lets Domino out, the dog races around the tree in a broad circle, barking madly. The sight of his dog relieving its latent hysteria on several laps feeds Jeremy's own sense of panic. It is more than likely that one of the drivers they passed would recognise his unusual car racing against the Alfa. It would be useless now to deny his culpability in what just happened.

And that culpability is more than he wants to admit to himself, will admit to anyone. The drivers' windows on the stretch before

the curve were no more than a metre apart. He could have warned
Fabio as they approached, done something to attract his attention,
not only slow down just in time himself. He hated the arrogant
bastard, let that hatred grab hold of him, but Fabio's death is too
high a price for what sparked this disaster: Isabella's secret is now
safe.

It is very late afternoon before the police arrive. Jeremy
observes them approaching from the top of the villa.

'Here we go. Cheers to your lovely retreat, Riccardo,' Jeremy
says to himself before he gulps down his wine, emptying the glass.

The *carabinieri* drive up beside the villa and park in the courtyard
at the back. Jeremy moves out of sight, stepping back from the
terrace parapet, waiting for the angel to knock on his back door.
He can feel the jolt through his body when the police slam their
car doors shut. But there is no knock on his door. Jeremy returns
to peer over the parapet and sees the two policemen at his BMW,
exchanging comments he cannot catch, before they walk slowly up
the path to the stone dwelling. Of course, family first. He hears
them calling out to the open window Jeremy can see clearly from
his vantage point, framed by branches of the oak tree at the corner
of the courtyard.

Is there anybody home? Fabio's father is out in the fields
tending the flock with Fabio's sisters, whose playful squeals Jeremy
hears in the distance as they chase each other and the sheep.

The horror that contorts Fabio's mother's face the instant she
comes to the window and sees the police on the path below shocks
Jeremy into recognition of what he is really guilty of. The terrifying
shrieks and hysterical pleading to God as she races through the
house, down the stairs, and out the entrance, pierce with their
suffering. Jeremy's own throat at once feels the tourniquet he has
twisted tight on the lifeblood of Fabio's mother. She fights to free
herself of its choking pain, pounding the chest of the policeman
who delivers the news she has always feared . He sees her go limp,
sobbing uncontrollably, as both policemen carry her inside.

Standing there at the parapet looking down on them, Jeremy
remembers Dom Pietro standing impassively on the terrace as he
watched Fabio's dead dog being dragged away behind the moped

on a rope, the priest selectively eliminating that scene and its bead from a rosary that denied any attachment to heartfelt emotions. Jeremy will not call up any for Fabio, the malignant bead his mother must now petition for in her Fatima prayers with all the power of her devout soul.

There was no knock on his door, no angel hammering for his attention in his practice room where he hammered notes out of his oboe at random, cutting out the day's horrors in an ugly high-pitched staccato tour de force.

One false step

There is a knock at his door the following afternoon. It caught him lying in bed, trying to get some rest after a fitful night. The dogs were howling and barking non-stop, including Domino. In Jeremy's imagination, news of the dog hater's deeds and his demise was being relayed throughout the canine world.

He gets up, slips into his trousers, T-shirt, and sandals, and goes to the door, taking a deep breath and practicing a sober but friendly face for the policemen before he opens it.

For Isabella.

He looks worn out, older, she thinks. 'Oh, I have woken you.'

'Just having a nap . . . siesta. Come in.'

A loud wail from Fabio's mother through the open window of the shepherd's house freezes them both in the open doorway.

Isabella looks back towards the dwelling. 'È una tragedia.'

When she looks back at Jeremy, his head is bent. He lifts it, looks at her. 'Yes. And I am to blame.'

'Comme?'

'Come in. I'll tell you all about it.'

They are having coffee in the kitchen, standing at the table, when Jeremy spins his tale. 'He must have asked me five times about the test drive, and I refused. I knew about his plans to buy the Alfa. I thought it was a ridiculous idea, but I didn't try to persuade him against it. I guess that pushed him to buy it, to prove himself to me.' He bows his head. 'A test drive with me in the BMW might have calmed him down for a while.'

'You must not blame you, Jeremy.'

'Yes, I suppose you're right. Everybody else already has. I haven't yet faced his poor mother, but I think his father would have killed me this morning, or have his guard dogs do so, if he thought he could get away with it.'

Isabella silently studies her empty espresso cup, not knowing how to break the news, aware that she is also being studied by

Jeremy. 'That is why I come today. To tell you. But you know maybe. It will be more hard for you in the village now.'

'Signora Tendri already warned me this morning. The rumour is I raced him. I should have traded cars with Dom Pietro when I arrived. That was a joke. Ha ha.'

'The padre says nothing bad about you. He says it is Fabio alone. He goes on a bad path.'

'He was probably racing to the devil. Sorry, not the right thing to say. Does anybody know what really happened?'

'No. There was a big fire. Only when they put it out, they find him. His car.'

'No other car? No accident?'

'No, the police only come when they discover the car. We have fires often here.'

'Where did it happen?'

'We have drive on the road together.'

'To the olive tree? The abbey road?'

'That is where, yes.'

'Oh, no.'

'What is wrong, Jeremy?'

'The fire. I saw it. I went to lunch on Wednesday, in the abbey town. I was on that road. I passed it.' He collects the cups off the table, moves to the stove to refill them. 'I've misjudged my speed on those curves myself, so I know they're dangerous. But Fabio was a speed fanatic.'

'They say on that road it is only harm to outsiders for fast driving. People from here know the danger. This is a puzzle, the police say.'

'Maybe Fabio was racing against the clock, wanted to break his own speed record. Each time he drives faster. And faster. And faster. And then he loses control.'

'You know this?'

'I know about speed, how thrilling and dangerous it is. See this scar on my arm? The accident was my own fault. Almost cost me my life, as a musician as well.' Jeremy moves towards Isabella to offer her a closer look at his arm. They are very close.

'Almost a tragedy.'

'It can still be one, Isabella, if I don't find a way to recover my

177

old talent, find a different way to play here like I did before I came.' Jeremy says it slowly, holding the forearm she had extended to hold his.

When she looks up from the wound to his face, Isabella feels the intimacy he has sneaked in. 'The CDs are before the accident?'

'Yes. When I played for you last time, it felt like something was happening I thought I may have lost forever.'

Isabella instantly realises the something he is talking about is not just music but has to do with her too. She turns away from him. 'I am so glad for you! I love your music!'

When she completes the turn and looks at him across the table, she sees his deeply inset eyes looking up at her from a slight downward tilt of his head and a smile she recognises from the last time she was here sitting across from him at the lunch table.

'I will always remember the look on your face when you heard it for the first time, on our little trip together.'

There is no mistaking that smile now, the tone of his voice. But how can it be dangerous, across this table, to acknowledge that that day means so much to her?

'Your music is something new for me. È stato un bellissimo giorno per me.'

Jeremy misreads her smile, the simple sincerity she intends. 'For me, too, Isabella. I have been there again. To remember it.'

Isabella matches Jeremy's cautious steps to the first corner of the table around to her, she moving to the opposite corner, trailing her hand on the tabletop and trying hard to appear casual. 'You went to the tree?'

'Yes. To say hello to my namesake.'

'Comme?'

'Aginulfo. The prince.'

'Ah, sì! Did you play?' She tries to laugh at the idea.

'That's not the real story, is it? Not why you took me there and gave me his name.'

Isabella's forced gaiety disappears. The real legend has caught up with her, his role and hers. 'La mia fantasia, it is better. It is only about you,' she says.

'I like the romantic one.'

'Ma non è reale, Jeremy.'

178

Jeremy moves in earnest now. Isabella keeps his pace and the space between them.

'Isabella, *we* are *real*. I am not a medieval prince who will force himself on you; you are not a poor village girl named Artemia with no choices of her own. There is no romance in that. Let go. Trust yourself. Let's write our own fabulous story.'

'I do not want romance now. La mia storia è più importante per me.'

'Let's stop this.'

They both stop circling the table.

'Jeremy, the city, it is still far away?'

'Very far. I am here, now, more who I want to be because I do not want to hide my feelings from you. Don't be frightened of them.'

'I am not frightened. You are not a bad man. Your ideas is too much different. It is not a good match to what I think. It is too soon to understand it for me.'

Jeremy notices a faint plea in her voice, in her eyes. This he decides is the first hint of wanting to give in. The 'good match' inspires him instantly, a dating show he once watched on TV years ago with a distant cousin her age who had a crush on him. They played it afterwards, alone, and ignored the family tree.

'Isabella? There's a lot we like about each other. Let's at least find out now what those things are so we *both* understand what the other person thinks. It's a silly game, OK? We each take one step at a time. If I take one towards you, you must take one towards me, or I stop. I'll go first.'

They are at opposite corners of the table. Jeremy takes a tiny step.

'This one is for the joy of hearing you laugh,' he says.

This idea catches Isabella completely off guard, and a small giggle escapes her before she can stifle it. It's true, he has made her laugh many times, put some joy back into her life. She should show she appreciates the fun they have had together, and the courage that came from meeting him. Will he stop when she does?

'This one is for . . . funny English,' she says.

'This one is for the fun of making lunch together,' he says.

'Fun with you. *Sì!* Snooker!'

179

'This one is for my inspiring listener.'

'This is for your music, for feeling free, inside.'

Jeremy takes a step backwards. 'Against anything that makes you feel stuck.'

'Tolleranza!' She adds another step. 'E rispetto per me!'

'To a passionate rebel!' He adds a step. 'And to a brave and beautiful woman.'

She retreats a step. 'Per la sua virtù.'

'To hidden desire.'

'To be not beautiful. To his understanding.' She retreats another step.

Jeremy waits; this game is not decided yet. 'Let go, Isabella. Turn the corner and be the woman you really are. Not the village girl, nor the city girl I do not want you to be. For God's sake, trust me. I can make you feel more beautiful than you already are in every way.'

Her beauty is God's challenge her mother said. He is a stranger to her feelings. Maybe girls in the city give in more easily to men they like, but she does not want to. She wants deeper feelings attached than this soapy praise for her looks, and a stupid legend is no reason to break his promise and question her own sincerity. She wants to run out; she feels guilty for coming here, for challenging him against what every man wants, for letting this happen to her. He is moving slowly towards her. She feels trapped and deserted at the same time, vulnerable, lonely in her fear. Her shoulders slump, and she crosses her arms around them as if she could console herself. She feels his arms encircle the small of her back. This is OK, she thinks before his hands slowly begin to move, gently stroking her back, taking possession.

'No, Jeremy!'

She pushes him away with her bent arms, a shove with all her might he was not expecting, could not prevent, being deliberately gentle and holding back surging passion at the feel of her body.

'But . . . Isabella, there's no reason to be frightened.'

'This is not my meaning! It is not right.'

It is not going to happen, then. It is not the first time he has been pushed back at the last moment. He has never pressed, and to depreciate his own desire by not feeling it returned when it is stronger for this girl-woman than any other, he would belittle himself.

'If it's not right for you, Isabella, it's not right for me.'

This appeases her; he can see the tension leave her. If he can be a good sport about it, he might even get another chance when Vicky has come and gone and Isabella sees the stakes are even— appear so, at least.

'Your Marco is a lucky man.'

Her face contorts as soon as he says it. He has seen beautiful women turn ugly when he really hurt them, but he is shocked at this unexplainable transformation; the venom in her voice when she speaks tells him there will not be another chance.

'I am unlucky girl to have meet with you. Sei solo un estraneo con le stesse idee sbagliate su di me. I do not belong you or any man!'

Isabella bolts out of the villa before he can even think of a reply. But she is right to accuse him, a stranger, of having the wrong ideas about her. He encouraged her to show herself for what she stands for to people who want her obedience, and he did not know until now how imprisoned she feels by the sway of her beauty. He thought wrongly that boosting her confidence to be her own woman would persuade her to give in and become one for him. Nothing could be farther from the truth in the contest 'per la sua virtù'.

You are mine!

Isabella runs. Out the gate and down the path to the bottom of the valley, punishing her feet on sharp stones in her flimsy sandals, until the pain stops her. She brought this on herself, visiting a second time, impatient to trust in herself.

She looks back at the villa, can just make out a corner of the roof terrace. Now he ruined that trust. She danced on the roof of its promise, the space it offered her, but he does not want to share it on her terms, accept her for who she is.

Jeremy is in his music room. She is gone. This shows him that what he genuinely wants to feel makes no difference. He must stick to type, to Vicky. No experiments anymore, simplicity. Sex, reeds, music. Who cares what his music inspires or who inspires his music? That story, too, he need not pretend exists. He will play a piece to spite her distress and overcome his own: Mozart, C major, Rondo Allegro, on his best-ever blue-wound miracle reed.

Jeremy is on the opening bars of the piece when Isabella hears the moped, turns, and sees Marco racing towards her. He has been hiding, waiting for her, somehow sure when he rang her bell and her mother did not know where she was that he knew where to find her.

He felt it, her distance, even after the church affair was cleared up, forgiven. He wanted to believe that bullshit about Mass, how wrong it was of everyone there to ignore anyone in the true practice of faith. He forced himself to swallow that dry wafer for her sake, defend her for once. He even kept his doubts to himself about what Fabio told him later. He does not need that dead fat ass to confirm anything now. How many times has she been here? She knows better than Angelina? How far has she gone with the pretending Catholic creep? There is no need to hear her out. Marco will find out, now, whether she is his or any man's woman.

Isabella cannot deny where she has been. This *is* about her virtue. And it is not a test. It is a grab. Panic grips her. She finds an opening in the hedge, a cornfield beyond it to get lost in.

Her run is faster than the notes Mozart wrote for Jeremy's oboe, and he is playing for her now, in the villa, with inspired abandon.

Marco sees Isabella duck into the hedge, sees what he thinks is another weak spot in it, leans forward, and charges though it on his moped, hoping to cut her off before she reaches the cornfield that will hide her.

The moped loses momentum as he crashes through the hedge and stalls. He is at once engulfed by a million blowflies that are still devouring the sizable corpse of Fabio's sheepdog. They think they may have found another meal, ignoring the distraction that this one still moves, as Marco frantically tries to fend them off from his eyes and face, inhaling a few of them, coughing them up, and scrambling to get up when he trips and tries to get away from the buzz of their thick swarm. He is on his feet and running before they finally give up on him. He cannot tell where Isabella entered the cornfield.

Isabella cannot hear the moped. He is chasing her on foot now.

'Isabella, you cannot hide anymore. I only want what was promised—to me!'

She tries to guess where his angry shouting is coming from. Somewhere behind her, to her right? She runs, trips, stumbles, runs on. She must reach the other path on the other side of this cornfield which will take her to the back of the nursery, to safety.

'I won't hurt you. I want you, only you, forever.'

This has a more pleading tone. It is closer, to her right. He has not found her trail through the field yet. She runs on. The thin back strap on one of her sandals breaks. The sandal slips off; it trails and flaps behind her, held on to her foot by the ankle strap.

'I am yours, you are mine. Remember? Forget the lying Inglese. Don't run from the truth!'

This again angrier shout tells her he is moving up on her left now; he has crossed her track without seeing it. She decides to go farther right of him and turn back to the original path through the valley, losing him in the cornfield.

There is a slight pause in Jeremy's playing, a few bars from the orchestra, before Mozart invites him to take up the lively race again between oboe and orchestra all the way to a final pause for breath followed by the cadenza that ends the movement.

Marco, too, stops his chase for a moment, catches his breath, hoping to hear anything that will give away where she is. He hears her stifled cry in pain, the sharp rustle of cornstalks where she has fallen.

It was only a matter of time before her bare foot came down on a sharp something on the hardened soil. She was expecting it to happen but could not control the reflex when it did. Her leg gives way, and she crashes into the stalks ahead of her. They lessen the impact of her fall, but she has given herself away. She scrambles to her feet, manages a few steps, and falls again.

Mozart has Jeremy keep pace playfully with Isabella's repeated attempts to flee, taking him quickly through short high-pitched staccato runs and a few longer-held notes that plead with her to carry on. He is on one of the last runs before the orchestra gives way to his cadenza when the reed splits; the notes on the way to the top screech to a halt.

'Fuck!' Jeremy says.

Marco runs through the few rows of corn that hide him, directly onto Isabella's track. She collides into him.

Jeremy will not let the reed break him; he will carry on. The cadenza is his; he can tame the reed enough to get through it.

Marco loses his balance, takes Isabella down with him, flattening the stalks around them in their struggle into a makeshift bed. He holds her down. 'Now it's my turn to ask for a kiss, carissima Isabella.'

She turns her head away, but fighting him, she knows, is useless. 'You will never be forgiven for this, Marco.'

'Maybe I will have to forgive you if I am not the first.'

She can feel his hands rise to her breasts, ripping her bra away. Pleading is useless too, although she tries, and so is the crying to which she succumbs when his hands move down to her thighs and raise her skirt.

The soloists each fight their demons. Jeremy brings Mozart's movement to an end with as much flourish as his reed will allow. Marco brings his hot-wired lust to an end soon after the last spark of recognition leaves Isabella's face and he takes what he claims is his without resistance. He met different resistance when he thrust his way into her and she screamed in pain. She is the one who will have to forgive him.

Jeremy removes the miracle reed from his oboe, examines it, and throws it on the floor in disgust.

Enter prima donna

'How could you keep me waiting for so long? In this heat!'

Jeremy had agreed with Vicky he would pick her up directly outside Terminal 1. He could see her under the entrance awning from the Kiss&Go parking spots across the road when he arrived—half an hour late. She was surrounded by men and enjoying the attention, leaning back, her bare arms stretched out behind her on the bench she sat on, throwing her breasts forward, swivelling her head casually around, surveying her admirers without pausing to look at any of them directly. She stopped when she saw Jeremy coming across the road, stood up, and crossed her arms across her breasts in perfect curtain-call modesty, but without a bow. Show over.

Or not quite. When Jeremy reached her and put his arms on her shoulders, bending forward to give her a light greeting kiss on the lips, she quickly uncrossed her arms and transformed the kiss into a more passionate, tongue-searching variety.

'Che uomo fortunato!' one of the men ventured. What a lucky man.

'Vero! Vero!' another man replied.

Jeremy held her face from his, smiled, and took the handles of two sizable roll suitcases. How long was she really intending to stay?

Vicky took no notice of the new car when they reached it, more intent on picking her bone with him about being late.

'I had to drive halfway round Rome to get here. There was a jam. It took ages. I thought I'd be too early, not late. Sorry.'

'Telephone?'

'My cell phone is dead, I told you.'

'Convenient.'

'Yes. Outside of an occasional call from you, I haven't missed it here.'

That lie appeases Vicky long enough to register the new car. 'It is beautiful. And it has already been scratched?'

'Drive into Rome at your peril.'

Jeremy chooses to hide what he assumed from the start must be Marco's rancour at work and his being spurned by the villagers. In her mannerisms and fashionable appearance, it is unlikely Vicky will be better received by the villagers than he has been, even if she is Italian and speaks it.

'Riccardo has been fighting hard for me. What I lack in confidence, he certainly does not.'

'When will you know?'

'I'm expecting a call.'

'Coverage is weak out here. There's no reception out at the villa.'

'Then I will call them. Let's hope we have something to celebrate. Scala is a big step for me, Jeremy.'

'I know. And Riccardo is right to fight for you.'

'I owe him a favour. I've packed a few outfits.'

'I'm not with you.'

'Concert? He said it sounds like a major event in the village. He would be here if he could, to represent the family. He's counting on us to do that now.'

'I didn't think you would want to. I've said as much to the priest, Dom Pietro.'

'Who wanted to see us perform together?'

'Who has been insisting you would sing. Now I know why.'

They have just turned onto the ring road around Rome. Jeremy tells her how the idea of a concert came to be, about his debates with Dom Pietro, the miracle reed, his visit to Mass.

'You're turning into a good Catholic boy again? Take me back to the airport.'

'I only went to hear the organ. It sounds OK. Angelo is pretty good on it, I think. He knows Adalena, by the way.'

'My holier-than-thou sister. Maybe you should go after her.'

'I would give it a go if she is as good-looking as you.'

'Always Prince Charming.'

'Anyway, I didn't understand too much. Dom Pietro's stage presence is pretty good though, convincing.'

'I think this isolation is not good for you.'

'It has kept your charming prince out of trouble. Well, almost.'

'Meaning?'

'In church I discovered not all Good Samaritans are welcome in the village. I gave a girl a lift in this car one day and apparently breached protocol between her and her Romeo. I'm accused of disturbing their gilt pact—the village's "copia dorata".'

'When did you start talking like this? You picked up a loose village girl, had some fun with her, and found out she's already hooked up with someone. Why are you telling me?'

'Hang on! You're as bad as the villagers are!'

Jeremy primes Vicky for what she might hear about him and Isabella, and the false accusations that he is responsible for Fabio's fatal recklessness.

'Completely idiotic! I've been scandalised just for driving this car and giving the girl a lift in it. The only person sticking up for me is the priest, but it's his preaching that put this small-minded bigotry in everyone's head in the first place.'

Vicky hears Jeremy out and stays silent for a while before delivering her verdict. 'It sounds like a fun village. But we don't have to mingle too often with the locals, do we? That's not what I came for. Isolation with you suits me fine.'

She reaches over with her right hand to Jeremy's thigh, travelling up.

'Vicky, please, I'm driving.'

'And I'm here to drive you mad, bring out the devil in you the villagers take you for.'

'What a drab place,' Vicky says smiling, holding the serenity of an unperturbed diva while they drive slowly across the village square, passing the stares of dour-faced villagers mingling under the olive trees and near the bar.

'Is that the church?' she asks.

'Your local Scala. Built by Riccardo's family.'

'What on earth did he have in mind? The looks we're getting. Not sure I want to sing here, if there is an audience at all.'

'Dom Pietro assures me we will have a captive audience.' He will let Dom Pietro do the explaining.

At the top end of the village road leading down through the valley and across to the villa, Jeremy can only see smoke at the other end. Black clouds of it. Is the villa on fire? He instantly has visions of his music room in flames, weeks of work on his reeds ruined. He looks over to Vicky, tries to suppress the waver in his voice.

'Got to get to the villa fast, Vicky. Hold on tight.'

The hand that has teased him for most of the trip from the airport misreads the emergency and does as it is told as Jeremy takes on the rutted path at speed, grappling with alarm and pleasure, his gaspy breath in that struggle encouraging the hand to get bolder until the steroid/cortisol mix in his blood threatens to wreck them halfway across.

'Vicky, the villa is on fire!'

'Oh! You could have told me!' she says, pulling her hand away.

Only when they reach the entrance gate is his panic relieved—replaced by the stink of burning and smouldering plastic, rubber, and whatever else landed on the garbage tip he chose to forget about after discovering it on his first day.

Vicky is not taken by this reception, the immediate surroundings, nor the sparsely furnished villa. 'This is a dump! We cannot even cook a proper meal in this kitchen. How could you possibly imagine inviting me here?'

'Oh, come on, Vicky. It has a certain rustic charm. Don't play diva on me.'

'Me, diva? Yes, capital *D*. It is thoughtless of you to wreck my only holiday this year like this.'

'I thought you would find it rather . . . romantic.'

'Since when?'

'What?'

'Since when are you a romantic? Is this your idea of what it's all about? I prefer a few hours between rehearsals, in a nice, clean, cosy hotel room.'

'I can only offer you a new, comfortable sun lounger on a spectacular roof terrace. Meet you up there after your shower. Prosecco?'

'Yes, please.'

It is the golden hour, a warm glow on everything he sees, the perfect time to be up here, Jeremy thinks. He places the Prosecco and two glasses on the parapet wall. He remembers the day he arrived. The five weeks—or is it six?— seem like as many months. Wouldn't it have been better to stick it out alone till he was ready to leave? Relationships like the one he has with Vicky are all he knows, both of them pretending it is rooted in something more meaningful than lust, but that is basically the only satisfaction. Isabella rejected the feelings he expressed for her, hoping, if she believed him, that they would become real. Would they have become real? It is what he can have now, not the illusion he chased yesterday. That is gone.

What he can have now makes a dramatic entrance onto the terrace, sweeping onto her stage in a long, sheer, white, flowing silk kaftan that clings to her skin as she moves. It is almost transparent in the sunlight. Jeremy has only seconds to recall Isabella, as Vicky turns gracefully on her toes, his body aches for what he cannot do without, and the target of that addiction twirls towards him at the parapet, beaming her delight with outstretched arms. 'Oh, Jeremy, you are so right! It's so delightfully romantic here.'

Pure theatre, acting her part, Jeremy thinks, not at all natural, like Isabella. The touch of Vicky's body through the silk and the first light scent of perfume in ages arouse Jeremy instantly. Isabella disappears. Nothing can distract him. One hand is still around her waist as the other splashes out two glasses of Prosecco from the bottle while she leans into him and lets one hand glide slowly down his chest and stomach. Before she can reach the swell in his loose cotton trousers, he occupies that hand with a glass. He knows she likes the teasing bit.

'It's a spectacular view, don't you think? I'm very happy, now you've come.'

'I see a spectacle that makes me very happy. I've been looking forward to coming for a long time. That's why I'm here. Kiss me please. Now.'

190

His needs, and hers, are pure hunger for sex. Jeremy answers the urgency, and his reflexes obey their often-rehearsed role. Their eager hands, tongues, and lips deny passion the patient humility of cherishing and exploring sensuality. She feels beautiful, is beautiful, is she not? Jeremy asks himself. Your needs are perfectly matched. Slow down then. Take it one step at a time.

Banish the thought!

He pulls his head away from the kiss and leads her by the hand to the lounger. Still standing, he slides the loose V-neck of her kaftan out over her shoulders. It falls to the ground. She is completely naked, and yes, beautiful, gold. As she leans back on the lounger, he pulls off his shirt over his head, unbuckles, and strips in one practiced movement. He wants her now. Now! He lays on top of her and buries his head in her neck, positioning his loins between her legs. He meets some resistance, looks up at her face.

Vicky holds his head in her hands. 'Bad, bad man. We're on a slow train, not a flight to heaven. There's no hurry to get there. You know what I like.'

The ever so slight insistent force of her hands on his head takes him to her breasts, but he knows that is only an intermediate station on the way down to her Termini. By the time she signals she is ready to switch tracks from foreplay, the locomotive of his lust has derailed.

'You've never gone limp on me. Getting you aroused was hard work. What's the matter?' Vicky asks.

They are lying arm in arm on the lounger, looking up at the first stars as they appear in the last moments of dusk. This is not a discussion Jeremy wants.

'It's, well, the timing. It's not always right, is it?'

'Because I take care of my needs too?'

'I didn't say that, or mean it that way.'

'I don't deny I'm demanding, Jeremy. You can be too.'

The dogs bark incessantly through the night when they eventually go to bed, as if insisting that their complaints, to nobody in particular, be heard.

Unwelcome truth

Domino gets scolded by Vicky as soon as he appears at the breakfast table on the front terrace the next morning. 'You kept me awake all night!'

Domino looks up at her sitting at the table; his eyes are pure innocence. He saunters past her over to where Jeremy is sitting, on the same side of the table, facing the garden-that-was and a still-smouldering garbage tip behind the parapet wall. The dog sits, looks up at his master, swivels his head back to Vicky, then round again to Jeremy: who is this chick?

The tractor trailer arrives while they are still having breakfast. The trailer is loaded with large plastic containers and parks directly in front of the entrance to the oil cellar below the terrace. Jeremy goes to the balustrade of the terrace and looks down on Giorgio as he clambers off the tractor. He has wanted to speak with Giorgio about Fabio since the accident—if they are still on friendly terms. He takes a few tentative steps down the stairs.

'Buongiorno, Giorgio.'

Jeremy watches Giorgio unfasten the bolts holding up the side of the trailer opposite the cellar entrance, letting it flap down noisily, before turning to face him. There is a foreboding pause but not an angry face to match it.

'Buongiorno, Jeremy. Sorry to disturb you. We are taking the oil now to the bottling plant. It will be noisy down here for a few days. Buongiorno, signora.'

This explains the uncustomary politeness to Jeremy when he turns his head back to the top of the stairs and sees Vicky, in her stunning kimono, smiling down at Giorgio.

'Buongiorno, Signor Peroni. I am to send best greetings to you from Riccardo and congratulations on your success. Would you like a coffee before you continue your work?'

Both men are stunned twice each: Giorgio by her perfect Italian and a positive message from Riccardo, Jeremy by Vicky's casual takeover of the situation and what he does not know.

'I expect my workers to arrive any minute. Thank you, anyway, signora,' Giorgio says, taking off his hat to speak and holding it in front of him with both hands in a gesture of modesty Jeremy remembers seeing when Giorgio stood in front of Dom Pietro.

'Signora Costanza,' Vicky says, pronouncing her name with the self-confidence of someone used to being recognised. 'A very short coffee then,' she adds, also not used to being refused.

Giorgio pauses, puts his hat carefully back on, and moves towards the stairs, ushering Jeremy with his hands to move on ahead of him. The two men do not sit down immediately when Vicky goes to fetch a cup for Giorgio, whose silence when Vicky is gone suggests to Jeremy that their amicable relationship may be hanging in the balance now because of Fabio. They stand apart, both looking out from the terrace and not at each other.

'This garden . . . he hated me . . . and I don't know why.'

'It is unfortunate you came here. Your car made him foolish.'

'Am I to blame?'

'I knew it would happen, sometime.'

'I did not know. I wanted to ignore him.'

'He could not ignore you. That was the problem. He wanted to race you. He told me when he bought the car. I ignored him too.'

Jeremy feels a nervous spike in his stomach. 'I hear he was alone. No one else hurt.'

'His family will hurt now. Very badly. He has ruined them.'

Their exchange is interrupted by Vicky's reappearance. 'Caffè fresco!' When Jeremy finally turns around to her in the doorway, Vicky senses something went wrong while she was gone. 'What is it, Jeremy? You look . . . odd.'

'I think I've had enough coffee already.'

'They say in the village, Signora Costanza, you will be giving a concert,' Giorgio says, all eyes on her as he is motioned to sit down, and she pours him an espresso.

'I hope you will come to hear me,' Vicky says. 'And you must tell me what Riccardo is congratulating you for.'

If Jeremy had not avoided the village recently, he might have discovered that Signora Costanza is expected to be performing in

193

the church. He would also realise that his part in the now-announced concert hardly gets a mention and that the Costanza in question is mistakenly assumed to be Adalena, who someone in the village has heard perform.

His attention drifts from Giorgio riding again on his artigiano bandwagon, the tamed bully doing his best to keep his attention off Vicky's cleavage as he swells with pride over his olive-eyed obsession. Jeremy is thinking about what Giorgio said: Fabio's family will hurt; the only son has ruined them. How? Then he remembers Dom Pietro explaining that Fabio's mother's fear for the safety of her son was also the fear of losing their livelihood when they get too old to work. There is no one to take over the herd one day. Jeremy had not even given that any thought until now. But is that what Giorgio meant? Or does it have to do with the Alfa Fabio could not afford and he helped write off?

Vicky places a hand on Giorgio's arm on the table to interrupt his monologue, a gesture that electrifies him mid-sentence and earns her a suggestive smile she misses, her eyes on Jeremy. 'Jeremy? Where are you?'

'Oh, sorry, drifted off.' They are both looking at him, waiting for an explanation. 'Giorgio, what you mean to say Fabio's family will suffer more badly? They are in problems now?'

'I think I had better translate,' Vicky says, smiling inappropriately at his miserable Italian.

'It's about insurance for the car,' Giorgio says, looking down into his lap. 'It's a tragedy.'

'The car was not insured?' Jeremy asks, alarmed.

'It's complicated to explain.'

Fabio's father and mother came to Giorgio's office to ask for help with the car insurance policy their son had taken out. The next instalment to pay for the car has been refused by the bank, and the family's income backed Fabio's loan. They must urgently claim the insurance. Giorgio discovered to his horror that Fabio had agreed to a very high exemption to keep the monthly insurance rate down. The first five million lira in damages are not covered by the insurance.

'Five million! That is half what the family pays to live here for a whole year! He has ruined his own family!' Giorgio says. 'And I cannot help them!'

Roughly two thousand pounds. The selfish, cocksure bastard has wrecked his family's future, not just his car. They cannot be more self-sufficient than they already are.

Giorgio's workers show up, and he excuses himself with such gushy thanks to *la signora* for the coffee Jeremy might as well not be there. But he was stuck deep in thought after hearing Giorgio's story, trying to reconcile his not guilty plea for his part in it with the obligation he feels to help cover the consequences.

'Maybe we can help them,' Vicky says after Giorgio is gone.

'We? Why you?'

'Why not? Donations. We are giving a concert. So, let's turn it into a good cause.'

'It is bad casting: you're not Adalena and my stardom in the village certainly won't help the cause.'

'They will love us. Their donations will be generous.'

'You cannot ask the poor to help the poor. You heard Giorgio, what that family lives on. They don't have money around here. Which is why my holy friend in his boundless wisdom has indoctrinated the locals over the past three decades to believe it's a sin to own anything beyond bare necessities. So, copycat Fabio with his fancy car was a category-one sinner. He also killed a villager in another car before flaunting himself as an ace driver in the one he has just crashed. He is definitely not on anyone's do-good list.'

'*You* want to help the family, don't you?'

'What gives you that idea?'

'You're telling me why nobody else will.'

'I feel sorry for the mother. But I have no charitable memories whatsoever of her son. I'm not willing to cover his responsibility to the family.'

But Vicky hit the core of his conflict: if he feels an obligation, he must assume guilt.

Backtracking

Marco is sitting alone on the benches under the olive trees on the perimeter of the square. He called in sick again today at the electrical supplier where he works. Before he started his electrician's training, they would meet up here at around this time almost every day. His eyes are glued on Isabella's door across the square, willing her to come out, walk over, and take a seat next to him. He is trying hard to convince himself he had a right to do what he did, to believe she must come round to accepting him, but this is day three and she has not come out, and no one has seen her in the village at all, not even in the nursery.

'Don't you dare come near me ever again!' she shouted across the field when he went to recover his moped. She cannot possibly mean that. It is foolish, now that the big step has been taken. It was not the way he wanted to take it, either. Even if she was only flirting, as it turns out, why did she let the Inglese come between them? Why did she force him to take a stand? He just cannot understand it. He would have waited.

He is still waiting for Isabella an hour later, thinking of how he can reason with her, when the BMW comes up onto the square. There is a woman sitting next to the Inglese, her arm casually stretched over to him, her hand behind his neck. They park in front of the rectory, and almost as soon as they do, the padre appears. Loud classical music escapes the open rectory door. He waves to them gesturing 'I'll be with you in a minute' and goes back inside.

Marco watches them get out of the car and stand in front of it together, waiting for the padre to reappear, looking at the church. She leans into him. This stylishly dressed woman is Jeremy's woman, that's obvious: more his age, a city type, fancies herself. If Isabella saw this, she would know that he was right all along: the Inglese is false, and she could have fallen for him. He at least stopped her before it was too late, prevented something worse from happening she would never have wanted: to be this man's other woman. His chances to get her back just improved. The Inglese sights him on the bench, fixes him briefly, then scans the square quickly, all the way to the opposite end, in the direction of Isabella's house, making a connection to why he is sitting here.

Jeremy carefully disengages Vicky when he sees Marco; he must be waiting for Isabella. It is unfair to Isabella, appearing like this in public with Vicky clinging to him—simply bad form—and no telling how Isabella would react to his being with a woman he told her nothing about. She may not want anything more to do with him, but Vicky is sure to spot a facade she already suspects. It would be a relief to get inside the church before Isabella shows up.

Isabella has hardly stirred from her bed inside her small, dark room. She cannot bring herself to leave the darkness, the smallness, nor the ugliness of the fashionable worldly women cut out of magazines and pasted on her walls, spiting and looking down on her with demure condescension: *you* wanted to join *us*?

Lying on her back, trying to forge forgiving sleep that has not come to her for days, her breathing turns shallow again, as if pinned down by an oppressive weight. Returning to that horrible, brutal, painful moment of possession, her hand moves protectively between her thighs, and she hears herself scream, her eyes now, as then, crunched together tightly against the squeeze of tears, against the spasms of hate and despair. And when these subside, the cycle begins again, signalled by the thud-pause-thud of her heart's slow insistence on truth, if it is there, and will find its way out, even if she is ashamed to let it appear.

How can she pretend not to have known the risks she was taking? She was conscious of red-flag masculinity on its home ground, she knew the playing field she was on, and yet she still insisted Marco and Jeremy play by her rules. There was nothing virtuous in keeping Marco waiting, until it was too late to end the promise she did not want to keep. She played with beauty's challenge until Marco punished her conceit, after she bound Jeremy in chains she pretended did not exist and he could not unlock. She now cannot free herself from a cramping complicity she feels in her stomach that churns in rebuke of her innocence, until she turns to lie on it, her head buried deep in her pillow, suffocating her defencelessness before the ugly conscience of what happened to her starts the cycle again.

When she returned home that day, her mother was out. Isabella could not have explained the buttons ripped from her blouse, her braless breasts, and scratches all over her assaulted body. She washed and washed and washed that body, trying to scrub away as much as she could of herself and of him, his smell, his hands, his mouth on her skin, his seed. She then went to her room, mummifying herself in her bed sheets, and felt unclean, under a pyramid of fear that anyone should discover her and dig up how and why it happened, the shame of it. When her mother came home and looked in on her, Isabella could not speak, afraid the sound of her own voice would betray her, her pain, and her anger with herself and with her mother, whose blind dependence on her daughter to bury the broken dream of her own married life led only to Marco, and to this.

She had chosen to live the lie with Marco to not disappoint her mother, but all Isabella could say when she looked in was 'please, Mama, leave me alone' before turning in her bed to face the wall. Her mother did not wait at the door and press for more, herself familiar with the apathy and despondency that takes no prompting to show up, when even prayer to ease her own sense of dread during those bouts of depression seemed pointless to her.

Marco has today lost his patience with waiting. He would like to go over and bash the creep's head in, in front of his woman, for messing around with Isabella. Underneath the silent threat, made at a safe distance, is a loud truth that comes up to him on the bench and knocks him sideways. Where was he while Isabella was, as he imagined, under threat of this man messing around with her? Waiting his turn. He did not storm the villa to protect her. He waited for her instead, fuelling the confidence he needed to punish her afterwards for going there, to justify taking what he, too, wanted from her. What he did does not feel as right as before. He did it without respect for her, and she will never respect him. Even if he is maybe a father now and she is forced to marry him, it

198

remains a sin. He has abused her, his rights, with force. He has committed a real sin. It does not feel good.

Jeremy sees Marco stand up from the bench and walk away, no longer trying to stare him down, hands in pockets, head down as he walks, like a schoolboy ready to be called out any moment. That posture does not fit Marco at all, and Isabella has not shown up, maybe no longer belongs to him.

Delightful people

'What a pleasure to meet you, Signora Costanza. Welcome to our humble village and the home of the Patricelli family.'

Dom Pietro is laying it on a bit thick, Jeremy thinks, so eager to profess his pleasure that his hands are extended in front of him long before his bulky body can catch up to greet his visitors.

'Buongiorno, Padre,' Vicky says.

She extends her hand with courtesan affectation that suggests it could be Violetta's on stage, expecting to be kissed. Dom Pietro takes hers in both of his chubby hands and looks into her face with the practiced air of sincerity Jeremy has seen before. Really and truly thick, Jeremy thinks.

'It is so nice of you to visit us,' Dom Pietro says, and turning to him, 'Jeremy, you've been hiding. I thought of visiting you a few days ago.'

'I've been busy.'

Vicky laughs lightly and looks at the priest, then at Jeremy. 'He might soon be back in best form,' she says, 'but it's still a bit like hard work.'

'And the reeds?'

'The miracle was short-lived. But there are plenty of others.'

'Glad to hear it. Keep your faith.'

'In the new method certainly. It works. Shall we go inside? It's hot out here.'

'Yes. Angelo is waiting.'

'I honestly cannot see how you could find it appropriate to have a concert here directly after Mass,' Vicky says, looking around the church from the middle of the nave.

Dom Pietro is quick to quell the indignation Jeremy already warned him was likely. He takes the stage, standing in the middle of the chancel. 'Forgive me, signora, but it is absolutely appropriate. My homily for the service is already written. It is all about music, its power to heal the soul, to elevate us, to create goodwill, to bring us closer together—'

'Padre, please. I think you are confusing me with my sister, Adalena.'

'Not at all. God has bestowed the same gift on you, as your singing will confirm to us all.'

'I can assure you, there is no likeness between us.'

'But I am sure we will all like what we hear. After my congregation has entered Communion with God, they will welcome the privilege to hear from Him through you . . . and Jeremy, with the kind support of Angelo, of course.'

'Gladly, certainly, very gladly,' Angelo says.

'This is not what I had in mind,' Vicky says, visibly irritated.

'I'm sure you will open their minds to grasp some magic. We sorely miss it here in our humble daily lives.'

Vicky smiles.

Jeremy is sure Dom Pietro has no idea of the wickedness he has just invited into his church. But it is not his concert anymore. Let him collide with the dour villagers. Angelo must be thinking something similar; he and Jeremy share a discreet smile.

They decided on rehearsal at the abbey to avoid giving the surprise away to curious villagers and devout worshippers who happen into the church and because Vicky is sure to welcome lunch out at Jeremy's Trattoria there, as opposed to cooking at the villa. The first stop for today's lunch is the butcher.

The conversation between four older ladies sitting on benches across from each other to either side of the display counter stops at once as they enter through a curtain of hanging beads that serves as a fly-stop entrance. Jeremy's friendly 'buongiorno' is met by wordless forced smiles before conversation resumes in heavy Italian slang under the pretence of harmless chatter.

'A sinful hussy in fancy clothes, that's what this is.'

'A certain village girl will now see how wrong she was about him.'

'That won't stop the panty chaser going after her.'

Vicky is sure she heard correctly and wants to find out more, so she joins Jeremy at the counter, points at different cuts of meat inside the display, and pretends she is talking about them. 'Jeremy, I want to catch out the hags wagging their tongues in here. It's definitely juicy.'

'Veal or lamb, Vicky?'

'We are being shorn. Let's go with lamb.'

'This is what our prize girl would turn into? God forbid it,' one hag says.

'I saw them earlier going into *our* church with you-know-who.'

'How can he be so blind to how shameless they are?'

'Let in indecent rot, it soon invades.'

'Guess who says we must be more welcoming?'

'Too much tolerance, I say.'

'Count me out.'

'Me too.'

The meat has been packaged and Jeremy is paying.

Vicky turns from the counter to address the women in faultless Italian. 'This gentleman is certainly not chasing any of your village girls. It is a sin to talk about us like this. It is slanderous and evil, and the padre will hear about it. Pray for your forgiveness.'

The women are dumbstruck. Two of them cross themselves as Vicky and Jeremy leave; a cacophony of exasperated voices trail behind them as soon as they are outside.

'That was about?'

'Your excellent reputation here, Jeremy.'

'Delightful people, aren't they?'

Vicky is happier about her Italian origins when they meet with the genuinely delightful Signora Tendri. The old lady is taken right away by Vicky's elegance and fluency, without regard or excuse for her own dialect and shabby clothes.

'What a beautiful outfit you have. May I?' she asks and feels the fabric. 'Oh, this is so fine. It is silk? And God has blessed you with beauty too.'

'Thank you, signora. That is very kind.'

'We do not see many like you and Signor Jeremy here. A perfect match. Ah, now I know. You are Signora Costanza?'

'Yes, I am.'

'I have heard you sing. Beautiful.'

'I'm happy to hear you liked it. I—we—will be giving a concert here.'

'I have heard! It will be so different to listening on my poor old radio set. Ave Maria. Beautiful.'

'That would be my sister, Adalena. I am Victoria. I sing in the opera.'

'True? Opera? It is not music for religious old ladies like me,' the old lady says, subdued, before gushing with enthusiasm, 'but I love the opera! It is better. Emotions, tragedy, drama! You will surprise everyone!'

'I think so, if they are expecting my sister.'

'I will keep it secret. And will I hear Signor Jeremy at last?'

'I will play just for you, Signora Tendri.'

'It is wonderful. I am very excited.'

Just teasing

'Wonderful salad, Jeremy. Very fresh. The lamb is a bit strong for my taste, though.'

'Local breed probably. I'm glad you like this old goat's salad.'

'What makes you feel like an old goat?'

'My salad days are sadly over when I could claim to be—as Shakespeare put it—green in judgement, cold in blood.' He pours them both some wine, trying to dash the memory of Isabella sitting opposite at the same table.

'There's still something left of both bits, Jeremy. You are hesitant sometimes, which can make you lukewarm on me.'

'You're so tolerant. I feel younger already.'

'Does that make younger village girls more appealing?'

'You are no doubt referring to tongues wagging at the butcher's?'

'I'm not so sure they're mistaken about you.'

'I told you how the rumours started. I ignore them.'

'Do you like the girl? What's her name?'

'Are you serious?' He takes a swig of wine and squints to hide from her suspicious gaze. She could read men just by intonation, blindfolded. 'They are as sour mouthed in the village, in fact, as this wine. Isabella . . . I think Dom Pietro said her name is. I'm fetching something decent to drink.' He gets up and moves to the door, out of observation, but has not reached it.

'Jeremy, I don't believe you.'

'Believe what you like. That's what the locals do.'

How stupid, he thinks on the way to the kitchen; she now knows he has something to hide. But she is not so stupid: she will ignore it. She is an eager child on the hop-on, hop-off merry-go-round of the singers' and musicians' playground after hours, between rehearsals, behind the scenes. He returns to the main room with a bottle and corkscrew and opens the bottle at the table, pouring out two glasses.

'You've been here too long, Jeremy. Or you're not with me yet. You know I was just teasing you.'

'I may make you regret that. Later.'

'I cannot wait.'

'But after this,' he says, indicating his glass, 'I think I will practice for an hour or so.'

'I will go upstairs then, and warm up . . . my voice.'

'Then how about some fun afterwards? A game of snooker?'

'I would prefer a siesta. You know I don't care much for your real passion.'

'If the table is my bed, you are always the pocket I aim for.'

'I like that. Very original.'

Undisciplined

Jeremy stops his practice to listen. Her timbre is uncopiable, a voice of many colours: demonic red, angelic blue, holy purple. It is passionate, demanding, magnetic, and supplicating. She will soon be a big name; he is quite sure about that. And being given even more attention than she now has, to tend and tame her unpredictable moods, will no doubt end their affair. Her salacious provocation is seldom genuine anyway. It lacks conviction. It is more a need for confirmation she is looking for than sexual gratification. Hearing her sing, he asks himself why she needs it and, then more uncomfortably, whether his own rote conquests of other women and dependence on her follow the same need. His confidence in his music when they met after his accident was not the best opening bar.

His music has always covered over the empty gap that appears between conquests. She will soon leave another gap. But she will feel it less; the greater of her seductive powers, her voice, will be heard, in demand, while he is still not sure he will ever fully recover his own voice on the oboe. He continues his practice.

Vicky is clearly too impatient to be accurate, Jeremy thinks. She is playing for him because he asked her to, and playing with him, provocative at every turn, wanting to turn him on. He asked her to play because he wanted this correction. This is not Isabella. He does not need a cue from Vicky; he knows he has her consent, the confirmation she wants from him. But his awakened physical arousal is not strong enough yet. That day in this room is not simple to correct, when consent would not only have satisfied but also purified the extreme desire he felt, given new meaning to it. There is now no chance to share in Isabella's hesitation, to coax an innocent pleasure in her, for her, with her—until out of nothing, everything happens. There only this flaunted immodesty repeating itself, this brazen call to submit to his need and answer Vicky's obscene desire to assert her seductive power, to ply her infallible control over men's wants until they are made willing to do anything she might want from them. It is not persuasive but possessive, humiliating. He can be selfish, too, and is persuaded to be so when on her next shot she again poses her buttocks directly in front of him.

She misses the cue ball, merely scratching it so that it hardly moves. 'Oh, hell.'

Before she can straighten up again, she feels Jeremy right up against her. 'Let's take that again. Take your time and prepare for the shot.'

'Like this?'

'Yes. Move back a bit more, away from the ball. Bend right down on the table. That's a perfect position.'

Jeremy slides his hand up her skirt, along the inside of her thighs. She is wearing nothing underneath. He strips off his shorts with his other hand. 'I think my favourite pocket is a ready-made target. But maybe we should test the stroke first, glide in and out of it before we strike for real. Does this feel right?' He thrusts hard into her on each word. 'Nice . . . smooth . . . stroke.'

'Jeremy? You're hurting me.'

'Focus on what I like for a change, Vicky.'

'I'm not ready for this.'

He holds her down forcefully. 'No? I'm just following through on your foreplay. Stay in the game.'

'You are breaking the rules!'

'It's too late to disqualify me, Vicky.'

There is no search for pleasure in her, for her, or with her. It is a stubborn attempt to convince himself that rough-and-ready sex is all he wants. But it is off target, a forced shot at estrangement he does not want to believe in. He is humiliating her for being the wrong woman, for smashing the colourful rack of fantasies played out in this room, until they collapse, lifeless, as Vicky's body does, submitting to defeat in this unfairly matched round, refusing to play. Only then does he pull himself away from her, pull up his shorts, and walk to the door. He turns back to her before leaving.

'Sorry, Vicky.'

She lifts her head up off the table to look at him. There is no scorn for his humiliation on her face; he meets a brief questioning stare. She is looking at someone she is no longer sure she recognises.

The olive queen

Vicky does recognise the loudest voice she hears in the courtyard through the bedroom window the next morning. It belongs to one of the seven men seated on empty wooden crates at a long makeshift table—a wooden plank supported at each end by an empty barrel—an improvised arrangement that disguises the seriousness of the issue being loudly contested. The men Vicky and Jeremy hear from their bed are constantly interrupting each other so that their voices gradually swell to a crescendo until, at its peak, one voice holds the rest at bay and commands to be heard: Giorgio. This is followed by complete silence until the pattern is renewed.

'What do you think they are arguing about down there?' Jeremy asks.

Vicky gets up out of bed and goes to the window to look. 'I think I'll go and find out.' She grabs her silk nightgown, slung over a chair in the room, and slips it over her shoulders. Its deep V-neck and the clinging material outline her breasts and her figure in revealing detail.

'You cannot go out there like that, Vicky. You're not properly dressed.'

'I'm absolutely well dressed. It's nice you noticed for a change.'

'Temptress.'

'Brute,' she says at the doorway.

But the exchange is light-hearted. Jeremy lounges on the bed, grateful for a few minutes on his own. After the game of snooker he avoided her, went on a walk with Domino, and tried to forget what came over him. He did not have any answers and was relieved to find Vicky in a conciliatory mood when they finally cleared the air last night. His attitude towards her since her arrival felt lukewarm, she said: there was too little intensity. He seemed at a loss to make her feel really wanted, especially compared with their spontaneous coupling in London. She missed the hungry lover and

209

wanted to tease him back into being one. What she got was rough urgency, and she could not respond to it as she might have liked with more warning, and more regard for her objections.

'I honestly don't know what came over me, Vicky.'

'I think you do.'

'Then you tell me.'

'You've always been considerate. Maybe too considerate.'

'Meaning?'

'You were punishing me for always having it my way, always agreeing to my needs.'

'There could be some truth in that. Although, rough sex is not the sort of correction I want to fulfil my own needs.'

'It's not unusual for men to let their beast out of hiding every now and then. But let's put him back inside, until we both invite him out again another time, not tonight.'

He was surprised at how normal 'normal' felt with Vicky. Neither made demands, they followed an instinctive and not distinctive path that left neither behind. It was a sublimate rather than passionate experience. What would Isabella be like? This question falls tellingly on another crescendo outside the window that ends abruptly, at the peak of its volume and confusion, in silence.

Vicky goes out into the courtyard carrying a tray of cups and a large moka pot. Her appearance is Carmenesque as she makes the scene her habanera stage, stunning the men into an embarrassed silence.

Giorgio is the first to recover. 'Buongiorno, Signora Costanza.'

'Buongiorno, Signor Peroni.' She bends to place the tray on the low-lying tabletop, looking up past the row of bottles in the middle along its length to Giorgio at the other end.

The half peek the men are given just inside her gown is too much for the two men closest to her at her end of the table, and they look to Giorgio as if expecting him to speak. Vicky straightens up again and stretches out her arms—diva, diva—as if she has just gotten out of bed.

'I have heard you arguing with each other for the last hour, so I thought I might as well get up and serve you all some coffee.'

'My apologies for the noise, signora. But we are not arguing. We are debating our different tastes. In olive oil.'

'Ah, I see. Perhaps, then, coffee is the wrong idea.'

Various voices object, but only shyly, when she reaches for the tray again. Giorgio is more affirmative. 'No, no, Signora Costanza. We welcome the chance to switch to something different now. Especially if, like coffee, there is no disagreement about our tastes.'

Vicky smiles, a courtesan graciously accepting the insinuated compliment, responding to Giorgio's odd attempt at a fetching smile and the other men's forced attempts at smiles of equanimity. While she pours the coffee, Giorgio explains they are trying to find the right blend of three different olive oil varieties to bottle the perfect oil. After an hour they are down to a choice of three blends. Would she like to give her opinion?

'I trust my instincts in any choice I make, but that's no use for olive oil, I'm afraid. I know nothing about that.'

'And our choices are maybe too logical because we know too much?'

She is persuaded to not disappear, to not end her appearance as a briefly coveted apparition to these men. They remind her of the admiring eyes that followed her and her sisters when they were young, developing, needing affirmation. Adalena, she remembers, was horrified, while it nourished her own confidence; she would one day be a woman with plenty of choices.

She can dramatise the whole procedure here and make her appearance something, even beyond her looks, they will always remember. Years ago, still a girl dreaming of becoming an opera star, she memorised short descriptions she made up for starring roles in the opera. It does not matter which roles she assigns to which samples in the small beakers in front of her, but adding a bit of drama would be better than the 'nice', 'it's good', or 'interesting' that would spoil the fun.

'I know nothing about olive oil, but I know everything about opera, the starring roles for soprano. They each have a different character, so I will give each oil a name according to the character it has.'

'We will try to follow you, signora. It is an amusing idea.'

Vicky adapts as she sips appreciatively. 'Convincing, but what it promises dies too soon. I would call it Verdi's Violetta.' She places the beaker down and takes the next, looking through the clear plastic at its contents, swirling them around, as absorbed as she would pretend to be on stage. She takes the next sip. 'Fiery, but bitter at the back of the throat. Bizet's Carmen.' She likes that one, it was inspired, and she smiles as she puts Carmen down and takes the last beaker. 'A bit tricky, but genuine in the end. This is Donizetti's Norina.'

The men are agape at this foreign description, and being beyond their grasp, it holds them all in venerable silence. At each sip, their heads turn from Vicky to Giorgio as if hoping for a translation that could help them understand.

'So, I do not know anything about olive oil, but I do understand opera. Imagine if you could blend convincing, fiery, and a bit tricky in one bottle. Is that what you're looking for?'

Giorgio reflects on this for a few moments and then offers her a convincing and thoughtful smile. 'Will you sing for us, signora? Your description is very inspiring. I want to hear it.'

Vicky can see that he means it and feels mean now that what she described had little or nothing to do with differences in the oil she tasted: the roles she assigned to each of them were random attachments, vain footnotes, showing off. His admiration humbles her; it reminds her of the timid young girl she was in the company of men in her own village, three hours away, fifteen years ago.

She pulls her nightgown around her and folds her arms over her breasts. 'You will hear an aria from Violetta in the concert this Sunday, after Mass. You must all come. The padre said he would welcome more men in the church for a change. Now I must go back inside.'

Giorgio does not protest. He takes his last sip of coffee and passes the cup down the table. 'Thank you, signora. It was very kind of you.'

The other men do likewise, murmuring their thanks. The cups are back on the tray.

Vicky reaches for the moka pot. The sash of her gown snags on a splinter of wood at the rough end of the tabletop, almost undoing it. She catches her gown before it falls open completely. She can feel herself turning crimson. 'It was nice to share in your debate. I look forward to seeing you all. In church.' She picks up the tray and leaves, and for once there is nothing suggestive in her gait as she heads for the back door.

When she is gone, Giorgio asks for the three beakers Vicky sampled. He pours all three into one beaker, stirs the contents, and takes a sip. He is inspired to taste something different slipping down his throat: convincing, fiery, and a bit tricky. A smile stretches across his mouth.

When Vicky enters the bedroom, she finds Jeremy still lounging in bed. But he has been up, looking out the window.

'I followed what went on down there. You've turned a real brute, Giorgio, into a proper gentleman. Maybe you can do the same for me.'

'Oh, Jeremy, I hope not.' She lets her gown slip from her and crawls into bed with him.

'But, just the same, don't be rough, please.'

'I know what you like, Vicky, don't worry.'

An hour later, the men are clearing up their makeshift table, still talking between themselves, but more quietly, teasing Giorgio and each other. The sound of Vicky warming up her voice in one of the rooms of the villa stops whatever they are doing. They listen, eyebrows raised. She has given them a day to remember. They will be in church on Sunday.

Accidents happen

'That's where he went off,' Jeremy says, forgetting he is not supposed to know.

Jeremy and Vicky have just passed the clean break in the guard rail on the road to the abbey where Fabio met his end. This spot of the ravine they are driving around is black scorched earth. The guard rail has still not been repaired.

'Who? Fabio?'

'Yes.'

'How do you know?'

'Well, I was told it was this road, then the gap in the guard rail, and there has been a fire here. That makes it obvious, to me.'

He is defensive. Vicky assumes he still feels accused of encouraging the young man. 'It's horrible. What a tragedy. And the poor family now. But Jeremy, you are not to blame, are you?'

'The villagers and his parents say I am. It's my car that misled the poor sod, encouraged him to buy his own so he could race against me and become the ace driver he thought he was. They have to blame somebody.' Jeremy steps down on the accelerator to overtake a van and keeps driving fast, forgetting what he has just said, his thoughts elsewhere.

'Slow down, please. I would like to enjoy the view, and to arrive calm for rehearsal.'

'Oh, sorry, Vicky.' He slows down.

The driver has seen this car on this road before, he knows it, though he was in the smaller delivery van that time. There are no other cars like it. He does this route often, and he sees plenty of cars he recognises. It is a game he plays to keep himself awake during endless hours at the wheel in the heat. He is having to miss his siesta again to make up time and deliver punctually. Why should he recognise the car? Why is it important? He must have a short break—too tired to think.

'Ave Maria? Are you serious, Vicky?'

'And why not? They are expecting Adalena, aren't they?'

'But it's not really you.'

'Let me decide what that is, please.'

'Why don't you both perform it?' Angelo suggests. 'That would work. When you finish the Albinoni Adagio, we move into Ave Maria and then Signora Costanza—sorry, Vicky—enters to sing. Beautiful.'

'If I keep the volume down, we could probably do something with it together. Let's give it a go, see what works.' Jeremy starts to unpack his oboe and put it together.

'And Violetta?' Vicky asks, taking the score of the aria out of her handbag.

Angelo looks at the title page. 'You want to do opera? La Traviata?' he says.

'Vicky, I can't say I mind, but the padre might. We are in church, you know.'

'But, Jeremy, you know the libretto; there's nothing profane in it, as a recital. I will raise my head to the heavens, and it won't be Alfredo I'm singing to. It is God. It is about love, the pulse of the whole world—except, maybe, in the village. Dom Pietro wants to change that, doesn't he?'

Rehearsal begins.

The van driver pulls himself out of a roadside doze. He is barely awake when what he thought of earlier is suddenly at the top of his mind. The car he saw today was racing another one when he saw it last. The other one was a Sprinter, coupe. He remembers everything now. And why it could be important: there was recently an accident on this road he read about in the local paper. He passes the site every other day. Could the car that went over be the Alfa he remembers now? He will go to the police. They would want to know about the race maybe.

Mama!

Isabella's mother must find out what is wrong with her daughter, who has not left her room for days now. It has something to do with Marco, sitting for hours every day on the benches across the square near the church. He has not rung the bell and is not going to work; has he lost his job? Through her door, Isabella rejected the idea of letting him visit. He was very angry the last time he came asking after her a few days ago. Something serious has come between them. Maybe it is the decisive question of marriage and starting a family, which Isabella insists she is not ready for and Marco, she knows, wants to see happen at last.

That irresponsible Inglese has upset things, maybe more than she knows. Isabella likes him, said the padre obviously does too, which proves she was right, and everyone else, including her husband, are wrong: he is a decent and friendly man who does not deserve the mistrust shown him. Even if that is true, which she doubts, expecting Marco to accept that his future wife publicly sides with a stranger he and everyone else would like to be rid of is both untypical of her daughter's humility and humiliating for him. And the rot caused by this Inglese does not stop there. The padre himself has announced that the Inglese, together with a very tarty-looking singer he has appeared with in the village, will be giving a concert in their church this coming Sunday after Mass. It is all people are talking about: why is the padre doing this?

She left Isabella one of her pills again this morning. She does not know if this is the right remedy, but they have helped her get over her own depression in the past. Her husband has been as insensitive as he always is these days, threatening his daughter through her closed bedroom door that he will break it down and drag her out if she does not do so herself soon and tell them what is wrong with her. She must find a way to get Isabella out of her depressed state before that threat becomes a reality. She says a prayer to ask for guidance, crosses herself, and knocks gently.

'Bella?'

No response.

She tries again. 'Isabella?'

'Yes, Mama.'

'May I come in?'

'Only you? You promised: no visitors.'

'Only me.'

'OK then.'

Her mother is relieved to see her daughter sitting in bed, not lying down, her back propped up against the wall opposite the door of her narrow room and sipping water from a bottle, but the rest is a split-second test of her composure. Isabella's hair, unwashed for days, is matted against her head. She has headphones hitched around her neck and an old cassette recorder on the bed in front of her. The air in the small room is stale, sour. The room is in a shocking state: the pictures from fashion magazines her daughter had cut out and pasted on her walls over the years have all been torn down and left crumpled where they fell, leaving a mottled patchwork of lighter and darker shapes on the old wallpaper, and her chest of drawers has been emptied, the clothes separated into two piles on the floor. Her daughter is in serious distress. She must keep calm.

'You need some air in here. May I?' she says, reaching for the window.

'I am *so pleased* to see you. Yes, you may open the window.'

Is her daughter talking in tongues? She stares at her blankly and meets a faint smile that is equally demure and triumphant. She is confused by what she has just heard, confirming and questioning it at the same time. 'You speak English. You do? Since when?'

'I have taught myself English for the past two years.'

'But why? I mean, what for?'

'It is the most important language, everywhere. I want to know how to speak it.'

'You have been talking then . . . with the Inglese.'

'I want a proper job. I am not interested in Jeremy, his ways, his music, his games.'

'What do I not know?'

'I visited him, in the villa.'

She must remain calm. Isabella's mother reminds herself not to show alarm and speaks quietly. 'What happened there?'

'We played snooker. He played his music for me.'

'And . . . what else?'

'He didn't do anything wrong, Mama.'

'What is all this about, Bella? Your clothes. The pictures.'

'I am sorting my clothes. Those I do not want anymore,' Isabella says, pointing to one of the piles.

'But these . . . these are your best clothes.' Her mother bends down and picks up a sleeveless dress, delicate embroidery sewn in along the modestly low-cut neckline seam. 'This has always looked so beautiful on you!'

Isabella says nothing. Her head is bent into her chest. Examining her interwoven fingers in her lap, she presses her thumbs together until they turn white. When she does speak, it is a stream, an angry, hurt, defiant stream. 'What if I don't want to be beautiful anymore, don't want to accept God's challenge, Mama, don't want to be admired? What if I want people to see me for who I am? I am not here to . . . to decorate lives, men's lives. I want to live my own life, for me—what I can be, not what other people expect me to be. This place has become a prison! So, here I am. In *my* cell! Not Marco's girl, not any man's other woman, not where people fuss over me for the wrong reasons or accuse me of wanting to be friendly to an outsider for the wrong reasons. I don't want anything from Jeremy, and I don't want Marco. I don't want him anywhere near me ever again!'

There was more, lots more, that she found the right words for in her isolation but cannot remember now. But she has said enough, maybe even too strongly about Marco, so it was right to stop, to strangle further emotion. The tears swelling in her mother's eyes as she takes a seat on the bed tell Isabella no more needs to be said. She waits for her mother, and when she speaks, softly and falteringly but with years of bitter energy, it is the mother Isabella denied existed.

'A prison. Oh, Bella, I know your prison. I married one of the wardens. I have seen him walk down the corridor of his moods every day, barred from reaching him. I prayed in my cell for a better life. I found comfort in God, and he sent me you, the only thing that has given me joy. And what have I done with God's gift? It was given to me to repair my own broken hopes, through you, through what I might help you become. But I was selfish. I wanted to keep you for as long as I am here. I wanted to believe it would not be a prison for you too.

'How mistaken I was to mislead you—the only one, the only woman, who has the courage and the virtue to rebel against what keeps us all locked up here stabbing at each other's faults, smiling, pretending. I had the whole of Mass that Sunday to think of why I should be proud of you, and all I could feel was shame. Why? Because that is what was expected of me, and I knew nothing else nor why I should think anything else matters. Until now. English, yes, I understand. It is right for you to go away.'

Isabella lurches forward to embrace her mother. They lock and rock in each other's arms, neither able to speak for a long time.

Her mother's shame shrinks Isabella into her own. But in different ways, shame is shared now for the untruths they admitted only to themselves about Marco.

'I am yours, yours only. You are mine, mine only.' She can hear Marco in her head: loud, ugly, menacing. She is the only one her mother has. At least that is a pact she somehow will try to keep.

'I will not leave you, Mama. That is not what this is about.'

'True? Then let me be here for you, to help you brush away all the things you do not want that I accepted without understanding how different you are, and without realising how much I let living in this village I grew up in strangle every objection I had to it. I want to make a fresh start.' Her mother smiles weakly, asking permission.

'Yes, Mama, we should.'

'But, maybe, Bella, you should wash your hair first.'

This brings muted laughter, relief, a sad joy in each other. They flop backwards onto the bed, breathing in this moment together. Isabella feels relief at their honesty and to be accepted by her mother as a woman.

Her hand lands on one of the strewn pictures at the head of her bed. She picks it up, uncrumples it, looks at it, and then turns it to face her mother. 'This is not what I want to be. I want to be more like you, the person you want to be for me.'

They talk. The smallness of Isabella's room seemed to impose limits on the confidentiality each allowed themselves, to limit the size of emotions they can share after years of hiding them, but they try. They talk about the village, Isabella about her fear of the bubble closing her inside it and her mother about the generation she was born into.

'You remember my mother, I know. You were only small when she died, too small to know why she did not always recognise who you were, mistook you for me sometimes. She had dementia. I think God just wanted to be kind to her, to let her live out her last days without too many memories of her years of suffering, hard work, my disagreeable father. She spent days talking to herself, in her small room, probably no bigger than this one. When I tried to take her out, she refused. One day, when her head seemed clearer than usual, I asked her why she didn't want to walk around, maybe meet some villagers she knew. "The village lives in a bubble. I have my own now," she said. You just told me what she meant.'

Her mother made coffee, the first for Isabella for many days. And the deal was, Isabella would use the time to wash her hair. She was surprised when she came out of the bathroom and went into the main room that her mother was not there. Her mother was not in her maternal territory but in her daughter's room, seeking refuge, or comfort, in a space she knew too little about. Two small espresso cups stood on Isabella's small bedside table.

Isabella went to the window and opened the shutters a crack to let some light in, took a sip of her coffee, and sat on her bed to let her mother brush her hair.

'I was all wrong about Marco, wasn't I?'

'Mama, please, not now.'

'You said he must not come near you ever again. Those are strong words.'

What happened would make her mother's guilt unbearable, shame her for what she failed to see before now: his conceit, the arrogance. Isabella, too, must bury years of pretending the mismatch. She has been punished for that pretence, and it will take a long time before she can talk about what happened without punishing her mother. 'He did not respect me. He thought he owned a right to me, and that was enough for him since everyone acted like he did.'

'Did I act like that? Such a horrible mistake.'

'Didn't I, at times, behave like he did? It was my mistake too.'

'Hold your head steady. Here's a snag.'

The snag in their now-honest union is Bella's father.

A good man

There was still time for a late lunch after rehearsal and Jeremy took Vicky to his terraced trattoria. He saw her relax. She praised the food generously and smiled a lot, the poise of City Vicky replaced by something more natural. As the bottle of wine emptied, she reminisced readily about her childhood in her own village, her sisters, the church where they all learnt to sing, the boys they pretended not to hang out with, the insistent boy she left behind—also a Marco—who everybody thought was made for her. He married Adalena at nineteen, just a year after she left.

It would be like Vicky to resent that her suitor was not torn up about her for longer, Jeremy thinks. He remembers Marco's dejected walk away from the bench when last he saw him on the village square, and he now wonders if Isabella—who 'does not belong any man'—found the courage after all to put the golden couple behind her and ditch the jealous car vandal.

'Should I have married Marco, then?'

'Huh? What?'

'The boy, from my village.'

'Oh, for God's sake, no. Only Catholics have a motive to marry so early. What would you, the good Catholic girl you were at that time, have turned out to be? A mother of, say, ten?'

'Adalena has five, and still counting. All planned. Nothing spontaneous, I'm sure.'

'Was Marco good-looking?'

'Yes, by village standards, the golden boy. A bit vain about it, too.'

Get out, Isabella, for God's sake, Jeremy thinks. He takes a sip of wine and looks over the gently rolling terrain of the broad valley. Vicky, he realises, could only escape over the hills because she has talent; even young and untrained, her voice proved stronger than the inbreeding earworms of her village and its noisy young men. Isabella has nothing to help her get out. Is he not a little bit ashamed of pretending she does? After a little adventure across the valley from her village, he would have left her with nowhere to go.

'Calling Jeremy.'

'Oh, sorry, I was just thinking about village life around here, how it must make people feel closed in somehow. Lucky your voice gave you the ticket to leave yours.'

'There's a part of me that never wanted to leave, believe it or not. It is only three hours away from here, and yet I dread the thought of going back there. Too many questions I cannot answer honestly about what it feels like to have left.'

'Because you don't know . . .?'

'Because I don't know if what I left to become is more valuable. In my heart of hearts I may still be a village girl, longing for the support people gave me freely simply for being part of their lives. You're right, of course, they weren't exactly liberal. But it's still hard sometimes to live off respect only for what I do—the expectations people have of me—and not for who I am.'

Two very different women in different circumstances fighting the very same battle.

They set off to tour the town after lunch. As they ambled along the cobbled streets of the town centre, Vicky reached for his hand. It was an awkward moment, not only because he was thinking of Isabella when she took it but also because Vicky's call for this sort of affection took him by complete surprise, even if the impulse fit how vulnerable she admitted feeling, for the first time ever. He could see it made Vicky feel good, unaware she was standing in for Isabella, the thoughts of her she prints on his imagination of a village girl no longer imprisoned by her roots, who, self-assured enough of her feelings, might have tilled the ground with him.

They decide eventually on a small cafe on a quiet square for their coffee before heading home.

'I have an errand to run before we leave. It shouldn't take long. I'll be right back.'

'Jeremy, not the necklace with that gaudy cross. Don't buy it, please.'

'A nice holier-than-thou cross? Perfect disguise for the concert.'

'Don't you dare.'

'Ave Maria? I dare you to wear it.'

He goes back to the bank they passed on the main town square and hopes this is not going to be too complicated. It is, of course. The business takes half an hour, and on the way back to Vicky, he buys the necklace as a joke. But she is not amused. He takes a seat. She looks away from him, then back at him, the venom of indignation in her eyes every conductor has seen at least once.

'They drove a hard bargain, Vicky. I had to go to the bank.'

'What are you talking about?'

'Two thousand quid.' He quickly loops the necklace around her neck.

'Jeremy! Never! This is completely fake, don't you see?'

'Yes, I did, just in time. So, I paid them ten pounds for it. I think I'll donate the rest to Fabio's family.'

The venom disappears, her voice and eyes softer. 'Why do you joke about the good man you could be?'

'Maybe because it's a joke, me trying to be a good man.'

Back at the villa, Vicky helps write a letter to Fabio's family, enclosing the money in cash. This is a thick wad of forty-eight bills, each worth 100,000 lira. A couple from Caravaggio's painting *The Fortune Teller* and a portrait of the artist himself are depicted on the face side of each note. This donation is graced by an artist he admires, making the large gift almost personal.

The letter is more difficult. He must pretend he cared about the hateful, arrogant lout he knew. He has no motive to explain his generosity, other than guilt. Is he even supposed to know from Giorgio about the family's financial ruin? He dictates to Vicky that the signora expressed concern for her son's safety on several occasions and that he is aware of the dangerous influence his own car had on the son's love of cars—this sentiment marking the halfway point to any guilt he is ready to acknowledge. The tragedy fills him with deep sorrow for the suffering it has caused, and he feels sorrow for the other burdens the padre and Signor Peroni have told him the family will face through the loss of their son and the costs of the accident. He begs that they accept the enclosed donation as a response to God's wish that the family find faith in these troubling times.

'Jeremy. That is almost blasphemy, really not you.'

'No. It's not. But playing God's messenger is the only way they might accept the money.'

'And blame you less?'

'Like I said, it's a joke me trying to be a good man.'

When Jeremy and Vicky go for the late afternoon walk with Domino, they pass by the shepherd's dwelling. It is shuttered and eerily quiet, and even the sheep seem to be mourning in their sheepfold beside the house, offering only an occasional lifeless bleat. Jeremy slips the envelope under the entrance door.

'You want to say a prayer?'

'Vicky, please.'

'Just want to be sure it's only a make-believe role you're playing.'

A bit farther up the track, he picks up a stick and throws it for Domino to fetch. The dog is not in the mood for the silly games Fabio derided them for that day. His race companion in the BMW has not been keen on a ride in the car, either.

When they pass by the dwelling on their way back, the sheep are gone. There was someone at home earlier, then. And despite the gift, the shutters stay closed on his guilt.

Witnesses

Marco does not know why he is on the bench again, knowing Isabella will not come out; she will not come out and forgive him the sin he has committed against her. He had no right to force her. And if she is pregnant, how likely is she to toe the line now? She will say the child is his; she has no other choice. But if she refuses him, accuses him of . . . of force against her will, who will believe him if he denies it?

Can the Inglese be stuck with it?

The padre is praising Isabella's virtue to everyone, defended her 'true faith' with the Inglese at Mass, telling everybody else off for rejecting him. Now that this other woman has shown up, the Inglese is spoken for, not so easily accused of having been after Isabella the whole time. She always said she had felt safe in his company to anyone who warned her about him. And she was. Her innocence is real, and the more so his sin.

There is no way to fix it, to erase what disconnects them, what blows out all the lines he has that are good, things he was sure made him dependable, like wanting to be a good, responsible father. The horror on her face turned away from him, her fight against him, the sharp cry of pain as he entered her: it frightens him to know all that did not repel him. Her resistance angered then aroused him long enough to fire his lust, which he did just as her body went limp and offered itself to him.

Where did this bad current running through him come from? He was overloaded—he saw her falling for the Inglese—and that short-circuited his main line to her, the promise between them. But there is another circuit he could try and connect to. He can see it gives her a different kind of confidence and purpose. He has never found any faith in the Church; he only went for her sake, and to stay on her mother's good side. But even if there is no current there, maybe he needs to talk about what happened, confess his sin, then do penance and try to make it real enough for her to see he regrets hurting her feelings so badly. Prayer is make-believe, not him, but maybe it is not as essential as the padre says it is.

He sees Ramiro and Francesco approaching, full of themselves, laughing, nudging each other, sharing a private joke, not attuned to his mood at all.

'Hey, Marco, lucky man, why so serious?' Ramiro says.

'None of your business.'

'Is this what it does to you?' Francesco asks.

'What?'

'Your business!'

Ramiro and Francesco both laugh full throttle.

'Looking for trouble, you two?'

'Oh, no, no. In fact, that's why we're here, if it's not too late. To keep *you* out of trouble,' Ramiro says, handing Marco a plain paper bag. 'Hope they're the right size!'

Another round of laughter as Marco opens the bag to discover a packet of condoms.

Francesco says, 'You may get away with it the first time. But you never know—'

'When the mood hits you again,' Ramiro butts in. 'What a chase! We were rooting for you.'

They had followed the chase from the top of the path, looking down on the fields.

'Nothing happened. So push off and leave it!'

'*Hello?*' Ramiro says, drawing out the word, mocking Marco from their first encounter with the Inglese. 'He beat you to it?'

'No he didn't!' Marco's shoulders cave in at his own stupidity.

'Thought so. It didn't look like you were just playing hide-and-seek when she came out,' Ramiro says.

He has their word of honour before they leave, but he cannot count on it anymore. He is no longer in charge now that they have something on him. He is at their mercy. Admitting what he did is the only option. It is not just about being a good Catholic for her sake; he is sorry, really ashamed, and now that he has spoilt it, the promise they had means everything to him. But does he have the stomach to ask for pity so he can be forgiven?

The concert

A few of his congregation left after Mass, but many more have slipped into the church since, for the concert, competing in number with attendance on Easter Sunday when even the less faithful show up out of tradition and pretend belief. Dom Pietro seldom has today's opportunity to address them and encourage them to belong in spirit. Catholic influence is dwindling everywhere, three churches gone in his diocese alone last year.

But today is not the day to think about how long his parish will hold out. His core faithful are all here, maybe some of them only begrudgingly, because he personally asked them to attend, knowing they would not want to disappoint him. Despite his authority, he met with a lot of adamant scepticism; he was afraid the church would only be half full at best.

Signora Costanza is regarded by all the women in the village who have seen her—and even those who have not—as extravagant, licentious, and sinful. They resent her presence in their church and say she does not belong 'no matter how inspiring to our faith and goodwill, Padre, you say her God-given voice might be'. The first time he met her, he too had serious doubts about her taking part today; she is too provocative, putting his licence in allowing her to perform under severe scrutiny. Thankfully, Jeremy has her under control; it was a relief to welcome Signora Costanza in the rectory earlier wearing a free-flowing cape that concealed her figure with exceptional modesty, almost worthy of a nun, except for the extravagant lustre of the light-grey fabric—that might be overlooked, he hopes.

Dom Pietro has changed out of his decorative alb and chasuble into his black cassock before taking up his post at the screened window giving him a view of his congregation from the vestry. Some ardent sceptics of the concert have shown up whom he has admonished, after Alessia's confession, for the slander that led to the departure of the Accardi family and, with less vehemence, the circulating rumours that denigrate Jeremy. Their response to this effort to loosen tensions and seal loose tongues could be a turning point in village attitudes, for better or for worse.

He stood behind the man he is not sure he knows well enough to trust, and that man is putting their allegiance on trial today. Too much has happened since his bold announcement of the concert after Jeremy took Mass weeks ago. That was before Fabio raced to his death and ruined his family. Most parishioners hold the *estraneo* responsible for the accident one way or another, even if accusing Jeremy of racing him is ridiculous. His own outing with Jeremy to lunch quickly branded himself complicit in weakening the hold on self-restraint he has always preached. Then there is Isabella. Her mother told him confidentially that the golden couple is dead, and that is being made obvious today.

Not seen in the village for ten days at least, she is sitting with her mother, and Marco is here on his own at the opposite end of the pew in front of them. Does Jeremy have anything to do with it? Those who have seen him parading in the village with Vicky see him confirmed as a dangerous philanderer, and according to her mother, Isabella has visited the villa. Innocent unless proven guilty, but this is the man who must light a candle for him at the altar of God's honest and peaceful purpose in the village. He can only hope and pray Jeremy and Vicky do not blow them all out today.

There is animated discussion going on in whispered voices throughout the church, but few of the faces are smiling. Looking out for those, Dom Pietro is surprised to find Giorgio in the crowd accompanied by other men in the grower's circle the priest rarely sees—except at Easter, of course. Their wives, and most of the other women in the congregation, could take a cue from Signora Tendri, talking excitedly with her son, a bright smile on her face. What a happy, precious soul she is. Dom Pietro needs that sort of optimism now. He hears impatient heels stamp the stone floor of the vestry behind him and turns to face Signora Costanza.

'How much longer are we expected to wait?' she asks.

'Not much longer, I hope,' Dom Pietro says. 'The bishop's own Mass at the abbey ended an hour ago, so they should be here very soon.'

229

Dom Pietro was very surprised to get the call announcing His Excellency's attendance. He will soon know whether it is scrutiny or curiosity that has prompted the bishop to visit, whether the finger his superior now needs on his other hand—to count the six times he has visited the village in thirty years—points at his priest in admonition or admiration. He has put more of his reputation at stake than is comfortable. The church suddenly goes quiet. All stand. He's here.

Dom Pietro opens the door and walks as briskly as he can into the church to meet the bishop coming down the aisle, smiling and nodding discreetly to the congregation, accompanied by some members of diocesan curia. Dom Pietro just cannot explain this attention. His brow gives him away, pearls of sweat forming.

'There's no need to be nervous, Dom Pietro,' the bishop says, signalling to his congregation that they may all sit down as he takes his seat. 'We are here to celebrate your initiative, reinforce it. I have not seen any church so packed in ages. An admirable accomplishment.'

'Would Your Excellency care to say a few words?'

'I think not. I would prefer to remain in private, if I may.'

'Oh, certainly. Then we can begin.' Dom Pietro returns to the vestry. He did not hesitate to scrap his own planned speech, written before he knew of the bishop's attendance. He will not claim more responsibility as host of the event than he already has.

'What a surprise. I suppose the bishop is why the padre insisted we all stay,' her mother says.

Isabella was of two minds about breaking her isolation, not sure she was strong enough to hold her composure. She has only been able to because the people who have approached her are now like strangers. She feels no connection to them anymore. She is here because it is against her will to discard Jeremy and her own responsibility for his behaviour; she still feels a connection to him, a willingness to forgive him and herself. Contemplating her decision to come here, she listened to his CD this morning. She thought things over more logically. He did nothing forcibly wrong by expressing his feelings; he backed off. He does not deserve to be shunned because of the horror she suffered afterwards at the hands of the man only two aisles away staring at her—the other reason for her composure: she will never give Marco the satisfaction of knowing just how ashamed she is for her incautious behaviour and how disgusted she is by his cruelty. She will ignore him.

Isabella sees Dom Pietro re-enter the church and take his seat at a respectable distance from the bishop in his pew at the front of the nave. Only then do the organist and Jeremy appear. The organist takes his seat and spreads out his notes; Jeremy wets his reed and nods, smiling, to confirm he is ready.

He holds the smile; it is thoughtful and confident, inviting, but it finds only a few welcoming faces. The first bars of the Adagio in Albinoni's Concerto in D minor belong to the strings, in this case the organ, the notes stealing their way forward as if on tiptoes to his opening. This leaves Jeremy plenty of time to look for her. He has not been completely rejected. He turns to face her in a pew far back in the nave. He tries to lock her attention, to reach her with questioning humility on his brow she might recognise, before his knees and body bend slightly forward and he tenses his abdomen to hold the long notes of the theme that slowly rise in strength with his body as it straightens.

Isabella knows he has searched her out. The music she probably knows more about than anyone else in the church is hauntingly beautiful, melancholic, bringing tears before she can stop them. She can see her mother is likewise moved and places her hand gently on her mother's arm. They listen together. Isabella hides from Jeremy's gaze.

She closes her eyes, letting the music take her back to her first experience of it, the ride in his car. Those hopes she had for herself are not gone. He gave them to her, opened her world. She would never give him what—in the ways of his world—he wanted in return, but he respected her; she will respect him and not let those hopes die.

She looks around after the last notes on the organ trail off, sees many heads nodding and catches whispers of approval for Jeremy, the outcast. The reaction possibly redeems her, but approval is no longer important to her. Not wanting to find or protect her acceptance in the village feels a bit like freedom. A faint smile forms on her face when she looks at her mother's.

'We all knew nothing about this,' her mother says. 'It's so beautiful.'

Dom Pietro was at first too nervous to take the music in, but the more he let go, the more convinced he was that other listeners would too. He stole a glance, only to find the bishop looking at him. He is safe, so far. Jeremy deserves the applause he would have allowed, there is no liturgical norm against it after all, but regrettably only the bishop can give the cue, and he did not.

Jeremy stood still for a long time after the last note, perhaps waiting for the applause, but he should know that to conservative Catholics, this is all in honour of God, spiritual communion with Him, not the performers He blessed with the talent to inspire His followers. Jeremy returns to the vestry, and Angelo is now performing a piece by Bach he likes on the organ. No need to be nervous. Dom Pietro can enjoy it—not knowing what is going on in the vestry.

'No applause. Oh, what fun this is!'

'Maybe at the end, Vicky. It's probably up to the bishop.'

'These holier-than-thou fanatics give me the creeps. I'm not going out there.'

'Vicky, please. We cannot back out now.'

'You do your bit, then. Leave me out. Who am I supposed to be? An anonymous voice from heaven?'

'It has been described as heavenly before. Now's your chance to prove it.'

'Very funny. I'm not out to prove anything around here.'

'Give them a chance. I could tell just now they like what they're hearing. Do the Ave Maria, and then . . . we'll see.'

When it is time to go out again, Jeremy does not know whether Vicky will give in and join the piece as planned on the repeat, after he has introduced it on the oboe d'amore. He warns Angelo and they begin. On the last notes of the first ending, she suddenly appears at the entrance to the church, having slipped in largely unnoticed. Jeremy sees her, turns to play in Angelo's direction to alert him, and they return to the beginning.

Vicky can even make piety work for her, hands clasped in holy reverence in front of her flowing cape and the necklace cross he dared her to wear. She walks slowly forward, her voice filling the small church from the other end, turning heads that follow her down the central aisle; it is now her concert. She turns to face her audience when she reaches the chancel, opens out her palms, and at the most dramatic point in Schubert's music to the Latin prayer, stretches out her arms upwards in a theatrical supplicating gesture. She can be holier-than-thou, too, and makes a show of it.

The bishop frowns, Dom Pietro squirms in his seat, and eyebrows are raised in every pew behind them, the congregation aware, as Vicky is, that she is abusing a sacred gesture of Catholic ritual.

She finishes with her forearms crossed over her breasts, head bowed, a picture of humility worthy of Mother Mary herself. When she has sung the last note, she looks up, drops her arms to her side, and strides to the vestry door. End of act 1; she cannot be bothered about pretending to be Adalena, her sister.

Jeremy and Angelo continue with Bach's 'Arioso for organ and oboe' and then move on to Alessandro Marcello's 'Concerto in D minor'. This takes the audience by surprise, not being acquainted with any music that sounds less than sacred in their church.

Vicky comes out again for her act 2. She takes a chair next to the organ, repurposing the chancel to place it in the centre of her 'stage'. She stands behind the backrest of the chair, signalling to Jeremy and Angelo to wait. In perfect Italian, she introduces the three of them to the audience. This is a concert and not some spiritual exercise, and Dom Pietro had agreed to introduce them. She also quotes his ungiven speech, praising music's power to heal the soul, to elevate it, to create goodwill, and to bring people closer together. She can see he and the higher clergy are uncomfortable, and still more so when she announces she will sing an aria from Verdi's La Traviata, directly quoting the libretto:

> *To that love which is the throb*
> *Of the whole universe,*
> *Mysterious, proud,*
> *Cross and delight to the heart.*

There is very audible confused murmuring in the church. An opera? Here?

The bishop's face is changing colour, and cold sweat forms on Dom Pietro's brow. The performance must be stopped! Are the three of them not aware of how inappropriate this is?

'*È strano! È strano!*'

Vicky's solo voice introducing the aria invades the church, banishing the thought of how strange this is. The audience is transfixed; even the bishop looks as if an archangel has struck him down, slumped back in his pew. A rush of emotion, Vicky's aria pierces the air, hardly needing the sparse accompaniment from Angelo and Jeremy. She leans back in her chair, letting her arms hang behind her, her head thrown back; she lurches forward, bows her head, hands wringing; she stands behind then circles the chair, wanders off, returns to it, sits again. Every gesture magnifies the doubt, the longing, the fever the aria demands from her. Standing near Angelo on the organ and peering over his note stand occasionally, Vicky has Jeremy convinced: no one will ever match this. It builds up so much emotion inside everyone who hears and sees her that there is sure to be applause; it must escape, there is no way to contain it.

Were it not for the cross and its implacable rule in this church over the delight of the heart. Vicky was sure delight would win. She is sitting when she delivers the last notes on '*croce e delizia al cor*'. When she finishes, there is dead silence in the church which at any moment must explode. She waits. It is a painfully long wait.

Angelo turns on his seat at the organ, ready to stand and leave. When Vicky turns her head towards them, Jeremy can see the theatrical look of longing on her face change to one of bafflement and defiance. He smiles apologetically at her with a faint shrug of the shoulder. She shakes her head no, then lips the word both he and Angelo recognise at once:

'*Follie!*'

Jeremy is the first to respond, familiar enough with the first bars in the dramatic conclusion of the aria, while Angelo pivots back on his seat, turns to the next page of his bound score, and does what he can, following whatever cues Jeremy can give him on this extemporaneous dive into the whirlpool he hears. The villagers, Signora Tendri a notable exception, do not rejoice in the whirlpools of voluptuousness Vicky decides she will lead them to.

She throws off her loose-flowing cape in the middle of her foolishness to reveal bare shoulders and a deeply cut neckline, turning her into a courtesan dressed for the kill. It is not indecent on any opera stage, but completely abandoning all modesty is too much of a rebellion, as is the hedonism of the aria's libretto. Vicky's dramatic coloratura as she moves from joy to joy, swaying along the front of the chancel and facing her audience, stuns before it can offend, but ultimately the consensus reached by the panicked whispers relayed along the pews is that this performance is scandalous, and the first wounded souls leave before the aria is finished; to ever new delights their thoughts will not fly. Vicky does not wait for applause. She pointedly curtsies, fixing her eyes on the bishop, and heads for the vestry door.

But the bishop gives as good as he gets, and when eventually he stands, after what seems like minutes, the congregation follows, at once hushed.

'Vanity has no place in the house of God. How easy it is to misuse the talents God bestows on us. Let us not forget that today, or any other day.' When he passes Dom Pietro on his way out, he stops before he reaches the central aisle. 'A more vigilant mind would not have let this happen, Pater. It is a disgrace to the Church. I forbid you further experiments and expect a report of how this happened.'

Heads bow from the admonition on the bishop's grim face as he leaves: the cross wins.

And Dom Pietro has lost, feels under attack by the loud confusion of the villagers he faces as soon as the bishop is gone. The reverential distance between him and his flock is cut short by a rush of gesticulated comments and questions. What has just taken place is scandalous, and this scandal, like any other, is driven mostly by one question in a village accustomed to finding its scapegoat: who is the culprit? For the first time, Dom Pietro is on the wrong side of that question.

Isabella stays seated, staring straight ahead at the commotion surrounding the padre, her mother beside her, both ignoring the faces turned in their direction as the people file out of church.

Only Marco stops at the far end of their pew and waits until he can see no point in doing so when Isabella's mother looks at him angrily and orders him to go with a dismissive swing of her hand.

By the time Dom Pietro can make his way to the vestry, he finds only Angelo there. Jeremy and Vicky went home. They left quickly—driving off just as the bishop appeared on the square— and are already on their second bottle of wine.

Confirmed sinners

'The look on his face when I announced the aria was priceless.'

'Bishops don't like being upstaged, Vicky. Their s*acred* vanity keeps everyone obedient—in the name of God, of course.'

'Your holy friend, the padre, is in trouble now, I suppose. But it's his own fault. What was he thinking?'

Jeremy empties the rest of the bottle in their glasses and settles back in his chair on the front terrace. 'He's probably asking himself the same thing right now.'

'There's nothing unsuitable about an aria in a concert.'

'About life's sinful pleasures? *Follie?*'

'I had to show them how foolish they are. You heard me. I didn't want to sing on the backside of Mass devotion.'

'He wanted as many people as possible to attend. He got us a captive audience. And you were captivating; they just weren't allowed to show it. It is against the unwritten rules of good Catholics to be thinking about anything else but Him above in His house. You were a profane distraction, leading them down a sinful path.'

'How ridiculous, maddening! I was an inspiration! I sang Maria better than Adalena ever did.'

'She only sings in church. She has probably never had any applause, nothing to improve on.'

'What is it with Catholics? Why can't they find pleasure in anything? It makes me want to really sin just to show them how it's done.'

'According to their rulebook, you already live in sin.'

Vicky gasps, an awkward smile on her face. 'I just thought of one. It's really wicked.'

The smile was supposed to be wicked then; the wine is getting to them.

'Want to be a really wicked sinner with me, my Romeo?' Vicky asks.

'How can I be both at the same time?'

'The old altar boy has reservations, I see.'

'My sobering thought is we're nearly drunk.' Jeremy stands, slightly unsteady, and moves to go inside. 'We should eat something. I'll go fix us some lunch.'

'No appetite for sinful pleasures? Come find me when you're ready—'

'With lunch,' Jeremy calls behind him as he heads for the kitchen.

In the kitchen, Jeremy uncorks another bottle of wine and takes a big anti-nympho swig. He is not in the mood for sex, and his appetite for lunch is not any stronger when he goes to the fridge and takes things out at random, tired of the staple diet of pasta and salad and snacking on salami and cheese. Tomato, mozzarella, and basil? Not again. But they should eat; Dom Pietro is sure to be buzzing with sacerdotal fury, and he could pay them a visit this afternoon.

Vicky is right, though. Denying her any applause was ridiculous, and Dom Pietro could have warned them. It is easy to provoke Vicky to extremes; try to stop her at your peril. She couldn't care less. The priest will blame him for not cutting her off and will cut off any association with him. The question is: were they sort-of friends or just trying to bridge the great divide between them with opinionated banter?

He stands at the table looking at his lunch choices and takes another swig of wine. He couldn't bear to listen to another of the priest's monologues about faith, conformity, blah-blah, ignoring the hypocrisy of his own Church. What his cross bearing has done to his village was sacrificed to paganism by Vicky today, and everyone despised them for enjoying it. It is time to go, leave this run-down place, the ugly village, its hard-up, holed-up peasants. Why should he care about any of it? Let them all rot in their self-righteous bubble. He kicks the fridge door he left open. It slams shut with a rusted, squeaky, heavy thump.

She was there. He tried to connect with her when the stage was his alone, and she was alone, too, without Marco. She closed her eyes on him. She could be standing on the other side of the table right now, taking a step back: 'You did not tell me about her.' Maybe Marco plays poker, too, trying his luck with other village girls, which is why Isabella has decided she belongs to no man— although the cocky macho boy hardly counts as one, moping on the bench now that she has called his bluff and given him the shove. He has no hand left either that could win her over. Another lost cause, and he made a fool of himself playing in her game. Another reason to leave.

It was follie all right: pretending to want a more meaningful involvement with her was pure foolishness. He has never wanted it; every shared bed goes cold. Any match is trial and error, not anything to dwell on too much after the customary expressions of regret when, sooner or later, it is over. But Isabella left something on the unused bed he cannot crawl under and hide from. She made a sham of his longing for her, the irreversible pretence of it. She saw through him, rejected the feelings he wanted to believe were genuine for once, and exposed them as fake as soon as he expressed them. But she pretended too. She is not Artemia, the helpless, innocent village girl she made him believe she was through her own vain pretence of chaste attraction. Why he denied himself the licence to take her, as Aginulfo, the city prince, would have done, and he should have done, he does not know. It would have absolved them both.

Half the present bottle of wine already finished, he blesses the would-be consummate match with a graceless splash of olive oil on what will have to pass as a salad—ante-Isabella. The pasta is overcooked. Never mind. Arrabbiata sauce out of the jar. Never mind. Hunger. Eat, drink, sex, sleep: the routine feels very old already after these days with Vicky. There is no kick, no exploration left between them. He puts everything on a large tray to carry out to the front terrace.

He puts the tray down on the table with a clumsy bang. She is upstairs, waiting.

'Vicky! Lunch!'

He waits. No sign she has heard him. She must have fallen asleep. But his stomach is awake and his head aches. He takes the tray back into the cooler main room, sits, forks a few mouthfuls of pasta . . . this will not do. Wine dribbles from his mouth as he gulps another mouthful, and now he notices she took her glass with her.

'Wicked woman, what are you up to? Come and eat,' he shouts.

A few minutes later, he steadies himself on the railing and climbs the stairs. She is not in bed. She has left a note on the dresser, scrawled in haste. A small bottle, pipette cap, sits on the slip of paper, her wine glass next to it, empty.

'A love potion, my dear Romeo. Come take me in the most wicked way. Rush Into Pleasure with me.'

Her dress is thrown on the bed; the cape is missing. She must be wearing it. Where *is* she? What is this all about? The door to the snooker room was closed, he remembers now; is this an invitation to rough, rushed pleasure? He stumbles down, not sure he wants it now. She is not waiting there. On the roof terrace? She is mad! He lurches up the steps, fast out of breath.

'Vicky, no. It's too hot up here,' he says loudly as he steps out onto the roof. But she is not there either.

His dull, half-inebriated brain still functions well enough, despite the heat, to search for a clue in their conversation earlier, in the note she wrote. And there it is in capital letters: Rush Into Pleasure. RIP. He goes to the side of the terrace overlooking the chapel. The entrance door is ajar. When they went into the chapel on her first day, she said there could be no place cooler for it, more exciting than Romeo and Juliet. And what did he, the old altar boy, say? 'Vicky, you're sacrilegious as hell.' That must be her intention.

Domino, tail wagging energetically, is waiting for Jeremy outside the back courtyard door. He bends down to pat his dog.

'You know where the mistress is, don't you?'

Domino leads Jeremy towards the chapel. He leaves the dog outside.

'I need you here, mate. Be a good guard dog for me.'

He goes inside and pulls the chapel door behind him. The hinged marble slab covering the entrance is open. And as he peers into the deep dark, he sees Vicky, her naked body, face down, stretched out on her cape that covers the stone table in the centre of the crypt.

Well, altar boy, what now?

Jeremy's undisciplined alter ego takes control.

Priest in doubt

Dom Pietro can no longer view the scandals circulating in his village with equanimity; in them he reads a deep insecurity in his congregation. Abiding God's rules only lets people feel safe if no one is seen to stray: disobedience or laxity breeds distrust. And now this concert, his cautious departure from the strict morality he has preached for thirty years, has put him at the centre of the biggest public scandal ever; he will be seen as weak for not suspecting the profanity and indecency he invited into the church. He is closer than ever before to losing the trust of people who have depended on him for guidance and correction.

Because he misled himself, placing trust in a man who has not so much abused it as he has simply ignored it. And it was his own vanity that pushed things forward. He assumed he had the power to persuade Jeremy back towards belief, confronting not some simply constructed village soul wavering on the edge but an accomplished man of the world, of keen intellect, whose company he could and did enjoy sparring with. How arrogant and stupid he has been to think he had such persuasive power.

Jeremy is as close as he has come to sharing anything like a friendship since arriving here. But how in heaven could he believe he would pull Jeremy back to His Church? The truth is, he never believed it for a moment; the debate itself was more important, vocalising his convictions as Jeremy's inspired priest was more important, puffing up his role as the arbiter of good in the village was more important. Their relationship was more honestly a competition between vanities, and the concert today made him pay for his, for not keeping a vigilant mind, as the bishop said.

Why had he not vetted the programme? He vented his fury at Angelo in the vestry only to find out the poor organist had assumed he had done so and now feared consequences at the abbey for taking part. Angelo was surprised at the very liberal choice of the aria but thought permission was granted exceptionally because Signora Costanza is an opera singer. It was supposed to be a recital; he did know she would act the part nor had they rehearsed to the end of the full aria.

She is the one he should have been wary of, Dom Pietro thinks, it was obviously a mistake to believe Jeremy had her under control. He turns onto the path leading to the villa and inches his way forward on the strained suspension of the Cinquecento. She is as rutted in her morality as the track he is on. And Jeremy must have known that, and ignored it, ignored his common sense, his responsibility for how she behaves here, ignored the respect and tolerance shown him.

Dom Pietro will not be ignored, and God must forgive him the vanity of his rebuke. For his own sake he will insist they leave. The village is his home, and they are destroying his authority in it. Not that he wasted any time deploring the performance when surrounded by his congregation. He made it known that what they witnessed is something which he, in the name of the Church, or personally, would not tolerate. He faced a horde of loud 'I told you so's when he claimed he had been deceived. How relieved he is not to have made any speech before it all started, even if he had to suffer the indignity of being quoted by Madame in her false show of piety.

He will make a speech now, though, tell the two of them just what he thinks of their disrespect, their intolerance of people of faith, their hedonistic and selfish behaviour. In the words of a priest, not a friend, he will tell them both to go, leave the village alone.

He can see from the gate that the main door to the villa is open. They are home but not on the terrace: it is Jeremy's snooker hour. He parks at the bottom of the stairs and is out of breath when he has finally climbed them. Through the front entrance he can see the door to the snooker room on his left is closed. There are three wine bottles on the long table, a bit left in one of them beside a glass. He enters the main room, fills the glass, and toasts to the misery of his day. He has not even had time for lunch, but he will not invite himself to any horrid ready-made pasta. He passes his hand over it; it is still warm. The table was left in a hurry not long ago. For a drunken siesta? He strains his ears for telltale sounds:

they *are* asleep. He is not here to bless their disrespect with silence. He calls out loudly for Jeremy and wanders into the music room to wait for him.

There on the secretaire, Jeremy's workbench, he sees several reeds in progress. Jeremy has seen what faith can do and denied it. Dom Pietro remembers his silent invocation, and God stood His side of the bargain. Jeremy got what he needed and threw the invitation to reconcile in His priest's face; wherever his soul is at this moment, it denies any accountability.

Dom Pietro goes to the kitchen, calls Jeremy again. His throat is hoarse; he is wheezing with tension. He puts on the table the music score he brought as evidence of the scalding insult of the aria's libretto—never mind its scandalous performance. He fetches a glass from the cupboard and pours himself the last glass left in the water bottle on the table, gulping down courage for a confrontation. There is no sign of life from above. He will go and call from the courtyard outside. Maybe the bedroom window is open, or maybe their two bodies are in hot free-float alcoholic pursuit of pleasure on the roof terrace. He is not climbing any stairs to find out. But he is not leaving until Jeremy faces him.

The car in the back courtyard confirms they are home. Dom Pietro spots Jeremy's dog right away when he briefly looks beyond the car to the chapel and sees Domino spring to his feet, erect and alert, ears and head cocked in his direction.

Hear no evil, see no evil. Dom Pietro will later plead with God to erase his sin-infested intuition, to purify him of the sudden, horrible premonition that took him to the chapel door, to hear evil and to see it. He heard the telltale sounds first, coming from the crypt, the echoed hoarse grunts and moans blaspheming the chapel as he stood in shock at the door. Why did God want him to see it? Why was he compelled to move forward and peer through the entrance to the crypt? He wanted to rage against this sacrilegious evil. Why did God choke his voice?

He could not meet that evil face to face. He went to his car. He left, undiscovered. His emotions fragmented his mind into self-loathing and vengeance against Jeremy, a deep personal injury he felt for standing by as the Lord, his only true companion in life, was abased by the profane worship of selfish, sinful hedonism in

His Church. He could not have faced Jeremy. He instead faced Jeremy's naked ass, pointing up at him, just visible below, between the legs of his courtesan harlot. Both pairs of feet were pointing down. He knew instantly why God compelled him to look, what choked any rebuke.

Confession—sort of

Dom Pietro approaches the village church and decides he will pray. He will pray with all the shame and self-loathing he now finds in his soul, pray to find genuine contrition for his past disobedience, the eagerly sought consenting sexual encounters of his early priesthood, so much a part of his life until his conscience awoke to his dependence on them. He has never truly regretted them, or thought them ugly or truly sinful. Until today: lust mocked death in the crypt, mocked everlasting peace; today lust proved how degenerate those wants are, how they can maim the spirit, leaving it to crawl for new ways to perpetuate the thrill because the denier of sin is denied a merciful end to the soul's painful emptiness. Jeremy is too far gone; he can never find mercy for his soul, not in the here and now, not ever.

What he sees happening to Jeremy has given him new resolve as a priest. He confessed at the time, he had to, and his move to this off-map outpost of the Church's primacy dissuaded him from further temptation. But an emptiness lingers he feels more often than he should; his penitence has not been sincere enough, severe enough on his conscience. He must purify his authority.

But his prayers, Dom Pietro discovers, must wait.

'Buongiorno, Padre.'

The greeting is to his back as he unlocks the vestry door. Dom Pietro turns to face the young man. He was expecting Isabella to come to him at some point, not Marco. He can guess what this is about.

'Salve, figlio mio. What brings you to me?'

Marco is well groomed, as usual, but not as self-assured, running his fingers through his thick hair, his head bowed down as he speaks.

'I just missed you an hour ago. I have been waiting, over there on the bench. I . . . I was not able to take the Eucharist today.'

'I see.'

'Well, if you are busy . . . if it's bad time, then maybe tomorrow . . .'

'I can never be too busy to aid reconciliation. Nothing can be more important to us. Give me five minutes. I will see you in the church.'

Lust, again? Why is he assuming that, Dom Pietro thinks when he enters the vicarage, goes straight to the kitchen at the back, and combs the fridge. He takes out a salami, cuts off thick slices, and chews, and chews. Premarital sex, or less prettily, fornication: Catholic doctrines are clear, and clearly ignored these days by most people, though not, to his confessional knowledge, by many in his village. He fetches some bread, cuts a few stale and dry slices, and dribbles some olive oil on them. Bless you, Giorgio.

He cannot remember the last time Marco confessed; it is out of character. He has never considered Marco devout by any means, much too vain. Fornication? Isabella? Completely out of character. Maybe that is why she has been in hiding: shame. Marco is jumping her rightful place in the queue; she is the one with devout conscience. Or this is worse? Why has she left him? It was not premarital; it was another girl. Or worse still? It was Isabella, but not consensual. Oh, God forbid.

Marco takes a seat in the pew closest to the confessional. Maybe he should kneel, pretend he is praying. Is he going through with this? The Lord is not talking to him like everybody says He will in situations like this; He never has. That is not why he is here. He does not know how to begin. The few other times it was just things he said or did that he guessed were wrong somehow. Not this time. He knows that much. He hears the padre enter the church from the vestry and walk towards him. Instead of going to the confessional, the padre takes a pew behind him.

'We are alone, Marco. I will hear you here so you can turn to me at any time, should you wish to do so. There is no need to pretend anonymity. I know your circumstances very well.'

'So, you know about Isabella . . .'

246

'First, my son, why are we here?'

'Bless me, Father, for I have sinned.'

'Believe you will be forgiven if you speak the truth.'

'I . . . don't know where to begin. I guess I've always been proud that I was the one Isabella chose, too proud maybe.'

'Pride is a difficult beast for the soul to deal with.'

'My pride has been attacked . . . by the Inglese. She has broken up with me. He changed her, filled her with ideas I do not understand. So . . . I attacked her . . . I accused her of not wanting to keep our promise to each other. She denied it. But she not only took a ride in his car, she also visited him. Fabio'—Marco remembers to cross himself —'he saw her there, at the villa. It made me too angry for words.'

Dom Pietro remains dutifully silent. Even if Jeremy did not try anything on Isabella, and her mother thinks not, her visit will have driven the likes of proud Marco mad with jealousy and rage. So what did the boy do to avenge those feelings? He must collect himself; the power of lust is too much at the front of his mind. He must be patient. Most confessions come on their own if the soul is not too weak to face them. And this is likely not an easy one; a soul undone by jealous rage. 'Too angry for words. I see.'

'I wanted revenge, Father. I have kept faith in the rights she promised me, and I was sure they were being stolen from me.'

Another long pause.

'What did you do, my son?'

'I was too angry. I didn't know what I was doing.'

Be patient, Dom Pietro reminds himself, thinking about how severe the penance will have to be for Marco to salvage his soul, if what he did was not consensual, but out of jealousy, and cannot be made now to morph into premarital eagerness Isabella shared at the time.

'It was when he showed up at Mass, and she sided with him, put me down. That did it for me. I couldn't take any more. I wanted my rights back, my place in her life.'

'My son, these rights you claim for yourself, they are not real. The only rights we all have are to the promise God made to us of salvation, our place next to Him. And if you've found yourself unworthy, seek forgiveness. That is why I am here for you.'

'I see, yes, Father.'

There is still no confession. Another long silence.

'Believe me, Marco, you can speak the truth and sincere penance will heal any wrongs you feel have offended the Lord's sacrifice for us.'

'I was so angry. I wanted to scare him away from here, from her. I did not attend Mass that day. I walked out before it began. I was full of hate. I wanted him to know he must go. I took a sharp stone and scratched his flash car.'

Dom Pietro suspects this is not the whole truth. Marco's soul is too weak. Or is his own soul too soiled by what he saw an hour ago? Has the day led him to evil assumptions that question everyone's sanctity?

'But you defended Isabella, didn't you, for her behaviour towards Jeremy in church?'

'She said she did it out of true faith.'

'You didn't believe her?'

'I wanted to find forgiveness for what I did by forgiving her for putting me down. I wanted to show her that what she did, did not change my feelings for her. But she still turned away from me. I thought, maybe, it is because I live in disfavour, for my sinful hatred.'

'I see. It's true that the Lord does not look kindly on hatred. Reconciliation with Him is, thankfully, always possible for anything we choose to repent, even mortal sins. He waits for us to seek it, for our own good, so that we may become better people when we do.'

'Yes, Father.'

Did he imagine that Marco faltered?

'So, you came to confess this anger to the Lord and what it did to you. Pray for His forgiveness and you will find it. And pray for Jeremy, the Inglese.'

'I do not think I can do that, Father.'

'Try. Pray that he may avoid temptation, free himself of it, free himself of the presence of Isabella. Pray that he leaves before Isabella falls victim to city morality we must question, though she may not question it, being so accustomed to your own virtuous behaviour. Her beauty and purity are precious. You have honoured them for many years. Do so now.'

'Y-yes, Father.'

He did falter. Unmistakeably.

'You've both been an example of faithful temperance we all take pride in. Nothing should stand in the way of your reconciliation with her, and with God.'

There is a fat pause. The pew is uncomfortable. Dom Pietro can assume the hard truth is more than just uncomfortable for Marco.

'I have wronged her, Father.'

'How, my son?'

'I . . . I insulted her purity. I mistrusted her innocence, her promise to me. I refused to believe her.'

'That is . . . regrettable.'

'But she's pure, isn't she, like you said? Nothing can change that about her. But I . . . accused her . . . of being the opposite, with the Inglese. I . . . degraded her.'

'In front of others?'

'A few . . . yes, Father.'

'Slandering another soul is a grave sin, my son.'

'I know, Father. I repent that I have done her wrong, deeply, inside. But I do not know how to show her, and God, that I repent what I did.'

Dom Pietro must end this confession. His assumptions of graver sin against Isabella are probably correct. What is preventing him from accepting the face value of the sin against Isabella that Marco has confessed? The truth is that this confession is too weak to be urgent. Envy, jealousy, slander, he well knows are rife in the village. But he could turn Marco's confession into an act of attrition, too sure the truth is more than he has been told or maybe wants to hear. He is not the Inquisition.

'Marco, you need only seek repentance through the Lord. He will guide you and forgive you. You may go.' Dom Pietro is aware that this is cruelly abrupt, but he must stop.

Marco does not go and now turns in his pew to face him. 'But, Father, what can I do? Now? I need your help, Father, please help me.'

'How can I help you, my son?'

'Isabella's mother has always been so kind to me. She said nothing but good things about me before. But today, after the concert, she again brushed me away; she will not talk to me. I have no way to explain myself to her. Maybe if she knew about my shame, how deeply sorry I am for what I have done to make Isabella angry, she would help me repair the match she wanted so much.'

So, is *this* the missing truth? This is not about repentance before God but an attempt by Marco to correct sinful behaviour with false piety in the hope he can be persuaded to use his influence as a priest to intervene. He must rebuke this in the strongest terms.

'Marco, I will not speak to Isabella's mother on your behalf. If you truly seek the grace of God, go to the Inglese, confess your crime, and face his wrath. If you truly seek the grace of God, openly confess the slander you have set in motion and face the anger you will meet from people who have trusted you. Face these things that have wronged God with true repentance, the repentance of a man before God. You are no longer a boy. Pray that He will strengthen your purpose. And do not add insult to injury by taking Holy Communion again until you have shown me, in His name, you repent and can reveal all sins you harbour in your soul. I will pray for you now. Go.'

His dismissal scalds Marco's face as he leaves. He made a real confession, didn't he? It was all there until the padre gave him the choice of slander. So, he opted out. But now, instead of coming out clean, he has made himself an outcast. Everybody knows what it means if he must skip Communion at Mass: no sacrament without true confession, everything else is sacrilege. And the padre knows somehow he is hiding the obvious, why Isabella will have nothing to do with him. But he wants her back. The current cannot be lost for good.

Dom Pietro waits till he hears the church door close and then kneels. He is not blessed with the sacred sufferance he hoped for as the church grows dark. It was wrong to forbid Marco Holy Communion; he is assuming the boy's state of grace would make it a sacrilege. His thoughts are invaded by a darker past he himself had to confess, images resurrected from the crypt of his conscience, encounters he had thought buried and at peace, questioning his worthiness before God, his right to guide others now, in His name, whose souls at any time may look no different than his did then.

His early priesthood is a litany of emotion and human weakness; he has found no blessing in response to his petitions to erase them from his own life, no matter how hard he has since disciplined himself to embrace the sanctity of his vows. His Church demands something from him not even God, knowing human frailty, can expect from His priests: the purity of spirit and conduct that governs his sacerdotal right to offer forgiveness in His name.

He prays well into the night until he is forced to obey the more temporal challenges in life: to let go of his bladder and appease his stomach.

Amnesia

'I sang . . . in the church.'

'Yes.'

'And then we came here, had some wine.'

'Yes. Lots.'

'You left me.'

'I went to cook lunch.'

'I came up here. Took some drops. Liquid Ecstasy. I know I wanted to get high for some reason, but I can't remember what it was.'

'I've hidden them. They're too dangerous, Vicky. You don't remember anything. You were practically unconscious for the last two hours. What's the point?'

'It's not always like that. I wrote something down. I remember that.'

'A message, to me.' Jeremy digs out the note from his pocket. 'And then?'

Vicky lifts her head from the cushions Jeremy put there to prop her up in bed. 'Oh, sooo dizzy.' She looks out the window past him, sitting at the foot of the bed, as if he is not there. 'Outside. I was out there, at the back. Everything was bright, too bright, too hot. I went under the trees, sat down . . . your dog . . . came too close . . . then, nothing.' She drops back on the cushions.

So, her body responded but not her mind with it. He had suspected that. Are there any physical sensations she might, at some point, remember? Jeremy gives Vicky her note. She reads it with difficulty, unable to focus properly.

'Don't think I want to understand this.'

'Look, at the words you capitalised. Pretty clever, for the state you were in. I looked for you everywhere before I caught on.'

'R-I-P?'

'A mortifying poke at grave sin, I would say.'

'I went to the crypt? You're joking! I don't believe this.'

'You don't remember?'

'Once the high wears off, I don't remember anything that happened in it, or too much directly before it.'

'You've done this often?'

'Just two drops the first time. I felt . . . euphoric, like a high on champagne. A few more and everything turns magic. You feel nothing but pleasure, all the senses are sweet sensation, if you don't take too much. I've never knocked myself out.'

'Well, it knocked you for six, that's for sure.'

Vicky turns over the note. 'Oh, you're right. Six drops. I always write it down. That's too many on top of alcohol.'

'When we met at the bar at the George Hotel, just before I came out here? You were all over me.'

'Don't remember that.'

'I let it pass then. I thought it was the champagne. You raised a few eyebrows.'

'I probably didn't want to be angry about you leaving. Today I was upset about something too. But what has that got to do with where you found me?'

'We sat together on the terrace after the concert. You weren't exactly sober. I guess you remembered your fantasy from when we looked at the crypt together; you wanted to spite the Catholics, the bishop, who thought it was a sin just to applaud you in church.'

Vicky reads it again. 'Wicked . . . yes. Romeo and Juliet. The crypt. I must have been daring myself to do it. So, more drops. Must have been more than six. Was I naked?'

'Goosebumped, yes.'

'Did you have a good time with me?'

'Vicky, please. Let's put this behind us.'

'I trust you. Something to hide?'

'Let's just say you weren't passive. And you were loud.'

'Did you carry me here—afterwards?'

'Yes. You scared the hell out of me, though. You bolted, like you were in a trance, hallucinating. You couldn't take the stairs out of there. You kept saying "let me go, let me go" and kicking your legs, but I was only trying to push you up since I couldn't get past to pull you out. When I got out, you were standing in the middle of the chapel staring at Mary in the stained-glass window. I

253

covered you. We stumbled out. I led you to the back door. Then you, well . . . collapsed, crashed out suddenly. I only just caught you. Your knee is bruised.'

Vicky throws off the sheet and stares at it as if it could help her remember anything. 'We had wine before?'

'As I said, lots.'

'Bad idea.'

'How are you feeling now?'

'Like shit. Fuzzy in the head, queasy.'

'I didn't dare leave you for a minute. I'll go get you something to drink now.'

'The crypt? I cannot believe it. We're confirmed sinners now, aren't we?'

'You're more wicked than anyone I know. But relax. Guilt is a Catholic power grab. There's no punishment; wait in vain.'

The first thing Jeremy notices when he enters the kitchen is the music score on the table. Then the empty bottle of water, a new glass next to it. The empty wine bottle on the table in the main room confirms that the one person who would take this licence paid them a visit. A priest may have personally confirmed they are sinners. And if so, Fabio was right: Domino is no guard dog.

Funeral

What remained of Fabio's body is finally being put to rest, forensically examined and cleared of any use of drugs that might explain his high-speed accident while driving on a local road renowned for being dangerous.

Standard insurance procedure is at fault for the delay, but at last the time has come to display village grief for the family surviving a son no one particularly liked and who has driven them to ruin. This public outpouring is a chance to sow and show solidarity, as encouraged by their padre, and a large number are gathered in procession behind the baby-sized coffin. Since it is known the family will be moving away, Fabio's final resting place is a corner spot with the solos, the unmarriable.

The volunteer pall-bearers are Fabio's friends: Marco, keen to shore up good-citizen status; Ramiro and Francesco, who could ruin it for him; and other members of the gang. They are dressed appropriately for this solemn occasion, although their dark confirmation suits of yesteryear—in foresight oversized when they first wore them—have reached the limits of later alteration.

The church bell rings in apology for questionable sincerity in single tones, the long pause between them suggesting each strike remembers a year of the twenty-one prior to Fabio's meetup with the ultimate judge of his moral character. He is five when the coffin appears at the church's doorway and only twelve when the occasional howl of grief from his mother, walking directly behind the coffin within hand's reach, collides with the insistent beeping of Vicky's cell phone, placed beside her while she is sitting down on the steps of the cafe terrace to enjoy an ice cream—only reluctantly sold to them—and ignoring Jeremy's protest that she should stand and show some respect, which she is no mood to do for villagers who, in her opinion, have shown her none.

She hands her cone to Jeremy after many rings, not wanting to appear too eager to the person returning her call.

At the head of the procession, Dom Pietro, head bent reverently, steals an occasional glance at his sacrilegious sinners: Jeremy is standing, abashed by the looks he is attracting, unable to turn away from them, clownishly caught out, pantomiming sorrow with a melting ice cream in each hand. Madame, trying to hear and be heard on her cell phone, again ignores any sensitivity for where she is and again, more publicly expressed, any respect for the dead.

What Jeremy sees in the procession is a slow-motion retake of the faces he saw on the trailer the day he arrived, confirming their contemptuous disregard for him. One of those faces is particularly venomous, and he would hide from it if he could; Fabio's father cannot be bribed into accepting his innocence, and if he knew the real story, Jeremy would land up where Fabio is now going.

Vicky's conversation on the phone ends as the tail end of the procession passes by on the final bell of Fabio's life. She is upset when Jeremy returns her ice cream. She takes it from him and throws it angrily on the ground in front of her. La Scala is off. This unsweetened news is an unexpected gag on her career so far. She looks down the steep road leading off the square to see the bent backs of the procession's trailing mourners, brushes away Jeremy's consoling hand on her shoulder, stands, steps around the ugly mess she has just made, and turns back to him before heading for the car. 'I'm leaving on the first plane home tomorrow!'

Isabella is unnerved by the scene below her, seen from her mother's window. Who was the man she met? How can she compare what he expressed to her to his attraction for this brash woman? Her good looks, fine clothes, and voice cannot excuse this thoughtless behaviour. Jeremy is not like that. She saw him try to make her stand up, but she brushed his hand away. He is not the same in this woman's company: insecure, under her thumb.

Did she keep him under her thumb too? She was suspicious of his self-control, the tension she could feel in it, what was lurking behind it. She did not want to hear him admit it, to be left only with the choice of either refusing or giving in to him. She wanted to keep him where she put him, where he said he would stay. Is she any different from this woman outside her window, then? She made Jeremy dishonest, made him suppress feelings for her she could not return. But if those were genuine, what does he see in a woman like this singer? What could he get out of being with either of us?

The answer is in the procession below her: Marco pretending to be solemn, carrying the coffin of someone she knows he did not even like. The unwanted question about Jeremy takes her back out onto the field where Marco took what he wanted by the force pressing down on his offended ego. What he did is unforgivable— and her own fault, her own shame for pretending that what she could plainly see ignited both men could be left to burn and flicker at the altar of her chaste pride. That pride was real to her, nothing to do with belief but fidelity to the faith she wants to have in herself and what she feels.

Jeremy must have seen that; able to behave as a mature man, he obeyed when she refused what he wanted her to give in to. 'If it's not right for you, it's not right for me,' he said. Did he want something different from her? What he took in exchange is the woman she sees outside her window. She feels sorry for him, watching him unable to do anything about this woman's shameless disrespect, trying to express his sorrow for Fabio's family but standing there like an unwanted mourner, guiltily holding an ice cream in each hand. How awkward and unsure he looks compared to the man she first saw one morning sitting on the steps and drinking coffee. She can see that all heads in the procession are turned in his—their—direction. Any further visits to the village will be openly shunned from now on, and any further contact with him is definitely out.

His reputation in the village will nevertheless always weigh down on her own, even if she no longer feels the need to shield herself against rumours. If he and this singer are a couple, she can be thankful her pride has protected her. It is a shame, though, that the 'something different' she thought he saw in her was probably not real. Beauty will not let her be the person she wants people to see.

Dropped off

Vicky rejected any attempts by Jeremy to console her, refusing his offer in the car after the call to take her to the abbey town for lunch; she berated him instead for convincing her to join him 'in this dump', as if her visit was somehow the cause of her misfortune.

After cold cuts and salad for lunch—'You don't even have a proper kitchen to cook here!'—she went up for a siesta 'alone!'. The disquiet in the villa botched his attempt at making a reed, which split. She spent the whole afternoon licking her wounded pride in bed, then packed. He heard her in the shower and announced he was on the roof terrace. She did not join him; he drank the Prosecco on his own. When he went down and found her on the terrace, sulking through her own almost empty bottle of wine, he suggested with bravado that a few drops of euphoria might help her over her disappointment.

'You mean punishment, don't you?'

'It was not meant to be an encrypted reference.'

She went berserk, attempting with her glass to shatter the invisible Catholic seal on her conscience for good, leaving him to sweep it up in the candle-lit darkness.

By the time he dropped her off at the airport this morning— she not knowing what flight, if any, she could catch—it was clear that he was the one being dropped off. He could not help feeling a bit relieved, being no longer forced to cope with her mood swings for another four days and forgo the practice her presence had mostly denied him. He decided on the way home he must now wind up his stay at the villa. There is no longer any charm in it, and there will be no Vicky clamouring for his attention when he gets back to London. The only charm in staying is no longer within reach, defies any sense of proportion or logic he can apply to still wanting Isabella.

Interrogation

There was a more pressing reason to have left earlier and avoid everything that has happened since, he realises, when he drives around the side of the villa to the back courtyard, accompanied by Domino's ecstatic yelps and leaps. But there is no one waiting inside or beside the police car to meet him. Jeremy gets out of his car and bends down to greet Domino.

'Nice work, mate. Good guard dog. These guys are suspect, and you sent them running. When they come back, bark like hell. I'll be ready.'

Jeremy goes inside, his mind racing for answers to questions he can only guess, running through the race again as he rushes into the kitchen to quench his dry mouth. Any number of drivers could have reported seeing them; both of their cars were 'flash'. And swallowing a second glass more slowly, he remembers: it must be the delivery van, that was the closest call involving any other drivers—a near miss of a head-on collision for him. If you're right, you're one step ahead, he thinks. Now play dumb, and get busy. He rushes to the music room, picks up his oboe, and hears Domino barking. He smiles, terrified, wets the reed, and starts playing, waiting for the angel, again, to knock on his door. This time it does.

'Are you the owner of the BMW parked outside?'

'I am.'

'May we come inside, to ask you a few questions?'

'Ah, I know, about the registration? I was stopped a few times already. It is provisional. I picked up the car in Munich on my way here from England.'

'It is not about your registration. It's a more delicate matter. May we come in?'

'Of course.'

Jeremy faces questions from the inspector, whose near perfect English from working in a homicide unit in the US put him on this case. The second policeman waits outside the door to the main room. The two men are sitting at the long table.

'So, you know the road I am referring to?'

'Oh, yes, I have been on it quite often, in fact.'

'And two weeks ago?'

'That would be a Wednesday? Yes, I went for a drive. I visited the abbey town. I like going there to walk around. It's a bit prettier than the village here. Why do you ask?'

'Were you driving fast?'

'Well, I admit, I still occasionally misjudge the speed of my car. It's new, you see. Have I earned a fine?'

The inspector ignores this. 'Very fast? Maybe racing?'

'On these roads? Can I ask what this is about?'

'The description of your car matches one we have of a car that was racing against the red Alfa, owned by your neighbour, before he crashed and died.'

'Fabio. His accident was on the same day, of course. It was on that road, then?'

'You deny you raced against him?'

'I think evil gossip is causing some confusion here. Everybody assumes I'm out to prove something with my car. I'm not, and certainly not on that dangerous road.'

'But you did meet the red Alfa on that day, according to our account.'

'He did pass me on the road that day, yes. I didn't think anything of it until now. I certainly didn't make any connection to what happened to him when I heard about it. I didn't know where he crashed.'

'Do you remember when he overtook you? Where that was?'

'Which part of the road? No. I don't know it *that* well.'

'So, you remember he passed you.'

'Yes. I was trailing behind a delivery van at the time, I think.'

'And then?'

'Then what?'

'You didn't chase him?'

'Oh, please, why on earth would I do that? Look, I had an accident myself just a few months ago, on a motorbike, going too fast. It was my own fault. Nearly cost me my career as a musician. If I was reckless then, I certainly am not now.'

'Our account says you both overtook his van on a bend?'

'We were coming out of it, I think. Right-hand drive makes it impossible for me to overtake unless the road is straight or veering left; I cannot see what's coming otherwise. When Fabio passed me, I assumed the road was clear, so I followed him then, yes, overtaking the van. But that turned out to be a mistake. There were oncoming cars I only saw when he pulled in. I had no time to overtake myself. I had to brake hard and slip back behind. By the time I could overtake the van, he was gone, out of sight.'

'He was driving fast, then.'

'He must have been because I didn't see him again. It did not surprise me he was driving fast.'

'Because you knew he was expecting you to chase him?'

'Listen, from the first day I met Fabio, he could talk of nothing else but fast cars, of owning the Alfa. He wanted to drive the BMW, but I wouldn't let him. His mother begged me not to encourage him. I didn't. But that didn't stop her from accusing me of 'possessing him', as she put it, to buy the car. He was not a bad sort, their son, but maybe too proud to accept that what he saved every penny for was pure foolishness, and dangerous. I dare not go over there now to express my condolences. I am the devil incarnate—because of the car I own.'

'His father is extremely angry.'

'He has made that pretty obvious. And he should be, but with himself, not me. Why didn't *they* stop him buying the damned car? He evidently already had an accident some time ago.'

'It was not his fault, according to our records.'

'Does it matter? That was a tragedy. This is a tragedy for the whole family, also financially, according to Signor Peroni.'

'Is that why you gave them this?' The inspector holds out the envelope containing two thousand pounds in lira Jeremy left inside their door with the letter Vicky helped him write to them.

'They are poorer than poor now, Signor Peroni said, ruined. I wanted to help.'

'Maybe you feel guilt for what has happened?'

'Guilt? No. I certainly have nothing to feel guilty about. But I understand why I am accused. I understand that without intending it, I influenced the young man by having the money to do what he always wanted to do: buy a fast car. The damage is done. I decided I could help by paying the extortionate waiver on his insurance.'

'It is a lot of money here. Very generous.'

'It was a stupid policy, insane.'

'But I regret to tell you that Fabio's father is as proud as his son. He has asked me to return it, and your letter, to you.'

'Heh? Did I get this all wrong? I understood they needed a bailout.'

'I think it is more a private matter.'

'You may think so, but if they haven't accepted this because they know I'm suspected, unfairly, of racing their son, I will have to lock myself in here, especially from the father, or leave here at the peril of his dogs attacking me.'

'Details of any investigation are never discussed with any party. As I say, I think it's a private matter. You've explained the events that have somehow been misinterpreted by . . . another road user.'

'I wish I could put this blame game behind me.'

'I assumed that, even before I knocked on your door. No one is ever comfortable being accused, guilty or not. But we have to investigate everything, of course, in fatal incidents like this until we are sure.'

'And now?'

'I will close this case and return your money. Will you count it please?'

When Jeremy has finished thumbing through the bills, the amount is short. He knows why the inspector has not watched him count.

'Is everything in order?'

'Yes, fine. Thank you.'

Echoes and sounds

The longer notes are reliably stable now, the fingerwork involving his fourth and little finger on the right hand can still present a problem, especially D/E trills in Mozart's concerto. But, overall, he has managed to retrain his hold of the oboe so that he is relaxed enough to play as he would like; the endless hours of intense practice that have kept him in this godforsaken place for the last two weeks have at least accomplished what he needed them to do.

Less satisfactory of late is the reed making, every second one failing for one reason or another, giving him reason to doubt that his new method is blessed to replace the old curse of producing them. Luckily, he has a sufficient stock not to panic anymore about the tour; rehearsals start in four weeks.

The snooker room, once a place of respite, is now a satin-draped den of dark tension; the chandelier no longer brightens any improvement in his game. He more often messes up the clean shots he used to sink with ease, so when they do find the pocket, it is difficult to follow up on the next shot with any winning sense of purpose, or clarity, of delight and fun. The game has lost its innocent, seductive charm; Isabella and Vicky have left him to compete against himself, against the frustration with either pole the two women represent in his snookered ego.

His self-imposed isolation is coming to an end at a time when it could not be more severe. He has steered clear of the village since Vicky left, not wanting to absorb the animosity he is sure he would face. It would be strongest from Dom Pietro if he indeed saw them in the crypt; the discord sown by the concert was a petty misunderstanding compared to the screeching sacrilegious encore that followed it.

Jeremy is still unable to fathom why he played along, as if some undefined force possessed him, overriding reason, risk, reluctance. That he was half drunk when he discovered her naked, and at once felt the urge to take her as she lay there, does not explain it.

Abusing her drugged state of mind and not having to invoke her desire before he forced his own sodomitic lust on her were not just wildly carnal and wicked; he relished the unconditional possession of her body, belonging only to himself, obeying his incarnate wants. It was only afterwards as she lay comatose in bed that he felt fear for the uncontained and deliberate evil he was capable of—or more accurately—his fear of not fearing it.

After the inspector left that day, he was possessed by another fear: Fabio's dogs, or rather his father's. He had referred to it flippantly, but it was earnest. He had not ventured out on any walks with Domino before this afternoon. Now they are gone.

He woke up this morning to the noisy commotion of the family's departure outside his bedroom window. The sheep were all herded onto a transport, and behind it, on an open-bed truck, their meagre belongings were stacked and tied down.

This was the price they were willing to pay to reject him, to refuse his offer of help? Jeremy was lost about what he felt. Did his offer exonerate him? He could not compose an answer, but he could hear it standing at the window of his bedroom—the loud bleating of the sheep calling up an imagined orchestra out of control in the pit, the different instruments of his conscience trying to find some stability, a place to begin. His brassy pretence and strings of doubt whirled through the scales in frenzied search of a common key, any leading tone of integrity ignored; what was right about him could not be played through with any sense of synchrony, any good intentions scattered in noisy emotional confusion. *Mea culpa* jangled in his ears like loud clashing cymbals, and behind them, timpani drums pounded him insistently with guilt that a triangle soon strikes out, an indiscriminate cynical pitch to its ring.

Standing at the window, he forced the noises outside to take over: the sheep called back the day the garden was ravaged by them until it was naked, without redress for what was lost. A despicable lout was responsible for the scene below, not him. His generosity was innocent; he is the only one who could afford it, and that's all there is to it. As Vicky said, he is a 'good man'. But the cynical ring of the triangle returned as the small convoy started to move, and Fabio's mother looked up at his window as if she knew he was there.

'Fabio, what must he learn?'

'To find compassion.'

He had done his best to show compassion, he decided. He turned away from the window and resolved to believe nothing else. It was an accident.

The experiment

His compassion belongs to his one unquestioning faithful companion, lying next to him, looking up at him. Jeremy bends down from his chair on the terrace and strokes Domino's head, moving his hand from near the tip of the dog's nose up between and then around his ears.

'Don't worry, mate. We're sticking together. It's a long drive plus two weeks of quarantine, but we like dogs where I come from. You'll get used to the weather; we all do—it gives us something to talk about.'

His companion's obedient warmth consoles Jeremy, alleviates the morose mood the morning's events have put him in. He wants to escape that mood, the culpability attached to it. A few of Vicky's drops, just a few, might pick him up, help his escape.

He takes a few drops in a replenished glass of wine, sets up a rack on the snooker table, and begins to play. Many minutes go by without any effect: the dose is too weak. He refills his glass and adds a few more drops. A short while later, the journey he will never remember begins.

The colour of the balls on the table suddenly becomes so intense that he sees it trailing like a holographic stream behind the trajectory of any ball he hits, revealing its direct angle of approach to the pocket. He does not wait to see the result of one shot before taking the next. The balls are all full of energy; he can hear the loud clack when they clash and feel the sharp impact of the stroke shoot up his arm from the cue as he makes it. What fun! Clear the table! Forget the rules!

He stands at one end of the table and shoots with anything at anything at the other end, soon not sure if the ball he is trying to hit is still moving or if his focus is playing tricks. He waits until they must all have stopped before he continues, shoots again, hard, pots the eight ball.

'Brav—oh'

The ball miraculously pops out halfway through his bravo; the pocket is already full.

It feels a little bit like he is drunk, and not just his head but his whole body is light, as if suspended, underwater, a sensation that makes any movements seem hampered and effortless at the same time. His senses are all alive, hyperactive, even his clothes feel rough on his skin; he strips down to his underpants, feels the tingle of a faint warm breeze coming through the window as he moves there, greedily swigging the cool wine left in his refilled glass. It is beautiful at dusk here: opaque blue-grey sky with brilliant streaks of orange and red. The yellow tentacles of the violet-red bougainvillea just below the window hypnotise him until he reaches for one and pricks himself on a thorn.

Thumb bleeding, he continues his game at the table with a burst of restless energy, hitting at random, laughing at his hopeless coordination, a loud 'yahoo!' when he sinks anything. There is nothing left to focus on when at last the table is clean, and a dull, confused tiredness sucks him in, slowly removing any coherence that still clings to his fuzzy awareness. He must not stand here. He hears a voice in his head.

'Give in to it, Romeo.'

That's Vicky.

The cryptic mystic.

The creepy sleepy nympho.

'Jeremiah. My pleasure.'

'Stay high. Don't let go. Play something, you brute.'

Too fast. The door to his music room moves. He slams into the frame, falls, struggles to his feet, topples the music stand. Oboe? On its pedestal. Reed. The case snaps open and several reeds fall out onto the workbench, the floor. This one will do. The first short note crashes through his eardrums like a blaring high-pitched siren, rattling the dulled synapses in his head. His right elbow jabs into his body in an involuntary reflex. Strong, familiar routine allows him to play a few hardwired strains from pieces he has practiced that his memory calls up at random. But he can hardly bear the sound in this confined space. Up to the roof terrace! His open-air stage!

267

The height of each step changes as he climbs; his foot is either too high above or too far below the tread. He stamps and stumbles up, hanging on to the balustrade, the near falls catching his knees and shin bones—but at last he reaches the terrace, the open sky compelling a euphoric feeling of freedom, heroically achieved. He must play for Signora Tendri! But there are other associations with being up here. Randomly reduced, they are now scattered on what is left of cognitive thought, and one is invasive.

'This is for you, Mother!'

It is not melodious, not timed, notes played with beginner's fingerwork, foraging for meaning and context borrowed from any composition that fleetingly comes to mind only to disappear as quickly as it came to him: a modern piece, delightful. But the pressure is too much, all in his head, on his lips, punching his thorax. He stumbles to the sunbed, sits, falls back. The stars are falling on him, and the barking and howling dogs across the valley are moving towards him.

Blackout.

Hours later, he comes to. His slow-beating heart and sluggish blood leave him feeling cold in the temperate night air—the first sensation he is aware of before he forces his eyes open. He is outside, naked, on the sunbed. Up here? When? Why? Spasms through his body during his comatose spell threw off the oboe he held onto; he sees it lying on the terrace floor beside him, no longer conscious of having come up here to play. He feels nauseous, dizzy. His legs are covered in bruises; painful dark-blue welts on his pale skin betray the bleached-out memory he will never reclaim, trapped between illusion and reality. He tries to stand. It is difficult to move. This physical certainty gives him sufficient hold on himself to regain some orientation despite his dizziness, but the top flight of stairs is all his leaden body on aching knees will allow. He goes straight to his bedroom and collapses on his bed.

Rude awakening

It was late morning by the time insistent loud barking woke him up, vocalising fear and panic that immediately took hold of him. What happened? The sound took him back to what he could remember: sitting on the terrace with Domino, opening the concealed drawer in the secretaire, and putting a few drops of Vicky's love potion in his wine glass, then racking up in the billiard room. Then . . . nothing. Nothing? Yes, nothing.

He was afraid of what he would discover and was oddly comforted to see Domino, out of bounds, at the foot of the stairs. He walked into the main room and saw the main door wide open. The snooker room window was also wide open, his clothes on the floor, the chandelier still on. The upturned music stand and scattered unprotected reeds lying directly in the sun on the floor of the music room alarmed him. The bigger fright: his oboe was missing. Only then did he recall having been awake at some point during the night and where he was then, at least.

Amnesia is an appeal to shadows that have lost their source of light to show themselves. Jeremy sees his own against the wall of the music room now and imagines it will have its own secret life once the light from the window is gone. What his shadow did two nights ago is still a mystery; the trail of clues tell him only that whatever took place was uncontrolled, and as Vicky proved, would never be recaptured. She was practicing the next day by the afternoon, not at all disturbed by her experience. It took him two whole days to recover enough from his stupor and do more than get to the bathroom to puke his stomach out. He should not have experimented on his own. His missteps in the music room crushed two reeds he was particularly pleased with, but otherwise the night's damage was not as severe as it presumably could have been; his oboe survived its unexplainable role in the sleepwalk that also bruised his left forehead.

269

He has been practicing today with resolute concentration, as if he must rule out that his memory loss could return and must be compensated by as much diligence as his still torpid body will allow. He is deciding what to play next when a deep rumble invades the room. He cannot tell where it is coming from. It does not stop.

Two huge stone wheels rotating slowly in a trough filled with olives being crushed to a pulp are the source of the noise Jeremy heard, coming from the ground floor of the annex building. He sees them through wide open doors on the garden side of the villa. Giorgio and his workers do not notice him, as if hypnotised by the rotating wheels, their eyes fixed on them and the mush in the trough.

Giorgio nods, and the wheels are stopped. His workers lower the trough and begin to ladle the olive paste out of it with large metal scoops. Next to the crusher is a cylindrical column around which round fibre mats are stacked. The paste is spread onto a mat and then placed on top of the column, followed by another mat and more paste. When the trough under the crusher is empty, Giorgio nods again. An enormous heavy stone is slowly lowered onto the column of mats, pressing down on the sandwich. The liquid flows down to a tray with a siphon tap and is caught in wooden buckets that are carried to the waiting clay vats in the cellar next door.

Everything is raised and lowered with brute strength assisted by pulleys and cranks. Were it not for the heavy-duty motor that replaced oxen rotating the crusher wheels, Jeremy thinks, this would have been more medieval than *artigianale*. He cannot imagine what the advantage could be. He watches the bustle of the workers until Giorgio spots him—and turns away?

'Molto impressio*nan*te,' Jeremy offers as he goes over.

'Sono occupato, cosa vuoi?'

The bluntness is intentional, insulting. They have not met up for some time, but he is not prepared for this rude tone. There could be any number of reasons for it; he is not sure which apply, or if it is one he is even aware of.

270

'It's about the dog. I will be leaving soon, and we should talk.'

'The dog stays here. It is not a city dog.' Like you are, Giorgio might have added in the same derogatory tone.

'But he's very attached to me meanwhile,' Jeremy says, hoping '*vicino*' means 'close' as he intends it.

'You did not feed him for almost two days. Did you notice he was not hungry when you did?'

'I was . . . sick . . . in bed.'

'I took care of him before and will again.'

'And tie him up?'

'That is my business.'

'Giorgio, why?' Jeremy is pleading.

'You city types are not to be trusted. With your fancy fast cars, fancy clothes, fancy women who flatter themselves. Who do you think you are, Jeremy, messing around with our lives here? Go back to your own type, like Riccardo.' Giorgio turns and goes back to work.

This broadside, about-face contempt leaves Jeremy bewildered, not only for its vehemence but also because it is fake, must be fake, put on. Their fraternity in the cellar and since, the tasting session with Vicky that morning in the courtyard, the enthralled look on Giorgio's face he caught at the concert—it all tells him Giorgio must be pretending hostility he does not truly believe in. But where does it come from?

He knows his temporary negligence of Domino has already been forgiven. When the dog appears from around the side of the villa, Jeremy pats his knees to call him. Domino runs over and lets himself be coddled. Jeremy waits until he is sure Giorgio has taken this in. Bringing the point home is unlikely to change anything, but what happens to Domino is his business, not Giorgio's. He will steal away with the dog if necessary. He cannot leave him here.

Faithless departure

Giorgio again looks like an overgrown schoolboy, with scruffy cap in hand, in front of Dom Pietro in the back courtyard, seen again from the same bedroom window. Even if it is a lot less hot these days than last time he saw them standing there, Jeremy still has the urge to lie down in the afternoon for an hour or so, and after his recent experiment, it has no longer been optional. He was not sleeping when he heard their familiar voices. Dom Pietro's fingers are pointing accusingly in the direction of the BMW; Giorgio nods sadly as he listens before lifting an outstretched arm in the direction of Fabio's abandoned house.

The cliché gestures of Italians tell the whole story: Giorgio is toeing the priest's line, and Dom Pietro is inciting the animosity Isabella came that day to warn him about after the accident. It has only grown since in the village, for sure—maybe hers towards him, too, after Vicky's appearance? No doubt Vicky's 'holy man' has taken a hard hit on his reputation for associating with them, but he is the one who made the rules the community lives by, which means his coercive grip is not based on anything real. His hold on the locals, like Giorgio, is a fake reality, built on the self-serving, ridiculous pretence Pater Robinson revealed: 'Whatever you do as a human being, Jeremy, you have already pledged your soul to God through us, and it will never find salvation without our proper guidance.' This priest, at least, will want to axe communication with him; public association with him is a liability. His gamble has backfired.

And Jeremy plans to go, in his own time. He chooses a cleanly pressed smart outfit to change into from his shorts and T-shirt—both to hide his black-and-blue legs and to remind the priest he is not of the poor obedient village class that can be pushed around. City type? That's my dominion, you bet.

272

There is a knock at the back door; the priest is not just barging in unannounced as he pleases. That's a good start. He goes to the door.

'You are on your way out?'

'Oh, no, although I might go out after my practice.'

'Practice or dress rehearsal?'

'Whatever you make of it. Come in.'

Jeremy appeared at the door in a tailored, light-grey shirt, dark trousers, and an elegant pair of black Italian loafers he bought during his visit to Rome: it is most definitely fashionable city apparel. As he speaks, he leads Dom Pietro inside to the music room where he was working on a reed earlier in the day.

'You have it easy, Dom Pietro. You go around in the same outfit every day, and your image is safe, accepted everywhere. The rest of us are always rehearsing how to dress up our image and approval rating. I wore something similar for the concert. I thought I would give myself a head start, presuming you're here'— he turns to face the priest—'to give me a dressing down?'

'I think fancy clothes genuinely suit your character, Jeremy. You pretend to be one thing one day and are someone else the next.'

'Well, I didn't make any promises to fit the Catholic mould you preach and expect everyone to fill, so I haven't broken any.'

'It is what happens inside that mould, whether you should be afraid of breaking it because it protects you or something you choose to shatter and accept the consequences.'

'I was sure you'd given up on me. Don't try so hard if your heart's not in it. You sound like my old Pater Robinson.'

'He and I were both concerned for your welfare.'

'Forgive me, like hell he was. He was only interested in obedience to the Church.'

'That may be your view, but he remembers you well. He regrets you chose to rebel.'

'May I ask what gives you the right to be snooping around in my past?'

'I simply wanted to know, after the fact, if there was ever any point in anyone being concerned for your spiritual welfare.'

'The protective arm of the Church has reached out again. The seed cannot penetrate the barren soil. You must be disappointed.'

'Stay a soloist. You're on your own. Fight your own battles with yourself, alone.'

'Wasn't that how we met? Don't hold it against me. I don't hold your faith against you. It has been very helpful, in fact. If my success with these reeds isn't just coincidence, the good Lord above heard you and cannot think too badly of me either. I'm getting something to drink.'

Dom Pietro can see that Jeremy's vanity, his profanity, is out in full colour now, no longer masked. How could he have been so mistaken about him? He must rid himself of this obscene misuse of his trust, and his vain trust in his own judgement. Dom Pietro thinks about how he can force Jeremy's hand and make him leave when he realises the solution is in his hands.

When Jeremy returns with two glasses and a bottle of wine, he declines. He wants to leave as soon as he can. 'So, you've done what you set out to do, coming here?'

'Well, for the most part, yes.'

'You're sure you've done enough dishonour to the Church you despise?'

'Dom Pietro, please . . .'

'You're sure you've done enough damage to my reputation in my church?'

'Not guilty! Your indoctrination of the village against sin city outsiders like me decided my reputation the day I arrived. If your association with me has turned your pulpit into my pillory, join the club. Cheers. Blame yourself.'

'I only blame myself, Jeremy, for believing I could trust your sense of judgement, goodwill, and respect toward the people here.'

'And theirs towards me?'

'Your concert debased the sanctity of their church, and you know it.'

'Vicky was provoked by your pompous bishop. No applause, please, just a stone-faced audience that wasn't sure if it's OK to show they liked the performance.'

'It was hedonistic and profane.'

'If the straitjacket conformity you demand of your holier-than-thou following has backfired on you, it's your own doing. The goodwill you were aiming for was a bit one-sided.'

'Nevertheless, I must ask you to leave.'

'I am not under your fiefdom, Dom Pietro. I am here as a guest of Riccardo Patricelli, in his house, and I will leave it when I'm ready. I have no intention to return to your village.'

'But Riccardo does. People are judged by the company they keep.'

'That has not worked out for me in your company, unfortunately.'

'His family's reputation here matters to him. He is unable to reach you here by phone. He asked me to convey to you that you should leave before further conflicts arise.'

'Those only exist because of the intolerance you preach, the scaremongering scandal it breeds. I'll speak to him myself.'

'Jeremy, I think you fail to understand that what you think of us here makes no difference. Riccardo depends on the loyalty and goodwill of workers from the village to run this estate.'

'I don't think restoring the chapel on their backs is a cause he is attached to or that you have done much to create any goodwill for him. He could pay for the restoration himself if he saw any sense in it. Riccardo is a well-paid conductor, as far removed from your villagers as they are from him, or me, or Vicky. He doesn't need this place, and he's certainly not devout.'

'You are slandering your host!'

'Which can only mean I have at last fallen in line with your villagers. Get to grips with your sanctimonious following, Dom Pietro, they'll get over it.'

'And this from you? After you tried to bribe your way out of guilt for the accident you caused? After you've pretended faith to pry a village girl away from hers? You're as sacrilegious as they come, Jeremy, and I know how much delight you take in it. You will pay for it. But I warn you: stay out of the village. And hands off Isabella!' the priest shouts behind him as he leaves.

Jeremy is left with the untied knots of what the priest knows. Did the inspector talk? Does Fabio's father know? Is that what turned Giorgio against him? Has Isabella buckled and retreated under her bubble, talking him down? Were they seen in the crypt? Is Riccardo more tied down here than he let on? What in God's name is the point of thinking about these things?

It is time to send the orchestra in his head packing that again wants his attention. It is time to leave this orchestrated pit of fake morality. He is dressed now to go out and ignore it. Rome is too far. But a drive to the abbey town, for a late lunch at the trattoria and a grappa on the pleasant town square, is a good way to put it all behind him before he starts to pack tomorrow.

Take 2

Isabella knows she will have to prove herself. She is not really qualified for the job yet. They said that indirectly by admitting their first choice backed down. She doesn't know if the salary they offered is fair, but it is three times her nursery pay. And it is a start, a real job: a trainee export clerk, with her own desk, phone, and a typewriter. She has loads to learn, not to forget improving her English. It worries her they just took her word for it, and she is far from ready even though she has spent hours cramming her course since they asked her back.

Angelina was thrilled for her, also with the idea they could meet more often now. Her girlfriend insisted they have a glass of Prosecco to celebrate, and it turned into two, which made Isabella so light-headed she had to nap for an hour. But her mother knows where she went today and was relieved she would still be living in the village if she got the job. They both fear her father's reaction, though.

Anger is all he knows these days, threatening his daughter with 'Marco, or on your own, go!' until her mother screamed back at him with more heated anger than Isabella ever knew she had: 'She stays, or I go!' The shock is still there, her father spending even longer evenings at the card table but her mother visibly calmer now. 'Let's give it time,' she said, 'see what change the Lord is preparing us for.' Her mother has even tried a few words in English for the fun of it.

Jeremy on the way back from his late abbey lunch decided against provocation, circumventing rather than taking the shortcut through the village; he is heading down to take the track to the villa from the main trunk road, where Isabella just got off the bus. He sees her walking up to the village and slows right down. It is not the girl he met here months ago, he can see that in her walk, the smart clothes she is wearing, a proper handbag on her

277

shoulder, and her hair neatly clasped back from her face, a bewildered look on it on seeing his car. Her walk falters, and he does a U-turn up-road from her and waits.

He has a few moments to question why he did not simply greet her from the opposite side of the road and move on. But he is damned if he will do as he has been told by Dom Pietro and keep his distance; this is their last opportunity for a U-turn after she stormed out of the villa last time she visited. Her connection to him is the only one that has not been fake, not denied by prejudice forced upon her. Is that still the case?

He can see in his rear-view mirror how she has changed: quickly finding her composure, resuming her unhurried pace in elegant shoes, flicking her hair back from her neck; all this belongs to the poised behaviour of a woman, not a shy village girl.

And he made this happen, didn't he? Their meeting across the age gap transformed her awareness of herself. He turns around in his seat to look at her as she approaches the car. She does not immediately return his smile, annoyed perhaps by attraction she cannot hide when she sees him, answering its pull only slowly with a hesitant smile, afraid to let go of the girl and be the woman he is sure she wants him to see in her.

'Cara Isabella, how nice to see you.'

'Hello, Jeremy.'

'You look really smashing—sorry, I mean you look perfect in that outfit. It suits you.'

'Thank you. It is kind you say so.'

'But you will ruin those lovely shoes on this rough road. Let me give you a lift to the village.'

She looks away from him into the distance; the soft squint in her eyes is not against the late afternoon sun. 'There is too much talk, Jeremy. I am sorry to you about my village, but a lift is not OK now.'

'I know that, Isabella. I meant up to the village, not the *piazzale*.' Intentionally mispronounced.

'*Piazzale*,' she corrects with an amused lift of her now carefully trimmed and highlighted eyebrows.

'My Italian has not improved.'

'My English must get better than now . . . *significativo*'—she holds up a hand to stop him—'significantly.'

He beams a significant, delighted, and encouraging smile at her, earning a modest smile in return. 'Is your English still a secret?'

'No, it is necessary.'

'Ah, the clothes. No more nursery? You have a new job?'

She nods yes, sweeps her hand down in front of her fitted blouse and knee-length skirt. 'In an office, in town.'

'*Fantastico!* I want to hear more. A short drive? English only.'

'Jeremy, I am sorry. I must protect me.'

'Myself, protect myself. But not from me, I hope. I will not misunderstand you a second time. My hands stay here, promise, at the steering wheel. And the air con stays off today,' he chuckles.

The reminder still produces a tinge of bashful colour on her cheeks that he detects before her head bows and she thinks things over. She then looks at him with a calm directness new to him, and her, too, probably. 'OK, I like to drive with you and talk. But not to the village.' She motions to him to turn back around—the U-turn he was hoping for.

As soon as they reached the main trunk road, she directed him off it, along quieter country roads. His destination was to restore her confidence, hers was to find it at a safe distance ahead of him. He did his best to show he was excited about her new job. When he said, 'It's your ticket to freedom', she corrected him and said she intended to stay in the village. And then he corrected her by saying that he meant her independence, making new choices for herself. That was a good answer. He did understand her.

'It was a good concert in church. It was not understanded by the village.'

'It was not understood by the village.'

'Thank you.'

'Not surprising. Vicky treats her own independence as if other people's ideas are not important to her. You wouldn't do that. She did the last part without telling anyone in advance. She just kept singing.'

'It was very . . .'

'Passionate, provocante.'

'English only, Jeremy.'

'She went overboard. Over the top. Overdoing things.'

'These are sayings?'

'They all mean *troppo* one way or another. The bishop was not amused because she ignored that he, or the villagers, would have any doubts. She's not used to that.'

There is a pause. He knows what's coming.

'And for you? She's your woman friend, no?'

'Isabella, don't believe everything you think you see or what other people, like Marco, tell you. People in the city have a different connection with each other. I met her through Riccardo Patricelli; we're all colleagues, just friends. He sent her to the villa to have a holiday and said she should do a concert with me. It was Dom Pietro's idea. I guess once she was in the church, she wanted to show she was a better performer than her sister, who sings in churches all over Italy. So, the concert did not go according to plan. That's all there is to the story.' A fake story. But since any further attachment to Vicky is dead, it is only half a lie in favour of the story with Isabella he desperately wants now. His mention of Marco did not even raise an eyebrow.

The conversation falters after that, as if she is digesting what she has heard.

To prove his point, Jeremy puts on the recording of 'Follie'. Seeing Isabella shrink back at the reminder of full-throated passion she witnessed in church, halfway through he says loudly, above the music, 'Nobody can stop that once she gets going,' and dramatically punches the stop button. 'She's uncontrollable.'

Vicky is no longer a consideration, too foreign to Isabella's temperament to comprehend.

He encourages her to do most of the talking after that, asking her questions about her new job, assuming her parents must be proud of the achievement. He can see she is hesitant to discuss anything intimate, but she opens up a little, confessing she is worried about her English now that she really needs it, her lack of office experience, and whether real work will change her, how people see her. Marco stays conspicuously absent.

Jeremy withholds his own opinions about the village, venturing an occasional 'difficult' or 'unfortunate' in support of her misgivings, cautiously correcting her most obvious mistakes in English; she will be understood, and that's what matters. Lining up the words in a sentence properly and getting the right spin on the verb tense are not always as easy as it seems, but she learnt snooker quickly, didn't she? She did not understand the metaphor entirely, and he had to explain the analogy in more simple terms, but his inspired mention of snooker earns him an eight ball in the side pocket he was aiming for. She delights in the game, and that afternoon is a happy memory they can talk about, steering clear of her second visit to the villa.

On her insistence, he puts on another of his recordings, and he chooses Crusell. When, after an hour or so, he sees she has fully relaxed in his company, he suggests near the end of the drive that maybe she should come to the villa after her first day of work the next day to celebrate, play some snooker, and practice her English. The lively playful music can only partly mask the weight of what he is suggesting, and he can see through her smile and the almost inaudible 'maybe' at the top-end signature note of Crusell's adagio that she is sizing him up.

He tries as casually as he can to reassure her. 'Oh, don't worry, Isabella. You can trust me. I'd love to celebrate with you.'

When he drops her off on the bus route so she can make the trip home alone, he is not so sure she will show up—and whether he should want her to. But since it is purely by chance that they have met now, despite any attempt on his part to line her up, he cannot be blamed for making the most of the shot that was staring him in the face.

Packing it in

After breakfast the next day he starts to pack. At around four o'clock he has tidied everything up, returning the table and chairs on the front terrace to storage and packing everything in his car he does not need for the remaining night. He wants to leave early with Domino, who has become nervous watching him move around. The dog is also probably restless because Jeremy is skipping their evening walk in case Isabella shows up. He has thought of nothing else all day.

Catching her on the road has not felt as fortuitous today as it did yesterday. His immediate desire for the woman she suddenly is has been detached from what he now realises made it so important that any sexual bond with her be consensual. She was the girl he missed between the angry confused boy he was with no genuine sense of belonging, and the proud seducer he became with little courage to feel anything a relationship called for. She was the key, and he wanted her more than anything to unlock him. Now he is uncertain if seeing her again would lead to anything more than the will to seduce her and ignore the compulsion of yet another victory over reluctance, hers and his own. The invitation is a source of nervous tension that stings the self-confidence he has normally felt in situations like this.

Seeing her will decide whether either has patience with the other's truth, which note is played and whether they both tune into it. He decided not to pack up the music room just yet. His music has drawn her to him, so he must play for her, let his music make a play for her first, draw her closer than her caution might otherwise allow. Vicky removed too much of his own caution. He must not let that happen with Isabella, and instead find a way to weaken her resistance to what she wants as much as he does, since there could be no other reason for her to come.

The sun is low on the horizon, seen from the rooftop terrace, when he has given up, more than soured from the local wine he has been drinking and having to admit she is a no-show. Nothing can be unlocked, and he feels somehow relieved when he goes down to collect the Prosecco they were to share and drink it by himself. He has reached the bottom of the stairs when the angel knocks.

.

Nasty bubbles

'Addio, del passato bei sogni ridenti. . . .'

In the theatre, Vicky's dying Violetta takes on her last big aria in the final act of La Traviata, the libretto grieving her fading beauty and the end of 'past beautiful laughing dreams', wanting to be forgiven for her misguided soul. Jeremy removes the mask he has been wearing. The woman sitting next to him in the dress circle squirms in her seat. Stunned at the glimpse she has of him, she unconsciously touches her heavily made-up face as her owl eyes return to stare at the stage, as his do, but without seeing it.

He sees himself opening the door, taken aback for a moment: Isabella was a girl again. A natural beauty no matter what she wears, but a girl, not the woman in his mind's eye his imagination had jostled with all day. He at once felt older, less suited to her: the gap was back again, and this time round there was no way patience would bridge it.

Isabella told Angelina about her planned visit when she went to see her after work and changed into normal clothes: her simple calf-length, free-flowing skirt, a plain long-sleeved, loose-fitting blouse with rounded neck, and sandals on her feet. She stored her office outfit in her plain canvas shoulder bag.

She still felt guilty at the disappointment on her mother's face that morning when she told her she had agreed to celebrate her first day at work with Angelina afterwards; only then did her mother tell her she had planned a surprise dinner. But her shared excitement will hold, her mother assured her. They agreed to cook together, just the two of them, on another night; the family has not sat at the same table for weeks.

While she was changing, her girlfriend questioned whether she could take Jeremy at his word. On the other hand, if Isabella knows what he is like, what spells danger, he doesn't sound like a beast who would pounce on her, more like an older man totally taken by her looks. He embraced her and promised, like all men do, that he was looking for something more, then he backed off, like she said, when Isabella said stop. Besides, now that she has joined the real world, there will be plenty of men trying to get under her skirt, no matter how long it is, and she must start learning how to deal with that.

She was right to get rid of Marco: all he ever wanted was a right —in God's name through marriage—to push her into having sex; he is the worst type. Not all men are like him. She cannot be overcautious if she is curious, wants to enjoy life a bit, celebrate with a star musician, and have a good time for a change.

It was all a bit one-sided and overwhelming; it made Isabella on the bus home feel a bit like a virtue-stamped simpleton compared to her girlfriend, but that is only because she has kept what happened with Marco weeks ago to herself. Who would not be overcautious after that? If only Angelina knew the terror living inside her of being forced by a man again. And Jeremy? Is he also the worst type? He cannot be. The idea is simply too ugly. He is too smart, grown up, too sensitive to force himself on her. It just does not fit how thoughtful, happy and protected his music makes her feel. She must take Jeremy at his word or run scared of men entirely—seeing Marco in all of them.

She gets off the bus and stands there as it drives off, undecided still and like yesterday at the same spot instinctively fearing he could be there, hiding somewhere. She crosses the road. If Marco can see her, she can see him—if she is looking in the right direction. There is a rustle in the tall grass along the road from another direction that spooks her. The small flock of resting lark take flight. She watches them; she frightened them, but they are free. It sends her in the same direction as the bus along the trunk road; in a few hundred metres she reaches the dirt track leading to the villa. She is calm, looking forward to practicing her English, confident it will be fun, free to take flight herself if she needs to.

'Oh, well hello, Isabella, how lovely to see you. Come in!'

'Hello, Jeremy. It is also nice to see you. But it is late, I cannot stay for long.'

'Wow, that's perfect . . . your English, I mean. And the sun won't stay too long either. You must go up and see it from the roof. Everything has turned to gold! I'll join you in a minute.'

He is at once mesmerised by the soft sway of her hips as she climbs the stairs, the careless coyness in her steps. He darts through the kitchen door just as she turns on the landing to continue up; he has got to have her, but he cannot let her see that. 'Please, please, take me to heaven,' he says to himself as he fetches the Prosecco and fills two waiting glasses on the table. He then goes to the music room, to his secretaire, and returns to the kitchen with his oboe to collect the glasses.

He is at the foot of the stairs and knows beforehand: each step towards the heaven he worships will take him a step closer towards the inferno of her Catholic conscience. He must outpace his, too, can almost feel its hot breath on his neck as he climbs to her. The first step respects the heaven she worships. Can he do this? No, he cannot. Then, he will. Then, he won't do it. The last footfall lands on the first floor in front of his bedroom door: any solution to her consent is a mixed one, and not being aware of that fact beforehand, she will hopefully not have doubts about him afterwards. It has to be this way now. It would be a sin to be patient.

'But, Jeremy, you know I do not drink alcohol.'

'Well, I thought you might make a small exception, just to celebrate.' He clinks the two glasses together to punctuate his wish with a broad smile.

She smiles back but declines with a shake of her head.

But the shake is hesitant, does not convince him, and he goes for broke, stretching his hand with her glass over the parapet wall. 'You sure? Bit of a shame, really.'

'OK, one glass is safe maybe.'

They toast.

'Bit of a funny taste, this one, not as perky as I'm used to. Never mind. I would like to drink to our new beginnings.'

'Comme?'

He can see apprehension in her upturned brow. 'Beginnings, plural. You have one—a new job—and I hope I have my old talent back, on stage, live. Here's to us . . . I mean each other.'

They drink again.

'You are, how do you say it, back in form?'

'Correct. In every way. I've prepared everything I need to. So, no worries. That's a good Australian expression for you. No worries.'

'No worries. Senza preoccupazioni?'

'A bit like that, yes. Maybe more in the spirit of everything's going to work out fine. Here's to your own form, Isabella. It's sure to improve without any help from me now. Your English is getting better.'

They drink again and share a smile before her forehead lightly creases.

'What you say means you will be leaving soon?'

'Yes. But come visit. I will show you London if you want to see the big bad city Dom Pietro doesn't approve of because it is filled with people like me.'

'He laughed with you, I remember.'

'Cheers to your padre! But it is not funny he is so *severo* against joy in life.'

As they drink again, she unconsciously takes a healthy slug to her promise of joy in her life.

'Live more in the here and now, I say. It's more fun,' Jeremy adds, aware a promise is unfolding.

'London, it is like Rome? I have been there some times.'

'I think you mean you have been to Rome a few times?'

'Yes, in winter, when it is more quiet, most only Italians.'

'London is completely different. Very busy. Heaving! Oh, sorry, funny English . . . full of life, fun places to go, fun things to do, people from everywhere around the world.'

'Un mondo più grande!' The mock stern look on his face checks her. 'A bigger world?'

'A much bigger world. And I hope to see you in it sometime. Cheers.'

They drink again.

He then turns away from her, looking out over the countryside. She turns too, and he can feel her close to his arm, but they don't touch—much too early. He waits for the first signs. Patience.

'But you know, Isabella, London doesn't offer magnificent

views like this one. You won't find the quiet I have enjoyed so much here, away from it all. So, your home is good too, really, in a different way.'

'No worries. It is my home,' she says with less enthusiasm.

'And we'll drink to it, with these bubbles because they burst!'

She giggles self-consciously at the joke, he more openly. He raises his glass and drinks up. She does too, more hesitantly.

'On my first night, the peace up here inspired me.' He picks up the oboe he laid on the parapet wall. 'Signora Tendri heard me playing—badly—right across the valley in her garden. This time it's for you, Isabella, since it's not on your CD. And I hope I can prove I'm back in best form.'

It's a standard encore piece: the Bach Sinfonia. He walks to the middle of the terrace, turns to face her, wets his reed, and begins.

The long, solemn notes are not what she was expecting, and she would have preferred something more lively, more fun. She finds it hard to concentrate on what she is hearing; it is confusing her somehow. She likes the CD better, the sounds in the background that bring everything together so the music flows nicely. It feels silly standing here, watching him play all by himself, his head and body moving like a rubber man to the notes his cheeks and lips are squeezing out of that small thingy in his mouth. She wants to laugh. That would not be right.

Her gaze and her mind wander away from him. She wants the sun to stay over the horizon, wants to keep it there, its mild warmth on her body, colouring the streak behind an airplane overhead a fiery red. How nice it would be to fly, to go somewhere completely different, walking down busy streets full of people; she doesn't know them, and they don't trouble her. No worries! Free to go wherever she pleases . . . nice cafes! the cinema! . . . or the top of a skyscraper! On top of the world! She has never been to the top of a really tall building. What would it be like to look down, for real, over a whole city? Just imagining the sensation thrills her, sending a rush up her spine, unbelievably real, nice. It would be so much fun.

Especially together with her bestest best girlfriend. What a crazy idea! Go to London with Angelina! Lighten her big, heavy heart. Escape. Adventure! Having fun together. Flying there. How exciting! Way up in the air, a passing streak in the sky. It is gone.

Whoosh! They are on their way!

She has never felt so happy, so much joy, so light-headed, breathless, and she aches to move, which makes her realise the music has stopped. How long ago? No matter. He looks happy too. She would hate to hurt his feelings. What a nice smile he has, such a handsome, funny man. They should do something silly together, now, have some fun!

Jeremy could see soon after he started playing the short piece that she was not really listening to him. He gives her a generous smile when he is finished; there is a small pause before she 'comes back'. She was not smiling at him but at her own thoughts, and they were livelier than his music. The dazed euphoric look leaves her face, and she suddenly becomes a girlish burst of enthusiasm, hopping to him, her hand squeezing his arm.

'Oh, Jeremy, Jeremy! I like you to play again! Please! Something pam-titty-bam . . . piena di gioia! I will dance!'

Her exuberance is infectious, his loud laugh triumphant. What a miraculous transformation; all he could hope for. 'You will?'

'Yes, yes, play!'

'OK. OK. Let's go with this one. Ready?'

She curtsies, laughs, and then begins her improvisation to the runs of Cimarosa's *Allegro* that he joins seamlessly into a continuous dance. It is controlled at first, beautiful, in flow; her long hair and extended arms sweep through the air as she spins and glides on her feet in all directions. She giggles, whoops, and twirls all over the rooftop, his gaze on her, her movements sometimes following the rise and fall of his oboe. It soon gets wilder, frenzied; her delirium turns her from nymph to overexcited dancing chimp. He can see what is going to happen before it does. She continues to spin around even when he stops playing. He goes to her and catches her with his free arm just in time.

'Whoa! Steady, girl.'

She laughs hysterically, out of breath, wants to start up again, and breaks free of his hold. 'Ancora, di più, di più, di piùùù, carissimo Jeremy.'

His laugh is forced; he plays along. He does not know what to do. He had not reckoned with this.

'You were great, Isabella, *magnifico!* I can't play anymore. We'll do it again tomorrow.'

'No more dancing?'

'Now it is time for? . . . Snooker!' He could be talking to a child, as the synapses in her adult brain are shutting down fast enough to grab her with the next distraction. 'Come on! Time for our favourite game.' He grabs her hand and moves towards the door and stairs, not sure if she will resist. He needs to be ahead of her . . . in case.

'I beat you. You see,' she says.

She has difficulty with the stairs, but she does not seem to mind, giggling and laughing at her missteps on the first flight down. On the second flight, when he reaches the landing, she begins to sway dangerously behind him. He looks back at her.

She smiles weakly, puts a hand on his shoulder. 'Portami giù,' she slurs and puts her arms around his neck. He holds one of her legs around him with his free hand in a very lopsided piggyback to the bottom. She is very unsteady on her feet when she goes to the snooker table. Her movements around it become frantic. She takes a cue and strikes the cue ball with surprising accuracy and force to hit the frame he had prepared earlier. She plays a few shots, totally self-absorbed, before the inertia she is fighting strikes her, hits her hard.

He watches her. Was he like this?

She does not move, even as some of the balls bounce back in her direction, one of them glancing her chin, which has almost come to rest on the baize. 'Che bello . . .' It is almost a whisper.

He goes to her, afraid she will pass out, gently coaxing her off the table, pulling her body up by her upper arms, then turning her towards him, brushing her hair away from her face. 'Isabella, I think you need to lie down.'

She touches his cheek affectionately with her hand, her faint smile awry, her voice warbled. 'Tutto va bene, no? Ci capiamo l'un l'altro.'

He smiles. Her senses are in limbo. It is now or never. He jumps over the low bar, and in the middle of their first kiss, just as she is beginning to respond, he holds her up as she goes limp.

A gap

He is nervous, sitting here exposed in the theatre, recalling the next scene, quietly scratching the scar through his long-sleeved shirt. He feels hot.

..
No.
.....
I can't think about it.
....
You . . . *must* . . . own it!
....
It was a mistake!
....
Stop!

..
I can't look.

The village is my home

He feigns surprise at the amount she drank: one glass of bubbly on the roof terrace, three more while playing snooker. She only remembers the first glass and him playing something slow on the oboe. She has never been this drunk.

'I thought you said you have been once, in tilt?'

'Non è vero, fantasia.'

'I'm sorry. I should have stopped you sooner.'

He is covered.

She was out for two hours. He finds no consolation in the fact that her drug-induced hangover might not last beyond tomorrow, with only one glass of nasty bubbly to clear from her system. He knows how she must physically feel—the enormously heavy, dull head, the confusion, the nausea, and the exhaustion. She woke up on 'her' single bed, where she had once fallen asleep while hiding from Dom Pietro.

His own stomach churns too, remembering how spellbound he was when he discovered her that afternoon lying on the same bed, seeing the terrible state his lunacy has put her in tonight—not even counting those inflictions hidden by her amnesiac shadow conscience when the lights went out on her, went out on his insane unbuttoned hope to find the desire and enchantment her seduction had promised.

She agrees he will drive her to the edge of the village, off the abbey road. Buried still too deep inside her confusion is anger (with herself or with him) she has no energy to express. She hisses and waves him back weakly when he tries to help her up, insisting on getting to the car by herself, although she can barely walk; he doubts she will make it up the road to the square. She falls asleep again almost as soon as she sits in the car.

When he reaches the turn-off, he decides it won't matter to him now anyway. He turns off his headlights and approaches the farthest edge of the square. The bar is closed, no lights through the shuttered windows; he hopes for her sake and his that everyone is asleep, but at the last moment he stops before driving her to her door. He wakes her up, tells her where she is, and hands over her shoulder bag.

She struggles out, steadies herself on the open door, and peers inside. 'Goodbye, Jeremy.'

The door slams shut on him. It feels intentional, even if not. He veers off the square at once, along the main village road, not wanting to replace her lithe walk across to her door the afternoon they met with the sight of her drugged unsteady wobble home tonight.

But there is always someone looking out the window. She has been worried sick; the last bus was an hour ago, and her daughter is so late. Isabella's horrified mother rushes down to her when she stumbles and falls.

Kindling thoughts of sin

The car door was slammed shut on him. How could it not have been intentional, he concludes as he drinks from the bottle of horrible grappa he forgot he had and washes it down with the last of the sour local wine he has left, looking up at the stars from the roof terrace.

He has shamed her, is ashamed himself, angry, disgusted by the compulsive, cynical, sordid sense of purpose with which he went through with it, manipulated the trust that made her his unconscious victim. Is the crime less real if she never finds out it was committed? Her mind was dead, her reflexes partly alive. But there was no passion in it at all; it was a mistake, a total mistake in every possible way, with possible consequences he dares not imagine.

Not having her consent, he must now admit his ardour was fake, not about sharing any sense of belonging with her. He can try to believe the temptation was too strong: she challenged him, he could not resist, had to fail, his defences were too weak. He did dishonestly what he intended from the start: find the weak point in her own defences and forge his way in, penetrate her will, her body. The crime will be real for him regardless how he tries to wipe away that hour from his memory, as he did his seed when he realised to his horror that he had pulled out too late.

In God's name, how could he have done this! What possessed him to treat Isabella this way? Is it because the young goddess refused his carnal worship? Did that spurn him on to punish her for the abstinence she enforced, tying down the brute force of his kickback lust, the vain pride he took in his conquests and consensual seductions? The endless hours in isolation he spent thinking of nothing else but her do not excuse this sick id, this sin against her, this real, punishable sin. He looks up again.

'So, Mother, you were right. It was in me all the time. You happy now?'

His wine and the horrible grappa are both finished. He goes straight to bed, drunk, still in his clothes.

Inferno

Vengeance has waited, waited to see a light upstairs go on, then out. Vengeance made friends with the barking mongrel while Jeremy was away and stole into the oil cellar, tipping over clay vats of oil onto the floor, soaking everything that would ignite quickly: old cloth rags and discarded fibre mats from the oil press. And now this is all vengeance needs: the siphoned petrol from the Englishman's car, spilled generously everywhere, christening the deed. Open the cellar doors wide. Light a match.

The dog starts barking. Vengeance transforms itself into fire.

Three hours later, where the air-nourished oil-fed flames from the cellar first bit into the beams and planks holding up the terracotta floor, the structure underneath the reception room collapses. The inferno throughout the cellar below is given free reign of the floor above, and after building up for so long, it wastes no time claiming the new space, its flames soaring with delight.

The deep rumble of terracotta tiles, the long table, and benches falling into the pit of fire wake Jeremy at last with what sounds like thunder. His half-sober head is still puzzling what he heard when shortly after, the weakened floor of the snooker room directly below him collapses under the weight of the snooker table. His floor and bed shudder, and panic grips him. He can hear Domino barking outside. He slips on his shoes, opens the bedroom door, and smells smoke as it travels up the stairs, the stairwell now a chimney leading through to the roof terrace door he left open.

The adrenaline wakes up his brain, and he remembers: he has not packed up the music room! He can see the reed cases on the workbench, the work that cannot be replaced. He rushes down the stairs, does not even look in the kitchen. He can see smoke creeping through cracks in the heavy wooden door from the reception room into the hallway. He has no time to waste. He pushes open the right half of the double door, his left foot

296

stepping into—

The shock stuns and delays him. One, two—whoosh!—too late. His right hand on the handle of the door he swung open, and his left hand braced against the other closed half of the double door, hold him mid-motion from falling into the inferno. The tall flames propelled from below through the open cellar entrance door leap at him like a flamethrower, escaping the pit into the hallway so fast he cannot escape them.

For a few seconds he has no free arm to protect his face, and he feels the painful sting as it is singed by pointed tongues of flame. Before he can regain his balance and move out of their way, his clothes and hair catch fire. He screams, recoils from the doorway, bats his head, rips off his shirt, lurches to the kitchen sink, and puts his head under water. He grabs tea towels, soaks them, and slaps them dripping onto the burns on his arms and chest. His wallet, keys, and a bottle of water wait on the kitchen table for the planned early-morning departure, now tonight's escape.

From what? Jeremy's conviction that somebody is trying to kill him burns through his skin, flows into his blood, penetrates any belief that this is an accident. Whoever it is will be waiting outside. But there is no way out. The back door is blocked, the hallway is now impassable, and smoke and flames are eating their way up the stairwell. The kitchen windows are too high up the wall to reach. The storerooms, off the kitchen, behind Giorgio's office—there must be a way out through there. He rushes in, now in greater panic, until he spots the frame of a door blocked with old furniture. He topples the stack, pushes it to one side. The door is locked, does not budge when he kicks it. He looks around him and sees an old dresser on a roller. He clears a wider path to the door. With all the strength he has left, he pushes the dresser a few metres to crash it through the door into Giorgio's office. It is the sixth key he finds unmarked on a rack next to the outside door that opens it.

He opens it cautiously. Peers out. Is there somebody waiting? Where? Out front? Back here? His car is a five-second sprint away. He sees Domino run towards him, barking hoarsely after three hours of trying to warn his master from outside. His companion is at his heels, sharing his panic.

'I need help! I cannot take you. I'll be back for you, I promise!'

The dog is insistent he keeps his promise now, until there is no choice left but the stern command he remembers, pointing at the compost heap.

'*Torna al tuo posto!*'

Domino stares at him, moves back, and turns to stare at him again, the last glimpse Jeremy has of his faithful companion before he lowers himself into his car.

Escape

Domino's barking and whining while chasing the car as far as he dares, break Jeremy down as he hurtles down the track he first climbed to the villa, jolting shocks to his undercarriage ignored now, mental shock erasing time, as if this track was a mistaken turn he could correct months later. There is no turning back. He reaches the main trunk road.

It is 11 p.m. The road is clear. Pain obstructs thought, jams his mind, punctures the deeper layers of welted red-brown skin on his singed face; it hurts to cry, but he cannot stop doing so. The only thing that works are his reflexes at the wheel. It takes merely a few minutes to reach the autostrada, where he stops to wrap the tea towel soaked in water around his face, collect his toll ticket, and race on, abandoning any help that might be found in Rome.

Desperate to go back in time, to not be where its passage took him, he heads straight to where he set out from, a place at once fixed in his mind like a pin on a map—north, 900 kilometres away—and a face that must still recognise his own, return it to what it was, return him to where his life was when he met Tammara in the beer garden. This bizarre logic convinces Jeremy to drive north, far away from his punishment, as if distance could disprove he deserved it here and now.

Maybe all uniformed watchdogs are asleep at this hour, but their radar and cameras are not. He is a celebrity of sorts who cannot avoid the flashing recognition he receives for this masked race through mobbing physical and emotional pain, accelerated by his panicked attempt to outrun this blitzkrieg and a possible blockade of his further passage at the next toll station.

One by one he passes them, and bit by bit what lies ahead becomes more present in his mind than the hatred left burning out of control behind him—a flight for help more than a flight from vengeance. He does not know who. He does not dare touch, look, or face up to his fear—what it could mean that he feels nothing when his tongue passes over the left side of his mouth; the burning sensation higher up, on his brow and cheek; the excruciatingly painful scalding of his arms and chest, barely alleviated by the car's icy stream of air directed at them full blast under the long-sleeved shirt he put on and doused with water.

When he must stop for petrol near Florence, he has the money ready when he goes in to pay. At 2 a.m. there are a few truck drivers. He digs a hoodie out of his luggage and enters without face cover, afraid to be mistaken for a robber. He is a phantom the cashier recoils at, catching a glimpse of Jeremy when he places the counted notes on the counter and dashes out again. At toll booths he is sitting on the wrong side for collectors to see more than his outstretched arm towards their booth through the passenger window. He races off with unrestrained horsepower as soon as the barrier is up. Go, go, go!

Anyone venturing into the overtaking lane is excused for misjudging the speed of his approach: two warning flashes of his headlights and he is right on their bumper. Jeremy's blood is flooded with adrenaline, and he drives in an alert trance, outside himself, pain being the only conscious part of this surreal experience. He becomes one with the stream of moving lights cutting through the blackness of the Po Valley in moonless night; his mind is in suspension as he drives over the towns and villages on the elevated Brenner Pass motorway; and he sees the opaque conclusion of life as he knew it, in the first shimmer of light, as he approaches Rosenheim under a hazy sky—to meet crawling, gnawing pain in early-morning traffic into Munich on the crowded autobahn.

It is 7.30 a.m. when he reaches Tammara's clinic and enters emergency reception to ask for her. He is sure he sees her wince before she reaches the half-inclined stretcher he was placed on and he passes out.

Wildly enthusiastic applause, a standing ovation, as the curtains close on the final scene of La Traviata.

Jeremiah suffers

Thy way and thy doings have procured these things unto thee;
this is thy wickedness, because it is bitter, because it reacheth unto
thine heart.
Book of Jeremiah 4:18

The burns on his body were second degree, but the tongue of flames that struck the left side of his face was pointedly vicious to the third degree, at the edge of his mouth and crease of his smile, and the skin had to be grafted. Those nerves were dead. He drooled. He would drink from a straw, chew with a hand pressed over his mouth, and speak with a slur when his mummy-wrapped face and the truth unravelled.

His car was towed away and sold at a punitive loss, its leather-cased contents—out-of-season summer clothes and music scores he would never play again—stacked in the corner of his hospital room. That's where the ten-day search for him ended following the trail of blurred photographs of a masked fugitive testing the speed-control cameras' fastest aperture speeds.

There would be no feather bed future ahead of him now, and not any kind of bed that would be shared with him. In his half-reclined hospital bed, he stared out the window in a sedated daze, feeling the pain, the itch of his second-degree burns, while late autumn shed its last heat and withered chestnut leaves the colour of his burnt skin fell from the tree outside.

If he could have spoken through his bandages in those first few days, he would not have been able to explain his insane flight to this clinic. Partly to blame were the excesses of histamine and adrenaline coursing through his body, creating a paranoic anxiety well beyond fight or flight instincts. He knows it must have been arson, that someone had tried to kill him. But what burned that night through the dermis of his blistered reasoning was the speed

301

of retribution. By driving here, he was trying to erase the here and now of punishment, leave behind what he claimed he would accept. The here must be elsewhere, and the now must be put in the past; His castigation could be stalled.

Whoever it was, was unaware that they were not meant to kill him but to punish him for life. The life he still has is as gutted as the burnt-out core of the villa, its metre-thick outer walls still standing.

The pictures were presented to him by Riccardo, who stopped off on his way back to London from there. It was arson. No further investigation required, a search for the criminal unlikely to lead anywhere. The villa was not covered by its out-of-date insurance policy, a total loss. Where else could Riccardo's anger be directed other than at him? There was no commiseration or sympathy for his own fate. Jeremy had destroyed Riccardo's ancestral home, and as his guest, the family's reputation in the village.

The Inglese incited this, that was the unanimous verdict behind the venomous remarks of everyone who deigned to speak to a Patricelli in the village. Going after a village girl less than half his age, breaking up her planned marriage, getting her blind drunk and dumping her on the village square for everyone to see? Was he mad? Did he not know where he was? Jeremy had raced a boy to his death and then tried to convince the family of his innocence with a falsely solicitous bribe. He gave everyone a reason to burn the place down, including Dom Pietro himself, for a sacrilegious crime so horrible the priest refused to talk about it, shouting through red-faced anger that Jeremy had brought every sin cursed by Jeremiah to the village and then called on Vicky for good measure to sing praises to them.

The accusations and his bandaged mouth rendered him speechless; he had no means to articulate a defence if he had one. When the nurse came in to change his bandages and asked if Riccardo could stay in the room, he nodded yes, hoping he would be able to say something intelligible before the new bandages went on. As the old ones came off, his eyes shut in loud pain he could not silence. The nurse went to fetch new bandages. He had no strength left; he could only manage a half-truth through one side of his mouth in a gravelly grasp for words.

'I . . . lost . . . control of Wik-key. I'm sorry.'

'She tells a very different story, I'm afraid. Backed up by your other female victim.'

'Isabvella liked to wisit me. Not my vaught.'

'No, of course not. Vicky was too much to handle, so you switch to a nice, young, innocent village girlie you can impress with pious sincerity and a few CDs—now valuable artifacts—and ply her with a few . . . drinks? Nothing wrong with that, is there? Did you get anywhere with her?'

'Stophit. This is all not true.'

'You're not indulgent, Jeremy, you're evil.'

'There waz no race. Geeorschio nose awout the bwoy.'

'I have friends in the local police. You pay to cover things up, I pay to uncover them. I have seen the accident file. Giorgio confirmed the guilty bribe to the family. You're lying.'

'The dog . . . Domwino—'

'Is dead.'

Jeremy made a sweep with his arms, swatting away despair that stung with more pain than his burns. The nurse returned and asked Riccardo to leave. He stopped at the door before going out.

'A word from Dom Pietro: do not ever expect forgiveness.'

As if to prove the point, the skin graft and the burns on his face became infected and would leave an ugly permanent scar.

The soloist

A substitute was found for the tour that could no longer be undone. The thought that he would never play again undid Jeremy. There was nothing to hold on to, nothing left to smother the hostility he was accountable for, no tuning his screeching mental orchestra, stuck in the pit every waking hour. He tried to dig his way out with accusing letters to Vicky but tore them all up. He fell into deep depression while still in the clinic, a monosyllabic patient kept afloat on a drip cocktail of antibiotics and pain killers.

After eight weeks, in the gloom of onsetting winter, Tammara had his further treatment transferred to a colleague at a private skin clinic in London. He left his music behind to be disposed of. He left hooded and masked; the immigration officer at Heathrow apologised for the 'inconvenience' of verifying he was no longer who he was.

His post, collected by a neighbour, covered his snooker table in the apartment. The first thing that caught his eye amongst the envelopes was a small package with Italian postage stamps. It came from the village, Dom Pietro: postmarked a couple of days before his departure? He tore it open. Inside the bubble wrap were his concert reeds. And one handwritten line: Stay a soloist. Do not seek His grace.

The felt-lined case he had looked to retrieve from his secretaire workbench the night his career came to its fiery end was emptied by the priest on his last visit and mailed the same day in the hope of forcing Jeremy homewards. He left the rest of his mail unopened, fetched a half bottle of whiskey, and guzzled it down in less than an hour sitting in his armchair, not moving even as he wet himself.

It took days to recover from the shock, not helped by traffic fines from Italy and Germany totalling three thousand pounds and notification from the UK Department of Transport to hand over his driving licence. Complete and utter despair was avoided thanks to prudence about insuring himself; his health insurance was private, and his 100 per cent payout from the professional disability insurance was sufficient for a decent if not extravagant life. He was rude with investors who somehow found out about it, the only ones who rang and harangued him.

'Hello, am I speaking to Jeremy Sinclair? My name is—'

'Bugger off!'

He threw out all copies of his own recordings.

A few months on, he sold his apartment in Chelsea and moved to a smaller one on Muswell Hill. There was no room for his snooker table.

Resting on a bench under street lights on the long way home after the opera, he looks back on that first year. He returned to London a shadow of the man he once was, without the benefit of amnesia for what had happened to him, without enough light to outline what he could still do.

At the skin clinic, they suggested they could graft away the ugliest scars left on his face by the infected burns. He turned down the operation because he had no faith it would lead him anywhere if he could not return to music. And without his calling as a musician, there was nothing to counter his acquiescence about being disfigured; the deceit his old face had hidden, what it once persuaded other people to believe about him, was now exposed. Cosmetics could not hide the truth when he saw Isabellas in other young women, dogs like Domino, chasing or fetching in the parks, a red Alfa Sprinter parked opposite where he sat having a coffee one day, old women who look like Fabio's mother, begging on the streets.

He began sorting out his totally neglected flat and tried to put some order back in his life. The half-open boxes of kitchenware and cutlery presented the first question. He had unpacked two dinner sets after the move from Chelsea and a few cups and glasses that he needed for himself. What did he need more for? His whole social life had centred around music, the people he worked with, and the women he inevitably chose to abandon. Very few people called to find out what had happened to him; he was practically a recluse. How likely was that to change?

The front room was crowded with stacked boxes of books packed by the movers, still waiting to return to empty bookshelves. He missed the snooker table, though not the game on his own. He had gone out to play one evening and found the place he went to neon shabby; his mask put people off playing with him. He left after one frame, apologising. A rather loud young woman a table away reminded him of how charmed he had been by Isabella's playful laughter under a grand chandelier. Going home on the Tube that night, he passed through Mornington Crescent station, where the PA system reminded him of her again.

'Mind the gap!'

There were other gaps that were easier to remove, interests appearing on his bookshelves that were not part of this afterlife, reminding him of the glossy delight he once took in books on cars and on erotic photography, music scores, and autobiographies of the famous in music history; he kept the book written by Jansen on teaching and interpretation with its personal dedication: You will soar and surprise them all. Believe in yourself!

At the bottom of one box was his leather-bound boyhood copy of King James Bible, the prophecies and laws against believing in himself. He had no recollection of having kept it. His mother must have snuck it behind other books on his shelves the one time she visited him in Chelsea before she passed away. She had hardcovered guilt into his life, and he resolved to read his way out of it.

What convinced people of gospel truth, the power the Church exercised in its name? The story's power mystified him, the will to reduce the human cause to achieving blissful, immortal innocence. How convinced his mother was in her beliefs he will never know, but she used them to hammer him. What struck down on him from her heaven was the opposite of blissful; it was a daily assault on the map of his conscience, and anywhere he moved on it was wrong, sinful. To give authenticity to her accusations, he wilfully disobeyed, until disobedience unconsciously shaped his life, his compulsion to test everyone else's weakness and compunction. And in the end, she won the battle. His mother, not any god, left the indelible mark that made guilt a reality he could not remove.

There was no other explanation for believing he finally got the punishment she had always denied him.

Revelations

The old man in a long, heavy, woollen, loose-fitting winter coat fastened with a thin belt—too warmly dressed for late spring—comes and sits beside him on the bench. He sees the man stare at the bible.

'If you ask me, no such thing as the afterlife. This is all there is, innit?'

Jeremy thinks about a reply, whether he wants to offer one and if so what to say, before he turns from reading to face the man on his left, relieved there is no alcohol on the old man's breath that would persuade him to get up and leave. He takes in a pallid, slightly jaundiced face, a scraggly collection of long grey hair, deeply inset eyes, and a downturned mouth trying to forge a smile that looks Mephistophelian on him. Jeremy can imagine himself in the company of a malnourished medieval peasant heretic who would have suffered gravely in his days for what he has just asserted.

'If you deny it exists, some people will assume you have reasons not to look forward to it.'

'No sense thinking about it, all the same.'

'I guess not, if you've no need to wonder your life has gone to hell already. '

'You a skeleton underneath that mask, then?'

'Just seen the fire.' Jeremy pulls down his mask.

The old man doesn't flinch. 'That's a hell of a scar. Punishing, that is. Was it an accident?'

'Was it an accident, or was I punished for something I did? I can't say for sure. If, like you say, I have nothing to fear or hope for after this life, then the punishment is not eternal, as they claim in this book, even if punishment down here can split your life in two.'

'Done something wrong, no forgiveness down here. Wounnit be nice, though, if you could wipe the slate clean, get accepted like, for who you are . . . somewhere else? Imagine that. I can't say I ever have. Have to forgive yourself where you are and get on.'

Assuming the man is used to talking about such things but not wanting to be asked back, Jeremy holds off asking what the man has done wrong. He hears about it anyway.

'Afterlife, down here, I get that someways. This is me afterlife for second degree, accidently on purpose. Came out two years ago. Nice to be outside today. Heavenly. You a churchgoer, then?'

'I was a Catholic a long time ago. Just thought I'd read parts of this story and make up my own mind about what it says, not what I was told it had to mean.'

'Read a bit o' the book meself, inside, for show, good behaviour. Know who God is?'

'You're going to tell me.'

'It's everybody in that book, everyone who has ever lived. We're the bloody miracle; this planet is the miracle. Just depends what we do with it. It ain't to be forced in one direction, 'cause we're all different. Ain't no such thing as common sense. People come and go, and the next carry on where we left off.'

'Where is God, yours at least, leading us, then?'

'Well, that's the biggest bloody miracle, innit? That nobody sees the miracle anymore, nobody's paying attention, and if we don't watch out—whoosh!—we're all gone, disappear, end of the show.'

'Accidently on purpose . . . sorry, it just fit.'

'That's all right. I'm mending me ways, what I leave behind, as best I can. If everybody does that, we'll be all right. Don't need no church.'

'Have you ever been in one?'

'Good Protestant boy, me. I went for me mum, back then. Couldn't stand the place.'

'That's my story too. Have you ever been in a Catholic church?'

'Yeah, now you mention it, down Marylebone way.'

'Out of curiosity?'

'I was walkin' about, yeah. I was like curious an' it was cold, so I just went in and sat down for a while to warm up. Real posh inside, by Protestant standards. When a priest showed up, I was ready to hop it, but he was real friendly like, asked me to stop for a bit of a chat. I told him I wasn't Catholic, an' he jokes an' says,

309

"What, you don't speak Latin?" A right funny priest. Anyway, we's talkin' an' I says to him, straight off the bat, "I am not believing in any judgement day, and doing penance, and all those things." Didn't bother him neither. He says, "If you repair bad things you might have done with good things and thoughts, you don't need to ask if anything comes after life; you'll feel good in this one, and maybe get another." Ha! I really liked that. They got a street kitchen, too. I been back a few times. Once for a Sunday service an' all.'

'Holy Mass.'

'Yeah, blow me, what a ceremony: fancy dress, incense, bells, loads of things in Latin sing-song—not like, you know, a singalong. I sat it out, but it was, well, a bit spooky really.'

As Jeremy gets up from the bench and continues his long walk home from Covent Garden, he remembers the old man, how their talk on another park bench had stuck with him, persuaded him months later to go through the door of the 'spooky' Catholic church in Marylebone.

He had taken a bus to Camden Town that day, intending to walk through Regent's and then Hyde Park; the church was right between the two, although he does not remember looking for it deliberately.

It was an unusually hot Saturday, and while many bought their way through the heat in high street air conditioning, Jeremy opted for the parks after picking his way briefly through a now disappointingly commercial Camden Market.

On the Broad Walk in Regent's Park, he came across a young bride and her two bridesmaids being photographed for the big day; they were laughing and joking around, each pointing at one of the winged lions holding up the massive Griffin Tazza flower bed, each naming one of the lions after the man in their lives as if to say, while they still could, how silly men were to believe in their arcane notions of prowess.

What sort of big day would the 'golden couple' have had, if any? Still fighting awakened self-contempt for his abuse of Isabella, he arrived in front of the church, awakening his older contempt for the Catholic faith, the power it unexplainably still held over him deep in his conscience. He found himself suddenly ready to open the door, to hear himself admit the heinous, callous crime he was responsible for. Yes, he would confess, he needed to. He needed to cleanse himself of the Church's pretence, let himself be judged for the last time by a priest no less mortally weak, fallible, and unworthy than he was. He would have himself declared a sinner against the Holy Phantom of morality, and then deny these ritualistic rites any meaning in their totemic pursuit of remorse and expiation. Who, after all, other than those he had made to suffer, could forgive him? Only when he had put the Church behind him, all it had written into his life, would he be free to convert to the old man's miracle, make amends, and get on— without forgiveness—here and now. He had to clean his slate of the confused emotional epitaphs scribbled on his conscience by his mother and her Church so something else could be written on it.

He looked at his watch and made his way to the confessional. He was alone in the church. There was half an hour left, according to the notice outside the church, and then confessions were over. A Father Peter, the sign said outside the curtained booth he entered, was on duty. Only once he sat down on the hard bench and drew the curtain closed did he realise he might be confronted by the friendly priest the old man met in this church. He would remain firm in excommunicating himself and could already feel his anger rising at the mere thought of protocol before being allowed to confess his crimes.

'Bless me, Father, for I have sinned. My last confession was thirty years ago.'

The second admission, Jeremy unkindly thought of the priest, was the reason why no reply came for a long time: the priest is annoyed, thinking lunch will probably have to wait.

'Jeremiah believed it was never too late to repent. No one listened, Jeremy, and Jerusalem fell.'

Reckoning

Jeremy reaches Muswell Hill and home, kicks off his shoes, pours two fingers of whiskey earned by his two-hour walk, and sits down in his armchair facing his bookshelves, without turning on the reading light, in the half darkness of street lights. Facing the ugly man he became over two years ago had not, as he had hoped, brought him any closer to making peace with himself. Running through the whole story again, trying to understand the compulsion that blocked any correction of his behaviour back then, did not remove the shame he still felt; his vigil at the opera tonight did not free him from further introspection that would lead nowhere.

The restlessness he felt when the performance ended was even more acute from seeing Riccardo and Vicky creating the magic their music offered in a moving performance, from them following the musical career they had promised themselves. He was left in a space nothing could fill. No punishment was more severe, not even his lost attraction for women. He could not bring himself to look for companionship in a dog. Dom Pietro would say this emptiness was purgatory: his file upstairs was still open.

Jeremy's original purpose that first day in the church quickly evaporated. Rebellious confession was pointless; Dom Pietro had already excommunicated him. But Jeremy wanted another form of absolution for his conscience only this priest could give him: an end to endless premonitions and answers at last to what had happened to Isabella, Fabio's family, Domino, Giorgio, and, now, why the priest had come to London, abandoned the village he was so dedicated to.

Jeremy was stunned when they both left the confessional and faced each other. The priest he remembered had lost at least a third of his bulk, judging by the straight fall of his cassock and the leaner face that openly stared at his mask. Jeremy instinctively felt the need to pull it off, to acknowledge he, too, had radically changed.

Only the faintest gasp through a slight part in lips that quickly closed revealed the priest's shock at his once-handsome, now-disfigured face. They were both immobilised by the truth they each confronted: the aborted confession could not have been taken by a priest whose visible distain for him matched Jeremy's faithless pretence of his rights to one.

'If you wish to speak to me, be at the rectory at two o'clock Monday afternoon.'

Dom Pietro turned on his heel and left, a determined pace in his stride to ignore anything Jeremy might say as he walked away.

Dom Pietro, alias Father Peter, sat at a large oak desk in a comfortable leather-upholstered swivel chair that would never have held his former bulk. Were it not for the large cross facing him, Jeremy, in his straight-backed wooden chair opposite the priest, might have mistaken the room's venerate aura for that of a distinguished advocate's chamber, the bookshelves here crammed with old volumes of theological wisdom serving the Church unto its own precedence and doctrines. The air of authority had an obstinate musty smell that gave it away as old and past its prime. Dressed, to Jeremy's surprise, in a plain, white, long-sleeved shirt, Dom Pietro's off-duty civvies were not intended to put Jeremy at his ease. On the contrary, plain clothes meant plain speaking, divesting the priest of higher spiritual obligations and sobriety that might forbid a not-so-sacral punch at today's petitioner for the truth.

The wheezing congestion to Dom Pietro's breathing went away with its near obese cause, the sumptuous meals and wine he now forbade himself, the priest explaining this to Jeremy as he poured them both a proper cup of jasmine tea, which the priest took without sugar.

Dom Pietro left the village when it became obvious to him that he no longer had the complete trust of his congregation. This coincided with planned further consolidation in the parishes by the bishop. Dom Pietro had no desire to be a visiting priest to other villages and looked for a new incardination that might give him new insights on his calling under a different bishop. He had decided it had to be a city, where most of the stray Catholics lived; he wanted to help them recover their faith.

Prior to his transfer to this new post, the priest spent a few months in a Benedictine monastery. In that peaceful seclusion, he reflected on his time in the Church and in the village. His practice of faith had become too doctrinaire, he sees now, missing the understanding people who sinned against their better judgement needed; prayer, strict devotion, and penitence did not in themselves prevent the likelihood of sin and should not be the placeholder for finding true forgiveness. He wants to reach out to people and regrets that his Church is failing to do so, too caught up in its own contradictions.

The priest continued at length about his newly discovered inspiration for his 'job', but as he narrowed in on the issue of sin his tone sharpened, and it was obvious that even with this new attitude to human error, Jeremy fell through the sieve of Dom Pietro's tolerance.

'In the Church's eyes you are a sinner, someone who must seek salvation before it is too late, but to me, outside the vestments of my priesthood, you are simply too evil a man to want it or find it. That takes penitence. I honestly do not know why you are here today.'

'I know I harmed people. I thought you would tell me how.'

'Ah, curiosity.'

'That is vindictive. Will you tell me or not?'

The priest swivelled around almost playfully in his chair, half smiling with upraised brows as he came full circle to face Jeremy. 'Where to begin, where to begin? Let me begin, then, with the mother of the young man you raced and sent flying off the road to his death.'

'I slowed down to warn him the curve ahead was dangerous, to stop the race. He ignored me.'

'He could do everything but that. And you knew it. You hated him.'

'That's true. I hated him for his cruelty, but not enough to want his death. I liked his mother; I knew how frightened for him she was. The boy was a lunatic. It was an accident.'

'For which you tried to pay off your responsibility.'

'I tried to help the family that Fabio's irresponsibility ruined.'

'Fabio's mother told me it was more money than they had ever seen. You probably unfairly assumed your then friend, Riccardo, would throw them off the property if they could not come up with their lease. But they learned about the suspected race from the detective and left to avoid bringing sin on the family. Fabio's mother feared his father would kill you. She protected you.'

'I wanted to protect them from ruin.'

'They saw your money for what it was: an attempt to bribe your way out of responsibility for what you did to their son. Their son and their sheep—that was their pension plan. Your form of penitence is fraud and it couldn't help them.'

'You are making this very difficult for me. Don't pretend I don't know what it means to them to have lost their son. I just wanted to help them survive and get on.'

'When I met Fabio's mother on a visit to the village to tend her son's grave, one of the most pious women I have ever known admitted wanting revenge for her son's death. When I told her you were badly burned in the fire and would no longer be a musician, she said, "La fine della sua vocazione per la fine della vita di mio figlio." The fact that you paid for her son's death with what she knew was your calling in life did help her "get on", I suppose, and to know God had taken vengeance she dared not ask Him for.'

Jeremy's own past cynicism is being thrown back at him in Dom Pietro's off-the-record break from his priesthood. 'You can pin as much on me as you see fit. The fire in the villa was not an accident. Fabio's father knew where to find me.'

'Speculate all you like.'

'You're saying you don't need to.'

'You were about to make use of the sacramental seal yourself a couple of days ago.'

'I am not hiding from the truth. It's unfair if you do.'

'Oh, well, one motive for arson was hidden away as quickly as possible. They married, she bore a son I had the pleasure to christen before I left, and not much later the golden couple split, went their different ways—you drugged her that night, didn't you?'

Jeremy gags at the swift, well-timed accusation on the last sip of tea halfway down his throat and sputters it back into his cup, or most of it.

Dom Pietro casually pulls two tissues from the box on his desk, hands one to Jeremy, and wipes the splatter on his desk with the other. 'I'll take that as affirmative. Isabella's mother told me that her daughter couldn't remember anything about what had taken place the night you dumped her on the village square. I was only able to put two and two together once I arrived here, in the bright cosmopolitan city of London, and learned to my horror about date-rape drugs, calling up—I will not hesitate to say—the sight of you in the crypt fornicating another half-dead woman—'

'Stop!'

Jeremy jumps out of his chair, unable to counter this assault. Dom Pietro sees his anguish, the disorientation his harsh words have sent pacing around the room until Jeremy stops at the window. He looks out onto the rectory garden and church beyond, trying to collect himself, immobilised by shame he has not been confronted with, except in his own mind.

'Are these the sort of events you wanted to confess?'

'It was never who I really am. I'm not trying to justify anything. The only explanation I have is that I lost control in my isolation out there, the pressure to save my career, then Vicky. I confess: I only asked her over because I thought her appetites would pull me out of a fixation on Isabella I could not stop . . .'

'Fascinating, isn't it, how one sinful, degenerate idea, uncorrected, leads to another?'

Jeremy turns on the priest. 'I'm sure you have always followed the Commandments to the letter and confessed when you haven't, which your Church believes gives you the right to that sort of high-minded arrogance—missteps amended until the next confession, guilt absolved.'

'Isn't that what you were after last Saturday?'

'I wanted to rid myself of the illusion that confession changes anything, call the bluff on authority the Church assumes it has to decide on penitence it claims will absolve me. I know what I've done, but not what the consequences are for those I wronged. Only you can tell me that. I want to hold myself accountable to them, not to anyone who claims to speak for the Almighty. I'm not looking for absolution or salvation in His eyes.'

'Well, the Lord will be most disappointed in you, although he was kind enough to accept your wish to be punished in the here and now for your sins.'

'I've left the psychotic Catholic world behind which my mother brought me up in. I live in the real world, not inside any holy bubble that decides what sin is, that suffocated and slandered anyone who chose not to obey your doctrinaire understanding of "rectitude" in the village you deserted.'

Dom Pietro feels indicted by his admission at the start of their conversation, but he will not let it be used to question the sincerity of his intentions as a priest. 'Faith changes people, Jeremy. If what I believed in and preached was wrong, I was given the opportunity with His help to get to the bottom of it.' The priest bows his head in thought before continuing. 'Let me help you to a full conscience of what you should feel guilty about, since that is what you want.' He lifts his head and points at the chair.

Jeremy reluctantly takes it. 'No sermon, please. I want to know what happened to Isabella, Giorgio, Domino.'

'Oh, the list is a bit longer, I'm afraid. I can include the whole congregation. I had spoken out on your behalf, insisting villagers must prove the strength of their personal faith by being kinder and more tolerant towards outsiders like yourself. And some villagers did take that to heart. The stupid thing is, the faithful you and Vicky baptised in tolerance, who chose to turn a blind eye to the pagan profanity of your concert, ended up fighting those who toed the bishop's line about it. What should have been a passing scandal brought up all sorts of buried personal resentments. Infighting soon infected everyone in the congregation. Many just stopped coming to church.'

'The bell rope broke.'

'You cut it, and I helped you.'

'So you left, came here.'

'And you'll be happy to know: feeling miserably guilty for not finding the right path for the people I served.'

Jeremy remembers their lunch together in the abbey town after Mass, the priest's mea culpa for the villagers' misreading of the faith he wanted to establish. But his conciliatory tone might tilt now into something a lot less guarded.

'What happened to Isabella, after she split with Marco?'

'Not too much sympathy on your part for the young man, I see. And an interesting assumption: that she split with him, not the other way around. But let's begin with the man who wanted to deface your sparkle by scratching your car. You knew it was Marco, of course, but kept it to yourself, obviously knowing what had sent him into a jealous rage. Even that did not stop you, did it, from interfering after I told you not to?'

'She came to visit me. What was I to do? Turn her away?'

'Against your own invitation? I was not so welcome that day, I guess, when I found two cues on the snooker table from your interrupted game with her. You gave each cue a role, I remember. I'm sure you were saintly cautious with Isabella, not undisciplined at all, which the only eyewitness of her visit might have confirmed, had he survived your race to cover it up.'

'That is slander, Dom Pietro!' Jeremy gets up from his chair again, the truth biting into him, the role Isabella had played in motivating him to race Fabio.

'Just pieces of the puzzle we put together after you left. No one but you knows the truth, and I don't think I want to see the bottom of it. But Isabella didn't make out so well on her second secret visit to the villa. Her lucky man was waiting to catch her out as she was going home. Unfortunately for him, he was observed by two members of his own gang.'

'What are you talking about?'

'Do you think a scratch on your car was enough to put Marco's crashed pride to rest? After thinking he lost a promise he had waited years for? When he guessed correctly that she was visiting you, he chased her. Even if you did it without her knowing at the time, you were not the first to rape her.'

Jeremy is stunned into painful silence. Knowing he abused her scorched his conscience, but this magnified the abuse, made it uglier than his face mirrored in the window. 'Oh my God.'

'Do not blaspheme, Jeremy,' Dom Pietro says from his swivel chair. 'We have in fact not reached rock bottom. You wanted to know the consequences. I'm afraid I cannot even describe the torment that young woman must have gone through: a day she could not forget, a night she remembered nothing about, and through the shame of her aborted chastity and the abuse she suffered, the need to protect and love the child forced on her. She held it all inside for as long as she could, refusing to give up her job and refusing Marco.

'But Francesco and Ramiro confirmed Marco was the father and how he became one—not you, as most assumed, although only Isabella knows. Marco became so penitent that everyone took his sin to be "maybe what happened"; he could be forgiven for being too eager to seal their expected marriage. She tried to fight her parents' wishes, then gave in, married, and then rejected him anyway, spending most of her time up to delivery with her mother. Then came the christening, and after weaning, she went straight back to work.

'This was not Marco's idea of family life. End of penitence. Marco's aggression towards her convinced people his sin must have been deliberate after all, and they rejected him. The fathers, once inseparable friends, fought out their own blame game after the fallout. Marco disappeared, like you did, and was never heard from again. Despite my own best efforts, Isabella's mother went into clinical depression. Isabella left with her child, despite her father's appeals, to live with her girlfriend Angelina. At the bottom of the rubble you left behind, there is a son, and only Isabella knows who the father is.'

Jeremy did not want a name attached to taking Isabella's choice away, a name that would etch itself into his conscience. But could he choose to deny his abuse, when she was reminded of it every day? 'What is the boy's name?'

'Do not search for clues, Jeremy.'

Jeremy was paralysed by conflicts that would have left him standing at the window for hours. 'What can I do?'

Dom Pietro rose from his chair and came up behind him. 'Don't look for her. Look for the truth about yourself, in yourself, with or without God's help. Do not look for it in the lives of others you have wronged. You're right: confession does not heal our sins or forgive us our guilt for them. These are a path to recognition, reconciliation with who we are. I have come down hard on the Jeremy I knew, who abused my personal trust and did things that caused unspeakable harm. But I am not your judge. What I saw and heard, I think, is not the truth of who you are now. It takes courage to look back. Doing so does not always give us the answers we need. Look forward, Jeremy. Make amends now, keep the balance, and get on with your life. Isabella and the boy are safe.'

Jeremy takes the rest of the whiskey he had ignored in his hand in one gulp. From tomorrow he will think of what he can do to amend his life. The opera tonight took him back, but seeing everything more clearly still does not allow him to turn away the stranger to himself he was. The stranger will always follow him, and if to blame, would be the real father, denying him any moral right to claim the boy is his, spiting him for the role he would so wish for now. He desperately wants to, but he will not look for them.

His guilt-driven presumptions of ruined lives he left behind were thankfully not fulfilled elsewhere. In the half dark of his sitting room he sees the pile of food magazines he has bought over the last few months to teach himself to cook with more imagination. He found a picture of Giorgio in one of them, his smiling square face featured in an article about olive oil. He had heard from Dom Pietro that the artigiano managed to bring in the crop when the villa burned down but had to go elsewhere to process the olives. He became the manager of a big grower and an advocate for high-tech processing he once despised, earning a good reputation for his oil since. The magazine article featured a bottle labelled with the name Carmen.

And Domino, the priest confessed, did not die. That was an assumption he made when the dog was nowhere to be found after the fire. Domino had strayed. Dom Pietro spotted a completely emaciated dog on the square one day outside the rectory window, too weak to run away when he went out for a closer look. Only when he called out his name could the priest confirm it was Domino. He kept Domino for a few weeks until he found someone whom he could trust to care for the dog with love.

Two years later

It is a beautiful afternoon, sunny but mildly warm. Jeremy is glad rehearsals went well enough to dismiss the choir earlier than expected. They were really getting better, even though infrequent rehearsal opportunities meant that it has taken two years to move them from motets to their first cantata. He loves conducting, having jumped in at the deep end when Dom Pietro's choirmaster fell seriously ill.

He was wary of the priest's motives when asked, but the priest has proved genuine in his desire to help people; the congregation he took over has grown steadily. They have put aside discussing what the Church means to either of them, and they are much too guarded with each other these days to ever become friends. Even so, Father Peter is a lot more tolerant than Dom Pietro was, and not all of the members of his small choir are stout Catholics; some have even come to dinner. And even if Jeremy still does feel uncomfortable in church, music is back in his life, which is all that matters.

And this hope, he says to himself. He is back on the old man's bench in Regent's Park because he is grateful to remember the simple truths that helped to mend his contorted conscience. But that is not the only reason he comes to sit here so often. Three months or so ago, before his operation, he was sitting here all wrapped up against a much cooler day.

When he saw the dog running after a tennis ball, heading in his direction, he was reminded at once of Domino, grateful his companion was in safe hands in the village far away but missing him terribly all of a sudden, the likeness uncanny, too real. The dog snatched up the ball while it was still rolling, was about to turn and run back, stopped, and dropped the ball from its mouth, looking directly at him with an endearing and familiar questioning tilt of its head. Jeremy froze, seized up inside, fighting the urge to reach out and acknowledge what seconds later sent a jolt through his body.

'Domino, vieni! Vieni qui!'

His eyes followed the cheerful voice, quite far away but close enough to recognise its radiant accompanying smile on Isabella's face. She was standing next to another woman her age, and between them a little boy, who in that moment broke into a run towards 'Mino! Mino!' He stumbled and fell. Domino picked up his ball at once and ran towards the boy, reaching him just before his mother picked him up under his arms, hoisting him high, and on the way down, turning on the spot to spin him around, both of them laughing and Domino barking and hopping around them, wanting part of the fun, all of them romping around together. Jeremy's chin dropped into his chest; tears were coming.

She had danced for him the very last time he played, on the villa's rooftop. His sunken head felt the weight of what that dance to his malevolent tune had cost him: the chance ever to be a part of this one. He looked up again. In all his painful premonitions of the suffering his abuse had caused her, how could he have forgotten the tenacity of her spirit, her search for joy in her life on her own terms? If she ever could forgive his cowardly abuse of her trust, then this escape from under the village bubble that had imprisoned her was her reward for courage.

In the few seconds he allowed himself to look, Jeremy knew the boy was his. His son, Isabella with her closest friend, Angelina, and Domino: they had made a new life for themselves here, had been here all along. They followed Dom Pietro here. He knew Isabella and the boy were safe and has kept them so; that was why their protector kept him at a guarded distance all this time and decided to help him out of his misery: there was nothing to be miserable about any longer, after all, and the priest was not his judge. His son is loved; they are happy—no worries!

He was fighting a breakdown in his resolve not to be discovered when he got up from the bench, his entire body shaking against the urge to walk towards them, and not away from them. He paced his retreat, counting a hundred yards before he did look back, and they were gone.

He stopped then, trying to freeze the film in his head and regain control of his senses. He pulled off his mask, wiped his face, and walked on. After another twenty paces or so, it hit him. He pulled off his mask again. He was sure somehow that when he wiped his face just moments before, he had felt his whole face, even where his burnt facial nerves were dead. Whether that was true or his imagination that day three months ago, does not matter now, sitting here again. For a fleeting moment it felt like forgiveness. Since then, he has allowed himself to believe that part of the stranger to himself he once was has at last been wiped away. His face in the mirror is indeed no longer as ugly as it was.

Dom Pietro does not know that his secret has been discovered, that Jeremy has waited several times on this bench. Will they come to the park today?

La Traviata aria: 'fors'é lui...'

È strano! è strano! in core
Scolpiti ho quegli accenti!
Saria per me sventura un serio amore?
Che risolvi, o turbata anima mia?
Null'uomo ancora t'accendeva O gioia
Ch'io non conobbi, essere amata amando!
E sdegnarla poss'io
Per l'aride follie del viver mio?
Ah, fors'è lui che l'anima
Solinga ne' tumulti
Godea sovente pingere
De' suoi colori occulti!
Lui che modesto e vigile
All'egre soglie ascese,
E nuova febbre accese,
Destandomi all'amor.
A quell'amor ch'è palpito
Dell'universo intero,
Misterioso, altero,
Croce e delizia al cor.

How strange! How strange!
Those words I have carved in my heart!
Will serious love be my misfortune?
What will you decide, troubled soul?
No man has yet ignited you, O joy
I never knew, to be loved by loving!
And can I disdain it
For the arid follies of my life?
Ah, perhaps it is he whom the soul
Lonely in its tumults
often enjoyed painting
With its hidden colours!
He who modest and vigilant
Ascended the high thresholds
and ignited a new fever,
awakening me to love.
To that love which is the throb
Of the whole universe,
Mysterious, proud,
Cross and delight to the heart.

Resta concentrata un istante, poi dice

She remains concentrated for a moment, then says

Follie! follie delirio vano è questo!
Povera donna, sola
Abbandonata in questo
Popoloso deserto
Che appellano Parigi,
Che spero or più?
Che far degg'io!
Gioire,
Di voluttà nei vortici perire.
Sempre libera degg'io
Folleggiar di gioia in gioia,
Vo' che scorra il viver mio
Per i sentieri del piacer,
Nasca il giorno, o il giorno muoia,
Sempre lieta ne' ritrovi
A diletti sempre nuovi
Dee volare il mio pensier.

Foolishness! Foolish is this vain delirium!
Poor woman, alone,
Abandoned in this
Populous desert
Which they call Paris,
What more can I hope for?
What can I do?
Rejoice!
To perish in whirlpools of voluptuousness.
I must always be free
to float from joy to joy,
I want my life to flow
Along the paths of pleasure,
Let the day dawn, or let the day die,
Always happy to meet again
To ever new delights
My thoughts should fly.

Acknowledgements

My sincere thanks to Simon Dent for all that I learned from him about the oboe, for his inspiring recordings, and not least for his ideas. I am highly indebted to Leslie Stradinger for her patient, dedicated and skilful editing of the manuscript, and to Christiane Suppé for her well-thought-out design of the book's cover. Thanks also to Amanda De Paolis and Pablo Cabrera for enabling my visit to the villa in Italy, and to Fabien Vitali for checking the Italian content. I was greatly encouraged by my first readers to refine the story and trim it of a debut author's excesses: many thanks to Claudia Whitney for her multiple reviews at all stages of writing, and to Judith Erber, Henriette Mayer-Ravenstein, Roger Houghton, Sheba Wetters and Simon Dent for their reading of the initial versions of the manuscript. I owe my sustained efforts to reach the finishing line to Birgit Berger, who lovingly supported my writing as an impromptu critic throughout and reminded me—only when absolutely necessary—that to eat, sleep and get some exercise were not to be dismissed as distractions from my desk.

About the author

Anton Van Iersel was born in Holland. He was brought up in the
Caribbean, the US and England, and has travelled widely on the
European continent and in Africa. He is a translator, editor and
copywriter and ran his own translation agency based in Munich
for 27 years before devoting his time to creative writing. This is
his first novel.

Author's note

In the early 1990s I was looking for a place to write in peace and was invited to stay in a run-down villa north of Rome. No sooner had I mentioned the purpose of my stay to an adorable old signora who sold me my veggies than everyone in the village seemed to know what I was doing there. The village priest was a well-educated man who visited the villa on several occasions. It was all genuinely very friendly. And yes, the local wine was barely palatable, the olive oil to die for.

Looking back, I came up with a very different scenario. As it took shape I needed an urban protagonist who would be caught off guard by the foreign rural culture he encounters. I have always loved music as much as writing, so these mutually inspiring arts created a musician with other reasons to choose seclusion I myself experienced.

I encourage readers to listen, if possible, to the compositions that correspond to what Jeremy plays on the oboe at different points in the story, and of course to Verdi's opera *La Traviata*.

In my memory, the Catholic Church held considerable authority in the village back then, and the abuses that have meanwhile eroded that authority elsewhere still today remain largely buried in Italy. I fictionalised an extremely closeted and intolerant village congregation that would nevertheless not be conceivable in today's wide-open smartphone-internet world. So, the point in time had to be preserved.

As for my own stay, I did not have a landline in the villa nor yet a mobile phone, and had to make appointed calls to the outside world from the village bar's pay phone. There is no nostalgia about having to compete to be heard above the noise of the card players.

Owning and running a translation agency that grew over the years after my stay in Italy, postponed my continuing ambition to write creatively. I sold my agency in 2019. Writing a full-length novel proved a harder accomplishment than I imagined: the idea was fine, but I hadn't reckoned with the research and rewrites until a real book emerged which, in my own eyes and my editors', could count as one that belonged alongside established authors on my bookshelf.

Have I, as newcomer, earned a place as an author on your bookshelf? Your review, alternatively a star rating, are the only way other readers will know whether or why I succeeded in convincing you. Your comments on writing style, characterisation, topic, storyline, pace, or anything that comes to mind, are all valuable pointers to me as I work now on my second novel. Please do click any follow button you find where you found me if you want to know when it comes out (next year, I hope!). Many heartfelt thanks for your support!

Printed in Great Britain
by Amazon